CONVERGENCE ON THE 42ND PARALLEL

NIC D'ALESSANDRO

For Frances, who believed in this from page one.

And for all those who serve their nations on,
beneath, and above the seas.

PROLOGUE

By three methods we may learn wisdom:
first, by reflection, which is noblest; second,
by imitation, which is easiest; and third
by experience, which is the bitterest.

—Confucius

7 December 1941

The United States Army major general sat at an awkward angle in the front seat of the jeep, twisting around to take in the full view. His driver had taken them to a vantage point in the hills to the north-east of Wheeler Army Airfield. Perhaps the major general hoped the situation would appear less disastrous from there. Yet reality—the full truth then before him—was horrific.

To the south, thick pillars of black smoke belched into the sky. A concoction of fuel and munitions fed fires beneath. Dozens of stricken ships wallowed in various stages of destruction. Some were sinking. Harbour facilities and buildings burned in sympathy. The usual bright morning sky was obscured by a thick dark smoke haze covering the harbour, its dark trail growing along the leeward side of the island. He took in the distant rumblings, secondary explosions, the wail of sirens still to be extinguished, and a growing putrid smell of gunpowder and fire, and their victims.

To his right and farther to the east, smaller plumes rose into the sky from what remained of Wheeler Army Airfield. Other airfields burned in the far distance.

A line from a letter to the major general and Admiral Kimmel—from the Secretary of the Navy earlier that year—echoed painfully in the major general's mind:

... if war eventuates with Japan, it is believed easily possible that hostilities would be initiated by a surprise attack upon the fleet or the naval base at Pearl Harbor.

The major general knew, right or wrong, that they'd have his head for this. They'd blame him for the devastation in front of him, and for the ensuing shame and fury from the U.S. Navy, the U.S. government, and the American people. This was the beginning of the end of his career.

*   *   *   *

For the United States, the attack on Pearl Harbor was a colossal failure of intelligence, command, communication, and preparedness. The unthinkable had happened in a place the armed forces did not expect, at a time they could not predict, and in a strategic move both they and their government could not believe was possible.

For the Japanese, it was a triumph of cunning and skill, of detailed planning, intelligence and counterintelligence, deception, and diversion. But they would pay dearly for their triumph, as history tells. An American World War II propaganda poster that emerged after the attack cleverly borrowed a line from President Lincoln's Gettysburg Address: "... we here highly resolve that these dead shall not have died in vain ..." The main caption on the poster read REMEMBER DEC. 7TH!, which became a popular war cry throughout America and the armed forces.

Remember it, they did. The United States would regroup and rebuild, and apply the lessons learned from the bitter experience of Pearl Harbor throughout the Pacific War. Many of its battleships were disabled or destroyed in Pearl Harbor, but instead of building many more of the same, the U.S. Navy shifted its focus to an emerging new breed of ship. A super-ship like none before it. And perhaps ironically, the same breed of ship that the Japanese used to launch their attack on Pearl Harbor.

The age of the aircraft carrier had come.

*   *   *   *

And today? The events of 7 December 1941 are still part of the American psyche. The pain of the battle is reinforced to any visitor to Pearl Harbor as they contemplate the memorial built over the rusted wreck of USS *Arizona*. The battleship sits where it sank—a tomb for many of her sailors.

The surviving class of super-ship, the American aircraft carrier, has cemented its place as a strategic weapon with global influence. American carriers continue to dominate the oceans, and their sheer presence and military clout have a profound effect on modern geopolitics. *Power projection*, as the Americans so eloquently put it.

Doubts are emerging, however. Are carriers becoming vulnerable to emerging weapons and technologies to the point they are no longer sustainable? Yet one undeniable fact remains. Of the many carriers built by the United States since World War II, *none* have been successfully attacked by an aggressor.

Not yet, that is.

CHAPTER ONE

*Success is not final, failure is not fatal: it is the courage
to continue that counts.*

—Winston Churchill

11 April 2019, 5:20 am

Grey. Flat, unremarkable grey.

The wall in Ben Cai's view held no particular features to hold his gaze, yet to his irritation he couldn't look away. His thoughts floated vaguely as his eyes wandered over nothing much at all.

Much of the room was painted in the same flat grey. The flooring being the exception—black linoleum crudely disguised as tiles. A rubber mat, placed there in the previous century, sat by the closed door.

Predawn light cast on a wall from a high-mounted window, the orange glow the only visible trace of colour. The small desk on the far side of the room was barely discernible, with Ben's only possession—his backpack—propped against a rickety chair.

His thoughts drifted beyond the tiny room and out to the facility surrounding him. The place held little visual interest, and no apparent beauty. Yes, there were others working there, but most had succumbed to this grey world. They were, to Ben, like worker bees in a hive with no honey. And no queen.

What else should I expect? he thought to himself. *This is a military facility, after all.*

His thoughts transported thousands of kilometres west. Pulsating streets teeming with life, distant mist-topped green hills and patches of blueish sea and sky, and at night, more brightly coloured neon lights than a person could hope to comprehend. Hong Kong. A long, long way from here and not just in distance.

Ben glanced at his phone—5:32 AM—and turned his attention to the day ahead. He'd been ordered to report to the central meeting hall at 0600 hours to undergo yet another test. Of the test itself he knew nothing, but that wasn't out of the ordinary. He'd faced many tests during the past four months of training, often without explanation. Ben had learned not to worry. He'd learned that particular lesson the hard way.

After a good long drink of water, running his hands through his hair, and donning the standard uniform of loose cotton pants and a thick over-tunic, he was ready to get moving.

*　　*　　*　　*

5:52 AM

Ben had spent the previous twenty minutes at one of the few places in the camp offering any sense of the natural world. The browning patch of neglected grass sat at the southern end of the training camp, a contrast to the rows of squat stone and timber buildings, each as nondescript and architecturally barren as its neighbours. A tall wire fence and a line of trees ran along the outer boundary. The trees were still leafless given that spring had just begun.

The camp appeared deserted. The facility had once served as a military air base, but it had been many years since an aircraft had taken off or landed on the disused runway.

There on the patch of grass, as was his custom every morning, Ben worked through a routine of quiet meditation and slow, deliberate body movement. He practised the traditions his father had taught him, repeating them with religious determination. His bare feet tapped into the sensations of the crisp grass and the cold earth beneath. He descended into the quiet and peace of the surroundings, sensing the sun breaking the horizon and the first hint of solar warmth playing on his skin.

*　　*　　*　　*

Ben approached the timber doors of the hall at precisely 0600 and used both hands to swing them inward. Tired hinges squealed to a crescendo. They repeated their cry as the doors returned to a closed position with a hollow thump.

Cooler air greeted him as he entered. His nose took in the blend of burning candle wax and an underlying aroma of vintage dust. The hall was lit, but only just, and Ben squinted to adjust to the dimness. Sparse candles mounted in small metal holders flickered along the two longest walls.

Ben made a short, pronounced bow to the person in the distance. His gaze stayed low to the floor as he formally greeted the man. "Master Park."

The man returned the bow—not as low as Ben's, and its duration much shorter. "Yong-sun," he said as he motioned for Ben to come to him.

Ben's local name—Jeong Yong-sun—was his only name in this place. And *Ben* wasn't the name on his Hong Kong birth certificate. His official name in Hong Kong was Cai Chen, *Cai* being his family name, *Chen* his given name. He had selected his other given name of *Ben* because it rhymed with *Chen*. He was not alone in having an English name, as the generational roots of many Hongkongers are still firmly and proudly British.

But in the place where he stood that British *munt* of a name was never to be mentioned. If someone addressed him as *Ben*, or even *Chen*, they could expect a lesson in local etiquette delivered with a swift force that would never be forgotten. Remembering, in this place, was highly recommended.

Ben walked towards Master Park, keeping his gaze respectfully low but chancing some upward glances. His eyes took in two monstrous portraits hanging high at the far end of the hall, yet his conscious mind paid no notice. Images of the two men were everywhere here.

Master Park Jon Chan stood tall with all five-foot-six of his increasingly short and tubby stature. His time as a physically powerful, lean, and athletic servant of the state had long passed. Yet his military rank of Sojwa—equivalent to a major in Western militaries—and Master of Taekwondo with a black belt to the level of sixth Dan were still intact and would never be challenged. Respect for him as a revered master had grown with him as he aged, and in his sixty-seventh year he was regarded by his colleagues and students as a legend of their craft.

Park showed no hint of emotion. The deepening lines of his face portrayed all his years, their ridges and valleys accentuated in the low candlelight as he spoke to Ben. "Your test, Yong-sun, is simply this." He pointed towards the opposite end of the hall.

Ben's eyes had adjusted to the dim light. At the end of the hall he could make out a vase sitting on a small table. It was delicate and ornate, with graceful lines stretching from its base. Between it and Ben stood two lines of seven equally spaced men.

Ben recognised them. Teachers and masters of varying rank and experience faced their counterparts like statues, staring straight ahead. Some held lengths of bamboo by their sides—some thick, others thin as whips.

"The vase," Master Park continued, "was crafted by our Goryeo Dynasty ancestors in the fourteenth century. It has survived many generations and foreign invasions. This vase is of tremendous pride and value to our great state."

Ben nodded curtly, acknowledging the significance of the master's words.

"You must go between the two lines before you and bring the vase to me undamaged." Master Park's voice deepened. "My student, you must focus upon your mission, and on the mission only ... *do not fail me on this.*"

With that, Master Park folded his arms. He turned to his right and faced the vase in the dim distance.

Thoughts tumbled through Ben's mind as he contemplated the seemingly bizarre mission. He began the walk towards the gantlet, moving with enough pace to demonstrate his confidence, tempered to show neither arrogance nor fear. His focus fixed on the vase fifty metres away at the end of the hall.

Ben passed between the first two men. He advanced another few steps towards the second pair, their eyes still fixed forward and not acknowledging his presence. Ben sensed a sudden whoosh of air from behind and then felt a sharp, cracking thump on his back. The first man to his left had swung a thick piece of bamboo, striking him across both shoulder blades. Before Ben's mind could deal with the searing pain across his back, he took a sharp kick to his right thigh.

Keep moving now, don't stop ...

Ben's right leg seized in a paralysis of numbing pain as he took his next step. He took a deep breath and limped forward, passing the second pair of men

Keep walking, eyes ahead ...

Another kick, this time into his stomach. A Taekwondo move executed with skill and to perfection. Ben recoiled and buckled as the wind was knocked from him. He faltered for a few seconds as he resisted the urge to cradle his injured abdomen with his hands.

Gather yourself, be strong, and above all else do not stop moving ...

The test became a blur of hands, feet, elbows, fists, and bamboo. A sharp jab to his upper arm, another to his face, an intense thwack across the back of his head, a bamboo whip across his lower back ripping the skin deep and raw, and more kicks than he could comprehend. His vision blurred and spun, his body reeled from the building, searing pain.

Somehow Ben kept moving forward.

Eyes on the mission, focus on the vase. I must not fail ...

Finally, after some eighty endless seconds, Ben had passed the final two men. His path took a drunken curve as he staggered to the table. He stopped and reached out to touch the vase.

No. No! ... Think!

Ben tried to push away the cascade of pain signals overwhelming his brain. It dimly occurred to him that Master Park had not stated a time limit. He could pause, control the moment, and gather himself.

Other thoughts surfaced in his mind. Lessons from his endless training were calling back to him, their echoes growing louder as he steadied himself.

Ben consciously took control of his breath. He slowed his rate of respiration. He focused his mind on the feeling of breath as it entered his nose, and as it expelled through his throat and mouth.

A peace of sorts moved through his body and mind. His heart rate slowed towards normal.

Ben had learned the ancient practice of the conscious control of pain. He'd been given ample opportunities to practise the skill in the past four months of his training, and in the time before that. The pain and the various injuries at its root were still very much alive at that moment, but Ben was regaining control. He moved sequentially through his body in his thoughts, from his feet through to the top of his head. Ben identified the major sources of pain, isolating them in his mind and consciously lowering the volume of the nerve messages. He released his feelings of anger and the urge to take revenge. The fog in his thinking dissipated. Clarity of thought was returning.

And now what to do? What is my next move?

Ben withdrew his hand, leaving the vase untouched. He turned in the opposite direction, facing the gantlet. The men were still standing motionless in their two regimented lines, their faces like stone. A trail of red spots on the floor marked the path to where he stood.

Ben moved towards the first pair, slowly at first. His limp was still plain to see, his left shoulder drooped, his tunic stained with the darkness of dripping blood. He gathered his pace, not to a run, but with greater speed and purpose than his first walk through the gantlet.

At the far end, Master Park shifted his stance.

As Ben neared the first pair, the man on his right flickered his eyes ever so slightly towards Ben. Now it was *his* turn to wonder what might happen next. Ben struck the man before he'd finished turning his gaze with a swift roundhouse kick to the chest with all of Ben's weight and strength channelled into the side of his foot. The man's body rocketed backwards and then sprawled to the floor.

The man opposite, still taking in what he had witnessed, was equally unprepared. Ben leapt, unfurling his legs across the front and back of the man's torso in a locking grip and sharply twisting to flatten the man to the floor. Three rapid hand strikes to the head and that was that.

Master Park remained frozen to his spot, his mouth dropping slightly open.

I must not fail. I will not fail …

The third man was still holding the long bamboo whip in his left hand. The two deep bloody gouges across Ben's back sang with recognition of their perpetrator.

The remaining men stood still, exchanging worried glances between them. The two at the far end looked to Master Park for direction but found nothing.

The third man instinctively crept backwards. He raised the bamboo whip above his head. Before he could strike, Ben caught him on the chin with a foot pointed like a dagger. The man staggered back a few steps before falling to his knees, both hands above his head in an attempt to protect himself from the next strike to come.

"*Stop!*" Master Park's shout echoed from the walls before silence returned.

Ben took one step back, bowed his head, and stilled himself, his gaze firmly at the floor beyond his feet. The man before him continued to cower.

The mission. The mission must be completed.

Ben returned to the table, his feet barely making a sound. He reached for the vase and carefully lifted it with both hands. Ben cradled it like a newborn child, laying its length along his right forearm as his left hand held the base. He took in its colour and quality for a moment. An exquisite blend of earthy green shades each imperceptibly merging into the other in gracious, flowing long swirls, the delicate ceramic cool to the touch.

The other men were as good as invisible to Ben as he strode forward. Some took another step back when he passed, but his focus remained firmly upon the master.

"Master," Ben whispered as he bowed. He kept his eyes to the floor and extended the vase.

Master Park searched Ben's face, as if attempting to divine something from the young man's soul. Seconds passed before he took the vase.

Ben would never know that it was a cheap fake. It had served its purpose.

Master Park gave a bow of sorts, so curtailed that it was barely distinguishable from a nod. "Return to your barracks, Yong-sun. Report to administration at 1400 hours."

"Master," Ben replied softly, bowing low again.

Test over.

Mission complete.

CHAPTER TWO

Doesn't expecting the unexpected make the unexpected expected?

—Bob Dylan

11 April 2019

Grey. Flat, unremarkable grey.

The ceiling in Katherine Marlowe's view held no particular features to hold her gaze, yet to her irritation she couldn't look away. Her thoughts floating vaguely as her eyes wandered over nothing much at all.

Katherine could appreciate the rare morning slumber. Her roommate, Lieutenant Brzezinski, had been assigned to a task elsewhere and wouldn't return until the next week. She had the tiny quarters to herself that morning and wasn't due on watch until 1200 hours.

She relaxed into the behemoth's rolling, pitching motion. There would sometimes be a hint of yaw in the ship's movement as it skidded around its central axis, but she sensed none this morning. Combined yaw and roll on the sea were never comfortable for Katherine. She hadn't been seasick since the early days, but sometimes the old discomfort would stir inside her belly. Not that anyone would know.

If there'd been a porthole for her to gaze at the sea as it slid by, she might have propped herself on the upper rack and taken a look at the outside world. But a narrow double bunk, closets built into the bulkheads, and some cramped bench spaces were all that adorned these quarters. Colour appeared only in photos of distant family members stuck on the walls, in the dark-blue privacy curtains slung along the line of each bunk, and in a faded ship insignia hanging lopsided on the back of the door.

A cruise ship? Not on your life. This behemoth of the seas—USS *Princeton*—was herself a celebration of all things grey. As a *Ticonderoga*-class guided missile cruiser of the United States Navy, *Princeton* was one of the many prides of the fleet. This lethal anti-air, anti-surface, and anti-submarine platform with a plethora of advanced weaponry and defence systems was formidable as a ship of war on the high seas. And despite her size and her age, she was quick, very quick.

But pretty? Well, not so much, and the blandness was something that Katherine had hated about her job since her first deployment at the age of twenty-one. But the sea, ships, and anything that floated was in her blood ever since she'd earned her stripes, so to speak, by racing sailboats as a teenager—even if she'd never felt at home in the endless maze of corridors, bulkheads, pipes, ladders, and hatches of a warship.

But Katherine had another inspiration. A greater love that kept her focused and sane. This too was decorated in bland tones, but she ignored that regrettable fact. It was waiting for her on the aft deck of the *Princeton*—out in the wind and spray of the sea.

*   *   *   *

0820 hours

Lieutenant Katherine Marlowe was dressed in operational uniform—a green one-piece flight suit. She pulled on her well-worn HSM-85 cap and made her way to the Officers Wardroom.

Breakfast, like all meals served on board day and night, was substantial, with an array of eggs made to order, and sausage, bacon, vegetables, and hash browns sweltering in steam pans. The ingredients were the same as for the enlisted crew, but they were cooked in much smaller quantities for the officers and therefore with more finesse.

After the server handed Katherine her plate she chose an almost-empty table and slid into a seat. At the opposite corner of the table a heavyset man with small glasses was inhaling his breakfast. A good twenty seconds passed before he noticed her presence. He flicked his gaze left with a start. "Morning," he said with a nod.

"Mornin'," Katherine replied, barely looking at him.

The man pulled out his earphones. "So, uh, when you on watch?"

"1200 for me. You?"

"Just finished. I'll be hitting my rack soon."

"Mm."

His face was vaguely familiar, but she had no idea what his role was or where he worked on the ship. She'd only been on *Princeton* for two weeks and there were still many places and faces to know.

A minute passed as the officer resumed his meal and Katherine worked up the motivation to take her first bite. He took a few fleeting glances towards her, then spoke again.

"You work with the helos?" he asked.

"Yup."

"Tough job?"

"Some days."

Katherine kept her focus towards her plate, twirling a long strand of spinach on her fork, but the man wasn't giving up so easily. "If you helo guys have a bad day, then we're all *totally* screwed. Or so I'm told."

"Is that so?" Katherine asked without asking.

"Yeah, if you're not up doing detection, then we're sitting ducks for any enemy submarines out there. Nothing else matters that much."

"This ship has a lot more than a helicopter protecting it. You would know that."

"I *do* know that," he half-snapped, "but apparently what others do on this ship doesn't count the same as what *you* do."

"Matter of opinion, I guess."

"Yeah? And what's your opinion?"

The intensity of Katherine's spinach-twirling had increased. "Um, I don't really have one. I just do my job and hope everybody does theirs."

"Oh, spare me the modesty. I know how it is with you aviator types."

Katherine looked up from her plate and glowered at him. Now it was his turn to look down. "We can't all be heroes, I guess," he mumbled to his plate.

He's got some issues, Katherine thought. *Something way up his ass. Maybe he's got a problem with pilots, maybe it's women. Or maybe he's bitter about pushing forty and still only a lieutenant.*

"Look, I'm not trying to be a hero," she said. "Like I said, I'm just doing a job."

He looked up. "Really? Seems like a waste. All that training, the prestige, the rush ... and it's just some desk job to you?"

Katherine frowned. This wasn't the time to be thinking about big questions. Not that there ever was. Thinking like that had never done her any good. But she was stuck at the table with him and her rapidly cooling spinach. "I signed up because it was the best option I had at the time. I wanted to fly; I knew that. But serving my country, maybe going to war, being some sorta hero in a flight suit one day ... I wasn't thinking like that."

"Uh, huh. And what about now?"

"It's the same." She looked down, then took the first bite of the spinach. It was bitter and watery.

Another minute of silence followed before he dropped his knife and fork to his plate with a clang, then rose to his feet. "Well, you have yourself a good navy day out there," he said.

"Yup. You too."

She didn't look up as he shuffled from his seat and left.

*   *   *   *

1210 hours

Katherine had met her crew in the ready room. The forty-eight-million-dollar machine sitting out on the flight deck was to be crewed that day by Lieutenant Corey Moretti, an airborne tactical officer with 435 hours of flight time; Al Denholm, an enlisted crewman with the role of crew chief in the rear; and Larry Cruz, a U.S. Navy diver and rescue specialist referred to as "the rescue swimmer".

Lieutenant Katherine Marlowe took charge as the officer in command of the team and the primary pilot of their machine—a U.S. Navy MH-60R Seahawk helicopter. She had significant flight and command experience with more than two thousand flight hours over her nine-year navy career.

The team would be on watch for the next four hours at least, and on a Ready-15 state, prepared to be airborne within fifteen minutes.

The *Princeton*, like any warship at sea, is in a constant state of readiness. Anything and everything can happen. For all her defences and weapons, the ship had a few key vulnerabilities. The threat of low-flying supersonic air- or surface-launched missiles, and torpedoes from submarines operating undetected below the surface, kept her officers alert, both on and off watch.

She had some good cards of her own though, and the MH-60R Seahawk was at the top of the pack. Variants of the helicopter were deployed to various classes of U.S. Navy ships where their primary role was to provide early detection of enemy submarines—and, if required, to engage those submarines. *Engaging* was a typically passive navy word that meant "manoeuvre to kill" and then blow the bastard to kingdom come. The Seahawk was fitted with an impressive suite of electronic-warfare equipment and not to be messed with—often packing significant punch with Hellfire missiles, air-launched torpedoes, and a mounted machine gun in the rear. Secondary missions for the Seahawk—or Romeo as it was called in the navy—included search and rescue, logistics support, personnel transport, and medical evacuation.

The helicopter on *Princeton* had been tasked for a secondary mission—on standby for logistics support and combat search and rescue, should circumstance demand it. And the crew had heard a whisper their operations might be "unusual" that day. This explained the presence of their rescue swimmer, as they rarely carried a second rear crewman for their primary role.

Lieutenant Moretti had conducted a pre-flight check in, on, and around the aircraft. The tail section and the four main rotor blades had been swung into their flight positions, ready to go. Katherine had also made general checks on the helicopter, as she always did. Moretti was thorough, but she couldn't help herself, and he'd learned not to be miffed by her need to double-check.

Katherine and Moretti had discussed the weather forecasts, as well as the load-out weights of their fuel, personnel, and equipment to ensure that they were within operational limits. The latter was hardly necessary, given they weren't carrying heavy weapons, though they carried a full fuel load to maximise their time on patrol.

As Katherine briefed the crew, Moretti noted again how meticulous she was, leaving nothing to chance. He wouldn't say it aloud, but he liked how she did that. He'd flown with Lieutenant Marlowe for five months and they worked together well—most of the time. *She could loosen up some*, he sometimes thought. *Wouldn't hurt to relax some more with the others.*

She finished her briefing with her typical emphasis: "As always, remember we're a team out there. Everyone knows their role. You see a hazard or a risk affecting our safety, speak up about it. You have a suggestion about how we're doin' things—don't you dare be shy now."

She paused. "Any comments, questions?"

"No, ma'am," Denholm murmured, and the other two men shook their heads.

*   *   *   *

As the hours ticked by, the Seahawk crew monitored operational and weather changes and stayed alert to operations in their area by checking the various tactical feeds. They engaged in quiet conversation and bantered here and there, but they would not relax while on watch. And especially not on Ready-15.

Their whole watch could have played out like that, all tension but no release, but a direct order mercifully came through at 1526 hours. Katherine took the call on an intercom phone, talking with a controller in the Combat Information Center. She scribbled down a thirty-second brief before she dropped the receiver back into its cradle with a solid whack.

"Showtime, guys. Let's move!"

Each of the four moved in unison. They grabbed their flight vests and threw them on, then picked up their flight bags and helmets.

Katherine's voice grew louder as they came through the hangar doors and onto the aft flight deck. "We got an F-18 down. Hopefully, the pilot ejected okay, but we don't know. We'll find out more airborne."

They pulled on their caps and combat helmets. Moretti and Katherine dropped their dark helmet visors as they emerged into the harsh sunlight. They were both scanning the helicopter with their eyes: checking, double-checking, looking for anything out of place. The ground crew was preparing to remove the chocks and safety chains from the landing gear as both pilots strapped into their cockpit seats.

The Seahawk sat poised on the deck. Ready to go, almost eager, her shape looking all business. If viewed from the side in silhouette, the machine resembled the shape of a dolphin—minus the flippers and dorsal. But to the crews who flew the Seahawk, it was a proud member of the Black Wolves, the Helicopter Maritime Strike Squadron 85—as the three wolves painted in stark black on the Seahawk's tail testified. Two wolves were in a fierce attacking pose and the other was baying to the moon.

As the crew prepared for departure, everything about them conveyed an air of professionalism and duty. With the electrical systems switched on, the machine began its transition from a cold-and-dark state to ready to fly. The cockpit had none of the old-style round instrument dials—that would be so twentieth century. Instead, four large flat panel display screens and two smaller flight-management units come to life in bright colour, providing pilots with everything they needed to monitor aircraft speed, altitude, and attitude, along with information on aircraft status, systems, navigation, moving maps, communications, and tactical data.

There were far fewer switches and knobs in this modern cockpit, with many replaced by multifunction buttons surrounding the displays.

Katherine and Moretti worked through the pre-start checklist. With the full electrical system operating and the fuel pumps on, Katherine engaged the engine-one starter. She was rewarded with a developing whine from the GE-T700 gas turbine engine mounted above and behind the cockpit. The whine built into a crescendo as the engine started and came up to operating temperature and pressure. The second engine then joined the din.

Their checklist procedure gathered pace. Moretti read the items as Katherine checked the item in the cockpit and responded.

"RPM percent one and two." … "Both checked."

"Transmission pressure." … "Checked."

"Hydraulic caution lights." … "Yup. One and two off."

"Hydraulic A pressure." … "Checked—"

And on it went. Both pilots had been through the checklists often enough to see them in their sleep. But they treated every journey through the procedure with wide-eyed concentration.

One of Moretti's instructors had once told him, in his broad Texan drawl, "It's just like sex, son. *Make every time like the first time.*" Moretti didn't think much of the analogy, considering how losing his virginity had gone. But the message was clear enough: *do this like your life depends on it, every time.*

Katherine eased the engine power control lever out of the idle position. The four rotor blades began a slow circular motion overhead as the transmission progressively engaged the rotor head to the mechanical power from the engines.

They ran the pre-take-off checklist as the ground crew took shelter from the rotor wash near the hangar door. The signal officer gave the pilots a thumbs-up to confirm that all chains and chocks were clear of the helicopter, and that the controller had cleared them for take-off.

"Y'all folks good to go back there?" Katherine asked on the intercom. She craned her head around to look back into the rear cabin.

Denholm and Cruz signalled their own thumbs-up from the rear cabin. They came back to Katherine on the intercom: "Yup." "All good."

The next part of the procedure still gave Katherine a buzz, even then after hundreds of similar take-offs. The moment when the Seahawk is transformed from a land- or ship-captured beast to a bird of the air. Katherine reached for the collective-control lever next to her seat. She rotated the power grip and eased the collective upward. The Seahawk responded eagerly by lifting a fraction lighter on its undercarriage. As the whine of the engines increased to a roar and the thumping *whacka-whacka* sound of the rotor blades built to a climax, the helicopter left the deck and hovered free a few feet in the air.

Katherine had never forgotten her first time in a helicopter. The experience was etched in her memory as one of her most treasured experiences.

At age seventeen, and with financial help from her grandfather, she'd saved enough money frying chicken at a Bojangles to start her flying lessons.

She signed up at a small airfield and won over Old Mitch Parker, its veteran flying instructor, who told her she "got what it takes" after her very first lesson in a fixed-wing Piper Cherokee. Encouraged, she continued to scrape money together for lessons whenever she could. She went solo with only eleven hours in her logbook. Six months later she passed her private pilot licence test with ease.

All was going to plan until a Robinson R44 helicopter landed at the airfield for an overnight stay. Katherine got talking to the pilot. He was so impressed with her knowledge and enthusiasm that he offered to take her for a quick five-minute hop over the bay. She accepted his invitation, nearly hysterical with excitement for the first time in her reserved young life.

It was *that* moment—the amazing, incredible, beautiful moment when the helicopter left the ground, turned, and accelerated away in one smooth effortless motion—that Katherine was truly hooked. Hook, line, and sinker.

"The view, the view," Katherine yelled into the phone later that day to her grandfather. "There's no better way to see everything. You can slow down, take it all in, hover, land where you want. I loved it!"

"Ah, alrighty," was all Grandpa could muster in response. He'd been in helicopters himself—many times. But that had been decades ago in a different country and under vastly different circumstances.

A gentle push forward and left on the cyclic control column in Katherine's hand eased the Seahawk from the hover. With further control inputs, and a push on the left anti-torque pedal at her feet, the helicopter banked and climbed over the open sea.

*　　*　　*　　*

1531 hours

As they cleared the ship, Moretti reported in by radio to the controller in the CIC: "Princeton, Black-Wolf Seven-Ten, airborne, initial track two-niner-five, four on board, endurance two-forty."

Moretti patched the radio frequency into the Seahawk's crew intercom to let the crew hear the CIC brief.

"Black-Wolf Seven-Ten, maintain present track," the operations controller radioed back. "Stand by for further ops details."

Within a few minutes the crew were given a more detailed brief. GPS coordinates of the location where the F/A-18E fighter jet had last been seen on radar were received via datalink into the Seahawk's flight management system. With a few button presses, Moretti plugged the coordinates into their route profile. A diamond target symbol and a magenta direct-route line were then displayed on their navigation screen. Katherine turned the helicopter towards the route line, tracking outbound from the ship.

Their destination was farther southwest and well out to sea at a distance of seventy-two nautical miles. At their cruising speed of one hundred and forty knots, it would take around thirty-five minutes to arrive.

"Thirty-five minutes is a hell of a long time to be floating in that ocean," Moretti remarked.

"Yeah, and when we get there, we still gotta' find him," Katherine said. "Could take a while. The Hawkeye that overflew didn't pick up an SLB, so we have to assume it's not pinging. It'll be all eyes outside today, guys."

The SLB was designed to activate during the ejection procedure, transmitting its GPS location. If it had malfunctioned, that would make their mission much more challenging.

"Mets, let's start runnin' the fuel and endurance numbers," Katherine ordered.

Katherine usually called him "Mets" when they were airborne. It was a far less unflattering callsign than the one she'd been cursed with—Flare, an unfortunate reference to how the air force's less manly pilots, unlike those on the navy's carriers, could safely flare their fighter jets to land on their endless runways. Air force pilots, as they said in the navy, would "flare to land and squat to pee."

"Our time on station will be one-twenty minutes," Moretti reported.

"Check," Katherine responded, running the figures through her mind. She was aware that they had a twenty-minute fuel reserve, and *Princeton* was moving towards their position at fifteen miles every hour. "Keep a real close check on actual fuel; I gotta feelin' we're gonna need every drop we got."

Moretti sensed an uncharacteristic tension in her voice. She didn't often express herself in terms of her feelings, and he wondered what she was thinking.

*　　*　　*　　*

GPS position 31.027923, -119.419521,
Pacific Ocean   1612 hours

The Seahawk arrived on station four minutes after the estimate due to an unfavourable headwind. Katherine surveyed the bland, flat scene. A low grey overcast hung over the sea, draining the afternoon light from the sun, and robbing the swell of any clear visual definition, aside from the occasional white breaker as a wave would rise to fight the wind.

Hmm. This is not going to be easy. "Heads on a swivel," Katherine ordered. "Let's find this guy."

Moretti, Cruz, and Denholm were straining through the windows, scanning the water for anything interrupting the black of the sea. They were hoping to see something to guide them, maybe part of the aircraft, or even the pilot floating in a pool of bright orange marker fluid.

But no, nothing. The pilot was nowhere to be seen. And the Seahawk's radar suite had nothing to report.

"Be alert," Katherine said. "We don't know why this fighter fell outta the sky. We have to assume it could be the result of hostile action. *Eyes out.*"

The crew's silence acknowledged the grim possibility. They'd all been briefed on the operational environment for the day and were aware of potential hostile threats.

Moretti had prepared a standard grid search pattern before they arrived on station. The Seahawk began its sequenced path across the sky, radiating in lines from the initial GPS search position. Mile after mile, minute after minute of burning holes in the air. But still, nothing.

At 1817 hours, Moretti said what they all knew was coming: "We're joker fuel and approaching bingo. I've rerun the numbers and we got seven more minutes before we gotta head back."

Katherine didn't respond at first. Her mind worked overtime, calculating time, distance, and fuel burn. "Let's keep at it," she said.

Cruz had been perched at the left side of the Seahawk for two hours straight. He rubbed his eyes hard and slow as he strained to see in the failing light. He spoke up on the intercom: "If this guy was on the surface, I think we'd a found him by now."

The others didn't respond.

Cruz took a risk and continued: "We ain't gonna see him in this light."

"Keep looking," Katherine shot back.

For ten more minutes they searched on. With the low overcast still hanging in the sky, the light dissipated even faster than the forecast time for last light.

Moretti broke the silence: "Katherine, we're past bingo fuel and into our fixed reserve. We gotta bug out."

His words only confirmed her own logic. It was time to put her feelings aside and head for home, despite the drive to succeed boiling within her. They would be landing on fumes, but Katherine was certain they'd be alright. With the ship traveling towards them, their return trip would be at least thirty miles shorter.

The crew kept to themselves as they cruised back to the ship. They each reflected on the past hours, and their disappointment.

*　　*　　*　　*

1834 hours

"Contact—three o'clock low in the water!" Denholm, on the right-side of the Seahawk, had picked up a flash of something in his peripheral vision.

Katherine hit the right anti-torque pedal and banked hard right, reefing the nose of the helicopter around to the three o'clock position. She eased the cyclic control back and lowered the collective to bring the helicopter to a creeping hover.

"Searchlight on." Moretti had hit the switch. And there, bobbing in the swell eighty yards away, they spotted the yellow of a life vest—visible for fleeting moments at the top of each swell.

"Stand by for recovery," Katherine said.

"Katherine—*fuel state!*"

"Mets, we ain't leaving this guy. *No way.*"

She manoeuvred the Seahawk to a safe hover altitude downwind of the pilot's position. In no time, Denholm had Cruz out on the hoist and was lowering him to the surface.

With a few yards to go, Cruz flipped the harness latch and dropped into the sea, flippers first. The pilot was unresponsive as Cruz fitted the harness over his shoulders and under his arms, reattached the hoist line, and gave the thumbs-up to Denholm to hoist-away.

Cruz and the pilot were barely inside the cabin when Katherine swung the Seahawk back onto their departure heading. "We're outta here! Mets, give *Princeton* our ETA and tell 'em we need a green deck with the lights burning."

Katherine waited until the radio conversation with the *Princeton* CIC had finished, then spoke on the intercom: "Guys. How's our pilot back there?"

"He's not good, Captain," Denholm replied with his best attempt at a thick Scottish accent. "And I cannae change the laws of the sea."

"Oh, boy," Katherine said, shaking her head.

Denholm then switched to a deep deadpan American accent, mimicking a certain doctor of 1960s TV fame. "He's *dead,* Katherine."

The stress and strain of the past few hours broke as the four allowed themselves to smile and chuckle. The pilot was indeed dead—in a sense, at least. He wasn't breathing when the navy placed his lifeless body there in the ocean three hours ago.

Cruz was not to be outdone. "Skipper, if you don't mind, I'll make our customer here more comfortable?"

"Granted," Katherine replied.

Ten seconds later, the rescued "pilot" appeared in the cockpit. Cruz plopped him at the back of the avionics pedestal between Moretti and Katherine. "Meet Oscar," he said. The burlap mannequin, stuffed with polyurethane into the rough shape of a person, stared stupidly at the instrument panel with its head drooped towards Moretti. And to add insult to no injury, Denholm had jammed a piece of stiff cigar-shaped tube into its mouth.

But dummy pilot or not, Katherine and crew were returning to the ship knowing they'd completed a tough mission in challenging conditions.

Princeton's crew, including those in the Seahawk, were taking part in

Strongarm, a pre-deployment exercise within Carrier Air Wing 11 and the ships of Carrier Strike Group 11. The exercise would continue for another five days, preparing the group for their next major deployment out on the world's oceans.

The late evening fell into full-blown darkness as the Seahawk settled onto the *Princeton*'s flight deck.

Test over.

Mission complete.

CHAPTER THREE

Science is about predictions based on predictable fact.
Life is about surprises based on the unpredictable
reality.

—Ori Hofmekler

11 April 2019

A cool breeze picked up as the afternoon began to fade. A few dry leaves blew along, dancing over the path, under Ben's seat, and into the open bus station. He sat still, waiting, his patience tested but holding true.

Bus services in the remote region were listed on schedules published for all to see. But a schedule in South Hamgyong was more of an aspiration rather than a promise by the state-run bus company—a stark contrast to Singapore, for example, where a schedule is as sacred as a Bible, or a Koran, whatever the flavour may be.

With this knowledge back of mind, Ben did not distract himself with frustration or anxiety, tempting as it was. He'd been waiting two hours for the bus bound for Pyongyang.

Ben had reported at the military base administration building at 1400 hours that afternoon. He'd been met by a senior officer and their interaction was brief. The officer informed Ben the current phase of his training was complete and ordered him to return home and wait for further orders.

No congratulations or handshake, no medals, or bars, or insignia. Just his travel documents and the return of his Chinese passport. The officer gave him ten minutes to get his belongings and catch a ride to the bus station.

None of this surprised Ben. The course was his seventh over the preceding three years, and each one had ended—and began—just as abruptly.

He set his mind towards home, thinking of his parents for the first time in a few days. Dormant emotions of belonging and connection arose, and he didn't try to suppress them. It would be good to be home again.

Ben had travelled the route to and from North Korea since his father first took him there at the age of thirteen. The journey had become routine. The bus from South Hamgyong would take him to Pyongyang, where he would take the China-DPRK train service, leaving North Korea via the Chinese border city of Dandong. From there it was onto Beijing, and then a China Southern domestic flight to the far south-west corner of China, landing at Shenzhen Bao'an International Airport.

Ben would use his fake Chinese passport for most of the journey. Issued by the Chinese embassy in Pyongyang, it was as credible as any regular Chinese passport.

From the airport, Ben would take the next local bus for the brief journey to the domestic border with Hong Kong. He'd take the last leg of his journey on the MRT subway train into Hong Kong proper, arriving at his parents' apartment in a high-rise building in Fu Chan Estate, Hammer Hill.

And then the identity of the young man known in his birth country of North Korea to be Jeong Yong-sun, would transform once again back to Cai "Ben" Chen in his long-adopted second home.

*　*　*　*

North Sea Fleet Headquarters, Qingdao, China
30 April 2019, 1850 hours

It had been another long day for Rear Admiral Pengcheng Tao.

There were many such days for the rear admiral, given his position as commander of the Chinese Navy's North Sea Fleet. But the sheer volume of information, opinions, facts, and figures coming at him were stressing even his limits. Pengcheng had been on duty since 0500 hours. He would be unlikely to get out of the naval headquarters building and back to his nearby apartment before midnight.

Of Pengcheng's fifty-nine years on earth, he had served forty-two years in the navy. He became the People's Liberation Army Navy's youngest-ever captain and commanding officer of a ship at thirty-two, and was promoted to rear admiral at forty-eight. Yet despite his years he hadn't lost two of his most recognisable attributes: his torso resembled a small bull's—stocky and muscled with little excess fat—and his head was almost as square and accented by an abrupt flat top of hair that remained stubbornly jet black.

"Sir, you have a call on a secure line from Pyongyang," his executive secretary said, his tone apologetic.

Pengcheng, a consummate professional, let out a long breath. "Put it through to my office," he ordered, striding from the operations centre and into the corridor.

He covered the one hundred and forty metres to his office in less than a minute. An indicator light blinked on his desk phone. He picked up the receiver. "Speak."

"Sir, the call is from Pyongyang … a Colonel General Kim Hyun-woo."

"Proceed."

Pengcheng heard the click as the call was transferred. "Colonel General Kim, this is Rear Admiral Pengcheng. Greetings to you."

"Greetings to you from Pyongyang, Rear Admiral, and thank you."

Formalities over, the two men lowered their diplomatic screens.

"Hyun-woo, it's good to speak with you again," Pengcheng said, his tone now far less formal.

"And you also, my good friend." Kim paused before getting straight down to business. "The American pig bastards have done it again, it would seem?"

Kim Hyun-woo had posed what he thought to be a rhetorical question, but Pengcheng was not drawn easily. "Not so quickly, Hyun-woo. There is still much at play."

"Maybe so, but the Americans did not take your bait in Chinese Taipei and now we have them at our doorstep!" Kim had to walk a line between expressing his frustration while maintaining his nation's diplomatic relationship with China. "Tao, forgive me," he continued. "Our supreme leader is furious, as you may imagine. I have just come from a difficult meeting with my superiors. He is threatening retaliatory action."

"Please, Hyun-woo. You must counsel your superiors to manage their response. This is not a time to make rash threats or sudden movements. We are not at war. Not at all."

Kim understood that he'd been given a not-so-subtle order. "I will do as I can, my good friend," he responded. "But do not forget—we are *always* at war."

Pengcheng was confident that Kim would do whatever he could to get his superiors to ease down. Their relationship was a key back channel between the two nations where much of the diplomatic and strategic work transpired. He could trust Kim in this.

The two nations had recently renewed their fifty-year alliance. The agreement included, for the first time, a commitment to joint military exercises in and around the Korean Peninsula. In the days preceding their phone call, the first exercise had played out in the seas between China and the Democratic People's Republic of Korea.

Both men were located close to the action. As they spoke, Rear Admiral Pengcheng Tao sat in the headquarters of the PLAN's North Sea Fleet in Qingdao. Three hundred and sixty miles to the east, Colonel General Kim Hyun-woo sat in his office in Pyongyang, on the opposite shore of the Yellow Sea.

Kim had worked with the DPRK Navy to assemble a coastal assault force of amphibious vessels and landing craft. They were supported by two helicopter frigates, six patrol boats, and three diesel-electric submarines.

The assembly of such a force for an exercise in the Yellow Sea was not unusual, but the exercise was provocative. A fleet of assault craft had headed straight for South Korea's Baengnyeong Island, crossing the Northern Limit Line, a boundary set by the United Nations following the Korean War, in what appeared to be the first stage of an all-out attack on the tiny island. The fleet then turned east and conducted a mock beach assault on the North Korean mainland.

The South Koreans were furious. There'd been other altercations in recent years between the two nations in the same stretch of disputed waters. DPRK Navy vessels had breached the NLL on more than one occasion, and some incidents had resulted in short naval battles with damage to vessels and casualties on both sides.

This exercise was bolstered for the first time by ships from China's PLAN under orders from Pengcheng, who had sent a Luhu-class destroyer and two Jiangkai II–class frigates from the North Sea Fleet. The ships remained farther out to sea, sailing along the international boundary. A formation of four Chinese fighter-attack jets and two long-range bombers had also patrolled adjacent to the region while remaining in neutral airspace. It was both an obvious show of Chinese military force and a demonstration that their commitment to joint exercises with the DPRK was more than sabre-rattling rhetoric.

And the world was listening.

"Where are the Americans now?" Kim asked.

"The carrier group turned north yesterday and have proceeded at high speed into the Yellow Sea. They are west of Jeju Island, near the Korean coast."

Kim paused. "I never thought they would make such a move."

"Neither did we, my friend. This is the bizarre strategic world we now live in, with an American president who is not afraid to make speedy decisions as he goes. Gone are the days when we could predict the advice of the U.S. military and national security advisers for their president, and his eventual agreement to their advice."

"Do you think their advice yesterday was for the carrier group to continue towards Chinese Taipei?"

"Yes, most certainly. Our build-up near Chinese Taipei would have remained their prime concern. But their president had other ideas it would seem."

Pengcheng's mind drifted as he was composing his next words. The Chinese had no intention of invading Chinese Taipei—or Taiwan as it is otherwise known—but it had been many years since they had tested the full resolve of the U.S. in the region. The provocation would determine how close the Americans would place one of their carrier groups to Chinese Taipei—vital information that would inform future Chinese strategy.

In 1996 the USA had sent two aircraft carriers—USS *Independence* and later USS *Nimitz*—and their respective strike groups into the region in response to the Chinese firing missiles into the sea close to major cities on the coast of Chinese Taipei. USS *Independence* had taken up position closest to the conflict zone—to the east of the island, both within the operating range of the carrier's strike aircraft into the region and a safe distance from Chinese anti-ship missiles and submarines operating from the Chinese coast. Contrary to popular myth, neither of the carriers had sailed through the strait, but the Americans had made their point nonetheless.

The 1996 conflict subsided without major incident. The Chinese Navy, which was much smaller at the time, had no choice but to stand-down. Pengcheng remembered the humiliation and embarrassment all too well. Once again, the might of the USA had imposed itself on a conflict that was no business of their own. The Chinese became obsessed with the strategic power of the U.S. aircraft carriers, and the desire to build and use their own carriers grew.

Pengcheng would sometimes see them in his nightmares—a U.S. Navy aircraft carrier carving through the South China Sea at thirty knots with dozens of lethal aircraft buzzing to and from its flight deck. The best of the world's surface ships in formation behind, struggling to keep up with their almighty lead carrier.

"The Americans would have given our Yellow Sea exercise some attention though, surely?" Kim asked.

"Yes, but not with the attention of a whole carrier group." Pengcheng paused. "Though the recent tests of your larger medium-range rockets have rattled the Americans, it must be said. And they haven't conducted a major joint-exercise with the South Koreans for over three years."

"Indeed. The supreme leader does not appreciate the outrageous actions of the U.S. president. Rockets are his preferred reply!"

Both men laughed.

"How much closer do you think this carrier group will come?" Kim asked.

"They won't risk putting the carrier in close range of our anti-ship missiles or submarine patrols. We think they will take up station close to where they are now."

"Yes. And then they will sit there and *humiliate us*."

"We cannot risk a significant conflict," Pengcheng said. "Not with a carrier strike group. This would be suicide."

"And this is why you have pulled your three ships back from our joint exercise?"

Pengcheng wasn't sure whether Kim had made a statement or had asked another of his unnerving rhetorical questions. "Unfortunately, my dear Hyun-woo, yes, that is the case. We started this game and we have been out-manoeuvred."

"The game of chess we are playing appears one-sided, as if the Americans have extra pieces, or are playing with different rules."

"Insightful as always, Hyun-woo. While the Americans can move freely around the globe with their aircraft carriers, we will always play this game at a great disadvantage."

"But for how much longer must we be humiliated like this?" Kim asked. "How much longer will these aggressor pigs dictate our lives?"

Pengcheng had no reply to Kim's questions. The conversation had reached its conclusion. Both men signed off with cordial pleasantries and a commitment to discuss matters further. The rear admiral remained at his desk after ending the call and stared into the dark room—the perfect incubator for his bleak thoughts.

There must be another way, there must be.

CHAPTER FOUR

Words empty as the wind are best left unsaid.

—Homer

8 November 2020

How ironic, Katherine thought, more damned ocean! The vast Atlantic filled her view, but with a welcome twist. She was back on terra firma and no longer bound by the pitching, rolling, insular world of a navy ship.

From her window seat at the Buoy 48 Seafood Grill, she took in the wide expanse of Chic's Beach and the Chesapeake Bay beyond. Beyond the capes lay the Atlantic Ocean, but Katherine ignored that unwelcome detail. She was home on four weeks leave and the open sea would be the last thing on her mind.

Try as she might though, it seemed impossible to erase the navy from her thinking. Norfolk, Virginia, on the mid-Atlantic coast of the United States, crawled with sailors. And the tall superstructures of aircraft carriers at dock were ever-present, towering over everything nearby. Naval Station Norfolk occupied fifteen miles of waterfront and was the largest naval base on the planet. The base was home to four carrier strike groups and more than fifty navy vessels, along with the countless facilities for naval air support, fleet support, and fleet command spread throughout Norfolk and the Hampton Roads region. *Navy, navy, everywhere I look.*

The first few days of leave always stirred a strange mix of emotions. Katherine had spent the last weeks of her recent deployment pining for home and longing to get her feet back on solid ground. But she couldn't help feeling disconnected after the initial emotions of seeing her family and hometown had waned. She struggled with a gnawing realisation she was someone from somewhere else. She'd been away for eleven months, yet life here had carried on just fine without her.

Strange too was the sudden lack of structure, order, and routine. Gone were the uniforms, ranks, duties, and times on and off watch. No whistles, bells, or bitch-box announcements. Weeks would pass before the hum of the ship disappeared from her subconscious hearing.

And so as always, Katherine planned to spend only a week at home with her parents before taking off somewhere on her own. Somewhere inland and well away from the sea.

But not today. There were things to do in Norfolk today.

The divine goodness of late-season steamed blue crab wafted past as a waitress carried a tray to another table nearby and Katherine suppressed a shudder of pleasure. And there were other benefits to being on leave that Katherine was taking full advantage of. A khaki flight-suit and straight tied-back hair? Not on your life! Instead she was wearing an actual goddamn dress, makeup, perfume, and the necklace her mother had given her for graduation, and her hair was all the way down.

Katherine watched the boats sailing on the bay and allowed her thoughts to drift. It had been thirteen years since Katherine had sailed on Chesapeake Bay. Her navy career, ironically, had put an end to that. Her most cherished memories as a young girl were with her grandfather out on the bay in his little twenty-footer, *Lady Blue*. She grew to love the water, the wind, and the peace of sailing. As a young teen she'd joined a local yacht club and competed in club competitions whenever she could during the season.

As she watched a yacht sail through the gap between Cape Henry and Cape Charles, Katherine's mind went back to a race when she was sixteen.

"He's tacking, *he's tacking!*" Toph yelled from the front of the J/29 sailboat where he managed the headsails. Katherine stood bolt upright at the helm. They were running a close second in the last race of the regatta, a half-mile from the finish line with a genuine chance of winning. Just up ahead on their starboard side, the lead boat from another club was doing the unthinkable.

"Katherine!" Sarah yelled from the starboard side, crouching to act as counterbalance as the boat keeled hard to port. "Watch his line!"

Their adversary had done the unexpected and changed tack just ahead of them. Their boat was on the same line as Katherine's and just fifty yards away. Both crews could hear the flap of their opponents' sails, the barked commands of their skippers, the swish and thump of the hulls through the water as they drew closer. There would be a collision in about thirty seconds if both skippers refused to flinch.

Katherine froze for a few seconds as their adversary came even closer. So close that she could make out the self-satisfied smirk spread over the face of William D. Baxter Jr.—or Billy the Kid, as his friends and crew called him. He took a moment to look her straight in the eye.

A surge of emotion welled within Katherine. Powerful. Primeval. Her body seemed abandoned to it. Her eyes narrowed to slits of focused darkness as she gripped the tiller. She adjusted the boat's heading to get the best angle on the breeze—squeezing out every knot of speed she could. "Pete, tighten the main sheet."

"The little shit's playin' chicken," Sarah said, shaking her head in disbelief.

Katherine knew the rules, as did Billy. The boat to the windward side had to give way and fall in behind. But the direction of the breeze that evening did not favour either boat and kept shifting either side of their tacking line. In the split-second before the collision would become unavoidable, someone had to give.

It was Katherine. "Prepare to tack!"

Sarah had just responded "Ready" when Katherine drove the tiller hard to the right. The boat groaned as it changed tack and the deck angle rolled to the opposite side. Sarah ducked as the mainsail boom rocketed past, just grazing her back. The startled look on her face told Katherine how close Sarah had come to going overboard. Neither said a word.

Katherine had no choice but to give way. Billy's rich parents could buy him another boat, but she was sailing a boat borrowed from a club member. There was no way she could risk damaging it.

Billy predicted her evasive move and changed tack again. He eased the boat back onto a starboard tack, putting Katherine's boat another twenty yards back.

Both boats were again on the same tack and only two hundred and fifty yards from the finish. There would be no room for any further manoeuvres. Just a matter of trimming the sails, heads down, and a straight sprint to the finish.

It was going to be close. Katherine's boat had been better trimmed for the wind and had a few knots more speed. They gained on their adversary, drawing them in closer once more.

"What the *hell's* he doing now? He can't do that!" Katherine was incredulous. There was a right way and a wrong way to do something. But Billy the Kid would do things his way.

He changed his boat's direction—just enough to stay on course for the finish line—and also enough for his boat's sails to be fully upwind of Katherine's boat. A classic move known in the business as an *overbear*, or in lay terms as *stealing one's wind*.

Katherine's boat fell into the shadow of their adversary and the wind literally fell out of their sails. She and her crew looked up in unison at the mast and stared with disbelief as the sheets of cloth sagged and flapped impotently in the stale air. Their forward speed dropped almost to a stop.

A sharp blast of the horn from the steward's boat confirmed what they already knew. The race was lost.

*　*　*　*

"We need to protest! He broke the rules!" Katherine complained to her grandfather.

"Steady, Kat. Take a breath." Her grandfather had an economy with words, and a knack for knowing what to say, and when.

But hell hath no fury like a young woman cheated in a regatta. "Take a breath? That piece of shit stole our wind and you're tellin' *me* to take a breath?"

Her grandfather looked straight at her, even and calm, and she finally took a much-needed breath.

"What rule did he break?" he asked.

"I don't know, there must be a rule about it somewhere!"

"Nope."

Katherine scowled. His economy of words could be plain infuriating. "Well if there ain't a rule covering what he did," Katherine said, "then somebody should damn well write one!"

"I got pen and paper in the truck," he said with a cheeky smile.

Katherine had no immediate reply. She looked away, trying her best to hide a grin. He had a way, which was why she loved him so much, even when he was annoying her with a life lesson.

Having pushed the grin away, she tried to remonstrate further, but her furious tempest no longer billowed her psychological sails. "Rules or no rules, Grandpa, it just ain't right."

"He sailed within the rules. He outplayed you. It might not feel right, but he did nothing illegal. If ya only see the world in black and white, you're gonna be awful frustrated when shady stuff happens. And shady stuff happens a lot, believe me."

*　*　*　*

"Katherine!" Thomas Delaney's voice shook her back from her daydream. He strode through the restaurant with a beaming smile.

"Tom, hey, it's so great to see you!" Katherine said, getting up to greet him.

As he walked towards her, Katherine recognised his signature broad smile and kind eyes. He was about her height, a few inches under six feet.

She noticed he'd put on weight around his waist since she last saw him a year and a half ago. His dark hair had thinned, and he had changed his hairstyle. But he was the Tom she knew.

The two had met in high school and became close friends. After Katherine moved to San Diego for the navy, they'd meet up whenever she could get back East on leave. And they kept up a tradition of writing to each other every few months—old-fashioned pen and paper style—which helped Katherine cope with the loneliness of navy life.

The next ten minutes were a mad rush of catching up, laughing, ordering their meals, and basking in each other's company. No matter how long they'd been apart, it always seemed like they had seen each other the day before.

"So tell me Tomboy—" Tom hated the nickname, which was why Katherine used it— "you still doin' your *thang* at City Hall?"

"Yeah, yeah, I'm mayor now. Didn't you hear the goss?"

"Well, I'll be damned. Promoted from second-rate legal counsel to mayor just like that, huh?"

"Ooh, totally roasted!" Tom shot back, grinning. "We can't all be flying whirlybirds looking for mermaids."

"Mermaids, huh? Last 'mermaid' I found was four hundred feet long, black, and weighed, oh, six thousand tons."

"Wow, she sounds like my kinda girl."

Katherine giggled. "Yeah, well, I plugged her with a torpedo right up where the sun don't shine."

Tom, halfway through a sip of beer, snorted and coughed.

Katherine waited for him to compose himself. "So, when ya gonna, like, lose that job and do something you *really* wanna do?"

"Ah, that's easy. I'll do that when you finally ditch the navy like you're always saying you will."

"Well, this next deployment will be my last. I'm done."

Tom maintained his smile. "Where have I heard *that* before," he said.

"Here ya go," the waitress interrupted, setting down their tray of crabs.

Tom and Katherine fell silent as they dove into the ritual of prying off shells, removing the mustard, and dipping buttery crabmeat into vinegar. It was a welcome break in the conversation. They both needed to rest up before they resumed their banter, which neither of them wanted to get the worst of, friendly though it always was.

Despite the efforts of their families and friends, Katherine and Tom's friendship had never developed into anything more. Katherine's mother, Rachel, was the worst offender, but even her grandfather had dropped a hint or two.

Katherine's longest romantic relationship lasted just five months. The long deployments were too much to bear for him. He broke it off with a "Dear Jane" email three months into her first deployment.

And Katherine had a strict rule against relationships in the workplace. As did the navy, though a few of her squadron mates had tried and failed.

As for her and Tom, neither of them had ever even broached the subject. But Katherine felt more reflective than usual, and uneasy in her own skin. "So, you think I should leave the navy?" she prodded.

"Ah, I didn't say that."

Katherine stared at Tom. "Do you *want* me to leave the navy?"

Tom popped a baby potato into his mouth, chewing for longer than he needed to as he composed himself. "Um. I want you to do what's best for you."

"Yup, but can't I ask my best friend for advice?"

"I guess ..."

"Well?"

Tom took a long sip of his Benchmark pilsner. A frown creased his forehead. "I don't think it should be on me. I mean, it's your life and you should do what you think's right for you. It shouldn't be my, ah ... responsibility."

It was Katherine's turn for a long sip of her beer. *Now there's a lawyer talking, if ever I heard one.* They sat in silence for a long awkward moment.

Tom looked perplexed. Katherine tried to fathom why she'd gone there. She'd surprised even herself.

So when in doubt, return to the teasing.

"At ease, sailor," Tom ordered in his best official voice.

Katherine smiled. "I'm a commissioned officer, I'll have you know. I give you orders, not the other way round. You got that, Delaney?"

"Anything you say, ma'am. Shall I drop and give you twenty, ma'am?"

"Hell, no. *Make it thirty!*"

And so it went. They talked about other things, ate, drank, and enjoyed each other's company as the cool fall afternoon rolled by.

CHAPTER FIVE

To put the world right in order, we must first put the nation in order; to put the nation in order, we must first put the family in order; to put the family in order, we must first cultivate our personal life; we must first set our hearts right.

—Confucius

Suffolk, Virginia, 24 November 2020

Things in the kitchen were already hectic. The only cook—Rachel Marlowe—appeared to be doing her best impression of a headless chicken.

Life in the Marlowe home in suburban Suffolk, Virginia, was hardly ever busy. Rachel both loved and loathed the annual Thanksgiving event. Growing up in Canada, she was unprepared for the complexities of preparing a traditional Thanksgiving dinner.

People in Canada are generally considered to be more laid back than in the United States, and Rachel Marlowe certainly fitted the bill. Of slight build and five foot three, she seemed in danger of being blown away if a strong wind were to rise. Her temperament was unflappable, her character reliable and even, and her humour dry and sparse. Her luxurious deep brown hair was giving way to an undercurrent of grey.

Rachel had moved to Virginia with her parents when she was nineteen. A budding artist with an obvious gift for drawing, sketching, and watercolour—Rachel's world had brimmed with promise. She planned to settle into the Hamptons region, get a part-time-job, and find a good art school where she could develop her talents. Her parents, Jacob and Helen Greenberg, were pleased she'd taken the move from Canada so well. Rachel saw the move as an opportunity to spread her wings—to engage with the big, wide creative world outside their small hometown. And to warm up a little.

For two years that is exactly what Rachel did: working as a waitress in Newport News and attending a local college. Her portfolio developed, and she expanded into photography—a natural extension of her interest in light, colour, and form.

"You look like you could use some help?"

Rachel spun from the kitchen counter and hurried across the kitchen to hug her only child without a word. Rachel's eyes welled as she took in the face of the person she loved most. "I'm *so* glad you made it back, honey," she said as she squeezed Katherine's hands. "You're home now."

They held their gaze for a few seconds, communicating through their eyes and smiles as only mothers and daughters can.

"Of course I'm back. I wouldn't miss this for anything," Katherine lied.

Rachel took a few seconds to compose herself. Managing outward displays of emotion wasn't something she had to concern herself with often. "So, tell me all about your trip. How'd it go?" she said as she dabbed her eyes with paper towel.

"All in good time. But first I think we got some cookin' to do, huh?"

Rachel smiled. "Oh, you think?" she asked as she looked around at the chaotic state of the small kitchen. Her creative flair was evident, but her administrative and organisational skills in the kitchen were, on the whole, awful.

"So gimme an apron. Let's do this."

Katherine was no master chef, but what she lacked in talent she made up with the good ole navy can-do attitude. It was just another mission after all: identify the objective, muster your resources, control the threats, then do it!

Mother and daughter's differing personalities complemented each other, and it wasn't long before the culinary chaos became more shipshape.

"I think we might just make it," Rachel said, looking around at their progress with a repeating nod. "So good to have your help."

"Yup, all good. But, um, when's the turkey flyin' on in?"

"When your uncle Jed gets here."

"Oh yeah ... Uncle Jed." Katherine rolled her eyes with a feigned half-smile.

"Katie!"

Richard Marlowe was standing at the open back door. His tall, lean frame filled the doorway, and his cropped steel-grey hair and beard were just visible in the morning light spilling in from behind. Richard was the only person who called her that. He'd only call her "Katherine" when she was in trouble—when *he* thought she was in trouble, that was.

"Dad," Katie said. She gave him a peck on the cheek.

A pot of potatoes steamed with excitement on the stove. Rachel pulled back the lid before things boiled over.

Richard strode through the kitchen with two small boxes in hand. "I'll put these in the dining room."

Rachel shot Katherine a knowing look. She blinked hard, pursed her lips, and forced an awkward smile before turning her attention back to the pie crust she was crimping into its pan.

Katherine was unmoved. She'd seen that look many times before.

* * * *

Relative calm had come over the Marlowe home by late morning, until pierced by the singing notes of a melodic car horn as a pickup truck pulled up on the street. This could mean only one thing: Jed and Barbara Marlowe were about to enter the building.

At age sixty-one, Jed was four years older than Richard. He stood a few inches taller than his little brother and his frame was more substantial. He had the neck and shoulders of a quarter-horse, and arms and legs you'd find on an antique dining table.

Brace yourself, Katherine thought.

Rachel took a deep breath as Richard went to the front door, followed by Rachel's father, Jacob, who had joined them for Thanksgiving.

"Hey, y'all. How's my favourite family?" Jed boomed, his arms out wide, his face beaming.

Richard extended a hand to his big brother, knowing full well that the gesture would be futile.

"Come here, ya big ole bear!" Jed growled as he put an arm around his brother's neck, pulled his head down, and messed up his hair.

Barbara Marlowe was still extricating herself from the pickup, all two hundred and sixty-five pounds of her. She let out a deep guttural laugh, enjoying the sight of brothers doin' what brothers do.

Thank god in heaven, Katherine almost said aloud as she saw that there were no other passengers in the truck. The couple's grown-up sons—cousins Josiah and Ezekiel—had not made the journey from Wayne County, West Virginia, that day.

Jed and Barbara worked their way down the welcoming line, kissing, hugging, and shaking hands. Barbara stepped back as she got to Katherine. "Oh my," she exclaimed, "you sure look awfully purdy."

Katherine smiled, understanding this to be a West Virginian compliment of the highest order.

Rachel stood last in line, as usual. She anticipated Jed would do his usual—picking her up in a bear hug and spinning her in a circle. But, thankfully, he was suffering from a pinched nerve in his lower back and had to content himself with a bear hug.

Everyone made their way inside, except for Jed, who halted on the last step. "Now y'all wait right there!" he said in his broadest accent. "I got me a lil somethin' in the pickup you'll all wanna see. Jacob, gimme a hand, will ya?—"

The two men ambled to the truck and Jed threw back the canvas cover. A few seconds later a small mountain appeared as the men lifted it up and over, with Jed wincing from "that goddamn nerve thing." The small mountain had been laid upon a thick slab of timber and wrapped in so much aluminium foil it could have survived re-entry from low earth orbit.

Jed and Jacob carried it up to the house and somehow manoeuvred it through the front door and into the kitchen. Everyone followed, transfixed by the object.

"And now, ma'am, may I present to you—" Jed spoke at a crawl and bowed to Rachel for dramatic effect— "Istanbul!"

Scattered applause followed, but the audience was not entirely sure what they were applauding.

Rachel had to ask, "Ah … Istanbul?"

"Hell yeah, girl. Istanbul … turkey!" Jed ripped off his hat and slapped it on his thigh as he laughed. Barbara, leaning against the kitchen doorway, erupted into supportive laughter—the effects likely to be detected at an earthquake monitoring centre somewhere.

The hapless Istanbul, as she'd been so cleverly named, weighed a good twenty-nine pounds. She could have fed a small army, let alone this small family standing wide-eyed around it.

"Well turkeys might fly," Jacob said in a quiet voice, "but that bird sure never did."

Katherine couldn't help a muffled giggle. *You shoulda called it Barbara*, she thought.

"Thank you so much, Jed. It's mighty kind of you and Barb to bring the bird this year," Rachel said as she peeled back the first layers of the aluminium foil. She wouldn't say it, but her mind raced in another direction. *How on earth am I gonna fit this bird in my oven?*

*　*　*　*

Preliminary Thanksgiving traditions had started in earnest. The television switched from the Macy's parade to the annual slaughter of the Lions. The men were eating crab dip while watching Deshaun Watson carve up Detroit's hapless defence, and the women kept their eye on Istanbul's progress as they caught up over a few too many coffees.

For all their bluster and theatrics, Uncle Jed and Aunt Barb were a warming influence on the home. They exuded an infectious simple love of life and family that made even Richard loosen up. His long-lost

West Virginian accent would surface every now and then as they traded stories.

Katherine excused herself from the kitchen and led Herman, their greying golden retriever, into the backyard. She sat in the hammock and scratched Herman's ears as she allowed her thoughts to wander.

The irony of leaving this place, going to college at Virginia Tech, and then joining the navy was still clear to Katherine. She had grown up in this strict Christian household where her dad was in command and the others—Katherine and her mom—knew their place. To change her career track in her second year of college was like taking her life into her own hands. Both figuratively and literally.

In an even greater irony, Katherine had been primed and ready for the command-and-control world of the armed forces when she'd started officer training at age twenty-one. She hadn't been surprised or disturbed by domineering male officers telling her what to do.

Was it all an escape? *Well, no ... but yes.*

Katherine thought back to the day when she told her parents she was switching her major from pre-med to engineering with an eye on joining the navy. Neither parent had seen it coming.

Her dad was furious. "No, you're not! I'm not gonna just stand here and watch you ruin your life."

For the first time in Katherine's young life, though, she'd made up her own mind about her future and she would defend it. "It's my future and it's my decision."

"And I'll stop paying your tuition."

"If that's what you have to do," Katherine said. "I can take out loans."

"I know what's best for you. You hear me?" Richard yelled, towering over her while slamming his fist into his other hand.

Things had disintegrated from there.

"No, you don't. You wouldn't have a clue who I am or what I'm capable of," she shot back.

"*I* brought you into this world, Katherine, and I know you better than you know yourself."

"Oh really? Just like ya know Mom, huh?"

"What?"

"Where's Mom's dreams? Why isn't she doing what she loves?"

Richard Marlowe was speechless.

And Katherine wasn't finished yet. "So you're gonna decide my future and crush who I am, just like you did to Mom?"

"Don't you dare, or I'll—"

"Or you'll *what*? You'll pray to your almighty loving God that he'll strike me dead?" She looked to the heavens. "Come on then, oh Great One up there somewhere, take me out!"

Seconds passed with no response from above.

"Look," she continued, her sarcasm pushed up to eleven, "I'm still here. Hmm, guess that settles that then!"

Many times since, she wished she'd handled things better that day, although she still didn't know how. There had been years of molten rock roiling inside her, and that day had been the appointed time for the volcano to blow.

She looked up as Grandpa opened the screen door. He leaned against the tree at the foot of her hammock and lit his pipe.

"Gettin' some peace and quiet?" he asked, the question rhetorical. "Only five hours to go."

Katherine laughed. "C'mon, old man. You can do it."

"Oh, I dunno. Pretty soon Jed and Barb will be joinin' ole Istanbul in that oven if I get my way."

"Well, good luck with that."

To everyone else, Grandpa and Katherine seemed to fit hand and glove. He had taught her to sail and drive, and even paid for some of her flying lessons—without her dad knowing, of course. He was the person she'd confide in and talk things through: her struggles at school, her thoughts of a flying career. Grandpa was the father figure she did not otherwise have, and Kat was the daughter he had lost.

"How's she doin'?" Katherine nodded towards the kitchen window.

Grandpa looked down and scratched the ground with the toe of his shoe. "Aw, you know."

"I think about her all the time. When I'm away at sea."

"Yeah."

"I'm thinkin' to leave the navy. Move back here somewhere."

"And do what?"

"Um, not real sure right now."

"Sounds like a plan then."

Katherine slumped deeper into the hammock. "I just, like … worry … about her."

"I know, Kat. I know."

Jacob had known it for thirty-four years. He had watched as Rachel had met a tall, handsome Richard Marlowe in her early twenties. They fell in love and married within a year. He'd grimaced as Richard morphed from a dashing, carefree young man, his clandestine God-fearing ways coming to the fore. And he watched as the life force of his youngest daughter drained from her, her world of colour and light dissolving imperceptibly into a dim grey existence. By age thirty, her hopes and dreams as an artist had all but disappeared, and by age fifty-four, she had become someone he could barely recognise.

"Your mom made her choices. You made yours," Jacob said at last.

Katherine thought aloud. "I got free, but she can't."

"Who says she can't?"

He was right, but also wrong, and they both knew it.

"Best thing you ever did, joining the navy," he said.

"Yup. I don't know for how much longer is all."

"Just live your life, Kat. You can't fix up other people." Jacob turned his pipe over and tapped out the ashes onto the dirt. "It's gettin' cold. We better head on in."

*   *   *   *

Istanbul made her grand entrance at 6:45 PM. This was an even-numbered year, so Jed was given the honour of carving her, and she sat

49

at his end of the table. She shared the space with an orchestra of mashed and scalloped potatoes, steamed and roasted vegetables, stuffing and gravy, and Barbara's famous mac and cheese with crumbled bacon. The remaining available space for the eight dinner guests was minimal.

Pastor Bill Mathers—senior pastor of the Children of the True Word Church—and his wife, Jolene, had joined the Thanksgiving dinner. Jacob had met the Mathers once before, but he wasn't a churchgoer and didn't know them well, and Katherine had never met them at all since she'd stopped attending her parents' church before its previous pastor retired.

"Thank ya so much, Richard and Rachel, for invitin' Jolene and me to dinner. Looking around the table I see y'all got much to be thankful for," Pastor Bill began, sounding more like he was opening a prayer meeting.

"Yes, we do, and we're also thankful you could join us," Richard replied.

Smiles all around.

"I'm smellin' turkey," Jed said, faking a whiffing motion with his nose as if tracking prey. "Can anyone else smell that?"

Barbara, who still found him funny even after all those years, shook with laughter. "Well hell yeah! I smell it somethin' good!"

Jolene, who had been the lucky one to score the seat next to Barb, looked down and cleared her throat with a small cough.

Pastor Bill held his smile without a flinch, much like a politician.

Richard, anticipating a mutiny, got the message and took further charge of proceedings. "Before we begin, Pastor Bill, we'd be mighty honoured if you would please say a Thanksgiving prayer for all us."

It was Jacob's turn to clear his throat. Katherine shot him a sideways look, but his gaze stayed narrow and down at the table.

Pastor Bill rose from his chair. He clasped his hands together in a firm grip, bowed his head, and closed his eyes tight. Getting a line to the Almighty was not to be rushed or taken lightly. "Our good and gracious Lord in Heaven, hear us today, your humble servants before you. We come before you as mortal souls, as mere men, ever thankful for your great and boundless gifts to us, and your ever-loving kindness toward us.

"We remind ourselves today, oh Lord, of our need to pause our busy lives, to take stock of all that surrounds us, and to be truly thankful for all we have. Thank you for our families, the people we love. Thank you for our communities and our great nation, the greatest nation on earth under God, the United States of America ..." His voice trembled as he uttered the words.

"Thank you, oh God, for our founding fathers, who on the first Thanksgiving celebrated a new world of freedom, justice, and liberty ... the foundations of our great nation to this very day. "Lord, we thank you for creating all things and for the gift of salvation through our Lord Jesus Christ. And to this we all say ... *amen!*"

Most at the table said "amen," or at least muttered the word, but Jacob would have none of it. Katherine had snuck several glances at him during the pastor's prayer and her grandfather had stared defiantly straight ahead the entire time.

The pastor deflated back into his chair. His eyes were still closed, as if in pain. The effects of the direct line of communication with the Almighty had taken their toll. Jolene grabbed his hand, grinning a little.

The room came to after a few seconds. "Before we partake," Richard said, "it's our tradition for each of us to say something we are thankful for. I will begin." He paused. "I am thankful for family and friends, and that Katie could be with us for this Thanksgiving."

Katherine was caught off guard. For the first time since she could remember, she could see a certain softness in his steely blue eyes.

"And I'm thankful we live in a land of the free where everyone can live life to the full and no one can stand in our way," Jed added.

Barb was thankful for her two sons, Jolene for the peace in their land, Bill for the wonder of God's creation, Jacob for all those serving their country overseas, and Rachel for the wonderful turkey.

And Katherine? "I, uh, I'm thankful for, um ... I'm thankful I have a home and family I can come back to. No matter how far away I am, or for how long, this is where my heart is."

The room was silent for a moment, and Richard appeared dumbfounded. "Jed," he managed, "would you please do us the honour of carving this mighty fine bird you have bestowed upon us?"

"I thought you'd never ask, lil brother," Jed replied. He looked every bit prepared as he rose from the table—taking on a similar reverence to Pastor Bill's earlier display. Jed revealed his favourite carving knife from under the table, withdrawing it with a dramatic relish from an old leather sheath. His eyes tracked along every inch of the blade's edge as he slowly revealed its entire length. The dining room lights reflected and dazzled on its perfect silver surface.

Barb snapped him out of his trance. "Darn it, Pa, there's no huntin' to be done. This turkey is stone dead already!"

Jed carved the turkey with the finesse and skill of a master artisan. Plates were filled, dishes passed around, and the room filled with the warmth of shared company and conversation. Jed, Barb, Katherine, and Jacob shared two bottles of red that Jacob had brought. The others abstained, of course.

"So, Katherine, what ya up to in the navy these days?" Jed asked.

"Oh, ya' know, same old same old. Sailing on ships. Flyin' helicopters."

"That right? Where you been this year?"

"It's *classified*, Uncle Jed," she said with a wink. "I could tell you, but then, you know ..."

"Aw c'mon. I got top secret security clearance, you know!"

"Yup, I'm sure you do. Well, mostly around the Pacific, up around Japan, China, South Korea, those parts."

"And what, you fly and rescue people and stuff?"

"Yeah sometimes, but it's more than that. We do logistics work and anti-submarine warfare."

Jed's eyes widened. "You girls are allowed to go fight these days?"

"You bet."

"So, you blown up any Chink subs then?"

"Ah, no, not quite."

"Well, ya get one them in your sights darlin', you go right ahead and torch them bastards for your ole Uncle Jed, yeah?"

Katherine was struggling to think of a response when Pastor Bill piped in: "Thank God our country has the best navy on earth. We can deliver his will swiftly when and where needed to keep the peace. Praise be."

"Especially in the Middle East," Jolene said. "I pray that we bring peace to that land."

"Yeah, Chinks, towel heads, Ruskies. I know what I'd do if I had the big red button," Jed added.

Jacob, two and a half red glasses of wine in, could stay silent no longer. "And why, exactly, would you do that, Jed?"

"Because they're all the same, those folks. Better world without 'em, I say."

"China is a godless nation if ever there was one," said Pastor Bill, shaking his head.

"You do realise there's like ... over a billion people in China?" Katherine interjected. "And you don't know one of them."

"Don't need to," Jed replied. "They all look the same, think the same, walk around in their pyjamas."

"Just like everyone in West Virginia wears overalls and chews tobacco?" Jacob asked.

Now things were getting interesting. Jed shifted forward in his chair. "And yer point would be?"

"If someone in Wayne County commits a crime, well, let's lock 'em all up. You're all the same, right?"

Richard joined the fray. "There's no equivalence. The Chinese have no concept of democracy or human rights. They throw the Uyghurs into concentration camps."

"Like we did in Iraq?" Jacob asked. "And how about the Muslim asylum seekers we arrested and forced to eat pork, just out of some sick spite?"

"There's a difference," Pastor Bill said. "The people of West Virginia are

God-fearing, good people, not heathens and terrorists."

"Muslims believe in the same God that you do," Katherine pointed out.

The pastor shook his head. "There's only one path to God, Katherine. Through the word of Jesus Christ and his Father."

"Funny. That's what they say about Mohammad."

Pastor Bill's eyes narrowed. "Yes. The Bible is the only path to salvation."

"How do you know?" Katherine asked.

"Because the Bible says so."

"So the Bible is the word of God because the Bible says it's the word of God. I see you've never taken a logic class."

"*Katherine!*" Richard said.

Pastor Bill was about to retort when he received a sharp kick under the table from Jolene.

"Well, I believe in God," Jed said. "And if he told me to send some towlie to his seventy virgins, I'd pull that damn trigger. You can count on it." He settled back in his chair and triumphantly crossed his arms.

"You ever shot a man, Jed?" Jacob asked.

"Nope, but I would if I had to. Bet you wouldn't, yeah?"

"I served in Vietnam. And I learned that the moment you pull that trigger, you'll never be the same again. *Ever.*"

Jed made no reply and slunk into his chair.

"Well, I think it might be time for pumpkin pie," Rachel announced.

With the circuit breaker pushed, the tension eased. Katherine and Rachel retired to the kitchen to arrange dessert; Barb and Jolene moved to the living room; and Jacob returned to the yard—desperate for the comforting caress of his pipe.

Out in the kitchen, Rachel furiously whisked a bowl of whipping cream for the pumpkin pie.

"You okay, Mom?" Katherine asked

"Oh, I don't know. It's the same every year. Someone has to have a stupid argument about something."

"Yeah. Part of the tradition, I suppose."

"You were kinda hard on the pastor."

"You think? I saw it as a good ole healthy debate. Not my problem if he wants to go all salty on us. Thing is, these people talk about other places in the world, other countries, but they've probably never even been there. I bet Jed and Barb have never been out of the country."

"Jed's a lot smarter than his accent lets on."

"I've got the same accent, and I've served in the places they were talking about, met some people there."

"Yes," Rachel replied, "but don't forget that some of those people from those places have been here to this country too. Remember 9/11? People in America have good reason to be afraid, and every right to wanna be safe."

Katherine meandered in her thoughts for a few moments before continuing. "I know, but villainizing people doesn't make us safer. The world's problems aren't simple, and the solutions are even harder. Truth is, the world out there is often kind of grey."

"Truth is," Rachel said as she strode towards the door, "those folks are waitin' for this pumpkin pie."

CHAPTER SIX

Children are the living messages we send to a time we will not see.

—John F. Kennedy

17 July 2021

The humidity and daily rainfall were becoming harder to bear as July rolled towards August. Still, it was the same year on year, and Ben had learned to live with the sticky, oppressive atmosphere in Hong Kong. The monsoon would reappear any day to do its thing, and then the welcome drier air would slide in as the end of the year approached.

A rush of humidity poured in to do battle with the air-conditioning as the main entrance doors to the apartment tower slid open. Ben paused to acclimatise for a few seconds before venturing further into the stickiness.

He relished in the knowledge Hong Kong never sleeps. At 6:50 in the morning, the city churned with pedestrians, bikes, vehicles, trains, ferries, and airliners arriving to and departing from Chek Lap Kok Airport.

The business of living rolls on. Everywhere Ben had been, people went about satisfying their fundamental needs for food, shelter, security, and community. He was bemused by how the basics of life never seemed to alter. Governments change, cultures shift, conflicts come and go, and even empires rise and fall. But the same rhythms of life somehow carry on.

And his home province of Hong Kong had experienced its share of change in the previous two years. The formerly British-controlled province was experiencing the pain of rebirth yet again. "One country, two systems," as China had coined it, had satisfied the citizens of Hong

Kong for the first few decades since British rule. They permitted Hong Kong to maintain its own economy, local government, and legal system as a Special Administrative Region of China with reasonable autonomy. But in 2019 building tension erupted with months of protest against what many perceived to be China muscling much further in on their way of life. The People's Liberation Army was eventually brought in, and the atmosphere in Hong Kong shifted discernibly as China strengthened its grip. The COVID-19 pandemic followed soon after, further extinguishing public dissent and protest.

This show of force—and the outside world's inability to deter it—was another milestone in China's return to power. Britain had once ruled much of the globe, thanks to its merchant ships and navy, and now the recent rise of China as a world super-power was borne on the back of their ever-expanding People's Liberation Army Navy. No longer a mediocre force only able to defend China's internal and regional interests, their navy had developed the technology, the vessels, and the sheer weight of numbers to push China's influence across the world.

China had been there before, however. In the fifteenth century their imperial fleets were a formidable force across Asia. The fleet's admiral—Zheng He—is often lauded by the Chinese as an exemplar of their nation's ability to conduct international expansion by peaceful and diplomatic means. Other historians, however, are not comfortable describing his exploits as diplomatic. Or peaceful.

Yet history shows the Chinese—in sharp contrast to the British— established trade routes and partnerships. Colonisation by force was left to the British and other European empires.

*   *   *   *

Ben made his way along Hammer Hill Road, taking a right turn near the roundabout. His destination, the Nan Lian Garden, was his favourite place in Hong Kong. He cherished the gardens as an oasis of the natural world nestled within a forest of high-rise buildings. Its three and a half acres were a magnificent tapestry of design in the tradition of the Tang Dynasty, featuring gardens with exquisite flora, meandering paths, serene water features, and low timber buildings exemplifying the ingenuity of ancient Chinese architecture.

At 7:00 AM the garden had just opened for the day and was mostly deserted. Ben went to a quiet corner near the waterfall to begin his daily routine of meditation and Tai Chi.

The quiet of the garden and the peace of meditation were a must for Ben. He had spent many hours learning the ancient ways there as a young boy with his father, who had been taught by his father as a boy in North Korea. Ben drew much from the practice, which centred him and helped him cope—to a degree—with his extraordinary double life.

His father, Cai Jiang, had some knowledge of the other life that Ben led. He too had been a servant of the North Korean state in his younger days—as an agent operating in South-east Asia. He'd been seriously wounded in the leg during a lucky escape on a mission in South Korea that left him with a pronounced limp. Jiang was then excused—or more accurately, removed—from the front-line service of the Supreme Leader.

The Democratic People's Republic of Korea moved Jiang and his wife to Hong Kong in 2001, when Ben was two years old. Jiang undertook limited clandestine work for the DPRK in Hong Kong, usually in the form of covert surveillance. The time between missions became longer and longer, and after five years they called upon him no more. His fervent commitment to the North Korean state and the Supreme Leader never waned, however.

Jiang taught Ben from an early age about their great homeland and the pre-eminence of the Supreme Leader. He tutored Ben on the history of the Korean peninsula, in particular on the scourge of *mignuk nom*—the American bastard, the evil aggressor with its subservient bastard allies from the West. Ben came to know the full truth about the American invader and their evil deeds, their bloodthirsty armed forces, and their vicious treatment of ordinary Korean people. He came to understand the American people to be ignorant, backward, and violent scum.

Ben's young mind drank in all his father could teach him. Since he could remember, he had been aware that Hong Kong was not his true homeland. As he grew, he sensed the pull of the Korean peninsula deep within his being.

Ben first travelled to North Korea with his father at age thirteen. He experienced the inconceivable breadth of China on the journey and observed the sharp contrast as they crossed the border into North Korea and into Pyongyang. The capital seemed manufactured and inauthentic to the young visitor. But on subsequent trips Ben moved past the mild culture shock of North Korea and his homesickness for Hong Kong. His cultural and historical ties took deeper root with every visit.

In his later teen years, Ben comprehended the ironic relationship North Korea had with the United States. Like most North Koreans, he could never articulate this and would never dare to try. For while North Korea was fundamentally self-sufficient and fiercely independent, its reasons for being, and how it functioned, were tied to the nation they most despised. If, for some unexplainable reason, the "American bastard" were to vanish somehow, the DPRK leadership would have little left to say or do.

It had been a matter of unavoidable destiny when Ben was accepted to attend selection training with a DPRK military special operations unit in North Korea at age sixteen. A proud day for his father, and of tremendous personal satisfaction given how his own career had made this possible.

Ben's mother, Cai Liling, knew little of Jiang's career with the DPRK, and even less of Ben's current involvement. Or at least that was what she had convinced herself.

Liling was not a native of either Hong Kong or North Korea, having been born in northern China. She met Jiang on a one-year work assignment in Pyongyang and they married within four months. She became a North Korean resident, living there with Jiang before they were moved to Hong Kong.

Liling, like many Chinese women, was the undisputed ruler of the household. She wielded cutting humour and quick wit, formidable verbal barrages when called for, and the undeniable fact that she was the coordinator who made their home tick so well. Jiang and Ben understood this to be true and conducted themselves accordingly.

But despite her undisputed ruling status, Liling was a loving partner and mother. She was proud of their family unit and had disciplined herself to ignore her husband's and her precious only child's secretive DPRK involvement, yet those ties tore at her soul. She would secretly fret every time Ben would leave Hong Kong for "work" on short notice, returning days or weeks later, often with bruises or cuts, and no word about where he had been.

*   *   *   *

"Pa, good morning," Ben said as he entered the tailor shop in Mong Kok near the centre of downtown Kowloon.

"Good morning. I'm glad you're here. We have much to do!"

Ben worked with his father whenever he could. The tailor shop was small but well known. Foreign customers would come to Hong Kong for Jiang's expert tailoring services. Jiang could produce a suit in an astonishingly short time, and to a level of fit and quality that always satisfied his devout customers.

"The next batch is ready for you," Jiang instructed. "Cut these out, then you can help me finish the two suits from yesterday."

Ben started on the first order. He retrieved a roll of cloth from the storage shelves, then laid out a pattern for a pair of trousers. He stared in awe at the size of the pattern before him. "Are we fitting a bull elephant today?"

"Yes, our favourite elephant visited again yesterday," Jiang said. "I thought I might need to enlarge the doorway for him. Never have I seen such a belly."

Ben smiled. "Ah yes, the elephant from France?"

"Yes. He has taken in even more cheese, and pastry, and red wine, and I fear he may burst one day soon."

"I hope it will take place outside of our shop. Perhaps on the plane?"

The morning pushed on with Jiang trying to keep up with their current orders, and he winced at the ding-a-ling of the doorbell as more customers came in.

*   *   *   *

"Pa, I received a message."

Jiang let out a sharp sigh. "Very well."

Ben had received a text from a friend via a secure messaging app on his phone, a greeting and a brief update on the friend's goings-on. He was no friend though, and Ben didn't know his real name. He had met him a few times, and he recognised his face and voice, but that was all.

Ben pulled his laptop from his backpack and slinked away into the small office at the back of the store. He launched a virtual private network application on the laptop to create a private internet connection between his computer and a remote server in Estonia. Ben created a further layer of security by launching the Tor internet browser. His internet connection was then 128-bit encrypted twice over, meaning it was double blind to any external entity on the Internet.

Ben re-checked the text he'd received from his DPRK handler. He decoded specific keywords from the message, translating them into meaningless strings of letters and numbers. He typed the first string into the Tor browser and added the https:// protocol before it.

A ding from his laptop confirmed the download had begun. The URL had pointed to a computer file hidden from search engines on the dark web. The download finished in under a minute and was deleted from the server a few minutes later.

He repeated the process, downloading three files to his laptop. Each had a different filename extension: .cx2, .3yy, and .w09. He changed all three file extensions to .psd. His computer then recognised them as Photoshop files.

Ben launched Photoshop and got to work. As he scanned the first image, he saw a large contemporary artwork—a complex digital creation of patterns, lines, shades, and colours. He had no idea what the image conveyed, nor did he care.

Ben created a new editing layer in the software, enabling him to adjust the primary red, green, and blue colours that made up the image. He isolated a specific range of colour in the red spectrum and made all other colours and ranges invisible. The resulting simplified image was still without meaning or recognisable form.

He worked on, performing the same process with the second image but in the green spectrum, and the same with the third image in the blue spectrum. He then had three meaningless images on three separate Photoshop layers, which he merged to form one large, cohesive image—a mission brief containing background notes, three photographs of a Russian man, and Ben's orders.

*   *   *   *

Shenzhen, China

It was always discernible—the moment when Ben left Hong Kong and crossed back into mainland China on the train. The landscape appeared the same, and China had done an incredible job of transforming the region of Shenzhen into a sizeable high-rise competitor to its close neighbour. Yet the differences were there. Perhaps it was the political atmosphere—the difference between a city grown on steroids by a totalitarian communist state and one developed under British influence and still hanging grimly to its fading democratic ties.

No, it's the people, Ben contemplated. *How different they are. Their use of language, their tone of speech, their facial expressions, their outlook on the world, and their responses to the world around them.*

As Ben picked his way out of the subway station, he braced for the expected cultural variations. The more gentle, peaceful people of his second home were not to be confused with the more direct, business-like, no-nonsense people of Shenzhen. Their pushiness, and what appeared to be their unrepentant selfishness, took some getting used to.

He was also aware as a Hongkonger in Shenzhen, they viewed him as a nonconforming individualist who did not understand his place as a tiny cog in a large communist machine. This didn't sit well with Ben, who felt a deep appreciation for his part of the greater good within his family, and within his true country of origin. Being an individual with individual rights and liberties was not high on his priority list, or on that list at all.

Ben made his way along Renmin South Road, then into the commercial district to find the small nondescript pharmacy tucked away in a shopping basement below a mega office tower. He greeted the lone pharmacist with a simple "*Nǐ hǎo.*"

The man seemed to recognise Ben, but skipped any greeting. "I have your prescription. Wait here," he said, then disappeared behind a bank of shelves. He returned a minute later with a small, unmarked package and handed it to Ben. No payment was expected or exchanged.

*   *   *   *

Hong Kong

19 July 2021, 5:25 PM

It was stifling outside and still unbearably hot, despite the sun having disappeared behind thick layers of rolling grey clouds. Steady light rain continued to fall. A non-local might be naïve enough to count on the rain as welcome relief from the unrelenting humidity, but it only made things worse. The rain collected in a thin greasy film on the street, with the rest returning to the heavens in the form of a humid mist. This was weather a person could touch and smell.

Ben had been perched against the corner of the laneway for some time. He was about to shift his position again to avoid unwanted attention when he saw a taxi turn off Nathan Road and onto the side street. The taxi pulled up past his position outside the Winchester Mongkok Hotel.

A moment later, Vasily Artamanov emerged from the back of the taxi. He was of average height but a girthy two hundred and twenty pounds. His bulbous frame dwarfed the tiny hotel porter who'd come to take his bag. Even in the weak light, Artamanov's red blotchy face was plain to see under his greying beard.

Hmm ... way too much vodka and stroganov, Ben thought.

The mission brief had described Artamanov as an accomplished ballistics engineer from Omsk, Siberia, and aged fifty-three. The DPRK military had contracted him to provide specialised ballistics consultancy on medium- and long-range missile designs. He'd worked in North Korea on three occasions in the past six months.

Artamanov would travel back to Russia via a circuitous route, staying a few nights in either Hong Kong or Macau. He had a weakness for gambling, and for young Chinese women of a certain look. He had shown himself to be loose with his tongue, and more so when intoxicated—which he often was. This had made him an easy target for an attractive female agent of Asian descent from the Central Intelligence Agency. And his liaison in Macau had been noticed by other players closer to home.

Ben watched Artamanov and the porter as they disappeared into the hotel lobby. He shifted location down the street and settled in, resigning himself to yet more hours of waiting.

*   *   *   *

7:40 PM

The rain had stopped at last, but there were still large wet patches and a few puddles on the street. Neon signs from the hotel building and a convenience store burned bright in the falling darkness, their reflections jiggling lazily in the water.

A larger-than-usual crowd moved along Nathan Road and its many side streets. The rain had kept most of the residents and tourists indoors, and now they were spilling into the city to take advantage of the break in the weather.

And sure enough, there he is. The wait had taken two hours, but Ben had been confident his target wouldn't take long to emerge. Artamanov had needs and was not one to waste time in having them satisfied. He'd worked two long weeks in North Korea with very little … entertainment. He had time now to live a little, or even a lot.

Artamanov glanced at the night sky to judge the weather, then turned right at the corner and melted into the crowd. Ben followed, keeping about fifteen metres back. The Russian's brisk pace was a surprise—he appeared to be on a mission of his own.

*   *   *   *

Artamanov came to a stop after three blocks. He checked his phone, made a left turn, and kept walking. After another few turns and another three blocks, he had entered an older and quieter section of Mong Kok that was not as well-lit. He found his destination in a quiet side alley. The tiny pink neon sign above the building's entrance was a certain giveaway of its inhabitants and their profession.

Inside, customers cruised the corridors and stopped outside apartment doors to read about the woman waiting inside, the services she was offering, and her prices. If the customer liked what he read, and her photo, he would knock. From there it was a simple exchange of cash, time, and bodily fluids.

Artamanov knew what he was looking for and it didn't take him long to find the smallest, youngest-looking Chinese girl in the building.

"Hello. How are you?" the tiny girl said in her best broken English. She somehow maintained her smile as she took in the blubbery beast in front of her, and the stench of alcohol on his panting breath.

"I will be very well. Soon," he said in his best broken English.

*   *   *   *

The deed was done twenty-three orgasmic minutes later.

Artamanov made his way outside. He was light-headed from his experience, or perhaps it was the Viagra. His appetite was quenched for a time, but it would return—most likely the next morning.

Ben had positioned himself in a dark stairwell below a fire escape just across the alley. He watched as Artamanov retrieved a cigarette and lighter from his back pocket and lit up. The Russian ambled towards the street corner at the end of the alley, his pace much slower than before.

Ben checked the alley, forward and back. It was empty. And he'd already confirmed that there was no CCTV in range.

Clear to kill.

Ben removed the cap of the hypodermic needle hidden in his hand and crept up behind his target without a sound, staying outside Artamanov's line of sight. He lifted the needle high and stabbed it deep into the Russian's thick neck, then drove the plunger down.

Artamanov dropped his cigarette and grabbed the side of his neck as if swatting at an overgrown tropical mosquito. He stumbled and shuffled, turning clumsily to see who or what had hit him from behind. A young man twenty metres distant was vanishing into the dim of the alley.

This would be the last thing on the earth Vasily Artamanov would see. Thiamylal coursed through his veins and spread into his brain and nervous system. A normal dose would induce a peaceful general anaesthetic, but he'd been poisoned with enough to drop a buffalo. Within three seconds Artamanov's vision faltered into an ever-narrowing tunnel. His world dimmed to grey, then eternal black.

*   *   *   *

Ben did not turn to check on the condition of his target. The man would be dead before he reached the other end of the alley.

He dropped the needle in a storm-water drain as he made his way back onto Nathan Road and blended into the crowds. Ben would take the short walk to Prince Edward MTR Station, then onto a train straight home.

Dinner will be waiting, His mother was making lamb noodles with Sichuan chilli oil, and his lips were already tingling.

He pulled his cap down tight and increased his pace. The rain had returned.

*   *   *   *

Pyongyang, North Korea
20 July 2021

Colonel General Kim Hyun-woo burst into his outer office as was his tradition on arrival each morning. He demanded his usual morning rice drink from his personal assistant as he barged through and disappeared into his internal office.

Standing at his desk, Kim rifled through a pile of documents placed there by his assistant for review. *More of the same, irrelevant, later, later, don't waste my time …*

The next one caught his eye. Jeong Yong-sun's handler had relayed a message from the young agent in Hong Kong:

The mission has been completed.

The colonel general eased around his desk and dropped himself into a leather chair as a satisfied grin spread across his face.

CHAPTER SEVEN

It is the ant, not the lion, which the elephant fears.

—Matshona Dhliwayo

San Diego, California
29 August 2021

Captain William A. Collins settled into the luxurious leather lounge chair. He savoured the sharp barley aroma in his nostrils and eyed the deep golden lustre of the liquid in his glass.

His dinner companion, Vice Admiral James Garrison Jr., seemed equally transfixed. "One hell of a single malt," he said before taking his first sip.

Collins took a short nip of the whisky and held it for a few seconds before allowing it down his throat, feeling the fierce burn and the singing tang of the aftertaste. "Now *that's* pretty darn good."

They were in civilian clothes and well away from the base at Point Loma, back over the bay. The meal at the fine-dining Japanese restaurant in Harbor Side had been superb, just as Garrison had promised. The subdued atmosphere among the bamboo shōji screens was a welcome change from the frenetic activity at fleet headquarters.

"Keep your feet dry and we can do this every week," Garrison said with a wink.

"Mmm. Or maybe I can get the chef on board to do some sashimi."

"You'll be lucky to get canned tuna a few weeks into the cruise, and the cook's probably from frickin' Tulsa."

Collins contemplated his choices for a moment, then shook his head. "No. Sailing a desk in some fancy office at Point Loma isn't for me. Give me the sea."

Garrison laughed. He had sailed with his old friend and colleague fifteen years earlier on the aircraft carrier USS *John C. Stennis*. At that time, Garrison was forty-nine years old and the commanding officer of the ship, and Collins was a senior officer at age forty-one. They served together on the *Stennis* for four years. Their careers had converged again in San Diego as senior officers in Third Fleet.

Garrison was a tad envious of his younger friend and didn't mind expressing it. He did sail a desk in a fancy office and sometimes missed the freedom of his own command on the open sea. He could think of no better man, though, than his friend Bill to be the first CO of a ship entering service with Third Fleet in the coming year.

The U.S. Navy had designated another officer to be the CO of the ship in 2020, but he had resigned from the navy early in 2021 due to a sudden chronic health condition. Collins had been next in line for command and Garrison did not hesitate to recommend him for the post, despite Collins having taken four weeks leave on compassionate grounds in the winter of 2020–21.

"J.F.K. *Ho-ly shit*," Garrison mused. "It'll be all over the navy and the media next week: Captain William A. Collins appointed as commanding officer of the soon to be commissioned USS *John F. Kennedy*."

"Then the fun begins."

"You could say that."

Both men understood the long road ahead. It would be a further eighteen months before the ship would set sail on her first deployment with Carrier Strike Group Eleven.

Collins held the moment in his mind. The moment when the ship would clear San Diego Bay and make for the open Pacific—leaving the ceremonies, politics, media appearances, interviews, sea trials, and pre-deployment exercises far behind. That moment, that goal, would keep him focused and sane in the months ahead.

His appointment as CO had brought him renewed energy. The preceding two years had been particularly hard, and Collins was ready for a fresh horizon and a new challenge. He had big shoes to fill, but he was up to the task.

The new ship had big shoes to fill of its own. USS *John F. Kennedy* would replace the retiring USS *Nimitz*, which had served with distinction for decades, whereas *John F. Kennedy* was to be the second of a new breed of aircraft carriers—the Ford class—and relatively untested.

"Has Paterson briefed you on plans for the first deployment?" Garrison asked, referring to the CO of CSG-11, Rear Admiral Susan Paterson.

"Yeah. We've had a few conversations. The details are still sketchy, but most of the cruise will be in the Persian Gulf and the Indian Ocean, and a little time in the Western Pacific."

"You might get up to Chinatown if the folks up there go nuts again."

"True. Let's hope Rocket Man keeps it in his pants."

"Who knows what that asshole will do next. What about exercises?"

"We're scheduled to join at least three," Collins said. "One in the Gulf, one off the Straits of Malacca, and a major one in northern Australia—at the end."

"Talisman Sabre?"

"Yup."

"And the port visits?" Garrison asked.

"Possibly Singapore, Chennai, and Bahrain, then an extended one after Talisman Sabre before we head home."

"Has Paterson suggested a port for it yet?"

"Nope," Collins said. "The plan is to spread the group around Australian ports, some goodwill visits, politics, all that crap."

"Keeping up good relations with our best friends." Garrison took another sip of scotch. "As CO of the carrier, you'll get your pick of the ports. What'll it be ... Sydney? Perth?"

"Not sure. Just somewhere good to finish the cruise."

"Well, let Paterson know sooner rather than later."

"Yeah," Collins paused, transfixed by his empty whisky glass. "Another one, Jim?"

"There ya' go again, reading my mind and all."

*　　*　　*　　*

Qinhuangdao, China,

12 December 2021

"That will be all," Rear Admiral Pengcheng Tao ordered.

The butler understood this as his signal to become scarce, and to order the other servants in the house to leave immediately and not return until the next day. He bowed with his hands clasped, shimmied backwards a few steps across the floor, then closed the two timber doors as he left the room.

The midday meal had been taken and the dishes removed. The four men were alone now, each enjoying a glass of one of Pengcheng's recently discovered pleasures. He'd been introduced to the delights of Portuguese fortified wine while being entertained in Hong Kong a year earlier. Pengcheng was beguiled by its rich, warm, smooth qualities; and by its shorthand name, "port," which seemed appropriate for a rear admiral of the Chinese navy.

Colonel General Kim Hyun-woo, seated to the left of Pengcheng, seemed the most impressed. Such brands and vintages were not available in North Korea. He was pleased to experience whatever minor pleasures he could on the rare occasions he travelled across the border into nearby China. Western sanctions made certain he could travel no further.

The view of the ocean outside was another simple pleasure. Pengcheng's third home was a moderately sized private mansion overlooking the beach at Beidaihe, Qinhuangdao, in north-east China. The home—located halfway between his primary residence in Beijing and his apartment at the naval base in Qingdao—was a sanctuary for the rear admiral and his family.

Pengcheng's home that day, however, was neither the scene of a retreat nor a holiday. He was using it as the location for a secretive discussion of the highest order. He would not have dared to conduct this discussion even in a military or government facility.

Each of the four had arrived at the house at different times, and in unmarked vehicles. They wore ordinary civilian clothing despite being from the highest ranks within their respective organisations. The usual aides and assistants had been left behind. All electronic devices were removed to the secure basement, and a sweep for devices had been completed before the meal began.

Across from Kim sat Li Guoliang, a lieutenant colonel in the People's Liberation Army and commander of the Jinan Military Region Special Forces Unit.

On Pengcheng's right, Special Commissary to the Defence Minister, civilian public servant Zhaoqing Feng. Zhaoqing was a short man with high stature in the Chinese Communist Party machine. He was wise and considered, and his calm, even expression would never reveal his strategic hand.

"Gentleman," Pengcheng began, "let us begin."

The three put down their glasses and sat upright.

"We welcome Kim Hyun-woo. It is an honour for us to collaborate with the Democratic People's Republic of Korea."

Kim nodded in acknowledgement.

"As you know, we are the only people to have any working knowledge of this operation. It is of the utmost importance we do not share this with anyone without my specific order to do so." He paused for effect. "Are we agreed?"

"This operation has been cleared at the highest level of the Ministry of National Defence and in the Party," Zhaoqing said. "I have complete discretion to act on behalf of the Ministry and the Party in this matter, and I am not required to divulge any detail of the operation to my colleagues or superiors. I am to advise the minister of National Defence when the operation has begun, but not before then unless requested by him."

"Indeed," Pengcheng replied. "For the purpose of this operation you *are* our government, and we are greatly pleased by your presence and contribution at these meetings."

Zhaoqing nodded. Though it all sounded manifestly grand, it did nothing for his ego. Status and power were the last thing on his mind. The significant responsibility he'd been given was foremost in his thoughts, with the unnerving possibility they could fail coming a close second. He knew the consequences should the unthinkable happen.

"And the DPRK leadership has provided me with full clearance to act in this operation as I see fit, in the best interests of our nation and our Supreme Leader," Kim added.

Li was not impressed by Kim, but few people ever impressed him. He would show the man due respect though, given Kim's position as commander of the DPRK Reconnaissance General Bureau, and his decorated history as a special operations commander. Li was also aware of the working relationship and friendship between Pengcheng and Kim, and he trusted Pengcheng's judgement on the matter.

Kim was equally aware of Li's rank and standing as commander of an elite special forces unit, and his reputation as a legendary special forces operative. Their joint intelligence, counterintelligence, and special operations experience would create a formidable partnership.

"It is time, gentleman," Pengcheng continued. "Time our nations reminded these high-nose foreign devils, these filthy old Americans, of their true place in the world. And of *our* true place in the world. For too long they have danced on our doorstep, dictating their policies, parading their powers, and supporting the traitors: those tiny-dicked ones from Chinese-Taipei, the dead-plank South Koreans, and those Japanese dwarf dogs."

Li and Zhaoqing chuckled. Hearing the rear admiral use such derogatory slang towards their South-east Asian neighbours was an unexpected delight.

"But it is not war we seek," Pengcheng said. "There may come a time for that. A time when our magnificent forces cannot be matched. It will be our nations who take to the world's oceans to demonstrate forever who is in charge of this region. We must draw together our collective hearts. Our resources. Our minds. We must apply new thinking and use new strategy. Our enemy may be formidable, but is *not* invincible. Not at all. We will show the world that this is true. *Heed my words.*"

Li was not sure of what to make of Pengcheng's fervour. Having known the rear admiral for eight years, he had not seen him like this before. Li had once watched a famous American evangelist in action on television. He found the experience to be bizarrely entertaining and psychologically disturbing, and the similarities to Pengcheng's oratory perplexed him.

"May I ask, Rear Admiral," Li began. "This operation ... what is the proposal?"

"Ah, Guoliang. A man of action." Pengcheng paused and smiled, as if realising he'd gotten carried away in his opening remarks. "This operation must be as no other. Military history shows us the Americans have three weaknesses. First, they believe they are invincible. Second, they do not seriously anticipate unconventional attacks—not even in their own war games. And the third, the sweetest of them all, my dear Kim," Pengcheng paused again for effect, "the Americans look to the future with such positive tunnel vision and in doing so they tend to forget the lessons of the past."

"Indeed," Kim said. "Their great strength may be their greatest weakness."

"Maybe so," Zhaoqing said. "But with respect, their military power is still greater than the combined strength of our nations at this point in time, is it not?"

"This is true," Pengcheng said. "And this is the reason we will not be attempting to match the strength of the Americans."

Li, Kim, and Zhaoqing leaned forward.

"No. We are going to attack the Americans in a *way* they cannot foresee. We will attack at a *time* they cannot predict. And we will attack them in a *place* they would never expect."

"Surely, Rear Admiral, terrorist attacks on the United States homeland have run their course," Zhaoqing said. "The Americans are well on guard and will see this coming."

"This operation cannot be on American soil," Pengcheng countered. "This is not a terrorist operation, not in reality, and it will not be against American civilians."

"Then what, may I ask, *is* this operation?" Li said.

"Name the Americans' most prized and most visible strategic asset. What tool do they proudly use to bully us in our region, and in every region of the world? Hmm?"

All three men knew the answer. Kim answered the rhetorical question, his words laced with a growling tone: "Ah yes. The American aircraft carrier."

Li looked away for a moment, staring at the view without actually seeing it. His mind raced with competing thoughts and ideas—a predator contemplating a distant prey.

Zhaoqing, in complete contrast, had turned pale. His pupils dilated as if he'd seen a ghost. "Rear Admiral, we are speaking of one of the best-protected military assets on the planet. An attack is likely to be detected early, and therefore to fail."

Pengcheng grimaced on hearing the dreaded f-word: *fail*. He too fought an internal battle with the word, although he would never show it. He eyed Zhaoqing. "Failure is not part of my plan." He paused, thinking through his next words. Zhaoqing was his commander and his government by proxy, after all.

"And this is why, my friend, we will not be using our forces to attack the asset directly," Pengcheng continued. "This is for two reasons. As you have wisely indicated, a direct attack by our ships, submarines, or aircraft would have a low probability of success. Each U.S. aircraft carrier is surrounded by a formidable strike force of ships and submarines, and squadrons of deployed aircraft. Their defences are second to none, it must be said."

"Yes, it would be suicide," Li said.

"Second, the operation must not be easily attributed to either of our nations. This is also why we have ruled out using our long-range anti-ship missiles. We must avoid American retaliation at all costs."

"But surely the Americans will work out where the attack has come from?" Kim asked.

"Maybe so. But if we are very clever, it will not be possible for them to link the attack directly to us or any specific nation."

"They would then look like fools at the United Nations and in the world media should they attempt it," Zhaoqing mused.

Seconds ticked by, each man within his thoughts. Pengcheng could almost hear Li's mind turning. The man of action needed details, as did Kim, his DPRK equivalent—himself a man of action and not so much of theory.

"If you wish to take down an elephant, it is foolish to use another elephant, or even a lion," Pengcheng said. "Instead, gentleman, *we shall use an ant*. And when it is done, this almighty elephant of the sea, this so-called invincible beast, will be stone dead where it sits.

"It is highly unlikely we can sink the carrier, but this is not the goal. Our goal is to cause enough damage to disable it, so they are forced to tow their prized possession back to America in shame for all the world to see. This will be a warning to them of the possibility of future attacks, and their vulnerability away from their homeland. We will disrupt their global naval strategy for decades to come. From that day forward, the authority of the American aircraft carrier to rule our oceans will decline, and one day vanish. *Forever*."

Kim had never heard of a story involving an ant and an elephant. Nor even of the biblical story of David and Goliath. But he had heard of the Rabbit and the Wolf. His small nation had long suffered in the shadow of the evil American aggressor, and the metaphor rang true with his memory.

For Li, the thought of attacking the great symbol of American power and purging the unspoken Chinese shame was utterly captivating. He would need all the details, yes, and he would need to plan it meticulously with the others, but he was fully in.

Zhaoqing, for once in his public service career, could not resort to a typical bureaucratic position. He could not say, "I shall confer with the minister and report back." There were no committees to consult or procedures he could follow.

Pengcheng braced for Zhaoqing's reaction. The response almost took Pengcheng's breath clean out of his lungs: "The task is significant, and especially so for an ant," Zhaoqing said, "but let us hunt this elephant!"

CHAPTER EIGHT

If you want to keep a secret, you must also hide it from yourself.

—George Orwell

San Diego, 15 December 2021

The view from the conference table in Rear Admiral Susan Paterson's office was straight down the length of San Diego Bay. Collins looked south over Naval Air Station North Island, Coronado Beach at the near end, and all the way to Imperial Beach shimmering in the fierce morning sun.

Paterson, CO of Carrier Strike Group 11, sat behind her desk on the other side of the room. She was dealing with a call that had interrupted their meeting. Collins could hear her sorting a scheduling problem in her typical no-nonsense, calm, and assertive leadership style. The person on the call would have been in no doubt about the gravity of the monumental screw-up, and what the CO thought of his or her performance.

When Collins received his command, Jim Garrison, Third Fleet Vice Admiral, had told him about his new boss's nickname within Third Fleet, "AMRAAM." "She can pack a hell of a punch, even outside visual range," he explained. It was then that Collins fully understood the analogy with the AIM-120 AMRAAM air-to-air missile used to target enemy aircraft.

Collins had been working with Paterson for six months and had stayed outside her launch range by adapting to her leadership style. He followed her lead without wavering, and he understood his role and what she required. And Paterson didn't play politics or mind games and seemed interested in his success.

As she continued the call, Collins had a few minutes to simply do nothing—an unfamiliar indulgence in his new role. Preparing a ship and crew for deployment was a time-consuming and serious business, but readying a brand-new ship for her first deployment was a whole other ball game that had required every ounce of the leadership, politicking, negotiation, planning, teamwork, and command skills he could muster. And then some. Garrison and Paterson had been solid mentors, and senior COs in CSG-11 were useful sounding boards when he'd needed them.

Time to stop and think, though, was something he neither enjoyed nor wanted. Staying on task and on mission was where he was and where he wanted to stay. He stared out the window at the colossal ship on the eastern side of the bay. An object so large it dwarfed everything nearby—even the city skyline in the distance. Sharp yet graceful lines and imposing yet refined bulk.

"You drifting out to sea, sailor?"

Collins jumped in his seat, jolted from his thoughts by Paterson's question as she sat down across from him.

"I must admit," Paterson confessed, "a few times since she's arrived, I sit here and stare too."

"Yeah, it's good to see her from a distance. A different perspective."

"Indeed."

Before the phone call had interrupted them, Collins had briefed the rear admiral on the progress of the ship, including reports from the recent work-up trials and training exercises. The sheer volume of items to work through was overwhelming. Every piece of equipment, weapon, and system needed to be thoroughly tested and analysed, and the results documented and reported. The integrations and interconnections between them all required the same level of scrutiny. Where deficiencies were found, they would be further analysed and fixed.

"What's your gut feel on COMPTUEX?" Paterson asked. "Are we gonna make the first week of July?"

Collins took a few seconds to consider her question. COMPTUEX, a Composite Training Unit Exercise, was to be a major three-week pre-deployment exercise involving many of the ships and units within CSG-11. This would be the first major test for the aircraft carrier, and a critical step before their first full deployment planned for 2023.

"My assessment is we will be operational and ready to take part in COMPTUEX."

"You sure, Bill? I'm not after hope or optimism. Just give me reality."

"I'm as sure as I can be. Our two major areas of concern are still the weapons elevators and MECALS reliability. But we're making progress and the engineering leads have assured me we're still on track."

Even a mention of MECALS—the Magno-Electric-Catapult Aircraft Launch System—gave Collins an icy shiver. MECALS had replaced the steam-powered catapults used on older carriers, promising greater reliability, system simplicity, less maintenance, and a faster aircraft launch rate.

"Where are you at with MECALS?" she asked.

"Same as before. Great when it works. And an absolute pain when it doesn't. Reliability stats have improved, but still below where I want them."

"Mmm."

Collins could tell that Paterson was calm, but nervous. The U.S. Navy and the U.S. government had been equally pensive about their Ford-class carriers. The first ship in the class, USS *Gerald R. Ford*, had been affected by unforeseen design issues and breakdowns in early testing, but all had been addressed over time. The second ship in the class—USS *John F. Kennedy*—would have smoother sailing, both literally and figuratively, it was hoped.

"It's trouble-shooting and maintenance," Collins continued. "Takes time to find the faults and get them fixed. Not something we'd want happening in the middle of an operation."

"Damn right," Paterson said. "And your people?"

"I'm satisfied," Collins said. "It's been a hell of a thing for all of us. So much to learn. Almost everything on the ship is different and new, but we're making good progress."

Collins held more reservations than he was letting on. He was reasonably certain of crew readiness by COMPTUEX, but not as confident as he wanted to be. His reservation stemmed partly from himself. System integration was one thing, but it was the human-to-system interfaces that concerned him the most. So many things on the ship were highly automated, with many of them based on computerised artificial intelligence control. Integrated systems made many of the decisions, leaving the humans to stand back and watch in awe. Or trepidation.

Collins knew the importance of understanding how humans interact with technology, with procedures, and other humans, and what happens when humans inevitably fail or don't perform as expected. He had come through the ranks when most of the systems were analogue and there to support the human—not the other way around—and he felt overwhelmed, out of the loop, and sometimes resentful at being relegated to observer status.

The warfare system contractors had assured him, time and time again, of the vast improvements in the integrated defence systems of the Ford-class carriers. But Collins was not fully convinced and kept a watchful and critical eye. He'd keep his thoughts to himself for the time being, not wanting to come across as an out-of-touch dinosaur or a cranky old skipper. And he was confident he could rely on his people.

Paterson gathered her papers and pushed back her chair. "Keep at it, Bill, and let me know if there's any major issues or delays. Don't hesitate to talk."

"One more thing, if I may?" Collins asked before she had a chance to stand.

"You got two more minutes. Shoot."

"The liberty port call for the carrier after Talisman Sabre ... I have a suggestion."

"Yes?"

"I request we go south for the week. Down to Hobart."

"Hobart ... ah yes, Tasmania. That'll be cold in August."

Collins shrugged. "Maybe."

"Okay. So why there?" Paterson asked.

"Did a port visit there when I was on the Chuckie-V back in '99. Fantastic visit, great people, nice place. Besides, I'm tired of the usual ports, and the navy has asked us to spread the love around more anyhow."

Collins could see Paterson was thinking hard. "Hobart ... isn't that where some goddamn fool jumped on one of our SSNs?" she asked.

"I'm not sure," Collins lied. He had hoped she wouldn't recall that incident, but her sharp mind had come through yet again.

Some years before he had first visited Hobart on USS *Carl Vinson*, a nuclear-powered Los Angeles–class submarine had made a four-day visit to Hobart. The trouble began when the submarine surfaced and made her way up the River Derwent towards Hobart. A small flotilla of welcoming craft and media met her mid-river. And unbeknown to the welcoming party, local environmental and anti-nuclear activists were waiting in motorboats and kayaks among them, and primed to share their views.

As the submarine made her way towards port, a motorboat breeched the exclusion zone and came alongside. The boat towed two kayakers, and as they neared the submarine, one of them jumped out of the kayak at just the right moment and clambered up the black rubberised hull of the two-billion-dollar nuclear-powered hunter-killer submarine. He unfurled his protest banner and danced along the hull. His protest ended two minutes later when a police boat pulled alongside and a pair of officers chased him down and arrested him.

"A major embarrassment for the navy brass," Paterson said. "I wouldn't want to risk anything like that happening on my watch."

"Understood, ma'am. However, I'm told the Tasmanian government is eager for us to resume our visits. I'm confident they'll manage things better this time."

"You damn well better be right, Collins. No Greenpeace nutcases will be using any of my ships as a stage for their propaganda."

"You have my word."

"I don't give a flying toss about your word, Bill. That was an *order*."

"Ma'am," Collins responded. He felt a wave of relief, but was careful not to show it.

"You'll excuse me then if I don't stay with the carrier for the visit," Paterson said as she rose from her seat. "I'll probably be heading off to Canberra or Sydney to press the flesh."

"Understood. No problem," Collins said, his reply coming a fraction too quickly.

*   *   *   *

Qinhuangdao, 28 February 2022

"Are we then agreed?" Pengcheng asked.

The other men nodded.

"Forgive me," Pengcheng pressed, "but I must *hear* you on this."

Kim shuffled in his seat. "Yes ... yes, I, ah ... we, the DPRK, we are in agreement."

Pengcheng looked at Li.

"Yes. I am in agreement. This will be done," Li said.

Pengcheng nodded, then turned to Zhaoqing.

"Yes, Admiral. I can agree to the terms and conditions," Zhaoqing said, his voice hushed.

Pengcheng's gaze narrowed further. "Zhaoqing. This decision is the point of no return for this operation. It is not relevant whether you *can* agree. It is only important whether you *do* or *do not* agree."

Zhaoqing took a slow breath and looked Pengcheng in the eye. "I do agree," he said.

Today's meeting, the third since the group first met in December, had been long and exhausting. Zhaoqing had gained a greater appreciation of the skill and resolve of military men. The volume of strategic options, detail, resourcing, scheduling, contingencies, and risk management for the operation was bewildering to him. He understood his role from that

83

point forward would become less significant, yet he would continue to meet with the group as required. Much of the fine-tuning would be left to Kim and Li, the special operations professionals. He would only speak up if he saw unmanageable political risks, or decisions incompatible with the ministry or the Party.

"Very well then. It is agreed." Pengcheng leaned back in his chair. "This will be all for today."

Pengcheng and Zhaoqing retired to their rooms, exhausted.

Kim sought fresh air and, ironically, a cigarette. As he lit up on the deck, he heard the door behind him open and close. "Cigarette?" he asked.

Li shook his head. "My wife would kill me."

Kim gestured the pack towards him, regardless. Li gave in, and Kim flicked the lighter for him.

Both men took a long, slow draw as they looked out at the moonlit beach and the ocean before them. The air had a deep chill, given the clear skies and calm winter weather. A low swell pounded the beach with an easy rhythm, with white caps on the breaking waves just visible in the low light.

Li broke the silence. "Were you concerned by any of the admiral's final requirements?"

Kim thought hard. He was careful with this man—he had to be—as if he were speaking to a Chinese clone of himself. He understood that everything said and done by men of his ilk was strategic. There were no wasted words.

"I would not say … *concerned*. No … it makes sense to me. China provides the logistics, equipment, and intelligence services. We provide the operatives on the ground."

"Yes. It's a logical plan. We will provide your operatives with every service. It will be as if they were our own."

"As if" your own? Kim thought to himself. Pengcheng's requirements were much as Kim had expected. China had superior weaponry and technology far in advance of the DPRK, and their intelligence services

had far greater reach, so it made sense the DPRK would provide the mission operatives on the ground.

But as sensible as it all was, something about the plan stung. Kim, more than anyone involved, was aware of the risks to the DPRK operatives. They would be exposed and left to their own devices, with a significant probability of being caught and/or stranded. The Chinese would be exposed to some risk, but their operatives would not be out in the open.

Kim knew the game. Should the operation fail, or should the nationality of the operatives be discovered, North Korea would take all the blame. Pengcheng had designed the operation this way. All the men understood this, yet it would stay unspoken between them. This was a risk Kim and the DPRK would have to take. The glorious prize was simply too tempting for his Supreme Leader.

"We both know the risks to your men," Li said. "Some of them may be caught."

"And at least one of them will die," Kim replied in a steady monotone.

"This is true."

Li was being typically factual. Not empathetic. Not even sympathetic. "Selection of the right man will be crucial," he said.

Kim took another long drag on his cigarette. He watched the trail of white smoke battle the cold air before it disappeared beyond the railing and into the dark.

"You have such a man?" Li asked. "An agent beyond your borders who could do this thing?"

"Yes, Colonel General," Kim responded. "We indeed have such a man."

CHAPTER NINE

*The trouble is not that I am single and likely to stay
single, but that I am lonely and likely to stay lonely.*

—Charlotte Brontë

San Diego, 1 April 2022

The slither of bright morning sunlight streaming in through a gap in the blinds awoke Katherine to a spasm of intense pain. The sun was often a bother in the morning as its intense light glared through the windows of her eleventh-floor east-facing apartment.

Katherine squinted open her left eye to find the source of the burning glare. Her right eye remained shut and buried in her pillow. Strands of hair lay straggled across her view.

Her brain was coming to. *Oh, god.*

As she lifted her head an inch from the pillow and attempted to focus on the other side of the bedroom, the floors and walls appeared to slide away before circling back to where they should be. Nausea swirled in her stomach when she sat up, and she fought back the urge to vomit.

What the hell did I do?

She struggled to piece her night back together, and why she was lying naked in bed and feeling so close to death. She recalled glimpses of noise and music, but it was a jumbled haze.

Then the first complete memory hit her. After finishing work at the base the previous afternoon, Katherine had made her way back to the apartment. Her mailbox in the lobby was usually empty, but she'd received a letter from Tom. She had written to him just six days ago, so it was a surprise to get a reply so soon. They'd usually take a few weeks to write back, which was a tradition they'd grown comfortable with over the years. Neither of them wanted the instantaneous demands of email, preferring old-fashioned snail mail instead.

Her memory was becoming clearer. She'd poured herself a glass of riesling and settled into a chair on the balcony before tearing open the envelope. The second surprise about Tom's letter was the size of it, or lack thereof. Just one page when there would often be three or four.

Hey Katherine,

Great to hear from you.

The new ship sounds awesome — you lucky thing! Hopefully, it won't be too much longer before the exercises are all over and you get away to sea again.

I guess it will be some time before you come back east.

Anyway, I've got news which I wanted to share with you.

I met a girl (no really!). Her name is Sam and we've been dating since last December. She's fantastic, I think you'd really like her.

Thing is, it's gotten serious pretty quick and we've fallen in love. She rocks my world and is everything I could ever dream of.

Katherine sensed what was coming and didn't want to read on.

Just yesterday, I asked Sam to marry me. And she said YES! So, we're engaged and looking to set a date for this fall. I wanted you to be one of the first people to know!

Thanks, Katherine thought with a strong tinge of sarcasm. *Yeah, Tom, really appreciate that.*

I'm guessing this will come as a surprise, but I know this is right for me. We'll reach out and send you a heads-up about the wedding arrangements when we know more. Hopefully, it will happen when you're still in San Diego and you can shoot over for the big day? We'd both love for you to be there.

Well, all the best for now. Stay safe and be good!
I hope we can catch up sometime when you're free.
Your good friend as always,
Tom

It hadn't been so much the words *marry* or even *wedding* that had stung her the most. It was his sign-off, the casual *I hope we can catch up sometime*. Tom never finished a letter that way. The phrasing indicated times had changed for them, and changed forever.

And then someone farted in the bed behind her. The hairs on the back of Katherine's neck bristled, and she reluctantly turned to see what she'd gotten into—and what she'd let get into her.

Fuck.

The reservoir of her memories from the previous night burst back into her mind in a gushing torrent. As he'd sidled up next to her at the bar, she'd noticed his chiselled features, strong shoulders, and a boyish clean face with impossibly good teeth and blue-grey eyes.

Enlisted, she'd thought, instantly writing him off. This was despite the fact they were both in civilian clothing. Navy people could pick navy people a mile off, uniform or not.

He'd looked towards her as he waited for his drink to come. A small nod, a subtle grin, and a partial flash of those white teeth as he offered to refill her drink was all it took.

She looked away from him as he lay still fast asleep and saw the trail of their clothes from the bedroom leading into the hallway to the entrance to the apartment. She was naked in bed with a naked enlisted sailor ten years her junior. And try as she might, she couldn't remember his name.

She stood up as quietly as she could and crept towards the bathroom. Suddenly the gurgling motion in her belly came back with full force. Katherine had barely stumbled into the bathroom before Mount Vesuvius did its thing, spewing vomit across the tiled floor and onto the shower door. She stumbled forward to kneel before the toilet as her abdominal and throat muscles purged her body of who knows how many shots of Fireball.

As she threw water on her face and washed away the filth in and around her mouth, she felt a little better, but somehow also worse.

Katherine Marlowe stared at herself in the bathroom mirror. A good, long, hard stare. What was she going to do with this person sleeping in her bed? This man without a name?

She shuffled back towards the bedroom as she tried to think of what to say. As she rounded the corner into the room, the sight of an empty bed greeted her. He was gone.

CHAPTER TEN

In America, anyone can become President. That's the problem.

—George Carlin

Hong Kong, 3 March 2022

"Ben … *Ben!*" Liling Cai called from the living room of the thirty-eighth-floor apartment.

"Yes, Ma," Ben said as he came into the room, his agitation plain to see.

The family spoke Mandarin at home—the native language of Liling's family in north-east China, and the nation's official language. They also spoke some Cantonese—the Chinese language traditionally used in Hong Kong and coastal regions of southern China—and some English when outside their home. Liling's English was rudimentary, but enough to get by. Ben and Jiang spoke English fluently, using it to converse with English-speaking customers and tourists from the West.

Speaking Korean in Hong Kong risked drawing unwanted attention to their ethnic roots and was therefore avoided. They had only done so in private when Jiang had taught Ben the language as a child, or after Jiang received a verbal drubbing from his wife. He would sometimes mutter a few swear words in Korean as he left the room, just to keep some semblance of testosterone-associated dignity.

"Aren't you working with your father today?" she asked.

"No."

"Then come to the market with me."

"I, ah—"

"Are you studying?"

"Not exactly," Ben admitted.

"Either you *are*, or you *are not*. If you are not, then you must help me."

Ben should have been studying. He was four years into his undergraduate computer science and engineering degree at the Chinese University of Hong Kong, but only two-thirds of the way to his degree. Chinese officials had persuaded the dean to grant him a flexible part-time status, an arrangement that allowed Ben to undertake his DPRK work whenever required.

"Yes, Ma."

"We'll leave in a few minutes. You can study this afternoon."

Ben lowered his gaze and made a small nod in defeat.

Liling read his body language like a book. "You *must* study! Your friends are all getting the best jobs in Shenzhen and Beijing, and you're sewing suits for your father."

"Yes. I know, but—"

She cut his off his response clean at the head. "Bah! Complete your education, then get a good job and find a nice girl to marry." Liling's tone softened. "That will be best for you and the family. You know this."

Ben feigned a smile. "I do."

"Good. Now let us be on our way."

*   *   *   *

The Fung Tak Market was a fifteen-minute walk from their apartment, in a sprawling basement beneath yet another cluster of high-rise buildings. As Liling and Ben made their way through the first row of open stores, the activity and noise were already near their peak. Ben had come to know shopping for fresh produce as an art form, developed over countless centuries of selling, bargaining, and purchasing. The act of buying is an established dance and an important facet of the social fabric.

Liling wove her way between the stores and smaller open stalls with Ben in tow. She did not have a shopping list. Everything she needed was catalogued in her mind, and she knew where to go for the best-quality items at the best prices.

And she could bargain. Even Ben would sometimes cringe at her tactics and stoic resolve. Liling would appear wounded, even devastated, by the price of an item, and then threaten to take her business elsewhere. Sometimes she won, but the shopkeepers had their victories too. And so the dance would go.

After yet another bargaining success buying stem lettuce and bok choi, Liling turned on her heel and hurried from the small store. Ben attempted to stuff the produce into the few remaining spaces in his overflowing basket while also trying to work out the direction his mother was headed.

As Ben coaxed the last clump of produce into the basket, he heard Liling yell in the distance. He dropped the basket and leapt into the walkway. He spotted his mother forty metres away. She grabbed at her shoulder—clutching for something that was no longer there.

As Ben sprinted towards his mother, he could see the object of her distress. A boy in his mid-teens was sprinting away at full speed with Liling's bag.

"Stay there," Ben said as he sprinted past her.

The boy turned his head and seemed shocked to see Ben gaining on him. He ran into a shopper and stumbled, then rounded a corner and continued his escape.

Ben hurried after him, but the trail had been lost. He picked his way through the crowd of shoppers, checking each store and aisle as he ran past. It was no use. There were too many escape routes and the boy had obviously known where he was going. Ben stopped at the next corner and made one last scan of the area before giving up.

He retraced his steps, dejected, to return to his distraught mother, who was still yelling and pointing. Several people had gathered around her.

"Excuse me," a voice said in a thick Western accent.

Ben ignored it, assuming the words weren't directed at him.

But the second attempt was louder. "Sir. Excuse me. *Over here.*"

A tall white man stood at a wall between a butcher's stall and a flower store. In one hand he held a different teenaged boy by his t-shirt, and clutched Liling's bag in his other hand. "I think this may belong to you?" the man asked.

"Yes. Yes." Ben said as he caught his breath.

"The kid who took it passed it to this guy as he ran off."

"I see," Ben replied, a bit at a loss for words.

"Classic pick-pocket strategy. Happens in all the tourist traps in Europe. Didn't think I'd see it happen here in Hong Kong, but here ya go!" The man was beaming, obviously thrilled with his catch of the day.

His catch said nothing, but the look of terror on his face was eloquent enough. He looked like a tiny cricket captured by a gigantic praying mantis that stood well over two metres tall.

Ben could hear the increasing commotion of his mother and her newfound entourage approaching behind him, and the sharp sound of a police whistle further back.

"Well, I'll be doggone. Here comes the cavalry!" the man said.

Liling strode towards them spouting a crazed mix of Mandarin, Cantonese, and English expletives, cursing the misguided youth of Hong Kong.

"Your bag, ma'am," the American said, handing it down to her.

Liling took the bag gingerly, then bowed, not taking her eyes off the human sun beaming above her. "Thank you. Sir. I thank you."

"No problem. Just call me Jake."

"I ... Mrs Cai."

The whistle-blowing policeman had made it to the group, his chest heaving from the run. "What happened?" he asked between wheezing breaths.

Ben explained the situation, and the policeman took the captured teen from the American and handcuffed him. After a few minutes spent gathering details, he led the boy away.

Liling was still effusively thanking the American man.

"Ah, it's nothing, ma'am, really. Just glad I could help. Right place, right time, you know—"

"You must come eat with us," Liling said, flicking her fingers towards him with her hand facing down.

"Look, really, there's no need, I—"

"No. You *must*. Is what we do. How we thank."

The American seemed caught between a rock and a soft place. He looked to Ben for guidance, who raised his eyebrows, shrugged his shoulders, and said nothing.

"Ben. Ben. *Address!*" Liling said, squiggling her index finger like a pen.

Ben and Jake exchanged first names and phone numbers. "I'll send you the address," Ben said, barely believing his own words as he heard himself speak.

"Dinner. Six," Liling said.

"Six. Oh yes, six it is, then. Thank you so much ma'am. I will see you both then."

With another bow and a smile to the American, Liling went on her way. She switched back to Mandarin. "Ben. Come now. Where is my basket?" she said as she walked off. "Silly child."

*　*　*　*

The intercom to the Cais' apartment buzzed at 5:59 PM. Liling seemed surprised, not expecting their guest to be on time. "Come," she said as she pressed the button to release the main entrance door. "Thirty-two-one-four".

Jiang still couldn't believe what was happening. *An American. In my house. And for dinner!* He shuddered in sour anticipation and muttered a foul Korean curse word under his breath.

Ben had warned Jiang about the American after the handbag incident. His father then risked life and limb by calling Liling to let his protest be known. "You invited a Western foreigner to my house!"

"No. To *my* house," Liling said.

"He could be from their government, or their army, some sort of spy!"

"Well, he will be good company for you then."

94

"I do not want the company of *Americans*! Cowardly, sadistic animals, all of them."

"Hmm. So much so he saved my bag and caught the criminal?"

Liling had Jiang there, and he knew it. He took a few seconds to respond. "I am busy in the shop. Won't be home for dinner."

"Dinner is at six. You will *not* be late."

Click.

And so there Jiang was. Home by six, as directed, and dreading the knock on the door.

Perhaps this is a dream. Yes. Must be. Or a nightmare. Wake up now man, wake up ...

And then the knock. Liling emerged from the kitchen steam and pointed at the door.

Jiang could not bring himself to it. "Ben, get the door."

Ben emerged from his bedroom a few reluctant seconds later. He shuffled towards the door as if approaching a rabid dog. There was no use resisting his parents, though.

"Hello again, Ben!" Jake said, thrusting out his hand.

Ben lost his breath for a few milliseconds. He had already forgotten how tall the American man was. And broad. "Hello, ah, Mr ...?" It was not polite to refer to a new acquaintance by their first name.

"Call me Jake," the American said as he shook Ben's hand with the force of an eighteen-wheeler shock absorber.

Ben nodded, out of habit, although it was so slight and fast it could easily be missed. "Please, Jake. Come in."

And there he was. This towering American with the big smile. Standing in the middle of the Cai apartment, his head practically scraping the ceiling.

Liling emerged again from the steam, extending both her hands to Jake and beaming. "Mr Jake. Mr Jake. Come in. *Come in.* Welcome to you. *Welcome!*"

"Thank you so much, Mrs Cai."

Liling motioned behind herself, wriggling her fingers at Jiang, who had refused to get up from his recliner. "Jiang. *Come!*" When Jiang hesitated, she raised her voice. "*Qǐchuáng!*" she demanded before transitioning back to English. "Silly man."

Jiang positioned himself beside and slightly behind his wife. He had all the stature of a deflated balloon. He'd dealt with Americans in his store, and he'd disciplined himself to handle them. But he didn't like or trust them. Too loud. Too arrogant. These were the wreckers of the united Korean nation, after all.

Jake grabbed Jiang's hand and gave it the full suspension experience. "Mr Cai. Great to meet you. It's an honour to be in your home." Jake bowed his head, still grinning.

"Hello," was all Jiang could manage. He nodded repeatedly, almost if he was having a fit of some sort.

"Sit, sit," Liling said, pulling out a dining chair for Jake. "You guest honour today."

"Thank you, ma'am."

"Eat, three minutes," she said as she disappeared into the kitchen.

The three men sat at the round dining table. Jiang and Ben did not know where to look and resorted to looking at each other.

"You have a lovely home," Jake said in heavily accented but surprisingly coherent Mandarin.

Jiang's face went pale. "You speak Chinese?" he asked.

Jake shrugged modestly. "I speak some, but not very well," he replied, still speaking in Mandarin.

Jiang switched back to English. "It is okay, though," he said. "We are comfortable speaking English. Please speak English with us."

"Yeah, sure. No problem," Jake said.

Liling returned from the kitchen in quick-fire visits. She placed a large bowl of rice before each of the men, followed by three steaming dishes in the centre of the table.

"Wow. This smells incredible!" Jake said, his eyes wide with anticipation.

"Oh, it is nothing," Liling said as she headed for the kitchen. "I get fork and knife for you."

"I prefer chopsticks," Jake replied in Mandarin with a cheeky grin.

Liling turned around in shock. *"Wā sāi, hēn méi xiǎng dào!"*

"He knows some Mandarin. But we will speak English," Jiang interjected.

"Oh. Yes. I get chopsticks."

Moments later, the meal was in full swing. Liling had cooked up a storm: noodles with black bean sauce, stir-fried cumin lamb, pork belly hot pot, and a small mountain of mantou steamed buns.

"Mrs Cai, your cooking is superb," Jake said. "It's such an honour to eat at your table."

Jiang noted how Jake seemed to understand the etiquette around the meal, and that he was deft with those chopsticks. "How is it you speak Mandarin?" he asked.

"Oh, I travelled through China in my early twenties with my girlfriend. She had lived in Guangzhou with her father, who worked in the American consulate there. She taught me some Mandarin, and I've learned more since I've been working here."

"Girlfriend? So marry now?" Liling asked.

"Yes, she is married, but I am not."

Liling appeared wounded by the thought, shaking her head. "Oh, oh. No, no."

"Perhaps she found a nice Chinese man instead?" Jiang joked.

"Haha, no, just another ugly American."

Jiang surprised himself by laughing in response. Ben stared at his father, although Jiang did not notice his frosty glare.

"You work here? In Hong Kong?" Jiang asked.

"Yes. I coach basketball at a sports academy."

"Ah. This explains your altitude."

Jake laughed. "Yeah, altitude, that's me!"

Liling wanted more. "Your mother, father. How old? Where living?"

"Ah, my mom and dad are in their early sixties. They live in Tyler, Texas, where I grew up."

"You do not live with them?" Jiang asked.

"Not anymore, no. I went to college in Austin and have been moving around ever since."

And so the conversation went. Liling asked what questions she could, direct as always. Jiang and Jake held the main conversation. Ben held back, saying little, and only if asked a direct question.

All three of the Cais were surprised, in varying amounts, by how Jiang relaxed over the meal. He seemed interested in this Mandarin-speaking, Hong Kong–living young man. As if, for a moment in time, he'd forgotten about the man's country of birth. As if that fact was not actually important.

*   *   *   *

Liling served tea after the meal. Sensing the imminent departure of their guest, Ben made a conscious decision to enter the conversation. They'd all been careful not to mention politics or world events. This would have been potentially offensive, and could have caused a loss of face for the guest and the hosts. But Ben struggled with a deep sense of dissonance—a disturbing confusion between the teachings of his father, his DPRK training, and almost everything he understood about Americans. His emotions disturbed him and he wanted a return to firm and familiar ground. "What of your president?" he blurted out. "Do you support such a man?"

Jiang attempted to cut him off, glowering at Ben as he did. "This is not a good question."

"It's okay," Jake said. "My dad says this president is the best thing for America right now. He's restoring America's place in the world and our role across the Pacific. He's taking it right to China. But personally, I don't support everything he does. I'm not into his aggressive version of America that much."

Jiang and Ben didn't know how to process this. Their Supreme Leader deserved their unwavering and undying commitment and must never be criticised. Anything other than undying devotion would most likely end with someone dying.

Liling, though, was not nearly as conflicted. She steered the conversation away from the impending minefield. "Mr Jake. Again. You saved me and bag today. Thank you. I thank you."

Jake might have been itching to ask what his hosts thought of the Chinese general secretary, or Hong Kong's deteriorating freedoms, but even if so, he resisted the urge. "It was my pleasure, Mrs Cai."

And as Jake's broad grin returned, the cloud of politics seemed to evaporate from the room.

Within a few minutes, Jake had said his goodbyes, Liling had thanked him another fifteen times, Jiang had thanked him once, and Ben had said nothing. Handshakes were offered and accepted, and then he was gone.

The three Cais stood staring at the closed door. Jiang was the first to come to with a small shake of his head. He saw the bewildered look on Ben's face—his eyes still focused on the closed door. "Ben. Understand ... this one was different. But *never* forget how the rest of them are."

"All of them?"

"Yes. *All of them.*"

CHAPTER ELEVEN

One thing you'll say for skeletons, they'll always give you a smile.

—Steve Aylett, *Slaughtermatic*

Jiaozhou/Jiaocheng Air Base, Shandong, China
10 April 2022, 0612 hours

The windsock near the southern end of the runway flapped hyperactively as a strong gusting wind from the north bit at the lieutenant's face. His uniform, jacket, and hat were no match for the weather and he shivered with every fresh gust of wind.

He ached for a cigarette to warm his lungs and use up some time. PLAAF rules said otherwise, and he would not dare disobey—not out in the open in the middle of a major airbase.

There were no fighter jets operating at the base that morning. The surrounding airspace, taxiways, and the single long runway were as quiet and desolate as ever. So, when he heard the distant sound of turboprop engines, he knew it signalled the approaching plane he was to meet.

Within a few moments, the Xian Y-7 transport had landed and taxied towards the apron. *What a sad specimen*, he thought as he contemplated the shape of the aircraft, which despite many design revisions and upgrades over many decades was still a 1950s-era Soviet-designed machine at heart. The outer half of its wings drooped down, giving it a defeated and tired pose. And the black rubber shapes beneath the forward cockpit windows had the look of an old man with deep dark bags of skin sagging beneath his eyes.

With the plane parked at the standoff bay and its engines shut down, the crewman opened the front passenger door and extended the flight of stairs. The PLAAF first lieutenant waited nearby. DPRK Colonel

General Kim Hyun-woo burst from the interior and descended the steps. A staffer and an old man in civilian clothing followed.

"Colonel General," the first lieutenant said, standing to attention as he spoke. He did not salute.

Kim stared at him, tightened his jacket against the wind, and said nothing.

"Welcome," the first lieutenant continued. "Please, I will take you to the meeting place." He motioned towards the staff car, which had pulled up close by.

*   *   *   *

PLA Lieutenant Colonel Li Guoliang stared at the video screen. For the past twenty minutes he had watched the series of video clips brought by the visiting officer from North Korea, Colonel General Kim Hyun-woo. He had watched the young operative in the videos undertaking training in North Korea, and he'd observed his performance in various demonstrations and tests. Some tests were outright bizarre and inhumane, even by Li's standards.

Kim had talked Li through the DPRK file on the operative while they had breakfast at the airbase, and they had discussed the young man's profile and history in forensic detail.

The two officers had met five times in the preceding months. They had planned the mission using their collective special operations knowledge and experience. But the decision they were to make that day would be the most important of the mission to come.

Li appeared mildly interested in what he saw, but not impressed. As a senior officer with significant operational experience, he was legendary among the Chinese special forces units. He could run three kilometres in ten minutes flat, endure inhuman levels of exertion and exhaustion, and survive in almost any conditions the planet could serve up. He maintained his peak operational condition even at forty-three years of age. And he could kill, efficiently and swiftly.

Li considered the young DPRK operative further. His Chinese roots and the fact he had lived in Hong Kong for much of his life interested him. This was the best of both worlds: a Chinese man for all intents and purposes, but of North Korean blood with DPRK training. These characteristics could be politically and strategically useful when the time came. Li also warmed to aspects of the young man's training. He recognised the man's use of Tai Chi and his significant martial arts skills. These elements aligned well with Li's own practice of qigong, an ancient Chinese practice of posture, movement, breathing, and meditation.

This young man has potential, he thought. *But does he have the stamina? Does he have the will power to finish a mission no matter what obstacles he faces? Can he be trusted to follow orders exactly and to act on his own?*

Li was looking for a unique balance of power and restraint, of cooperation and independence, and of energy and a disposition of inner calm. Yin and yang personified.

Kim could sense Li needed more. "I have one further test to show you," he said as he opened another folder on his laptop.

"Very well. But one more only for this candidate."

The video was hard to make out at first. The CCTV camera was mounted high up inside a cavernous hall and the lighting was dim. There were two lines of seven men on each side of the hall. They formed what looked to be a guard of honour with a narrow path between them. Li watched as their prospect made his way between the two lines of men and all the brutality that followed.

Li leaned forward as he watched the man stagger toward the small table and the vase at the far end. He saw the young man steady himself and close his eyes in quiet meditation.

Li's eyes widened as the next seconds unfolded. Even he was startled by the stunning attacks upon the young man's assailants. The strength, speed, power, and drive of this agent was something to behold. And especially so, given the injuries he had endured.

When the video ended, Li continued to stare at the screen. "This is our man," he finally said. "You have chosen well."

Kim nodded, unable to hide a hint of a grin.

*   *   *   *

Hong Kong, 4:55 PM

The day of study had been long, even tortuous. Advanced network architecture was not Ben's favourite topic, but with an exam looming in two days' time, he had no choice but to wallow in it.

The chime from his phone was a welcome distraction. The message from his "friend" was cloaked in friendly colloquial language, but the immediacy of the request was clear. There would be no encrypted mission package to retrieve from the dark web this time. His friend had invited him to meet at a nearby MTR subway station in thirty minutes time.

*   *   *   *

Ben returned within the hour. His parents were home and dinnertime was not far away. He retrieved a jacket from the hallway closet and made his way to his bedroom, hoping he could get on with his travel preparations undisturbed.

"Ben, a jacket?" Liling asked. "Where are you going?"

"I cannot say. I leave early tomorrow."

"*Cāo wǒ!*" she cursed.

Ben ignored her and slipped into his room.

Liling did not trouble him further or chastise him for his apparent rudeness. She had seen this many times before. When Ben had "work" to do, he would change—instantly. She would barely know the person he became at that moment, and she would not want to know him until he returned and became her Ben again.

*   *   *   *

Hobart, Tasmania

11 April 2022

Deputy Premier Matthew Cash burst into his outer office in the Executive Building, as was his tradition on arrival each morning. He demanded his usual morning double-shot espresso from his assistant as he barged through and disappeared into his internal office.

He'd been caught in frustrating peak-hour traffic that morning. Hobart, despite its relatively small population of around 225,000, was buried in a quagmire of traffic woes. The issues were caused to a degree by the local geography. Hobart was split in two by the expansive width of the River Derwent, and its suburbs were spread thin along its shores and hemmed in by steep hills and a mountain on the western side—the towering kunanyi/Mount Wellington.

But geography was not all to blame, for Hobart's residents were in love with their cars. The motor vehicle obsession was, perhaps, the natural result of a substandard public transport system. Or, perhaps, the public transport system was substandard because it could not compete with the all-conquering obsession with the motor vehicle.

No one knew the answer, including the government that Matthew Cash worked for. They had tried a few fixes, but had resorted to blaming the conga line of traffic consultants they had hired over the years—all of whom had concluded the traffic issue was too hard and too expensive to fix.

But those factors were not front of mind for Matthew Cash that morning. He had sat, bumper to bumper with thousands of other Tasmanians, in crawling traffic on the four-lane freeway from the outer suburb of Kingston, locally known as the Southern Outlet. It had taken him an hour and twenty minutes to crawl the twelve kilometres into Hobart's CBD, thanks to self-centred idiots who had combined their collective driving talents to produce a monumental three-car pileup.

The only positive for Cash was that he hadn't been driving. His government driver did that. Cash could sit back in his luxury government car and fume and curse at the traffic in comfort. But even so, he had an important cabinet meeting scheduled to start at ten o'clock. He would be "too late to the dairy," as he would say.

Cash scrambled to finish reading the never-ending pile of briefings and minute papers stacked on his desk. This was not the way he liked to start his day. He slammed a finger down on a well-worn button on his desk phone. "Michelle," he barked at his assistant in the next room, "set up a meeting with Rouse, you, and I for this afternoon at three. There'll be a shitload of actions out of the cabinet meeting to look at."

Cash sat back for a moment, threw down the last gulp of his cold coffee, and stared at the ceiling. On days like this he would wonder why on earth he remained in the god-forsaken bitch of a job. He'd fallen into politics sunny-side up, then slid all the way up to second in charge. Some would say he'd slid all the way down.

Cash's father had served two terms as a Member of Parliament in the 1990s. Their family held extensive agricultural land and assets across the north and north-east of the state, and they had dabbled in high-end tourism ventures on the east coast with some success.

Cash had first run for State Parliament twenty-two years earlier. He was a twenty-seven-year-old rural knock-about back then, still fresh-faced and wide-eyed. His father had suggested he "give it a crack" when a snap election was called.

He hadn't known much beyond his dairy farms back then, but Cash gave it a crack and succeeded on his first attempt. This was attributed to his prominent family name, and the sitting member on the other side being almost dead but somehow still dragging himself into Parliament House when required. The old ex-MP then "carked it"—an Australian term for dying—two weeks after the election.

Cash had dodged, weaved, and smiled his way through his political career. He survived by keeping his head down and mouth shut whenever he could. He would pick the alpha male of the political pack, then swear allegiance to him and work as a close ally in his shadow.

Cash had sniffed out and put down a few political coups in his career, protecting his leader at the time. This included the current premier, who, despite being grateful to his two-IC, had never expressed his gratitude.

And the top job? No. Not for him. He'd always known that. Cash would scoff at suggestions from journalists he should have a tilt at being premier one day. *You have to kidding me*, he'd think. *Nope. Deputy premier is as bad as it gets for me.*

And there were skeletons in the closet of the ever-smiling, mostly pleasant deputy premier. Some had come out to play. Others were yet to make their debut.

The rest of Cash's persona seemed to broadcast the wear and tear of a long political career. He'd maintained his farmer's physique and was not yet balding, but his hair had thinned and it wouldn't be long before the dastardly decision would have to be made between a comb-over or a shave-over. And for better or worse, the salt-and-pepper effect was in full swing as his once jet-black hair transitioned to silver. His wife seemed to like it, not that he ever noticed. They didn't cross paths often.

Cash glanced at the antique clock on the far wall. *Damn it!*

He had one minute to sprint to the cabinet meeting room. He hated being late.

CHAPTER TWELVE

*The successful warrior is the average man with laser-
like focus.*

—Bruce Lee

Qingdao International Airport, Shandong
11 April 2022

Ben was grateful for the business class seat. He didn't enjoy aeroplane travel and particularly not the longer flights. He had boarded the China Southern flight in Shenzhen at 7:35 AM, arriving in Qingdao in the north-east of China three hours and twenty minutes later.

It was a further relief when the flight attendant opened the cabin door. He grabbed his travel bag and coat and dashed down the aero bridge before the hordes from economy class could choke the walkway.

When Ben emerged into the arrivals hall, he scanned the waiting throng of people. There were a few drivers holding cards with names, but none displaying his.

"Mr Cai," whispered a voice beside him, "please follow me."

Stupid me, Ben thought. He realised the Chinese CCTV and the facial recognition system would have identified him as soon as he stepped off the plane. In fact, he had been tracked since he emerged from the elevator of his apartment building in Hong Kong that morning.

Ben followed the man out of the terminal. A black SUV with dark windows was waiting at the curb, engine running. The man opened the back door and motioned for him to get in. The driver said nothing, and Ben remained silent.

After a ten-minute drive to an industrial park on the opposite side of the airport, the SUV pulled up outside a small warehouse at the end of a quiet street. Another man approached the vehicle and opened the door.

Ben noted the tell-tale signs of a holster and handgun hidden beneath the man's jacket. He, like the driver and man at the airport, wore classic black business attire and dark sunglasses. *Must be the fashion*, Ben thought.

The man opened a small door within the main gate of the warehouse and gestured for Ben to step-in.

The interior was hollow and dim, lit only by a few high windows and a dirty skylight. The air inside was much cooler, with the aroma of a funeral home. As Ben's eyes adjusted to the light, he noticed a man at the far end. He was of short and portly stature, motionless, and looking straight at Ben.

"Yong-sun," the man said.

Ben recognised the voice and his mind transported to a time three years earlier. *Could this be?*

His silent question was answered without delay. "It is I, Master Park," the man said. He waved his hand for Ben to approach. "Come."

As Ben stood before him, Master Park read his eyes. "Yong-sun. This is not a test," he said.

"Master Park," Ben replied as he bowed.

"There is much to discuss," Master Park began. "Come … sit."

Ben pretended to relax.

"Your training has been completed and your missions have gone well. Your unique abilities have been put to the test and are well proven. They have been recognised by those who serve the Supreme Leader."

Ben nodded.

"I am meeting you today under the orders of our military, to discuss with you a mission of great importance, for which you, and only you, have been selected."

Master Park paused and exhaled. "There are few, very few, who have the opportunity to bring real victory for our glorious state. There are even fewer who have the skills and the discipline to seize the opportunity and bring it to pass. We believe you to be one of those few."

Ben stared straight ahead. He processed what he'd been told as best he could, but the "we" reference perplexed him. *Who are these people?* "I am honoured, Master Park," he said.

"You, as with all our compatriots, are a master of your own destiny. You have all you need. You do not rely on any external power to trounce our enemies. We have no need of a god, or a foreign power. We have *ourselves*."

Master Park seemed to be working towards something and sounding more like an orator with every sentence. Ben had not heard him speak this way before. *This must be big, whatever it is.*

"Today you will speak with senior officers of a mission of great importance. The colonel general you will meet is under direct orders from the Supreme Leader himself. He has conceived this mission in his supreme wisdom. He has decreed it to be so."

Ben bowed his head in recognition. This was convenient—it hid his look of surprise.

"Our magnificent nation has been given a profound opportunity to strike at the ignorant pig who seeks to control us and kill our people. It is time for us to strike back. We will show the world the genuine power of our people, the pre-eminence of our way of life, and the supremacy of our leader."

Master Park reached out, taking Ben's hands into his. "You will face much hardship. You will be called to sacrifice much."

"Master Park, I—"

"You will have many questions. I understand this. Many of these will be answered for you today. But not by me." Master Park released Ben's hands and stood up. "Remember all I have taught you, Yong-sun."

Ben also stood. "I will."

"And when the time comes, remember … the mission, and the mission only."

Ben looked into Master Park's eyes. He could see an emotion he could not quite fathom, as if they were about to separate before a long journey, or perhaps for the last time.

Master Park nodded towards a room at the rear of the warehouse. "Go now. They are waiting for you."

Ben bowed, then followed the order. He did not look back.

*　　*　　*　　*

As Ben entered the room, he first spotted a small table and faded plastic chairs. The room was lit by a single bulb that flickered every so often. A stale smell hung in the air. The room had not been used in quite some time, yet it had the distant stench of a thousand lunchtimes.

Two men sat at the table. Both were dressed in civilian clothing, though they had a military presence about them.

They both stood as he entered. "Agent Jeong Yong-sun," the older man said. "I am Colonel General Kim Hyun-woo, DPRK."

Ben stood to attention, slapping his heels together. "Sir."

"My colleague is a PLA commander, special forces. His name will not be made known to you."

Ben turned to the Chinese officer. "Sir." He did not salute.

"Be seated."

The three men each took a chair at the small table.

"You come highly commended by Master Park and his colleagues," Kim began.

Ben nodded, sensing to say nothing at that point.

"This mission is endorsed by the Supreme Leader and is to be led by our great nation. We are supported in this by our friends of the Communist Party of China, and the PLA."

The Chinese officer shifted uneasily in his seat.

The word *supported* amused Ben. With all the Supreme Leader's teachings on Juche—the nationalistic ideology of independence and self-sufficiency that drove the North Korean nation—it seemed odd the mission was to be supported by the Chinese.

For the next thirty minutes, Ben listened as Kim described the intent and nature of the mission, yet refraining from divulging details of planned dates, times, and locations. Ben asked a few questions about strategic and logistical matters, but for the most part he just listened and memorised details as best he could.

The Chinese officer said little. Ben could sense the man observing him—as if he were being inspected by a machine of some kind—scanned, probed, and analysed. Ben was careful to manage his words and his non-verbal cues. He only looked at the man when he spoke, and he used a careful economy of words.

Kim's briefing eventually came to a stop. Details of the mission were extensive, and he'd exhausted all he could remember. He sat back in his chair looking strained and tired.

"Agent," the Chinese officer said.

Ben met the man's piercing dark eyes.

"Do you comprehend this mission?"

"Yes, sir."

"You accept your orders?"

"Yes, sir. I do."

"Your parents will be proud. And your success will provide them with a secure future." He paused. "You understand?"

Ben resisted the instinct to ram the officer's head into the wall behind him. He nodded instead.

"Do you understand what it is you are being asked to sacrifice?" the officer asked.

"Yes. I do."

"These orders are extraordinary. You will sacrifice much. You have, therefore, until midday tomorrow to provide us with your final response."

Seconds ticked away as the room fell silent.

The officer broke the bizarre tranquillity. "Agent ... *acknowledge!*"

Ben rose from his chair without thinking. "Sir!" he snapped, not breaking eye contact with the man. He shifted his gaze to Kim. "I do not require further time to consider this. With respect. It will be of the highest honour to serve our Supreme Leader and our nation in this, and I will follow my orders to the end. I will execute the mission and I *will* succeed. This you can count on." He glared at the Chinese officer. "As can you."

CHAPTER THIRTEEN

*Power does not corrupt men; fools, however, if they get
into a position of power, corrupt power.*

—George Bernard Shaw

Hobart, 11 April 2022

"**S**hit, you're kidding me! What a joke."

But Deputy Premier Matthew Cash wasn't joking. "Does this look like a stand-up comedy joint to you, sump-plug?" Cash hissed.

Bradfurd Rouse—Cash's current chief of staff—sometimes drove the deputy premier to despair. He was good at his job, no question there. But Cash hated him. Rouse was everything Cash wasn't, which was why Cash needed him on his team.

Rouse would butt heads with the best of them. His many channels into the departments and agencies in the Tasmanian Public Service, and with the staffers of MPs on both sides of the political fence, were legendary, and he used them all with strategic aplomb. He was a master at manipulating the media, sending them into a frenzy by scattering titbits of information as if they were hungry chickens in a yard, while alienating and starving those who did not play the game his way. And he commanded a social media army of purported Tasmanian voters hailing from Ukraine and Belarus.

As Cash looked across the meeting table at Rouse, he took in a man of the city—a Millennial who acted like a mid-twenties Zoomer despite being thirty-six years old. His squat face was framed by delicate designer glasses of the square and trendy variety, and a frightening nest of scrawny red hair adorned his head, the hairstyle seemingly induced by two hundred and forty volts of pure Tasmanian hydro-electricity.

"Maybe not, but I'm still smiling," Rouse hissed back.

Michelle Weston, Cash's executive assistant, hadn't laughed either. She slumped further into her chair and rested her head in one hand.

Cash got down to business. "The premier doesn't see anything funny in the latest tourism figures."

"Okay, but what are we supposed to do about it?"

"Isn't that your job? Figure it out!"

Rouse shrugged. "I'm just the messenger. You're the statesman."

"Bull-crap. I'm not paying you to be a parrot."

Cash wasn't about to let this go. Tourism was part of his ministerial portfolio. "The visitor numbers from this summer show a dip of another six percent. And that's on top of similar declines for the last two years running. Something's not right."

"What's Slogan Tas saying?" Rouse asked, sarcastically referring to the government's tourism agency.

"Not much. They just spout these figures and not much else."

"Dickheads."

Weston chimed in. She, unlike Cash and Rouse, had read the full report. "International numbers are the most worrying. The drop is close to ten percent there."

Cash grimaced. "Stone the bloody crows. It doesn't make sense. All we've spent. And it's not like bloody MONA has closed down or anything."

He was referring to the great white knight of Tasmanian tourism and economy, the Museum of Old and New Art. It had opened in 2011, and the world fell in love with the museum and its many whacky festivals and offshoots. All of a sudden Tasmania, a forgotten little backwater at the bottom of the earth, was the place to be. Millions came to see MONA and join the fun, and tourism boomed throughout the island.

"What about the Chinese?" Rouse asked.

Weston flipped through the report. "Down by twenty-three percent this season."

Cash was getting a solid headache. No wonder the premier had gone off his nut in the cabinet meeting.

"The Chinese are travelling less and less." Cash mused, "and COVID-19 hit them hard."

"Yep. And our leftie Australian media just can't resist having a go," Rouse grumbled. Human rights, Hong Kong, Taiwan, ethnic minorities. I wish they'd leave the poor bastards alone."

Weston seemed unsure of Rouse's meaning. "You mean ... the Chinese need to leave them alone?"

"No. We can't be expected to maintain strong economic ties with China if our media constantly bashes them the way they do."

"Michelle, I want you to talk to the premier's people and float the idea of another trade mission to China," Cash said. "I think it's time we paid them another goodwill visit."

"You sure about that?" Rouse asked. "It's only been, what ... twelve months since the ah, ... *incident*."

Cash rolled his eyes. "That's done and dusted. You know that!"

"Nothing's *ever* done and dusted in this game. We both know that."

"Ah, gimme a break! This is Tasmanian politics, not a bloody episode of *The West Wing*!" Cash snarled.

Cash's comment stung Rouse, who glared back at his boss. Rouse had just finished rewatching the seventh season of his favourite TV series ever the weekend before. He adored that show.

Cash was stung too. The incident Rouse had referred to was the unfortunate discovery of a study tour that Cash and his wife had taken in China in early 2020. The tour itself had not been the issue, but the lavish dinners, shopping, hotels, resorts, and golfing destinations along the way certainly were. And especially so, given much of it had been organised and financed by a wealthy Chinese entrepreneur with emerging tourism interests in Tasmania and strong links to the Communist Party of China.

The allegations had been uncovered by a journalist who inadvertently crossed paths with Cash in Macau. Many uncomfortable questions were posed on a national current affairs program a week later. Cash went to ground and his then–chief of staff grossly mishandled the media response. Which was why, at the premier's direction, one Bradfurd Rouse then became his new chief of staff.

"It's not just the Chinese," Weston said in an attempt to get the two men back on subject. They were glowering at each other like primary school boys in a staring competition. "Cruise ship visits to Hobart are still way down. Just twenty-three this summer."

Cash was the first to drop his eyes. "Mmm, that's a worry. They still haven't recovered from the pandemic, I'm guessing."

"I'll get onto the cruise ship companies," Rouse said. "See what's happening from their end."

"Yes. And check with the Port Authority. There's gotta be something we can nail. An issue … something." A memory flickered in Cash's mind. "What was that press release we put out last year?" he asked. "Something about U.S. Navy visits?"

Rouse was onto it. "Oh yeah. That was Watson's office. The premier and her came up with some crazy-ass scheme to get the Americans back down here."

"So, ship visits 'n stuff?"

"Yeah. They figured getting another aircraft carrier or two would be a nice little boost to the economy."

"Mmm. But they don't compare much to dozens of cruise ships dropping all their passengers downtown."

"Maybe, but cruise ships only stay for a few hours and the bogan tight-arse passengers don't actually spend much. But you get a U.S. Navy carrier here with what … five thousand crew … they stay for like a week and it's freakin' Christmas. Those guys spend truckloads."

"Michelle, get me that press release. And Rouse, see what you can find out from Watson's office. What communication have they had with the U.S. government and the U.S. Navy on this?"

Cash spun his executive chair around from the meeting table to face the floor-to-ceiling windows. From there, on the seventh floor of the government building, he had one of the best views in Hobart. He could see over the city's historic maritime precinct and across the wharves, piers, and boats. And farther out, the hills of Tranmere sat in the hazy distance on the far shore of the River Derwent.

That will be the place, he thought to himself. *Where a U.S. Navy aircraft carrier will be anchored. The place from where thousands of crew will be desperate to disembark and get into our city.*

Matthew Cash relaxed into the view and smiled for the first time that day.

*   *   *   *

Hong Kong, 27 May 2022

The SUBMIT button loomed on Ben's laptop screen. He let the cursor hover as he went back through the online application in his mind. *Do I have everything? Have I answered all the questions correctly?*

The last thing he wanted were errors that could draw unwanted attention to himself. And he knew the Australian immigration authorities were no mugs. They did their checks and assessed the risks thoroughly.

Ben had applied to study in Australia as his handler had instructed. The flight school—Horizons Commercial Pilot Academy—had interviewed him on webcam, and even though he'd been sketchy on some aspects of aviation, they had accepted him for their eleven-month course for a Diploma of Aviation—Commercial Pilot Licence. Four weeks later, he received his letter of acceptance and a Certificate of Enrolment—the crucial step to gaining a subclass-500 Student Visa to study in Australia.

Ben inhaled, held his breath, and clicked the SUBMIT button. *What will be, will be.*

CHAPTER FOURTEEN

For where two or three come together in my name, I am there among them.

—Jesus (Matthew 18:20, translated)

26 January 2023, 1725 hours

Captain William A. Collins knew the time had come. He picked up the squarish microphone, wrestling its coiled cord out and away from the clip next to his captain's chair.

The shrill sound of the boatswain's whistle preceded his announcement over the 1MC—the communication circuit to the entire ship. He waited for a pre-announcement to end before keying the mic.

"This is the captain," he began. "Today we sail into history on the first deployment of our magnificent new ship, *John F. Kennedy.* I know you, like me, have been waiting a long time for this day to come. Well, we're here. We've completed our training and prep, Carrier Air Wing 11 has joined us on board, and now it's time to get on with our mission.

"Our first stop will be Pearl Harbor some days from now. Beyond that, we have a long deployment on the high seas. For those new to the navy, and even for the old hands who've done this before, there's always mixed feelings as we depart. But it's time to put those things behind us. We have much to look forward to in the service of our nation. We will see a lot, and we're gonna accomplish a lot of things. It's gonna be hard work. It will be tough sometimes. But I know we will serve our ship, our strike group, the navy, and our nation well.

"This ship, our ship, is the biggest and the best on these oceans. Make no doubt about it, we're sailing on *the* ultimate weapon. But I want you all to remember this: This ship is nothing without the people who serve on her. Our success will depend on how well each of us does our jobs.

And never forget—every single person is vital to everyone else. So let's each do our jobs to the absolute best we can.

"Folks, let's make our families, our communities, and our nation proud of what we do, and how we go about it. We take the United States of America with us to wherever we go. We bring our values of democracy, human rights, liberty, opportunity, and equality. The great American Dream. Let's do it with *everything* we've got. The world needs us now like never before ... this is the captain. Out."

Collins released the mic button. He sat back into his chair and exhaled a long, deliberate breath.

From his captain's perch high on the bridge of the carrier, the view was something to behold. The sun had only just set. Dusk light painted fluffy cumulus clouds on the horizon in soft shades of orange and pink.

On the flight deck below, the last of the Carrier Air Wing 11 aircraft, which had arrived on board that afternoon, were being towed into their parking positions. Two F-35 fighters were being taken on the elevators to the hangars below. Lights on the island—the multi-storey superstructure above the flight deck—cast a serene faint red glow over the lines of aircraft parked nearby.

The array of aircraft on board was formidable. Two squadrons of F-35C Joint Strike Fighters, another two squadrons of the older F/A-18E and F Hornet fighters, and a squadron each of E-2C Hawkeye early warning turboprops, EA-18G Growler electronic attack jets, and C-2A Greyhound logistics turboprops. There was also a squadron of MH-60S Seahawk sea combat helicopters, and a squadron of MH-60R Seahawk maritime strike helicopters—designated HSM-85, callsign "Black Wolf."

Behind and on either side of the ship, six other surface vessels deployed to the newly configured strike group sailed in lines, three abreast. The group included two Ticonderoga-class guided missile cruisers, three Arleigh-Burke–class guided missile destroyers, and a Supply-class ammunition/oiler/supply ship.

There were two other vessels in the group that, although Collins couldn't see them, he knew to be there. Hunter-killer fast-attack submarines—one Los Angeles–class and one Virginia-class—were patrolling some distance from the group, well below the surface.

It could have been another "pinch me" moment for Collins. He was finally on his way, captain of *John F. Kennedy* on its first-ever deployment. But his myriad of responsibilities would keep him busy, day and night, seven days a week, for the next seven months.

Just the way he liked it.

*　　*　　*　　*

Hong Kong, 31 January 2023

Awkward.

Ben had thought through the moment dozens of times in his head. He'd visualised how difficult their parting would be. His parents might get emotional. His mother might even cry. He'd prepared himself to be cool and collected when the time came. But where did cool end and cold begin?

The three Cais stood at the entrance to the passport control area— the last point before Ben would leave his parents and catch the airport subway train to Terminal One.

Ben maintained his usual control, but another more powerful force within his psyche was at work. The emotion, if that's what it was, was outside his experience. Arcane pangs of belonging, of place, of loyalty, spun within his mind and threatened to overwhelm him.

And looking into the pleading, forlorn, damp eyes of his mother was not helping. She was doing her level best not to break down, but Ben could tell it wouldn't be long until her emotions overtook her.

It had been over dinner, two months earlier, when Ben had told his parents about his decision to leave Hong Kong and study in Australia. Liling exploded, incredulous with shock and disappointment. Ben tried his best to convince her on the merits of the change, but it was an impossible task, given he had zero personal motivation to go to

Australia and become a commercial pilot. It took three days before Liling would speak to him, and even then, his relationship with his mother took on a frostiness that neither of them had experienced before.

And two months later, things had thawed little.

"I must go now," Ben said.

Liling pulled him to her in a death grip. Ben could feel her first tremors as she fought back her developing sobs. She released him, then moved away without a word, wiping her eyes as she went.

Alone then with his father, Ben didn't know what to do next.

Ben's missions were unspoken between them. Jiang would never ask, knowing the importance of absolute secrecy. Such things, in their game, could be the difference between life and death. And, more importantly, the difference between success and failure.

And Ben didn't know what, if anything, the DPRK was telling his father. He assumed his father was no longer informed at all. But a look behind his father's eyes, a look he hadn't seen before, expressed an unspoken level of understanding that chilled Ben to the core.

Jiang took his son's hands in his. "I will be with you in spirit, my son."

Ben nodded.

Jiang choked out his last words: "I know you will make us proud. *All of us.* Now go ... go now."

Ben made his way through passport control in a trance. He picked up his bag from the security scanner and took the few steps to the last exit leading to the subway train.

Ben knew he shouldn't. He told himself not to. But a powerful force within couldn't be ignored. He stopped for a moment at the top of the escalator, then turned his head to look back. In the distance, Jiang Cai was nearly doubled over and shaking in grief.

*   *   *   *

Western Pacific Ocean

19 March 2023

U.S. Navy Lieutenant Commander Katherine Marlowe was off watch for the morning. She'd had an early breakfast, hit the gym for an hour, and showered. The movies and TV series she'd downloaded to her laptop before leaving San Diego were all but watched, and the two books she'd brought with her were read. A third book she'd purchased in Hawaii had turned out to be melodramatic crap, and she'd tossed it down a rubbish chute.

It was easy to become bored some days, and Katherine had resorted to taking off for a long walk through the ship with nowhere in particular to go.

The sheer scale of USS *John F. Kennedy* still amazed her, and she was thankful for the assignment. Most of her colleagues had been stationed on other ships in the strike group, but she and her long-time colleague, Lieutenant Corey Moretti, had both scored the carrier.

She was still discovering new areas of the ship, even after two months at sea. And she enjoyed how the ship seemed so modern and spacious. The usual experience of tight, dim spaces and the pervasion of drab colours were mostly a thing of the past. And with around seven hundred fewer crew—thanks to the extensive automation on this class of carrier—there was more space for everyone on board.

Katherine strode down a long corridor on the O-5 deck and was nearing the forward end. She preferred to walk quickly rather than jog. As she stepped through yet another bulkhead doorway, she heard an unusual sound from behind her. She took a few steps back to investigate the source of the sound and pulled out her AirPods as she neared an open doorway.

It was the ship's chapel, and a Sunday church service was underway. Katherine lingered for a few seconds to listen to the congregation sing.

"Don't just stand there, Marlowe, get your butt inside!"

Katherine swung around to see who had delivered the instruction. "Oh. Yeah," she said with an awkward laugh.

Commander Owen, squadron leader of The Red Diamonds, wasn't joking. He gestured at the door to indicate he needed to get through. Katherine took the cue and walked into the chapel.

I really don't want to be here, she thought as she scanned the room. But something held her. About eighty people were standing and singing heartily. The back row was empty and Katherine took a seat at the far end, content to listen and observe. *Just for a few minutes,* she thought.

> *Every day as the sun rises*
> *I see the dawn of a new day*
> *I can't help but sing to you*
> *To sing your heavenly praises*
> *Through the day I will praise you*
> *I will sing to you every hour*
> *Even as the darkness comes ...*

The song moved on a chord progression—much like a modern ballad—and with an uplifting feel. Some of the congregation swayed to the rhythm, others had their eyes closed, some with their hands raised. Others followed the lyrics on the screen and sang along. Some only watched.

It had been six years since Katherine had stepped inside a church. She'd been to her parent's church in Suffolk a handful of times since she joined the navy, just to keep the peace with her father, and disliked almost every minute of the experience.

Up on stage, the minister led the band and congregation. His strong voice carried the melody with conviction, and he moved around the space with ease and a natural rhythm. Katherine was intrigued, having never experienced an African American minister leading a church service.

The worship song came to its climax, and a hush fell over the gathering. Many of the congregation's eyes were closed in quiet reflection.

Katherine's eyes were wide open. The hodgepodge of people attending had her thinking. Many were in their standard duty uniforms and she could see they were from departments and squadrons all over the ship. There were officers, chiefs, and enlisted sailors. The young and not so young. And every ethnic group on the ship seemed to be represented. Yet, at that moment, they all seemed as one.

All except Katherine, that was. But to her surprise, she did not feel a complete stranger.

"Praise be to God. Praise be," the minister began. "I welcome y'all to our service here today."

"God bless you, Pastor Abe," an armament fitter, still in his red outfit for flight deck operations, yelled out.

"And God bless you. Yes, God's rich blessing to y'all!" Pastor Abe said. "Now let's turn and welcome each other in the name of Jesus. C'mon now!"

Katherine had nowhere to go and nowhere to hide. After she'd shaken hands with a few people around her, she relaxed and enjoyed the experience. The welcome felt real and the people seemed happy to be together.

After a few minutes of milling around, Pastor Abe brought the focus back to the front. "Blessed be. Blessed be to God." His warm smile radiated as he spoke. "Friends, Matthew 6:34 tells us, 'So do not worry about tomorrow; for tomorrow will care for itself. Each day has enough trouble of its own.'"

He paused and beamed a broad smile, shifting his gaze across the room. "Folks. I don't know about you, but trouble seems to have a way of findin' me."

A few of the congregation rocked back and forth in their seats. Some clapped their hands a few times in recognition.

Pastor Abe looked down and shook his head as if in mental anguish. "Oh, glory be. Trouble, trouble, *so* much trouble … " He looked up. "We *all* have troubles, every one of us. Things that burden us, worry us. Things that knock the wind out of our sails just when we wanted a nice, easy cruise. Oh, troubles have a way of findin' all of us. That is the truth. Oh, glory be."

Murmurs of agreement rippled through the congregation.

"I don't know what your troubles are. Only you know … and Almighty God. We all have things that trouble us. Things we hide and push down and keep in secret. Things that eat away at our joy. Things that evaporate our hope. We struggle, we battle on, we do the best we can. So, brothers and sisters, search your heart today …. what is it *right now, right here today*, that troubles you?"

Katherine's thoughts drifted. Her mind searched her private world for troubles and didn't need to look far. As she continued to listen to the pastor, her mind went back two days ago.

She had called home on one of the crew phones. The telephones looked like ordinary payphones and were placed in high-traffic areas of the ship. They connected the caller via satellite to friends and family back home.

"Hello," Rachel said.

"Mom. It's Katherine."

"Oh, Katherine, it's so good to hear your voice. How are you, honey?"

They caught up for a few minutes, swapping the usual stories and gossip.

Rachel's tone changed. "Katherine. It's good you called. There's somethin' I need to let you know. It's … well, it's your grandfather. He, um, got some bad news last week. You probably saw his hand tremors when you were here last?"

"Ah, yeah. A little." Katherine had noticed the tremors, but she'd dismissed them as a natural sign of ageing.

"He's been having some struggles with balance too," Rachel continued. "And sore legs and arms. He's had some falls."

"What'd the doctor say?"

"Well, he ended up at a specialist and the thing is … the thing is, he's been diagnosed with Parkinson's."

Katherine struggled to process her mother's words in the seconds of silence that followed. "Are they sure?"

"Yes, honey. I'm sorry. There are treatments to help him, but you need to know ... the disease is quite advanced."

"So typical of him to keep this to himself! How long's this been goin' on?"

"Yeah, yeah, I know. He's stubborn."

"You okay?" Katherine asked.

"Yeah. You know me. I'm always okay."

Katherine had been half-listening to the pastor as his sermon continued.

"In all your ways acknowledge him and he will make your paths straight," he read from the book of Proverbs. "Jesus won't take your troubles away, but he will help you through them. He won't magically change your path for you, no, but he *will* help straighten it up for you. That I can guarantee you. Praise him."

"Praise be," someone called out.

Katherine's thoughts raced on. *Is Jesus just a crutch for these people? Is religion all about weak people needing a god, a divine being, or a hero? Is that how they deal with the uncomfortable truth of our pointless human existence, or with whatever shit that happens?*

She was sure this was the case, bet she still felt uneasy. There were people there in this congregation, and some she remembered from her parents' church, who were intelligent and reasonable. Good people who dealt with life as it happened. They just got on with it, much like anyone else.

So what do they get out of it then? And the news about her grandfather's condition had her thinking. *Does Grandpa need divine intervention? Not that he'd ever accept it, grumpy old atheist that he is.*

These thoughts made her shiver. She'd grown-up in a Christian movement at the more extreme end of the religious scale. By age nineteen she had come to see it as a human-centred, male-dominated organisation, and a racket of sorts.

She'd grown disillusioned by church leaders who got off on their power trips, and tired of seeing ordinary people manipulated by their cons. The pastors pretended to care about people but seemed far more interested in power and money. They demanded the absolute devotion of their followers, and those who offered criticism or proposals for change were driven from the church.

Katherine had been more than relieved to escape their clutches. Going to college and joining the navy were the perfect excuse to leave that world—and the home where her father ruled, as his church told him he must. The day she left for college felt like an escape from a totalitarian regime ruled by a ruthless dictator.

"Feels like I just jumped the North Korean border," she'd told Tom on the phone at the time.

But now here she was, sitting in a church—and on a navy ship, just to ramp up the weirdness level.

Pastor Abe turned to the band and nodded. The bass player launched into a slick rhythmic sequence of delicious thick notes that reverberated through the chapel. He repeated the riff over and over as other instruments joined in one by one.

The congregation stirred from quiet reflection and burst to life. Many clapped and gyrated. Some left their seats, dancing down the aisle front. They abandoned themselves to the beat, to the pure joy of the moment.

Pastor Abe joined in with the lyrics, supported by the harmony of three backup singers:

>*REJOICE! Gonna sing it from the mountaintop*
>*REJOICE! Sing, sing, sing, sing it now, yeah.*
>*JESUS! You set me free and broke my chains*
>*JESUS! Gave me freedom from my sin and pain—*

This was pure Black gospel in the best tradition. Katherine could not help moving to the groove and even clapped in time for a short while. She slipped out of the chapel just before the service closed.

*　　*　　*　　*

As Katherine made her way back to her quarters, the experience played over and over in her mind. She felt uplifted and somehow better, but she couldn't figure out why.

If God were real, she thought, *maybe that's how he'd want church to be?*

Katherine passed by the crew telephones in the passageway. She stopped, bit her bottom lip, and picked up a handset.

This was something she hadn't been able to bring herself to do. But at that moment, Katherine sensed an inner strength and calm as she dialled the sequence of numbers she remembered so well.

The phone rang endlessly before she heard the receiver click.

"Hello?"

"Grandpa? It's Katherine—"

CHAPTER FIFTEEN

The way to do is to be.

—Lao Tzu

Melbourne

1 February 2023

Ben made his way towards the Border Force checkpoint. He was surrounded by hordes of bleary-eyed travellers disembarking from international flights and doing their level best to get through the arrivals gantlet at Melbourne International Airport.

He'd only managed an hour's sleep on the overnight flight from Hong Kong, being unlucky enough to be seated near what seemed to be a childcare centre of screaming, crying, complaining little prats.

There were two Australians seated next to Ben—a couple in their sixties returning from a holiday in South-east Asia. It took them the whole first hour to get the hint Ben didn't wish to become their best friend. And then the man snored—with gusto.

"First time in Australia?" the Border Force officer mumbled as he flicked through Ben's passport and arrival card.

"Yes."

"Been to a few countries, I see. How long will you be staying here?"

"About a year. Maybe longer."

"Hmm." The officer checked the details of his visa. "What will you be studying in Australia?"

"Flying ... commercial pilot."

"And then what?"

"Get a job. Back in Hong Kong."

"Right. And what work will you be doing while you're here?"

"No work."

"You seem sure about that?"

"Yes. I will study only. No work here."

Ben did his best to keep his body still and his expression calm, and hold eye contact with his interrogator as he'd been trained. But he was uneasy. This was the first Western country he had visited, and he did not want to stumble at the first hurdle. And the Border Force person was intimidating, even more so than soldiers at the North Korean border. He was dressed in a striking almost-black uniform and kitted out with an array of equipment a Nazi SS officer would have been pleased to wear. His monotone voice and sharp gaze would cut through the defences of any guilty traveller.

The officer checked further details of the visa and eyed Ben a few times as he did. He handed Ben's passport back after what had seemed a century. "Make sure you follow all the conditions of your student visa. Welcome to Australia."

Ben took the passport from him and nodded. He could feel the stare of the officer following him as he made for the exit.

He picked up his bags and made his way through the quarantine inspection point with no issues. As he emerged into the arrivals forecourt, he paused to take in the moment. *Finally here! So far, so good.*

Ben's eyes adjusted to the bright morning daylight outside. The weather was much cooler and less humid than in Hong Kong—it reminded him of North Korea.

He scanned the arrivals area and saw a taxi-rank close by. He was in a taxi and away within a few minutes.

"So, where ya headed, mate?" the taxi driver asked.

The young man's broad Australian accent puzzled Ben. He looked to be a native of India or Pakistan, and dressed like one as well.

"Moorabbin, please. Moorabbin Airport."

"Rightio. Can't get enougha them planes, ay?"

Ben had little clue what the man had said. "Ah … planes. Yes."

"First time in Oz?"

"Yes," Ben replied, wondering if the taxi driver also worked for Australian Border Force.

"You from Malaysia?" the driver asked.

"No. Hong Kong."

"Ah, sorry, hard to pick sometimes," he said with a chuckle.

Ben's tiredness got the better of him. He let his guard down for a touch of evil sport. "You from India?" he asked.

"Yeah, nah, mate. Born right here in Ozstraya."

"Ah sorry, hard to pick sometimes," Ben snapped back.

He spent the rest of the fifty-five-minute journey in satisfying silence.

*   *   *   *

The first week at Horizons Commercial Pilot Academy had been a whirlwind. Ben spent the first two days settling in to the on-airport accommodation and attending tours of local services, shopping, and transport. *All very pedestrian.*

The course started the following Monday. After brief introductions to the instructors, and the twenty-four other students in the group, they were thrown straight into aviation theory. The classes continued for the next five days: theory of flight, the effects of controls, weather basics, aircraft radio. On and on it went.

By late Friday afternoon, the students were exhausted and their memories full. And they had yet to touch an aeroplane.

Ben lay on his bed, thinking back on the week. His room-mate, Justin Reynolds, sat on his bed, headphones on, escaping into a YouTube video on his laptop. He came from country Victoria and seemed friendly enough.

"Hey, you fellas comin' down the local? We're gonna' crack some coldies," said a voice from their doorway—a fellow student who'd taken it upon himself to organise the group's social activities.

It was at such times, Ben wondered if he should buy a translator app for his phone. Perhaps someone had created such a thing—something to translate Australian slang into the Queen's English? *What is this "local" and where is it? Do they smash ice there?* Ben had struggled with the Australian accent during the first week, not just with the slang. Some theory instructors mumbled and accentuated their vowels in ways he could not understand.

Justin pulled out his earphones. "Sorry, what?"

"We're all goin' down the pub. Youse comin' or what?"

At least Ben had then learned what *the local* was.

"C'mon on, Benny Boy," Justin said, slapping Ben on his knee. "Time to get out of this shithole."

So shithole must mean dormitory? And how did my name become Benny Boy?

There would be no refusing the invitation, and Ben soon found himself walking along the street with fifteen of his fellow students. Another two students had been sent back to change into plain clothes. They'd hoped their student pilot uniforms would bring them luck with the ladies that evening, but they'd only brought scorn and derision from their colleagues.

They entered a large local establishment and settled in at the bar. A live band throbbed out music on a nearby stage. Ben was familiar with rock and roll, but this was a raw pulsing sound from another planet.

"What ya' havin', luv?" shouted the bartender, who appeared to be bursting silicon out of her five-sizes-too-small tank top.

"Ah, same as him. Thank you," Ben replied, not having the faintest idea what Justin had ordered.

"No worries."

No worries ... why do they all say this here? Do they never worry?

Ben soon had a large drink in his hand, although he had no clue what it was. It tasted like Coke but had the bitter aftertaste of a cheap, nasty spirit.

The students swapped war stories from their first week of study. Ben only spoke if someone asked him a question. He kept his answers friendly and brief—just enough to appear engaged with the group, while keeping some distance.

He got to know a few of the students, including their names and their nicknames. For in Australia, he learned, your name is rarely what they call you. Stephen was now Steve-O; Simon, a redhead, had been dubbed Rust Nut; Jessica was Jezza; Damien was Dame-O; and so on. And Ben, it was becoming clear, was now Benny Boy. His mother would be horrified at such a thing. Thankfully, she was four and a half thousand miles to the north.

Then there was the generic name *mate*. Everyone, it seemed, was *mate* in this culture.

By seven o'clock, the place was teeming with workers from Moorabbin Airport and the surrounding industrial districts. It had become close-on impossible to take part in the conversations within their group, even if Ben had wanted to. The roar of the bar escalated as the rock band played even more loudly in return. Ben slipped out at the first opportunity. He had no desire to experience the strange culture any further, nor to become too friendly with his colleagues. Doing so would only interfere with his actual reason for being there.

*   *   *   *

23 March 2023

"Get your eyes *up* and outta the cockpit! For fuck's sake, Ben, how many times do we need to tell you!"

Ben grimaced and gritted his teeth, using all his self-control not to raise his right hand and deliver a fatal blow to the neck of Jamie Ingram, his flight instructor, who was seated next to him in the Cessna-172.

Six arduous weeks of theory and flight training had passed. Ben was excelling with aviation theory and he'd passed his first exam with a ninety-five percent mark. He'd started reasonably well with flight training, progressing to his first solo flight in the previous week. He had fifteen hours flight time in his logbook, which was about average within his student group.

Ben had spent weeks immersing himself in the foreign world of aviation before he left Hong Kong. He purchased flight simulation software and basic flight controls for his laptop, read flying tutorials, and practiced relentlessly. He would not look like a rookie, or an idiot. No. He would be top of his class. Anything less would be unacceptable.

Ben's Korean given name, Yong-sun, means "dragon in first position," and his father had chosen the name well. The only position that ever mattered was first place, and Ben would compete with the fire and ferocity of a dragon to achieve it. Ben's North Korean masters had seen him prove this many times during his training.

But there was a problem. Ben wasn't at the top of his class. Nowhere near it. One-third of his classmates were doing better than him in their flight lessons, including an eighteen-year-old girl, Mel, who was in front of the pack. She was the first to fly solo with just eight hours in her logbook, and already excelling in the advanced topics during the first phase of their flight training. Her age, gender, and easy confidence irritated Ben to the core.

What was she doing right? What am I doing wrong? And how can I fix this? These thoughts plagued him as he experienced serious self-doubt for the first time in his young life.

"Juliet-Yankee-Sierra, number three, follow the Foxbat on downwind, report turning final runway one-seven-left," the Moorabbin tower controller said. His calm voice rattled off the words like a well-worn machine gun in Ben's headset.

Ben had no choice in that moment—he had to do what his instructor had barked at him to do. He took his eyes off the instruments and looked out through the windshield.

"See what I mean?" his instructor asked rhetorically.

Ben could see exactly what the instructor meant. They were trailing a bright yellow plane just a quarter-mile ahead and a hundred feet below. The Foxbat pilot was conducting circuits on the same runway as Ben.

Flying circuits, as Ben had learned, involved a take-off and climb to a low altitude, flying a route that follows an imaginary rectangular path that leads to a final approach to the same runway. But after landing, the aircraft takes off again instead of coming to a stop. And then the process repeats, again and again. It's the tedious, repetitive, and necessary process of learning to take off an aeroplane and return it to the ground in one piece. Hopefully.

But Moorabbin Airport was no quiet little aerodrome for circuit training, with its five runways and multitude of taxiways, many intersecting. The skies were filled with aircraft, many of them piloted with novices.

Ben knew, from the air-traffic-controller's instruction, he was to follow the Foxbat ahead while keeping a safe distance. But they were gaining on it, and fast.

The instructor shook his head. "If you'd kept your eyes down on the instrument panel, we'd have flown right up the arse of that Foxbat."

"Yes, yes. I see."

"You'd better. We're trying to stop you from killing yourself, and me, and whoever else."

Ben eased back the throttle, reducing the engine RPM from 2,300 to 1,800. As the plane's airspeed slowed in response, he pulled back on the yoke to raise the nose and maintain their altitude.

"That's better. And look, you slowed us down and held altitude without looking at your instruments. Use your eyes, Ben. Look at the horizon, use your ears, feel what the plane is doing. Cross-check your instruments, but *don't* fixate on them. Got it?"

"Yes. I got it."

"Good. Now let's land this sucker and call it a day."

Landing was the ultimate challenge and Ben found it a real handful. He'd practiced it over and over on his laptop flight simulator and watched countless of videos on the subject. But somehow, to his dismay, he would perform a reasonable landing on one circuit, followed by an absolute shocker on the next. His frustration had become an obsession in his waking hours and would visit him as nightmarish dreams in his sleep.

Ben centred the control yoke and levelled the wings to line up for final approach. The Foxbat ahead had already landed and taken off again for another circuit.

Ben pushed the transmit button on the control yoke. "Juliet-Yankee-Sierra on final one-seven-left."

The controller's voice crackled in his headset: "Juliet-Yankee-Sierra, cleared to land."

"Cleared to land. Juliet-Yankee-Sierra," Ben responded.

Ben focused his eyes on the runway ahead. He was transfixed by the two large white markers at the near end of the runway—his intended touchdown point. *I'm going to fucking nail this one.*

He glanced down to check his instruments and controls: airspeed sixty-seven knots, rate of descent five hundred feet per minute, flaps thirty degrees. *All good.*

He looked up and his heart skipped a beat. The runway had moved. Or such was the sensation as the wind shifted direction, skewing the plane's nose five degrees to the left.

Ben banked the wings to the right to counteract the turn. He overdid it before correcting back the other way.

"Easy now," the instructor said. "Small inputs, and relax your grip on the yoke."

But the wind was having none of it. If he was going to nail this one, the conditions were going to make him work for it. What had been a nice easy five-knot headwind straight down the runway had shifted to the east and the speed had picked up to a blustery fifteen knots.

A further problem reared its head. With the higher wind speed, Ben's intended touchdown point appeared to be slipping up the windshield. He sensed the awful dread of sinking and slowing, of losing relative height and speed. Ben pulled back on the yoke to raise the nose and counteract the sink.

"Well, let's see how this pans out," the instructor said. He had his arms crossed and a smirk on his face.

Ben got what he wanted. With the nose raised, the plane's descent flattened out. For a few seconds it appeared to be regaining the proper glidepath to the runway.

But then the slowing and sinking sensation returned, and even more pronounced this time.

Damn this!

Ben had left the throttle at the same power setting. As he'd raised the nose, the plane had gained height for a few seconds, but also lost airspeed. Such is the physics of flying—the balancing of many actions with their equal and opposite reactions all happening at once.

Isaac Newton was not there to help. Indeed, it seemed his laws of physics were against Ben in that moment.

The stall-warning horn sounded and Ben's eyes dropped to the instrument panel to search for answers. *Airspeed fifty-nine knots, rate of descent eight-fifty, what the?*

The instructor lost his disinterest in a millisecond. "*Look up!* Add power. Your bloody airspeed is near the stall. For god's sake!"

Ben rammed the throttle forward. The Cessna jumped in response as it accelerated. He lowered the nose to stop the plane from climbing.

The runway threshold was only two hundred metres ahead. They were at least still aligned with the centreline.

Small mercies.

Ben could feel his hands trembling. His stomach muscles gripped hard with a blend of fear and anger.

The instructor leaned forward and fired off instructions like his life depended on it: "Ease the power back, lower the nose, look at the far end of the runway—"

The elusive runway numbers appeared in the right spot in Ben's view ahead. They weren't moving up or down the windshield, which meant the plane would touch down somewhere near them.

The Cessna crossed the airport boundary fence.

Fifty feet left to descend ...

Forty ...

The runway edge flashed by.

Thirty ...

"Hold it there, good, good ..."

Twenty ...

The ground came up fast.

"Power back to idle now ... yep, yep ..."

Ten ...

"Okay, ease up the nose ..."

The runway numbers were giant in Ben's view. He fixated on them as the final few feet of altitude frittered away.

Five ...

"Pull back. *Flare now!*"

Bang. The rear wheels of the Cessna hit the runway hard and the plane bounced a few feet.

Thump. Another hard bounce.

The quaint elegant squeal of the tires as they finally contacted and held the bitumen seemed a bitter and insensitive way for the whole horrid event to conclude. But they were still in one piece and rolling towards the taxiway exit ahead.

The instructor could see Ben had had enough. "Okay. I have control."

As they taxied back towards the apron, Ben shut his eyes. He slapped his forehead with the open palm of his hand. Once, twice, three times.

"C'mon, Ben. Don't do yourself in, young fella."

Ben opened his eyes and glared out his window, embarrassed and utterly frustrated.

"It's early days, Ben, nothing unusual. We all go through this," Ingram said.

Yeah, all except that Mel girl, Ben thought. He hoped to some unknown god she hadn't been watching his landing.

The instructor parked the Cessna and shut down the engine. "Well, that was quite an adventure," he said.

"I do not want such adventures. I want to get it *right*."

"Yep. But you gotta give yourself a chance, mate. You're all over the theory, the procedures—all that. You're well-prepared and dedicated and focused. You know all the numbers and checklists in your head."

Ben shrugged, not taking the compliments.

"But there's something you're missing."

Ben looked at his instructor.

"Yeah. Look mate, flying an aeroplane is a science *and* an art. You're getting the science bit down pat. It's the art side of things you ain't quite got yet."

"Art? I do not understand."

"Flying an aeroplane is also about how it *feels*. Let's take that so-called landing you did ... you kept looking at your instruments for the answers. But your eyes and your ears and the seat of your pants should have told you the wind direction and strength had shifted, and your approach profile had changed. You didn't sense the changes, so you missed it. You didn't react and that stuffed up your approach, which led to the crappy landing."

"Oh."

"A piece of advice, Ben. Get your head out of the books and away from your laptop. You can read about this stuff and practice it on a tiny screen till the cows come home and it won't do you one bit of good. Switch on the other side of your brain. Good flying takes thinking and logic, yep, but you gotta *feel* it too, mate. Use your instincts, use your senses, develop them, trust them."

"Okay. I will work on this."

"Good. But don't work *too* hard. Try to relax more and take it all in. Enjoy what you're doing. Yeah?"

The instructor thrust out his hand and Ben took it, feeling somewhat comforted by his handshake.

"You'll be alright, Benny Boy," the instructor said as he opened his door. "You'll be greasing your landings in no time, mate."

Ben could only hope he was right. And for the first time, he hadn't thought to be annoyed by the nickname.

CHAPTER SIXTEEN

Only echoes answer me.

—Anton Chekhov, *Swansong*

Timor Sea, one hundred and fifty-nine miles
from the West Australian coast
22 July 2023, 0700 hours

The stark sound from the bugler playing reveille across the 1MC of USS *John F. Kennedy* permeated every part of the ship, including the cramped ready room where officers of HSM-85 Black Wolf squadron had assembled.

Squadron members had been sitting in small groups before the daily bugle call began. Some sat on their own, lost in something enthralling on their phone. Others stared blank-faced at the television screen, or into space. The atmosphere could be mistaken as relaxed, but the overwhelming state in the ready room was fatigue.

After six months at sea, the Black Wolf crews, along with every other squadron and department aboard the carrier, had been ground down to a paste. Watch after watch, drill after drill, exercise after exercise, day after long exhausting day.

It was no secret among the senior officers and department chiefs that this deployment had been one of the toughest in memory. The commander of Carrier Strike Group 11, Rear Admiral Paterson, had driven its many crews and squadrons hard—sometimes to the limits of their endurance and ability. The commander of Carrier Air Wing 11 had raised issues of workload and fatigue at a recent CSG-11 command meeting, but to little effect. The push for the success of the group and the new carrier was relentless and Paterson expected the air wing to do its part.

The rumour mill whispered that the source of pressure came from the top of the navy hierarchy, and possibly above that. The United States of America had something further to prove, it seemed.

As the final few notes of reveille subsided, Lieutenant Commander Katherine Marlowe braced for what was to come. As the senior officer among those in her squadron deployed to the carrier, she had command responsibility for the six helicopters and crews on board.

Commander Pike had overall command of HSM-85 and was based on another ship in the group. He'd flown to the carrier that morning to address members of the squadron.

He cleared his throat to begin. "Okay, people. I have some good news and some bad news. Good news is, we're near the end of the operational phase of this deployment. This is the second-last day of the Talisman Sabre exercise and after that we'll sail away, find a nice friendly Australian port, and kick back. After that, we head for home."

There were a few mumblings among the officers. Some celebratory whistles and muted applause. "Better wash my happy sock," someone yelled. Not a celebration, though. They were way too tired for that.

"And the bad news, boss?" asked an officer at the back.

"Bad news is ... we're near the end of the operational phase of this deployment. We've had our fair share of danger over the past months, and we all accept that as part of our job. But when we feel like we're winding things down, that can be the most dangerous phase of all."

Commander Pike scanned the room. Their eyes were all on him. "Look, we're all tired. It's been a busy cruise. But this is *not* the time to slack off. I wanna see you disembark with me in San Diego soon ... and hug your partners, your kids, maybe your sidepiece—"

That got a laugh, and Pike smirked.

"What I *don't* wanna see is you being flown back early coz you're injured. Or in a body bag."

All remaining levity in the room evaporated.

"We've got two full days left of this exercise and our work won't stop after that either. So I expect *every single one* of you to be alert and give it everything you got. Stick with the routines, follow your orders, don't deviate from procedures. We all know what fatigue can do. Be alert to it. And above all else, look out for each other. Okay?"

There were nods and murmurs of acknowledgement.

After an operational briefing on the rest of the Talisman Sabre exercise, Pike left the ready room. Katherine accompanied him on the walk back up to the flight deck.

"Keep a close eye on them, specially those two young nuggets," Pike said as they strode through the O-2 level corridor.

"Yeah. You got it," Katherine replied.

"Captain told me some goddamn fool walked across the flight deck yesterday with an F-18 on short final. Pilot got a wave-off and had to go around. Tail hook near took the guy's head off."

"Yep. Whole ship's been talking about it."

Far up ahead, Katherine could see the bulky squat frame of a man marching towards them. The three letters emblazoned across his top— CMC—told her, and every enlisted sailor who got in his way, this was the command master chief. The Chief of Chiefs and the highest-ranking enlisted man on the ship.

He fired off orders as he went, dressing down almost every crew member he passed.

"Get your goddam uniform tucked in, crewman. Your mama ain't here to dress you now, huh?"

"You call that *clean*? I seen me shinier surfaces on a dump truck!"

"What you doing there? Standin' round, talking crap, causin' trouble is what you do. Get the hell outta my sight and go do your job, you puke."

Pike chuckled. "Well, looks like the CO's getting the word around."

"Hell yeah. This cruise sure ain't over yet," Katherine thought aloud.

* * * *

The bright midday sunlight sparkled on the mottled texture of the sea, dancing like diamonds in the eye of a hopeful bride-to-be. The waters beneath were a rich shade of mesmerising emerald. Lighter patches of aqua, where the white sands of the coastal shallows hinted from the deep, lay scattered across the expanse. With a striking blue sky above and not a menacing cloud in sight, it was a perfect day for a spot of flying.

The Black Wolf MH-60R Seahawk helicopter, tail number 703, cruised at fifteen hundred feet, headed south-east towards the West Australian coastline.

Lieutenant Corey Moretti leaned forward in his co-pilot seat with his safety harness at full stretch, peering ahead into the bright glare. "There's our two customers," he said as he pointed to two grey shapes on the horizon.

Katherine glanced down at the navigation display and noted the two yellow ship symbols. She looked again at the horizon. "Yup. That'd be them."

The symbols changed to blue a second later, indicating the ships were friendly. The two ships—USS *Portland*, a San Antonio–class amphibious transport dock ship; and JS *Suzunami*, a Takanami-class destroyer of the Japan Maritime Self-Defence Force—cruised as a pair towards the coastline forty miles farther to the south-east.

"They look lonely," Moretti said.

"Yeah. All out here on their own. You could forgive them for being nervous."

"Yup."

"Good thing the *Columbia* is with 'em," Katherine mused, contemplating the unseen Los Angeles–class attack submarine operating somewhere in their near vicinity. They were aware of the operational area, or "box", the *Columbia* was to operate in, but didn't know its exact position.

"Columbia's skipper must be cursin' though," Naval Air Crewman Second Class Emilio Perez chirped over the intercom. "It's so damn shallow and noisy down there. No real fun for a submarine."

"Yeah, no fun at all," Moretti agreed. "Much better up here."

"Let's hope so," Katherine said.

A good twenty seconds passed before Moretti began to sing. "Boom, boom ... boom, boom."

Katherine shook her head. "Oh no, here we go ..."

"Huh?" Perez asked.

Moretti was only too happy to explain. "I'm in the mood to shoot me some shit. It's time for some *boom, boom!*"

Katherine, ever the conservative and stickler for the rules, gave Moretti a quick sideways glance. He couldn't see her eyes through her dark helmet visor, nor could she see his. But he knew full well the look she was giving him in that moment.

All three understood there would be no real *boom, boom* that day. No one would shoot real bullets, missiles, or torpedoes. But the simulated fire would still have a profound psychological effect. Success on this exercise was as close as a crew could come to real success in battle, and failure as close to real failure.

CSG-11 had joined the Talisman Sabre exercise ten days earlier. The group's ships were split across two teams for the exercise: the invading aggressors on Team Red, and the defending Team Blue. The teams were supplemented by units from the Australian Navy, Air Force, and Army; the U.S. Marines and Army; ships from the Navies of New Zealand, Canada, and Japan; and, for the first time, one ship each from South Korea and India. Substantial air, land, and sea forces were split across the two teams, including 41,000 personnel.

The tactical designers of Talisman Sabre had made radical changes for the 2023 exercise. Previous exercises had been held off northern Queensland and it was time for a change of scenery. They centred the 2023 exercise off the Dampier Peninsula on Australia's north-west coast, where the topography and coastline were similar in many respects to places around the South China Sea.

It was also time for a change of tactics and strategy. This iteration of the exercise had surprised many by moving away from the traditional mode of littoral combat, where multiple waves of attack were focused on a singular beachhead assault. From the first day, Team Red's assault had split into smaller forces and staged unconventional attacks at unexpected locations.

In the final two days of the exercise, the strategy had been taken further with even smaller micro-forces going well north and south of the main tactical area to launch attacks on the far flanks of their opposition. This had stretched both forces and caused logistical and tactical headaches for the defending Team Blue.

The two ships and the unseen submarine that the helicopter was flying towards comprised one of those splinter micro-forces. They were on the attacking Team Red, along with USS *John F. Kennedy*, the air wing aircraft, and support ships back out to sea.

But Team Blue had surprises of their own. They had used tried-and-tested defensive tactics, but also upped the ante with pre-emptive attacks on the Team Red's ships with small fast-attack naval vessels, even smaller high-speed civilian vessels, plus swarms of small unmanned aerial vehicles. The exercise demonstrated a contemporary world of combat where brute size and strength didn't always win the day. Just like the Golden State Warriors had revolutionised the NBA, they were changing the game by going small ball.

"Okay, let's get busy," Katherine said. "Business time." She eased the nose of the helicopter lower as they approached the stern of JS *Suzunami* below them, giving them a bird's-eye view of the Japanese destroyer as they flew overhead.

Oh, the irony, Katherine thought. More than eighty years earlier, the Japanese had operated fighter-bomber aircraft in the area from a nearby base in Timor, attacking the outpost of Broome on the Australian coast. The assault, together with those on Darwin, sent shockwaves through Australia and its allies. The Americans were drawn into the fight to defend Australia, and the partnership set the foundation for a close military and diplomatic alliance between the two nations.

And now here they are, the Japanese helping to protect a U.S. Navy ship, Katherine mused. *It's bizarre how human conflict is so circular … it repeats and never ends. Enemies one day, allies the next.*

As they crossed the stern of the Japanese destroyer, they could see a lone helicopter sitting on the flight deck. The helo had returned to the ship with a mechanical failure and wasn't expected to re-join the exercise anytime soon. With no other helicopter on board either ship, they were vulnerable to attack from an enemy submarine.

The captain of the *Portland* had contacted Team Red command to request replacement anti-submarine air support. Though the submarine on his team—USS *Columbia*—was patrolling nearby, she was limited by the shallow underwater terrain and noisy acoustic conditions.

The order for immediate air support had come down to the Black Wolf squadron on board the carrier. There were two crews on standby and Katherine had decided to go. The other crew were more fatigued than hers, and far less experienced.

Moretti reported back to the Combat Direction Centre on the carrier: "Black-Wolf Seven-Zero-Three, reporting time on station 1227, commencing initial sweep south-east of the *Portland.*"

Katherine punched some keys on the flight management computer to check their fuel status. The trip from the carrier had been a long one: one hundred and ten nautical miles. The carrier had to keep at least one hundred and fifty miles away from the coast—the old saw from the Pacific War that carriers had a strong punch but a glass jaw still held true. "We got about ninety-five minutes of endurance on station. Let's make every minute count," she said. "Perry, we know there's a good chance there's an enemy sub down there. Let's find the sucker."

Perry, as they called Perez, was the Seahawk's rear crewman—a man with a multitude of roles. His primary task that day was to work the helicopter's sonar and radar systems in the hunt for a submarine.

"Okay, drop points for the first sonar spread are in," Moretti said. "Number one drop now designated." He had plotted a series of points between the two ships and their destination on the coast. The helicopter would drop sonobuoys into the water at those points, creating a line of passive sonar to listen beneath the surface.

"Got it," Katherine said as she steered the helicopter towards the first drop point.

As they flew over the point two minutes later, Perez jettisoned the first sonobuoy through the drop chute. The device dropped into the water with a splash, descended below the waves, and self-deployed. Its many sonar hydrophones began listening in all directions for everything and anything within range beneath the surface.

They dropped another seven sonobuoys at their pre-determined points, and the hunt began.

Perez worked his sonar and situation displays like a man possessed. With the line of sonobuoys transmitting acoustic information back to the helicopter's combat systems, he could see and hear the tell-tale signs of activity all around them.

Identifying the first two contacts was a piece of cake. Perez read the details over the intercom: "Two surface contacts. Designate Sierra-One, bearing zero-eight-zero, range four thousand yards—a San Antonio–class amphib—the *Portland*. And designate Sierra-Two, bearing zero-eight-four, range five thousand one hundred yards—a Takanami-class destroyer—the *Suzunami*."

The sonar detection system had accessed an acoustic database of all known surface and submarine craft to identify the respective types of the two ships through the unique acoustics of a ship's propellers, the acoustic signatures made by its movement through the water, and the transient sounds of systems operating on the ship.

The sonar system could then try to identify the exact ship, with some success, but Perez preferred to do this manually whenever time allowed. He had listened to the sounds of each ship through his headset and watched the waterfall display on his screen: a cascading visual depiction of the myriad of sound frequencies coming from the ship's bearing.

A good minute of silence followed on the intercom. Perez would be analysing the sonobuoy data for anything of interest, and they left him to work his magic.

"Possible submerged contact, bearing three-four-zero," Perez said.

Katherine's grip on the cyclic control tightened. *Game on.*

*   *   *   *

Melbourne

"Excuse me, Ben, is this seat taken?"

Ben was approaching brain-deadness while trying to absorb his *Commercial Pilot Flight Rules and Air Law* textbook. He sat up with a start. "Oh," he replied, "no, it is not taken."

Jia Jeong stood near his table in the academy's study zone, gripping her pile of books and laptop to her torso like a life vest. The room was empty, as it often was on a Saturday afternoon, except for the most dedicated students.

There were other tables, but Jia sat at Ben's, two seats away. She arranged her things, hardly making a sound.

Ben ignored her but remained on guard. He'd noted the girl when she started her course in the intake after his. She was Korean and obviously of the Southern kind. She was just barely over a metre and half tall and Ben wondered how she would even reach the rudder pedals in the airplane. But she had survived the course thus far. He looked up after a few minutes, pretending to gaze out the far window towards the airport apron.

Jia glanced up from her laptop and their eyes met. Her dark but radiant eyes and her generous smile could melt anything within a five-metre range it seemed.

Stop this! Control yourself. The silent words bounced through Ben's mind as his thinking-brain chastised the other.

But her smile would not relent.

What to do? Smile back? Say something? Or sit here like a dumb fool? "I'm Ben," his words tumbled out.

Jia smiled. "Yes. I know."

"Oh yes. Of course."

"I didn't mean to interrupt you."

"That's fine. If I read more of this air law nonsense, I think I'll lose my mind."

She smiled again, revealing perfect teeth. Ben couldn't help noticing the light flickering in her dark pupils, and the fall of her straight shoulder-length black hair as she flicked it away from her graceful neck. "What are you studying?" he asked.

"Oh, aerodynamics. I have to take the basic aeronautic exam next week."

"Ah, yes. I remember it."

"And how is your training, Ben?"

"It's going quite well. Only two theory exams left to do. My flying is on schedule now and I am about to begin the advanced flight lessons."

"Oh, so not long until you do your commercial licence test then?"

"I think about three months."

"That is good. I have so much further to go."

Ben thought back over the past six months of his training. He had blitzed the classroom study and theory exams. His struggles with specific manoeuvres were eventually overcome. His instructors were correct: he had been all theory and no feel. He had been so hell-bent on success and rapid progress that he'd turned the flight lessons into his enemy. Flying had been something to be defeated rather than learned, much less enjoyed. "Yes," he said, "there is much to do and learn. But it is achievable."

Jia seemed to be scanning Ben's face and eyes as he considered his options. He needed to indulge his classmates in at least some conversation to avoid being tagged with the reputation of being a distant, broody loner. But he couldn't be the centre of attention either. Staying out of mind was imperative—the mission demanded no less and his minders had been clear.

"I like how you practice your Tai Chi," Jai said.

"Ah ..."

"Forgive me. I noticed you practice early in the mornings."

Ben studied her face and it seemed to convey no malice. "Yes. It is beneficial for me," he said.

"I have done group Tai Chi, back in my country. Perhaps there could be a Tai Chi group here, at the academy?"

"I do not practice Tai Chi, not exactly. It is more than that, and different for me."

"Oh."

The room seemed to cool a few degrees.

Jia paused before uttering two foreign-sounding words. "*Singyeong zeugma*," she said.

Ben recognised the phrase but didn't let on. "Pardon?" he asked.

"I said 'never mind.'"

"Ah. I speak English and Mandarin. Not Korean," Ben lied.

"Oh, I see. I am sorry. I thought you might be Korean?"

"No. I am from Hong Kong. My parents are from northern China."

Jia looked confused. "It's just … you seem Korean to me."

Ben shook his head. "Hong Kong."

Jia seemed intent on keeping the conversation going. "It was a wonderful place, Hong Kong," she said.

"It still is."

"Oh yes. Sorry. I mean … different now since the Chinese takeover."

"It has always been Chinese."

"I thought the British—"

"They borrowed it for a short time, then gave it back. As it should be."

"So much trouble there, though. Difficult to go from democracy to communist rule."

"Maybe. But things there are more complicated."

"Complicated where I am from too, in South Korea. Democracy and communism along a stupid line on a map. It's strange, but I hope one day the north will see reason as we have."

The conversation was going south at a rapid rate. Ben could not tell if the girl was being young and naïve, or deliberately provocative. *Is she trying to flush out my past? Does she know more about me than she's letting on?*

Ben gathered his things. "It's been nice to speak with you. I must go now," he said with a forced smile.

Jia blinked. "Oh yes, yes. Thank you. Bye, then."

CHAPTER SEVENTEEN

Is this a dagger which I see before me, the handle toward my hand?

—William Shakespeare, *Macbeth*

Timor Sea, thirty-two miles from the West Australian coast
1247 hours

Precious seconds evaporated as Perez did all he could to locate and identify the submerged contact. Each second seemed more like a minute. "I'm pretty sure it's submerged and not biologic, but still inconclusive. Target strength is shit. No classification yet. Sorry."

"Any idea on range?" Moretti asked.

"Three to four thousand yards, maybe. But it's hazy. Very low reliability."

"Let's go take a look," Moretti said.

But Katherine already had the Seahawk in a steep left turn. "Keep up, Mets," she said.

He pretended to ignore her. "Perry, have the ships gone active at all?" he asked, referring to active sonar that transmits pings of sound energy, then measures the echo returns to find and track targets.

"Nope," Perry replied. "Probably too worried about giving their position away."

"I get it, but how else are we gonna find this sub? A few pings now and then ain't gonna pose a risk."

"Maybe," Perez said, "but tell that to the guys on the destroyer. If they're not experienced in shallow water operations, it would feel like they dropped their pants and bent over."

"I'd say they're relying on our sub to protect them," Katherine added. "But there's no way the *Columbia* is gonna go active in these conditions either."

"Which is where the good ole Romeo comes in," Moretti said with a self-assured smile, referring to the MH-60R's nickname. "Romeo, Romeo," he continued, "wherefore art thou, Romeo?"

"You're sitting in it," Katherine said with a groan. "One minute you're singing to us, the next it's Shakespeare."

"Just livin' the dream, baby. And *wherefore* means 'why,' not 'where.' We're supposed to find that sub, so are we gonna dip the girl or not?"

It was a standard joke between them. The passive sonobuoys were called "the boys," and the active dipping sonar was then called "the girl." Katherine didn't care about the sexist overtones. She thought some women made too much noise anyway.

"Yup," Katherine replied, "get her ready for a swim."

"The girl" was the AN/AQS-22 Active Dipping Sonar—a vital part of the helicopter's detection suite. The device transmitted and listened across multiple sound frequencies, and was among an enemy submarine crew's greatest fears.

Katherine brought the Seahawk to a low hover at the near end of the area Perez had identified. Perez set the cable in motion. The sonar unit dropped away from the belly of the helicopter and into the sea with a gentle plop. He let it descend ninety feet into the deep, where it self-activated and extended its many small arms, each lined with hydrophones to pick up echo returns.

The first burst of low frequency energy pierced the undersea environment and spread out from the unit in all directions. Nearby objects and the ocean floor reflected the sound waves, which were picked up by the unit's hydrophones on their return. Objects farther away would also reflect the ping, but their returns would take longer to echo back, and the echo would be weaker. And many of the echoes would be distorted not just by the sea floor but also the variable salinity, temperature, and pressure of the water.

The pings continued. The hydrophones received the returns and transmitted them through the cable into the helicopter's detection suite.

Perez listened and watched, entranced by the technology at his fingertips. He respected sonar technology as a powerful tool for detection, but he knew it to be both an art and a science. "In shallow water," he would say, "it's like using a pen light to find a penny in a house of bent mirrors."

Each ping provided additional information. If there was a submarine, its movement over time would give away its speed and direction. This information, together with bearing and distance, would give the helicopter crew a firing solution and the data they needed to attack with an air-launched Mark 54 torpedo.

The tension was clear in Perez's voice as he informed the crew: "Submerged contact, bearing zero-two-zero, standby."

Thirty seconds ticked by.

"Inconclusive. Suggest we dip on that bearing. Give it five hundred yards."

"Do it," Katherine agreed.

Perez set to work, winching the sonar unit to leave it hanging twenty feet in the air. "Girl's clear," he reported.

Katherine took the Seahawk out of the hover and moved it forward five hundred yards and twenty degrees north-east.

"I'm getting some better feeds, but it's a frickin' miss down there," Perez said a few minutes later. "Possible Los Angeles–class submarine now bearing zero-four-zero, range ... range unknown."

They knew they'd probably found their own submarine, the *Columbia*, but the information was still far from reliable. Perez struggled to make sense of the vagaries of sonar in shallow water. He could hear and see refracted and distorted echoes from the sea bottom, including large rock formations and possibly even shipwrecks. Added to that were the plethora of passive sounds from the biologics—including whale and dolphin songs and echolocations—plus the flow of currents along the sea floor, the waves and currents on the coastline, and sounds from the many commercial, fishing, naval, and pleasure craft operating in the region.

They continued to dip and listen, moving position every few minutes. They took up positions as best they could on the data collected, but the haphazardness of their search betrayed their lack of reliable information and growing frustration.

"What I'd do for another Romeo right now," Moretti thought aloud. Two Seahawks working as a pair would be far more effective in this situation. They would leapfrog each other, dipping continuously, sharing and triangulating their sonar data. A submarine—even in shallow water—would be found in time.

"Nope. It's just lil old us today," Katherine said.

"Yeah, and those damn Japanese too afraid to ping," Moretti said.

"The destroyer is twelve miles behind us now," Perez said. "Active pings would be pretty much useless at that range."

"Whattya got now?" Moretti asked.

"Not much better. I'm getting momentary glimpses of what appears to be the *Columbia*, but the other traces don't add up."

"Whattya mean?" Katherine asked.

"Well, for a few seconds there, the screw noise looked all Los Angeles–class, then something different … more like a diesel boat. And some transient noise that made no sense."

"You think there's *two* subs down there?" Moretti asked.

"Maybe. But I don't see how. When I pick up the traces, the returns are from the same bearing and range, but then I lose 'em again before I can analyse them. I checked the recordings, but they don't help us any."

"We got about four minutes left before we have to head home," Katherine said.

"If this weren't an exercise, would you bug out now?" Moretti asked, the words escaping before he'd thought them through. "Those ships are sitting back there like two fat ducks on day one of the hunting season."

"You got a better alternative?" she shot back.

"We can request another helo from the carrier come take over, but it'll take them close to an hour to get here. Or we could stop for gas."

Katherine recognised his idea as a good one. Moretti was an airborne tactical officer and one of the best. As an ATO his role was to think ahead of the helicopter, analysing options for both attack and defence. "Give 'em a call, Mets. You got your credit card?"

"Nope. Hope they got a pisser, though."

After a few tense minutes, Moretti had contacted the *Portland* and arranged for their arrival and refuelling. The ship's large flight deck, normally used for MV-22 Osprey aircraft, could accommodate the Seahawk helicopter. And especially one keeping them out of harm's way of a possible enemy submarine.

This tactic meant they could continue the hunt for forty more minutes. But after another thirty minutes in the air, they were still not much the wiser on what was below the waves, or where.

"Goddammit!" Perez cursed over the intercom.

They flew on, conducting further sonar dips. Katherine finally keyed the mic. "Five minutes, Perry, then it's time to go visit the *Portland*."

"Hold on ..." he replied, his voice strained. "I'm onto something ..."

Ten seconds of tense intercom silence followed.

"Bingo! We're almost on them. Confirm submerged contact, bearing three-five-eight, dead ahead, range twelve hundred yards, depth one-fifty."

"What classification?" Moretti asked.

"Possible SSK, doesn't appear to be the *Columbia*."

"You can't identify it?"

"The system's fighting me. The computer's putting its bets on an LA-class SSN with lowish probability. My ears and eyes see the signs of a diesel boat. I think it's the enemy sub."

"What's his track?"

"Stand by."

Ten seconds passed.

"He's heading away from us at about six knots, tracking three-three-zero."

"Towards the ships?"

"Yup."

"Okay. Perry, put through the firing solution."

"Will do, but I can only give you what I got."

Moretti's hands and fingers zipped across the Seahawk's tactical controls. He converted the firing solution from the sonar suite into launch parameters for the Mark 54 exercise torpedo. Within seconds, he had programmed the torpedo with presets for its hunt below the waves. Once launched, the unarmed torpedo would use the presets to begin its search. When it detected the submarine, it would finish the hunt on its own and harmlessly strike its hull.

Moretti continued his preparations, but Katherine needed more. "We need that classification, Perry."

"Working on it."

"Ready in all respects," Moretti reported curtly, indicating the torpedo was ready to launch.

"Stand by," Katherine ordered. She knew Moretti wouldn't fire without her final command. "Perry, what's our range to the ships?" she asked.

"Six miles now and closing."

"If that's an enemy sub down there," Katherine thought aloud, "he's getting close enough to get a decent sonar fix on 'em. Or he might be tempted to come up and take a peek."

"If his periscope breaks the surface for a second, we'll have him," Moretti said. "Radar will get him in a microsecond if I don't see his scope first."

"I don't get why he didn't run as soon as he heard our girl's first active ping," Perez said.

"Been thinkin' the same," Katherine said.

Moretti cut straight through the theorising: "We got him pinned. He's headed for our ships. It's time to engage."

Katherine stared at the ships in the distance, thinking hard. "Anything further, Perry?"

"Nope, sorry. That's the best I got."

"Okay. Lift the sonar. It's time to go get our fuel."

Moretti whipped his head around to glare at Katherine, but she kept her eyeline straight ahead of the helicopter.

"He'll get a firing solution on our ships any second," he said. "Then it's all over. You know that?"

Katherine waited before she responded. "We don't have a positive ID on the sub. It could be the *Columbia*, so I'm not taking chances on sending a hundred and twenty of our bubbleheads to the bottom."

"And if it's the enemy sub, like Perry said, how many more will die on our ships?"

"Perry didn't say that."

"No, I didn't," Perry confirmed. "I said I *thought* it was our enemy sub. But I don't have enough data to classify it with full certainty."

"There's enough information for me," Moretti said, "my gut tells me we sink this prick."

"No," Katherine shot back. "We're weapons-tight. We got permission to fire under our rules of engagement, but *only* if we've positively identified the attacker, and *only* if they're in a position to prosecute an attack."

"Fucking rules," Moretti grumbled."

"They *are* the rules though."

"Yeah, and my gut tells me otherwise."

"Enough!" Katherine said. "I gave my order."

"Yeah, and you're gonna get our people killed." With that, Moretti crossed his arms tight and stared hard out the window. A tactical withdrawal of sorts, or perhaps the reaction of a petulant child, or of an overworked mind desperate for quality sleep.

Moretti's words spun Katherine back to a distinct memory of her training. She had incurred the wrath of an instructor while struggling through a simulated intelligence, surveillance, and reconnaissance mission in a combat zone.

Katherine and her training crew had built what they thought to be a solid surface picture of the combat area and were identifying numerous surface vessels and reporting their details back to the CIC. She and her ATO were attempting to identify a civilian tanker when two small surface boats approached the ship at high speed.

The ATO identified the boats as potential PTGs—patrol torpedo gunboats. Katherine attempted to verify the nearest one by racing to intercept its track, but the conditions were humid and hazy, the boat was pounding through the swell at thirty knots, and the chatter on the primary radio frequency would not let up.

For a few precious seconds, Katherine froze. Her brain scrambled with information overload, her body pulsed with adrenaline, her conscience cartwheeled between uncertainties. Helmet fire, as it's known.

As Katherine struggled with her command decision, it was taken from her. A crewman on the boat fired an SA-7 GRAIL surface-to-air-missile off his shoulder. Her helicopter sustained a direct hit and exploded. She and her crew were terminated, in the simulated sense of the word.

Katherine sat motionless in the simulator, her mind and body still reeling.

"That Hellfire missile is there for a reason, you know," the instructor said.

"I know, it's just—"

'Just what, Marlowe? You were too scared to use it? The U.S. taxpayer is forking out well over a million to train you. And that helo you want to fly is worth a cool fifty mil. You freeze up like you did today and the bill's gonna be awful big."

The instructor paused for effect. "We train you to kill, and when it's time to kill, you kill. Got it? Remember this—in combat, the bad guy is gonna kill you if you don't kill him first. So, if you can't handle the pucker factor, then transfer out and go fly medivac or something."

Katherine's consciousness came back to the present with a jolt. She inhaled and collected herself. "Call the *Portland*, Mets. Tell 'em we're inbound for fuel."

*　　*　　*　　*

Within seven minutes they had reached the *Portland*, landed on the flight deck, and shut down. The receding whine of the turbine engines sounded like a long lullaby sung ever more softly. Katherine could have plonked her head on the side window, shut her eyes, and fallen asleep. But, before she could even begin to relax, she was hit by a rush of hot air laced with sea salt as Moretti opened the door on his side.

Katherine opened her door in reluctant unison. As she made her way onto the deck, the tropical sun burned like a pizza oven running on uranium.

The three made their way to the aircraft hangar and the cover of shade. They could sense the ship gathering speed. She lurched with each swell and swathes of spray flashed past either side. The deck vibrated hard from the engines and shafts running below at high power.

"Someone's in a hurry," Perez said.

Up ahead, two of the ship's crew, both with muted purple shirts and helmets, were moving a large rubber hose. The refuelers were heading for the helicopter. One held the donkey dick—the nozzle—and the other wrestled behind with the hose.

Katherine removed her helmet, hoping for some fresh air on her scalp. But the air was stifling and salty, and no real help at all.

One of the refuellers—the taller one—stopped in his tracks. His offsider couldn't drag the hose out farther by himself and had no choice but to stop. "What the?" he asked, looking at his colleague.

The tall refueller lifted his safety glasses and stared at Katherine.

As they drew closer, Katherine had an unwelcome flash of recognition: the chiselled features, strong shoulders, the boyish clean face with impossibly good teeth, the steely blue-grey eyes. *Shit. That's him.* She stared at the man she'd met at the bar in San Diego straight between the eyes as she drew closer. Without missing a beat, or a step, she yanked her left thumb backwards, pointing towards the helicopter behind her.

"Don't tell me," she said as she passed him, "you'd like to fill that for me?"

* * * *

As they entered the hangar area, Moretti had to ask, "You know that grape?"

"You could say that," Katherine conceded.

The hangar crew gave them a drink and a place to sit. The refuelling wouldn't take long, but the fifteen-minute break was welcome just the same.

"Katherine," Moretti began, "I, uh, I let things get away from me out there. I—"

Katherine put her hands up, palms open. "It's okay, Mets. There's nothing you need to say."

"No, it really wasn't okay. I stepped outta line and I wanna apologise."

Katherine took a moment to compose her words. She took in his face in the interim. His kind yet mischievous eyes were always a delight. There was a softness and a depth of emotion there, even when he was strained. "We're all *dog*-tired, Mets. I don't think any of us are thinkin' and doing things like normal. Plus, it's an exercise. Who knows what we'd do in a real battle."

Moretti bit his bottom lip and looked to the floor.

"Let's put it behind us, huh?"

"Okay," Moretti said.

They hadn't noticed the deck vibration had gone and the ship had slowed to a crawl.

"Officer on deck!"

Katherine, Moretti, and Perez stood to attention without thinking. Training will do that to you.

A tall man in blue-grey khaki wearing a USS *Portland* cap walked up—three stripes and a single star on his epaulettes. "As you were," he ordered. "I'm Commander Irving, XO of the *Portland*. Welcome aboard."

"Thank you, sir," Katherine said with a smile. "Lieutenant Commander Marlowe. I'm in command of the *Romeo*."

"Oh, I see," Irving said.

They shook hands.

"The CO has asked me to come down and fill you in. You guys can stand down and return to the carrier when you're ready. The exercise is done for us today."

"Yes, sir." Katherine paused. "*Done*, sir?"

"Yes. That enemy sub we've all been worried about? He was out there all right. Damned Collins-class boat. Just after you landed, he shot off four torpedos. Two at the destroyer. Two at us."

Katherine steadied herself, placing a hand on a nearby bulkhead wall.

"Turns out he'd been waiting for us in a trench we'd overlooked. He floated up behind the *Columbia* as they went over, then followed behind in their baffles at close range. The sonar guys on the *Columbia* didn't have their towed sonar array deployed in the shallows, so they never knew he was there."

Irving scratched his chin, replaying the tactical scene back in his mind. "Very clever, that skipper ... using the *Columbia* as a smoke-screen against you guys in the helo. All he had to do was wait till you left the scene. He obviously came to a stop to let the *Columbia* get out of range, then came up for a look with his periscope. That gave him a quick range and bearing on us, and his exercise torpedoes came next."

Perez put his head in his hands and groaned. It all made sense: the confusing sonar returns on identical bearings. Two submarines in close proximity—the first, their nuclear-powered Los Angeles–class SSN; the other, an Australian diesel-electric SSK on the blue team.

"The destroyer went to flank speed and ran," Irving continued. "Just managed to outrun the torpedoes. We were closer in and weren't so lucky. The tactical replay will show our countermeasures got one of 'em, but the second torpedo caught us port side of the stern. If the torpedo was for real, our engine room would be blown to hell and our rear compartments flooded right now. Maybe not sunk, but we'd be dead in the water, that's for damn sure. No beach landings for our guys tonight."

If the outcome affected him, Irving's monotonous, fact-heavy delivery of the news wasn't betraying it.

"I guess there's gonna be hell to pay in the exercise debriefs," Katherine said.

"More than likely," he replied. "But that's how these games play out sometimes, don't they? We play it hard and sometimes we fail. When we fail, we figure out why. Then we figure out how not to do that again. All part of a day's work."

Katherine couldn't think of what else to say. Moretti and Perez looked like they'd be happy for the deck to swallow them whole.

"Anyway, thanks for your efforts out there today," Irving said. "Godspeed."

With that, salutes were exchanged, and Commander Irving climbed up a ladder to the next deck.

Moretti concentrated on not looking at Katherine. There would be nothing to gain in that.

"Mets, you, uh ... I can't even—" Katherine stammered.

Moretti put his hands up. "It's okay. There's nothing you need to say."

CHAPTER EIGHTEEN

*What enables the wise sovereign and the good general
to strike and conquer, and achieve things beyond the
reach of ordinary men, is foreknowledge.*

—Sun Tzu, *The Art of War*

Melbourne, 30 July 2023

*Hey Ben. About the trip away we were thinking of doing. August
would work well, say around 14th to the 21st? Looks like an ideal
time to travel and everything is falling into place for me around
then. I know you're busy, so we could travel somewhere close to
Melbourne.*

The text message had dropped into Ben's secure messaging app
during a theory class. Ben stared at it for a few seconds to absorb the
words, then returned his attention to the instructor.

But unable to concentrate, Ben excused himself from the class five
minutes later. He locked himself in a stall in the men's toilet, then opened
the app with trepidation. He responded with a text message:

*Hello. Good to hear from you. Yes, I could use a short break. I
will arrange time off around those dates.*

* * * *

Indian Ocean, off the West Australian coast

1 August 2023, 1745 hours

It was a rarely used perch. A small platform at the stern of USS *John
F. Kennedy*, right on the starboard corner. The platform was down a
short ladder and a few yards below the flight deck. If you kept your
head down, you would be out of view from almost every point on the

flight deck, the island, and CCTV surveillance. Not the prettiest place, but it was quiet when flight recovery operations were suspended, and mercifully free of the thousands of other humans on board this floating town.

Katherine sat with her back leaning against the starboard-facing wall. The hard steel was cool to the touch, which was comforting in this humid sub-tropical air.

To her right, the sea churned to a foaming, bubbling, white cacophony of water and air, weaving and twisting from the ship's four giant propellers below. The churning settled to a long wispy line of wake, stretching back in a gentle curve to the northern horizon.

There were more expansive vantage points nearer the bow of the ship where a person could contemplate the sea ahead, but Katherine preferred this view. Contemplating where the ship had come, marked for a time by the ship's wake, was somehow more soothing.

Out past the starboard railing, the sun was setting on the Indian Ocean. She knew there was nothing between the ship's position—twenty miles off Western Australia—and all the way west to the African coast, too many miles away to contemplate.

Katherine closed her eyes and did her best to relax. The direct warmth of the last rays of sunlight and the persistent sounds of the sea hissing below seemed to caress her mind and soul. She'd been here before. Not at this place, but at this time. The exhaustion, the irritation, the boredom, the inescapable burning desire to get her feet on solid ground. To escape steel, and rubber, and sea. To quench her nauseating sickness for home. To feel her mother's tight embrace. To hear the warm timbre of her grandfather's voice. And to see her father.

There were other things too. Things even more mundane. The freedom to hop in a car and drive. To buy fast food. To shower alone. To sit somewhere aimlessly. To not have the nagging feeling she had to be somewhere else at a specific hour and minute.

It had always confounded Katherine since her first cruise how she would feel as the deployment turned for home. After six months at sea, the squadron, the air wing, and the ship had become more than a collection of teams, groups, and departments. This throng of humanity had morphed into something more. It seemed as if she were absorbed into another living being. Long-held bastions of individualism—privacy, secrecy, and self-determination, to name a few—had imperceptibly faded. It felt extraordinary to be part of an integrated larger whole—a team of thousands, and of hundreds, and of dozens, and of three—a collective being of humankind that could solve anything. Do anything. Conquer anything.

And yet other emotions still fought for her attention. Opposing thoughts bubbled below Katherine's surface and grew stronger by the day. Pangs of desire to regain a sense of self, of self-expression, to set her own agenda, and to be free of a uniform and what it symbolised.

It's time for this to end, she contemplated. *Time to disconnect from all this and get back to who I am ... whatever that is.*

Katherine leant her head against the wall with her eyes closed, resting into the mild rhythm of the ship as it pitched and rolled.

The sun had retreated below the horizon, but the warmth and humidity in the air persisted. True to form, though, the navy business had no sense of occasion and stopped for no one. The shrill of the boatswain's pipe over the 1MC blasted across the flight deck, smashing the serenity. "Stand by for words from the Group Commanding Officer," came the announcement over the loudspeakers.

"Men and women of Carrier Strike Group Eleven," she began, "this is your Commanding Officer, Rear Admiral Paterson. I want to congratulate you all on a successful Talisman Sabre. Everyone worked hard and did their part, and I, on behalf of all the commanding officers, thank you for your efforts. You should all be proud. We had many successes and some failures. We faced new challenges and handled new threats. We've learned more about how to assess and handle those threats. It goes to show how alert we must continue to be. We can't relax for a second, or think because we have the best equipment and people, we somehow have a right to success. We must continue to work hard, train hard, and always be ready. Our nation and our allies, the free countries of the world, are relying on us to keep the peace. We must be firm and assertive as we prosecute that peace. It's the only language our adversaries understand. It's how we, the United States, maintains liberty and stability across our world."

She paused.

"I appreciate this has been a long cruise for all of us. We've done many things, and we've been to many places. It won't be long before we turn for home and complete this deployment. We all look forward to that. And some shore time is coming up before then … a well-deserved break for many of you. Some will go to Fremantle, others to Adelaide, Melbourne, and Sydney. Our carrier will go further south to Hobart, where I'm told the welcome is warm and the food is outstanding. Your commanding officers will provide you with more information in coming days. In the meantime, we've all got jobs to do and we must continue to work hard and do our best. This is the commanding officer. Out."

Half-listening with her eyes closed, Katherine had barely taken in any of the rear admiral's words. The carrier's next destination—Hobart—was the only topic of slight interest. And she'd heard more than enough about Talisman Sabre in the hot wash debriefs.

Katherine looked up at the U.S. flag flapping hard in the stiff breeze—just along the ship's stern. Pledging allegiance to the flag was one of her earliest memories from elementary school, and she'd learned how the white of the flag signified purity and innocence; the blue symbolised vigilance, perseverance, and justice; and the red embodied valour and bravery. All the values a U.S. citizen and a U.S. Navy officer were to hold dear. And they were still there for Katherine. But there was a certain fading. An emotional distance between her and the flag right at that moment.

Are we making a difference in the world? Am I making a difference? Or are we wasting our time out here?

Relative silence had returned to the tiny platform as her thoughts drifted. For Katherine, there was nowhere to go and nothing to do but sit on the hard steel deck and daydream of being anywhere but there.

*　*　*　*

Hobart, 2 August 2023

Deputy Premier Matthew Cash didn't look up from the report as he read on. He responded to the buzz from his desk phone by hitting the intercom button. "Yes, Michelle," he said.

"I have Vice Admiral James Garrison from the U.S. Navy on line two for you."

"Are you sure? I was expecting a call from the U.S. Ambassador's office."

"Well, that's who he said he was. I don't think it's a prank call. It's on a secure line."

"Ah, okay. Put him through."

Cash's throat had tightened and he cleared before he spoke. "Hello. This is Matthew Cash, Deputy Premier."

"Mr Cash. Vice Admiral James Garrison, U.S. Third Fleet."

Cash felt a strange urge to stand or salute—or something. "Ah, yes, Vice Admiral—"

"Just go ahead and call me Jim. Thanks for taking my call."

"Oh, oh, yes … no problem, Admiral. I mean … Jim."

"I got off a call with our Ambassador in Canberra. He tells me our visit is ready to roll."

"Ah, yes. Yes, the carrier visit is mostly organised. We're looking forward to it."

"I'm sure you are. I bet our guys are too. Been a long time at sea for them."

"Yes, yes …"

"The carrier group are on their way down the coast, and we have an accurate ETA for JFK in Hobart now."

"Oh, good, good," Cash said while trying to unravel the navy acronyms in his mind.

"You can expect an update from my people real soon."

"Thank you."

"And how're things lookin' from your side?"

"Well, um … quite good. The Australian government has given its final approval for the port visit, and we're working hard on all the arrangements. It's coming together well, I think."

"Good to hear, Mr Cash."

"Oh, please … just call me Matthew."

"Okay. Matthew. The Ambassador's office is still going to call, but thought I'd brief you first … from a navy perspective."

"No worries."

"As you know, the expansion of our port visits is important to us. We want to better connect with our allies and tighten our bonds with your people."

"Yes, we're right behind that."

"Good. Good. Now, there have been some … sensitivities Down Under in the past, and a few unfortunate events down there in Hobart."

Cash stayed silent, his mind racing.

"We're keen to avoid those sorta complications, you know?" Garrison continued. "Anything that might embarrass either of our nations."

Cash cleared his throat again. "Yes, yes, absolutely."

"And I can trust you on that?"

"Yes, sir. I mean … yes, Jim." Cash hit his forehead in self-chastisement—he was glad it wasn't a video call.

"I'm glad we understand each other, Matthew."

"Certainly, Jim. You have my full commitment to this being a successful visit." Cash tried to lighten things up. "*She'll be right*, as we say over here."

"Ah … yes," Garrison acknowledged. "Well, my people will be in touch with all the details."

"Thank you."

"Oh, one more thing," Garrison said, sounding as if he had just remembered it. "I know some of your folks are nervous about nuclear-powered ships and all."

"Oh yes, just a few oddballs on the fringe who like to make some noise."

"Hah! Yeah, we've all got 'em. But the modern world has moved on from all that nonsense. We all know how safe our ships are. As an act of goodwill, can you please arrange for our ship to anchor much closer in this time?"

"Oh. Ah, I think we might be able—"

"It doesn't make sense to tell your best friend to park on the street when you've got space in your driveway, does it?"

"No, I guess not ..."

"Good Matthew, good. We're agreed then."

"Ah—"

"Well, you have yourself a good day."

"Thank you, and—"

Click.

Cash replaced the phone handset and slumped back in his chair. *I may not be in the navy,* he thought, *but bloody hell, have I just been given an order!* He hit the intercom button again. "Michelle!"

"Yes."

"Book me a meeting with the organising committee for the carrier visit, and tell them it's urgent."

"Yes, sir."

"Thanks. And what's with the 'sir' bullshit?"

"Oh, you know, just getting you ready for the navy ... *sir.*"

"Hilarious."

*   *   *   *

By 10:20 AM, Michelle Weston had called all the executive assistants of the main players to attend the meeting. She had worked out a time when most were available, created an invitation in the deputy premier's electronic calendar, and sent it off to the invitees.

She rushed a text message to Cash's phone:

All done. U.S. JFK visit organising committee this Friday 10 am.

An agent in the Ministry of State Security, Beijing Bureau, received the message five seconds after Cash.

It had been a simple courtesy for Cash—on his infamous tour of China in 2020—to hand his phone to the hostess at a dinner he attended with his Chinese entrepreneur friend. "This is a custom when doing business in China," she explained. It was a courtesy not to have devices at the table to "demonstrate a high degree of trust and commitment to the discussions."

Cash's phone was returned to him as he left the dinner in the wee hours of the morning, infected with sophisticated monitoring software of which neither he nor his government would ever be aware.

* * * *

Indian Ocean, off the West Australian coast
2340 hours

Petty Officer Third Class Eli Simmons had finally gotten off watch at balls o'clock—way past his schedule. He'd spent his shift sorting out issues brewing among the junior aviation ordnance man on his team. Tensions were on the rise, and fuses were short—not a good situation for a department that manages missiles, bombs, and bullets.

He'd be back on watch at 0600 the next morning, so sleep was next on his agenda. But he knew from experience it would take time to wind down, and tossing and turning in his rack wasn't the way to do it. Better to spend some time distracting himself. Eli flipped open his laptop and wrote an email to his wife:

Hi honey. We're finally on our way again and headed south. Not too long now till I get some shore time. I can't wait! I'm going to get a cheap room somewhere and collapse for a few days. Totally over all this navy crap. Gossip is ... our port visit will be down in the land of the spinning devil ;). I really don't care where it is, as long as I'm off this godforsaken tub. Missing you and the kids even worse than before. Soooo looking forward to seeing you all. Not long now!!! Love, your Eli xxxxxx

He hit send, then opened up Facebook to scan through his news feed. He had avoided any mention of the destination for their port visit, given the protocol not to divulge this detail until the commanding officer had announced the arrangements to the public. Something to do with security, or some other nonsense. Not that Eli cared. He'd be resigning from the navy straight after this deployment.

*   *   *   *

Montgomery, Alabama
2:28 PM

Faith Simmons wedged herself through the front door of the house with an over-stuffed shopping bag in each hand, plus her keys, phone, handbag, and the mail. She plonked them all down on the kitchen counter, then flicked through the mail. Just junk mail and bills.

The kids would be home from school soon, which meant she had about twenty peaceful minutes to herself. *Luxury, pure luxury.*

Faith grabbed a Coke from the refrigerator, gave it a decent shot of Jack Daniel's, and plopped herself on the couch. She opened her Surface tablet to check for messages. She read Eli's message with a smile, imagining the day when he would walk down the ship's gangway for the last time and into her arms.

Unbeknown to her, three keywords attracted the attention of a piece of software on her tablet: *navy*, *port*, and *visit*. The trojan had been installed months earlier after Faith had clicked a hyperlink to confirm her mailing address with her local bank.

Faith and her tablet weren't unique, though. Nearly two hundred other spouses, girlfriends, boyfriends, mothers, and fathers of the crew of USS *John F. Kennedy* had unwittingly downloaded the same trojan on their electronic devices.

The trojan on Faith's tablet sent an encrypted surveillance alert to the central intelligence system of the People's Liberation Army, General Political Department. The database-driven artificial intelligence system categorised and prioritised the message. The case was then flagged for urgent attention and assigned to one of the agency's countless human agents.

*   *   *   *

Beijing, China

The alert had the agent in Beijing sitting upright within seconds. With a few clicks, she had the screen of Faith Simmons's tablet in full view. The agent began recording the session.

She read the email from Eli with close interest and noted the words "land of the spinning devil." The phrase didn't make sense to her and required further investigation. Her search engine, which used Google by a remote proxy to browse the Internet of the West, displayed confusing results at first. Finally, she found a Quora page answering the question "Do Tasmanian devils spin?" and learned about Taz, an American cartoon character created in the 1950s.

The agent recorded her findings in the electronic case file and submitted her report. The system received the report and analysed the contents and metadata. Messages were automatically sent to high-level users in the Ministry of State Security, and the People's Liberation Army and Navy, who needed to know about a sailor on USS *John F. Kennedy* headed south to Tasmania.

Eleven minutes had elapsed since Faith Simmons had first checked her emails.

*   *   *   *

Hobart, 3 August 2023

Alix Zhao woke to find nine messages on her WeChat messaging app. She scanned down the list, looking for anything of interest.

A message from Lawrence Chen caught her eye. It'd been a good few months since she'd heard from the overseas study coordinator assigned to her by the Chinese Ministry of Education. She wasn't eager to see a message from him, however. The innocent-looking WeChat message was a prompt for her to download an encrypted task briefing, which she did with trepidation but no delay.

Alix had finished her studies with the University of Tasmania three years earlier, graduating with a Degree in Information Science with first-class honours. She'd then secured a position in the industry and had been granted Australian citizenship. However, things had not gone as planned since then. The company closed their Australian operation during the COVID-19 pandemic, and unable to find a permanent position since, she'd worked a string of casual jobs to get by.

Being a part-time spy, however, was not one of those casual jobs. The "job" paid her no wage at all, and she was certainly not a spy in the classic sense of the word. She studied, lived, and worked in Australia much the same as any nationalised Australian citizen. But Alix owed a debt to the Chinese state. As a proud Australian citizen, she felt little allegiance to her country of birth. But she would not fail her family in China. Not ever.

*   *   *   *

With the clock a few minutes from midnight, Alix's supervisor turned to her. "Going out for a smoke," she said in a low gravelled voice. "You got the phones."

Alix worked as a casual night concierge at the Hobart Royal Imperial Hotel, a two-hundred room establishment on the waterfront. She'd worked there long enough to know the desk supervisor would be outside for at least ten minutes, and she'd leave her computer unlocked.

Alix had observed desk staff using the hotel reservation system and knew what to do. She scrolled ahead to dates in the second and third weeks of August 2023, checking down the grid of reservations. She quickly found a single reservation for a block of forty-two rooms for the period 13 to 20 August. Guest names were not allocated to the rooms, which was odd, but the master booking had a single reference number: USN-PO-3F-23097765K.

She took an image of the computer screen with her phone, then returned the screen to its former state.

Alix wrote and encrypted her report on her laptop the following morning. She filed the report and the screen image via the secure file-transfer server, as specified in the task brief.

The Chinese intelligence system decrypted, categorised, and prioritised the report as it was received. The booking reference number Alix had reported was data-matched to its likely source. Messages were automatically sent to high-level users in the Ministry of State Security, and the People's Liberation Army and Navy, who needed to know about a purchase order created by the United States Navy for forty-two hotel rooms in Hobart, Tasmania, in less than two weeks' time.

CHAPTER NINETEEN

Hobart, 4 August 2023

Matthew Cash found the many roles he had to play as a senior politician in a small state to be a disadvantage. The Deputy Premier position had a certain level of responsibility and workload. Then there were his three ministerial portfolios: Tourism, Agriculture, and Police and Emergency Services.

It was quite a handful in any week, but more so when parliament sat. And how Cash *hated* those sitting weeks. The endless, mindless, soulless theatrics as he played his scripted part in the political drama on the floor of parliament. Then later—outside with the small but insatiable media pack—there would be the theatrics of manipulation, brand management, crisis control, and dodging, weaving, and redirecting. The practiced art of talking much and saying essentially nothing.

It was all in a day's work and Cash was competent at most of it, despite how it ran contrary to his straight-talking, no-nonsense country boy upbringing. And his current Chief of Staff, Bradfurd Rouse, had added cunning new tricks to Cash's repertoire. Some of the tricks so low they were downright subterranean.

As Cash sat at the head of the meeting table in the Police Tasmania Headquarters, he contemplated what a bizarre beast politics could sometimes be. Such unbidden thoughts occurred often and at the strangest times: during parliamentary question time, while he zoned out and pretended to be engaged during another boring community event, milking the cows back in Branxholm, or—as on this day—while chairing an intra-government committee of heavy-hitters.

Cash enjoyed the salacious, delicious notion of how a disadvantage in politics could become an advantage. These little gems would sometimes reveal themselves when he'd least expected it. *This is one of those days*, he thought, rubbing his chin as a grin snuck across his face. Managing multiple ministerial portfolios was often a royal pain in his arse, but it was precisely how he could steer this committee, and the meeting, the way he had planned.

Michael Cahill, the head of the State Emergency Service and chair of the Nuclear-Powered Ships Visits Committee, was wrapping up his detailed briefing on preparations: "The committee and the Ports Authority have completed final checks through the Port Safety Plan. We're satisfied all is on track, and all risk controls are being managed as per the plan. We've received the remaining sign-offs from the Commonwealth including the Attorney General's Department, and the Australian Radiation Protection and Nuclear Safety Agency."

"And the radiation monitoring?" asked Doctor Paula Smethurst, a representative from the state's Department of Health and Human Services.

"Yes," Cahill replied, "the Australian Navy will have its representatives here a few days before the carrier is due in. They will form the radiation monitoring group and conduct testing before, during, and after the carrier visit."

"Good," she acknowledged.

Cahill faced the projector screen. He clicked a button to call up the next graphic with a map of the River Derwent, the city of Hobart, and three anchorages designated for visiting nuclear-powered ships.

"The carrier will be moored here, at Anchorage B," he said, pointing at the centre of three blue circles marked on the map.

"For what reason?" Cash interjected. "Why there?"

"This is the standard mooring position for a ship of this type, and balances the safety risks while keeping the carrier within a reasonable distance of the Hobart docks."

"You call that a reasonable distance? Looks like quite a trip to me."

Cahill seemed surprised. "The distance is …" he mumbled as he rifled through his papers, "the distance is about eleven kilometres."

"That's too far," Cash said, flat as a cow pat.

"Ah, it's some distance, I know that, but—"

"We can't welcome our American friends to our city by saying 'G'day mate, good to see you, just park way down there out the back, will ya.'" Cash jabbed his extended thumb over his shoulder. "And then there's all the logistics to consider. Imagine telling the officers and crew they have to do a twenty-two-kilometre round trip on some bloody ferry to go ashore. And let's not forget, it's the end of winter. If they freeze their tits off, all we'll hear about is the cold and they'll never come back." Cash eyed Michael Cahill. "This is meant to be the first of *many* visits, Michael. Do not forget that. We must get this right."

The other attendees fell silent as awkwardness pervaded the room.

The police commissioner, Harry Jeffries, spoke first: "Yes, Matthew. We understand your concern. The Nuclear-Powered Ships Visits Committee has to find the right balance between convenience for our visitors and risk minimisation for the community."

"That's right. The risks are all documented and well controlled, are they not?" Cash said. "What difference is it going to make having the carrier parked at Anchorage A—" Cash pointed to the circle marked on the map two kilometres from the Hobart CBD— "or Anchorage B? If something goes wrong, it won't make any difference, surely. And anyway, when's the last time a U.S. nuclear-powered ship had a nuclear accident in port? Or anywhere? Huh?" Cash motioned towards Rouse.

Rouse seemed only too happy to respond to the question. "Never," he said. "Not once."

"There," Cash said, "that's the facts of the matter. We have to be mindful of risks, yes, but let's not go nuts over this."

"I beg to differ," Dr Smethurst said. "The consequences from a nuclear accident at Anchorage A are significantly higher. There would be immediate and uncontrollable radiation hazards at that range in the city and nearby suburbs. Even if the emergency response is perfect, as per the plan, we'd be looking at significant gamma radiation and airborne contamination. We'd have deaths on our hands soon after the accident and for months to come, and that's just for starters."

"Yes, and we'd have to evacuate the river and some suburbs, depending on the wind direction," Cahill added. "It would be catastrophic."

"Consequences are one thing. I get that," Cash countered. "But what some people in this room don't seem to be looking at is the *likelihood*. How *likely* is a nuclear reactor accident on a U.S. Navy ship?"

"We considered this when we reviewed the emergency plan a few years back," Maria Baldini, head of the Ports Authority, replied. "The thing is, if the likelihood was anything near significant, the Americans would be all over this and we'd know about that. Think about it this way … where do they position their nuclear-powered ships and submarines when they're at home? Go to Pearl Harbour, San Diego, Norfolk, and you'll find nuclear-powered vessels tied up at the docks, right in the middle of their cities. If the likelihood of a nuclear accident was anything but minuscule, they would not be doing that. I think we can be confident to follow the lead of the Americans on this. They are the experts, after all."

Cash settled back into his chair and folded his arms. Baldini had landed the killer blow with such precision it was as if she'd been scripted to say such a thing.

Rouse did his best to keep a poker face.

Commissioner Jeffries landed the final punch: "Michael, I think the committee should reconvene and consider this request."

Cahill nodded in abject defeat. His ashen face betrayed his simmering anger.

"I will have more to say on this at the meeting!" Dr Smethurst grumbled, tapping her index finger hard against the table-top.

"Of course," Jeffries said with a smile. "Your input on medical responses and preparedness are always valued and welcome."

You should have been a politician, Mister Commissioner, Cash was thinking. He'd found extra millions for Police Tasmania in the previous year's state budget, and he was heartened to see his political investments paying off at just the right time.

"Now," Cash said, placing both hands flat on the table. "There's lots more on the agenda. Let's keep moving ..."

*   *   *   *

Qinhuangdao

"As you can see, gentleman, the Americans have played further into our hands."

Rear Admiral Pengcheng Tao sat on the edge of his leather lounge chair with a manner exuding confidence and an eagerness to proceed. "We had contemplated and prepared for several Australian ports, but the choice of Hobart surprised us. However, I am pleased to say it is a *very* pleasant surprise. This port has the greatest distance from American and allied naval and air support. And it has a tiny population and police force, and almost no armed forces there whatsoever."

"Where is this place?" Zhaoqing Feng asked.

"Hobart is the capital of Tasmania, an island south of the Australian continent. The island is centred on the parallel 42 degrees south. There is nothing but open sea between Hobart and Antarctica."

Lieutenant Colonel Li Guoliang appeared to be on a battle footing already, despite being in civilian clothes and seated in the comfortable living room of Admiral Pengcheng's holiday home. "It is astounding, Admiral," he said. "Our intelligence tells us they will protect the carrier with a police launch, which is to maintain a one-hundred-metre exclusion zone around the ship." Li paused for effect. "And that is the sum of their protections."

"They have other protections on land and in the air, surely?" Zhaoqing asked.

"No. Nothing else."

Zhaoqing and DPRK Colonel General Kim Hyun-woo looked at

each other as if dumbfounded. They turned to Admiral Pengcheng for clarification, only to see him smiling back at them.

The four men, on perfect cue, erupted into unbridled laughter.

Kim was the first to regain his composure. "Forgive me, Li, I thought this could not possibly be."

"It is, my dear friend," Pengcheng replied. "These stupid Americans and their Australian lapdogs. They are so sure of themselves they protect their carrier with a speedboat and some traffic cops. It is legendary."

"There will be one, maybe two U.S. fast-attack submarines on patrol," Li said, "but they will be out to sea and not close by. Plus, the ship itself is always in a certain state of readiness. They have mounted machine guns and marines stationed at points around its perimeter."

"And what of the ship's weaponry?" Zhaoqing asked.

"Oh yes, formidable weaponry. Multi-band radar that feeds into computer-controlled defence systems. It has an array of defensive missiles and the radar-guided Phalanx cannon that fires three thousand twenty-millimetre per minute. Incoming objects do not stand a chance against this wall of lead."

"So how do we overcome it?" Zhaoqing asked.

"We cannot, which is why we will not try," Pengcheng said. "Most of the ship's defences are designed to repel attacks by fast-moving, sophisticated weaponry such as anti-ship missiles. We will not be using such a weapon. And their defensive weapons are designed for battle on the open sea. The carrier will sit in a winding river surrounded by hillside suburbs. These weapons are useless in such a place and will not be active."

Zhaoqing nodded. He did not doubt the admiral for a second, but he had to know the details. His superiors would expect nothing less. "Ah, yes," he said, his eyes narrowing. "The ant to bring down the elephant."

"Indeed," Pengcheng said, "but let us move onto other related matters. Li, please brief us on the status of the submarine."

"Yes, Admiral. *Shaanxi-2* is positioned near the Solomon Islands.

It has been refuelled and re-provisioned, and the two DPRK special forces soldiers are now on board. It departed yesterday and is transiting to the east coast of Tasmania in deep water at a conservative speed. It will arrive in the area in approximately twelve days' time, then transit down the coast while staying close to the shore."

Kim frowned. "What is the probability it will arrive as planned?" he asked.

Pengcheng sought to reassure him. "*Shaanxi-2* is our latest non-nuclear design and is top secret. We are confident our adversaries know little, if anything, of its existence or its capabilities. The sub uses an advanced air-independent power system, which means it does not have to surface regularly to run its diesel engines to charge the batteries. It can stay submerged for many days and travel much longer distances than our other conventional submarines. We have stripped it of torpedoes and non-essential equipment and reduced the crew to a minimum. It has the capacity to carry the mission payload, extra supplies, and extra fuel for the two long journeys. And by running deep and at low speed, it is virtually undetectable."

"And when they approach the coast, in the shallows," Kim prodded. "What then?"

"We have high-definition 3D mapping of the ocean floor throughout the Bass Strait, down Tasmania's eastern coast, and well out into the Southern Ocean." Pengcheng smiled. "This is courtesy of our Antarctic exploration ships, which have visited Hobart many times in recent years. They have advanced sonar and radar equipment that does much more for us than chart the ice.

"The *Shaanxi-2* will travel slowly and close to the coast with full navigational confidence. There is much ocean noise and shipping activity there, which will render our submarine undetectable—even to a U.S. submarine patrolling off the mouth of the river. Our captain will need to be careful and cunning, but the odds at the beginning will be on his side."

"And at the end?" Zhaoqing asked.

"An escape has been thoroughly planned. But yes, the odds will be more against them as they leave."

The men fell silent. They gazed at the map depicting the east coast of Tasmania and the wide mouth of the River Derwent. Each man seemed to play through the mission in his mind, considering the risks, the probabilities, the many dangers. And contemplating the ultimate prize.

"And what of our operative in Australia?" Pengcheng asked. "Is he ready?"

"Yes," Kim replied. "He will go to Tasmania and be briefed further, closer to the time."

Pengcheng paused. His countenance took on a deeper seriousness. "My dear Kim. Much will depend on this man. The mission will only succeed if he succeeds."

"He understands this. His commitment to the mission is unwavering."

"I have observed his skill and his determination," Li added. "He is the proper operative for this mission. I am confident of this."

Pengcheng and Zhaoqing nodded. The assessments of their special forces military colleagues reassured them. But all four men understood that in the end they were to rely on the skill, commitment, and determination of one solitary man.

*　　*　　*　　*

Hobart

Cash had managed the meeting with razor-sharp skill. He'd ensured the agenda items that mattered had been well covered while skimming those that were superfluous. Everyone had been given their say, including representatives of three local councils—all of whom failed to hide their voracious appetite for a slice of American pie.

"Very well then," Cash said. "Thanks everyone for your input today. However, there are some important points I must underline before we leave."

He paused and exhaled.

"We all know how important this visit is to our state. Diplomatically, strategically, economically. This is the first significant U.S. Navy visit in over a decade. There may be many more visits of this scale, but they will *only* happen if this one is a success. I emphasise to you all, again, of the importance of keeping the dates and final details of this visit confidential until we announce everything to the media and the public. There must be no leaks from this meeting. *None.*" Cash looked around the table. "Does everyone understand me?"

Everyone agreed. Some with a nod, others with a simple, "Yes."

"Good. There will be some anti-nuclear and anti-war protests. We can't stop those, but we must minimise their impact and visibility. As we've heard today, the police will have a substantial presence when the carrier arrives and departs. They will ensure there will be no idiots getting their five minutes of fame. And if the looney fringe only get a couple of days' notice to organise themselves, we are confident their presence and impact will be token at best."

The meeting room fell silent.

Cash smiled and nodded. "Okay. Good then. See you all at the next meeting."

*   *   *   *

Melbourne

6 August 2023

Ben gazed at his laptop screen, motionless and spellbound. His right index finger hovered over the trackpad. With the next simple push of his finger, everything was about to change.

He pressed down and three Photoshop layers merged into one. Three chaotic, indiscernible images became a single cohesive, detailed image.

Ben scrolled across and down the mission brief. Schedules, maps, locations, travel plans, actions, contacts, contingencies. All precise and succinct. And at the end, a detailed diagram of the ultimate target of his mission—a brand-new U.S. Navy Ford-class aircraft carrier with the name USS *John F. Kennedy.*

Ben did not breathe for a few moments as a cold shiver knifed through him. The sheer weight of the mission seeped uneasily into his being. His mind scrambled through the details he had scanned. The scale of the mission was alarming, and many elements would have to work in harmony for it to succeed.

But as he stared at the final diagram—the prize at the end—Ben took a much-needed breath. There would be many things he'd never know about the mission and its purpose, nor did he need to. He understood that. But he would follow his orders without question. He understood the meaning of the prize to his glorious country, to the Supreme Leader, and to their enemy … the American pig aggressors. He knew this would bring much glory to the nation of his birth, and would help attain the vision of a re-united and victorious Korea.

He also understood what it would mean to his father. And to his parents' safety and futures.

Ben scrolled back to the first page to begin a thorough read of the brief to memorise every word and detail. As he considered the travel schedule, it was clear his time as a student pilot in Melbourne would soon come to an end. He would be leaving in a week's time never to return.

*　*　*　*

11:13 AM

Leona Manning sat alone at a table in the back of the cafe. She'd chosen a table with a degree of privacy. She itched to order a coffee, but decided to wait for her friend to arrive.

It was no surprise that Martin Brady was late. He was late to the point of being reliably so. She'd given up on chastising him years ago. It never worked, and he was far too cheeky and charming for her to sustain her anger.

She scrolled through her phone between glances at customers in the café and the people passing by the windows looking onto Cygnet's main street. The locals in this smallish town in Tasmania's Huon Valley provided plenty of interest for people-watching. An eclectic blend of old-timers—mostly farmers, boaties, and fisherman, mixed with a growing number of the younger and middle-aged crowd. The blow-ins, as they were known, had brought crafts, artisan skills, New Age therapies, yoga, and folk music. And readily accessible marijuana, among other things.

But no matter how the demographics shifted, this little town seemed to have a firm grasp on its heritage and its natural, earthy, watery roots. The surrounding world—Tasmania, Australia, and everywhere else—could shift and change however they liked, but Cygnet seemed to stay true to its soul.

Which was why Leona often visited the place. She loved to escape the rat race of Hobart and her high-pressure job as Deputy General Manager of Glenorchy City Council. The simplicity of life, the connection to the environment, the people with no hidden agendas. Her mind would often wander through the forest of social delight as she wasted away an hour or two at her favourite café in Cygnet.

"G'day." Martin Brady had arrived fourteen minutes late. He had plopped himself on a chair opposite Leona. No apology given, and none expected.

"Well, look what the wind has blown in," Leona said.

"Hmm," he grunted with a contorted smile. "You ordered yet?"

"No. I was waiting for you."

"Never a good ploy, that."

"Yeah, so I keep telling myself."

He waved a waitress over. "Just gimme your biggest cooked brekkie and a large black coffee, thanks. What're you having, Leona?"

"A latte, skinny milk, please."

The waitress scribbled down the order, then made her way back to the drinks counter.

"You city slickers and your spewy lattes," Martin quipped.

"Up yours, Bush Boy."

"Oh well, that's just ace, ay? Make me drive all the way here so you can insult me."

Leona giggled. Her good friend had the driest humour around. They'd worked together on environmental projects with the Wellington Park Authority two years earlier. They hit it off from early on, then remained friends.

Martin, then aged thirty-one, was eighteen years her junior and too young to become anything more than a good friend. Although, to Leona's embarrassment, he would sometimes be the subject of the odd erotically charged dream of hers, and daytime meanderings about a life she never had. His boyish charm, his sense of humour, his weathered good looks were all encased in the roughish, muscly, six-foot build of a man from the bush—a rather intoxicating blend of what a good, attractive man should be. But her husband would never know how she felt, and neither would Martin Brady.

"So, what brings you to sunny Cygnet, Ms Manning?" he asked.

"Well, the sun, the coffee, you know ..."

"Bullshit."

"And to catch up with you."

"Yeah, yeah." Martin leaned forward, narrowed his gaze, and stared deep into her eyes. "You got something on your mind. I can always tell with you."

Leona shifted in her chair. He was right, and no one else would stare into her eyes like that, not since she could remember. The sensation was delectably unsettling. "Well, it's been a while, and I did *really* want to catch up with you."

"I sense a 'but' coming ..."

"But ..." She paused, trying to assemble the words. "There's some information I've come across. Something the people you mix with should know about."

The waitress placed the latte and long black on their table.

"Thanks," Leona said.

"You were saying?" Brady asked.

"You've got to swear you won't tell anyone who told you this, right?"

"You got it. Sounds intriguing."

"It is, I think. This info comes from the highest level of government."

"Uh-huh."

"Our General Manager was called to a meeting on Friday, but he's away on the mainland and asked me to take his place."

"Tasmanian government?" Brady asked.

"Yep."

"Those arseholes. Yep, go on."

Leona paused. "Yeah, well those arseholes are planning something behind everyone's back and they don't want your people to know about it. You know … the environment movement."

Brady shook his head. "I wonder why you put up with all that crap."

"Well, it comes with some influence. And sometimes it turns up juicy information."

"Okay. But you know I'm not one of those greenie people waving signs and chaining myself to bulldozers."

"Yeah, yeah. I get it. But you can pass on things I can't. It'd be way too risky for me to communicate this information directly."

Martin Brady stared again into Leona's brown eyes. "So, that's why you've come all the way down to Cygnet, then?"

"Yep. Can't be too careful."

"Okay. If it's *that* important, you better tell me what the hell is going on."

Leona took a good gulp of latte. "Righto. So … *John F. Kennedy*. You heard of him, yes?"

"Duh!"

"Well …"

CHAPTER TWENTY

In life, as in chess, forethought wins.

—Charles Buxton

North Sea Fleet Headquarters, Qingdao, China
7 August 2023

"**I** have just received word from the ministry, Rear Admiral. They have activated all the channels. The first communications release will begin today and continue throughout this week, as requested."

"Very good, Commissary Zhaoqing. This is most pleasing," Pengcheng Tao replied.

The two men were speaking on an encrypted secure phone connection, but they would not risk being anything less than professional. They knew there was no such thing as a fully private line within China itself, and the assumption someone else was listening was standard policy.

Individuals could only rise to high position, and survive there, with careful strategy. Pengcheng and Zhaoqing were fully cognisant their futures and the prosperity of their families depended on their continued usefulness to the state. This mission would either make them heroes among the military and the Party or bring their careers, and perhaps their lives, to a sudden conclusion.

"I will leave it to you to inform our partners," Zhaoqing said. "I wish you good fortune, Rear Admiral Pengcheng."

"And on you, Commissary Zhaoqing. We will speak soon."

Pengcheng ended the call. *There's no going back now*, he said to himself as he dropped the handset into its cradle.

He leant forward, his elbows resting on the desk and chin cradled in his clasped hands. He considered the sophisticated information strategy about to be unleashed by China's Ministry of State Security.

They—together with the People's Liberation Army, General Political Division—had crafted a tranche of minor information leaks and releases to occur over the three weeks to follow. These would begin later that day with leaked information through known vulnerabilities in Chinese information systems and to various individuals. Some would be Chinese operatives known to be double agents working for the West and only kept alive for purposes such as these. Others—American, Asian, and European defence and intelligence operatives conscripted or forced to work as double agents for China—would leak the information as instructed.

It wouldn't be long before the United States and its allies assembled the disparate pieces of information into a cohesive whole. They would become aware, perhaps within a day or two, that China was preparing a major military exercise along its coastline to commence on 19 August and to continue for a week, with North Korea and Russia as its joint-exercise partners.

Outside Pengcheng's office, the rising sun had breached the horizon. Intense rays of sunlight streamed through the window on the far wall, striking a small table positioned below it. Pengcheng's ornate Chinese chessboard lit in the golden light as if it were under a single spotlight upon a stage. The arrangement of the pieces revealed a game still in progress, and the thin smattering of dust upon them implied it had been a long time since the last move had been made. So long, he'd almost forgotten the game.

As he thought back, Pengcheng remembered making a bold move. He had placed his remaining chariot piece in a position to threaten both his opponent's guard pieces from afar. Pengcheng had hoped his opponent would be distracted from the immediate threat and would not see Pengcheng's true gambit to follow—a checkmate on his opponent's king piece.

*   *   *   *

210 miles west of Bass Strait
11 August 2023, 0805 hours

Captain Collins had completed his daily broadcast to the officers and crew aboard USS *John F. Kennedy*. He'd given the usual spiel about it being "another great day," provided further information about the port visit to Hobart, and bid farewell to the last remaining surface ship escorting the carrier.

The guided missile destroyer USS *Stockdale* had peeled away from the carrier's port side and set course for Port Phillip Bay and the city of Melbourne three hundred miles to the east. Rear Admiral Susan Paterson, Commanding Officer of Carrier Strike Group 11, had left the carrier and was aboard *Stockdale*. She'd be undertaking a few days of pressing the flesh in Melbourne, flying to Sydney to do more of the same, then a few days of rest and recreation.

The two fast-attack submarines assigned to CSG-11 would stay within proximity of the carrier all the way to southern Tasmania. There would be no shore leave for the officers and crew on either boat.

Collins was eager to be on their way. He turned to the quartermaster of the watch. "We are to intercept a south-easterly course along the Tasmanian west coast, not closer than one-five miles. Confirm your next turn."

"Aye, Captain," the officer responded. Right turn to intercept … right turn to course one-two-five."

Collins wasted no time. "Helm. Come right. Steer course one-two-five."

The conning officer at the helm spun the helm control wheel to the right while keeping a watchful eye on the digital heading indicator above her. "Come right steer course one-two-five, aye, sir. My rudder is right three degrees."

"Very well."

Collins sensed the carrier begin its gentle turn. Soon they would be established on their new course, headed for the north-west tip of the island of Tasmania.

With *Stockdale* disappearing into the distance, the carrier would be alone on the surface for the remaining two-day transit to Hobart. And with the departure of the rear admiral, Collins was the senior commanding officer. Not having the group CO hovering nearby was both a relief and a burden, but at that moment Collins felt only relief.

Collins contemplated what lay ahead as he watched an E-2 Hawkeye aircraft being prepared for launch at Catapult Two. At these rare moments—when he stopped to think about his impending shore leave—those beasts in his mind would return. They had lived on in the basement of his being—still imprisoned, yet still very much alive.

Collins inhaled, swallowed hard, and closed his eyes. He suppressed the memories and their cruel emotions like every time before. But he realised things were coming to an end. They had to. He could no longer imprison what curdled within him.

As the ship rolled out on the newly established course, Collins opened his eyes and stared at the sea. The island of Tasmania lay over the horizon, two hundred and fifty miles off the bow. And there, he knew, he would finally face his beasts within.

*　　*　　*　　*

Langley, Virginia

The CIA headquarters were always a hive of activity, but this day was busier than most. Meetings were in progress and reports were flying. Hushed rumours travelled as if on the wind.

For days, information had been pouring in from sources across the globe about a large-scale joint exercise between China, Russia, and North Korea. And the CIA's sources and American surveillance satellites were confirming the movement of ground, sea, and air assets across China; marine and navy forces from North Korea across the Yellow Sea; and Russian Navy ships and aircraft across their southern borders.

This was the first time the three nations had taken part in such a joint exercise, a development that had more than a few American eyebrows raised. The CIA and the Defense Intelligence Agency would soon brief the Joint Chiefs of Staff, and the military would deploy assets to monitor the exercises as best they could. Intelligence services would be placed on maximum alert to comb for every piece of information they could glean.

This would consume much of their attention and resources for the next two weeks at least. Other projects and priorities across the globe would not be forgotten, but they would not receive the same level of attention in the short term.

And a U.S. aircraft carrier undertaking a friendly visit to a distant port, way down south below the forty-second parallel, would be given almost no attention whatsoever.

*　　*　　*　　*

Melbourne, 7:40 PM

The repeating chime emanating from Ben's laptop persisted for fifteen seconds. And it had sounded twice in the preceding ten minutes.

When it chimed for the fourth time, Ben's roommate had had enough. "You gonna get that, Benny Boy?" Justin asked.

Ben flipped open the lid and clicked the green phone icon on the video-conferencing app in one smooth movement as he left the room, headed for the privacy of the dining hall. "Hello," he said in Mandarin as he moved down the corridor.

The video window on the laptop screen showed the fuzzy shape of a woman's forehead and hairline. Her head darted back and forth. "Ben. Ben. You hear me?"

"Yes, I can hear you."

"Can you see me?"

"Not really. Sit back from the screen."

"Oh." The face of Liling Cai came into focus. She seemed concerned or stressed.

Situation normal, Ben thought.

"Ah, Ben. There you are! Are you well?"

"Yes, Ma. I am well."

Liling had somehow managed to install a video conferencing app on the home computer and get it to work. They would video-call every two weeks or so, which had been as much as Ben could stand. Maintaining the lie his life had become was stressful work—especially with a person as perceptive as Liling.

He would sometimes hear a distant forced hello from his father across the room. Both men seemed resigned to the fact this was all they could manage. Liling couldn't understand their reticence and she would scold Jiang: "Silly man, speak to Ben now!" But Jiang always had an excuse, or didn't want to budge from his favourite chair.

Ben endured the repeating pattern of the video call. Liling, as always, checked on his health, his diet, his sleep, his studies. And his relationships, as if there would be any. He would tell her enough to keep her at bay.

But on this day, she needed more. "When are you coming home?" she asked. "It's been eight months. When will you be done?"

"Not until next year, maybe by mid-year."

"*Next year?* It cannot take so long to fly a silly plane!"

"It takes that long to become a commercial pilot."

Liling sighed angrily. "This is crap, this commercial flight nonsense."

"It's what I want to do."

"Where will you work? Cathay Pacific?"

"I don't know yet," Ben said.

"So many plans, yet so much you don't know about them. It doesn't fill me with confidence."

They fell silent. Mother and son stared at each other, seven thousand kilometres apart.

"Can you come home for a break soon, at least?" Liling almost pleaded.

"Maybe at the end of this year. I'll be busy for the next few months."

"We miss you," she said. "I miss you."

"I know."

"It's *too long.*"

Ben could feel the lump building in his throat. He focused on his breathing to keep a lid on his emotions and the physical reactions they could induce. "Ma, I have to go."

Liling forced a smile. "What, are you being attacked by kangaroos?"

Ben couldn't help smiling at that. "They're pretty vicious, you know."

But then her voice, and her facial expression, changed. "*Wǒ ài nǐ yī shēng yī shì,*" she whispered in Mandarin. The words, *I will love you forever,* knifed through Ben's defences. He inhaled sharply and held his breath, no longer thinking.

Neither of his parents had said anything like "I love you" to him before. They didn't need to. Like most parents in China, they expressed love for their children by fussing over them, protecting them, guiding them, giving them gifts. Those words, so valued in the West, were an awkward and embarrassing expression in Chinese culture.

Ben held his breath. His thoughts would not crystallise.

Liling sensed his dilemma. "My child," she said softly, "you don't need to say anything. Coming home is all you need to do."

CHAPTER TWENTY-ONE

There are only two emotions in a plane: boredom and terror.

—Orson Welles

12 August 2023, 2:40 PM

Deputy Premier Matthew Cash was no stranger to Hobart Airport. He'd flown in and out so many times on state business, he thought he should own shares in the place. But he suspected this trip would be different.

Cash heaved down on the flight helmet to force it onto his head. As he looked up, he saw Bradfurd Rouse kitted-out in his flight gear. And what a sight he was. Replete in a one-piece khaki jumpsuit, a yellow horse collar life vest around his neck, a large white helmet enveloping his head, all set off by an ungainly pair of thick black goggles stretched atop the helmet.

My goodness, how ridiculous he looks, Cash thought, but then realised he probably looked as ridiculous as Rouse.

The aircraft loadmaster, Second Aircrewman Sabatini, waved his hands upward to indicate they should both take off their helmets. He would have told them so, but their helmets were almost soundproof. "Just a dry run," he said. "May as well go ahead and leave 'em off till the others get here."

"We're supposed to leave at three o'clock," Cash mumbled to Rouse. "Where the hell are those TV people?"

"I'll call them," Rouse said, getting to work on his phone.

But on cue, the crew of two from Network-8 burst through the door of the corporate flight lounge.

"Sorry we're late. Traffic," Stephanie Sadler said. She waved one hand away as if to dismiss her own apology, then dropped an equipment case to the floor with a solid thud.

Sabatini smiled. "No problem, ma'am. Can I help you with those?"

"Oh yes, thanks," she said, as she dropped her other bags. Sadler's concept of chivalry would extend to carrying nothing at all for the rest of the journey.

"What the *fuck* is *she* doing here?" Cash asked Rouse in a rapid-fire whisper. "Where's De Vries?"

Sadler sensed his question. "Good afternoon, Deputy Premier. Peter went home sick this morning. I was available, so the newsroom gave me this assignment, like, just two hours ago. But should be fun, don't you reckon?"

Fun was the last thing on Cash's mind. Rouse had used his coercive talents to make sure Peter De Vries would be the journalist. De Vries was a known quantity and they could rely on him to carry the government's line. He shunned controversy and on-camera dramatics, precisely what they needed for this assignment.

Steph Sadler was as close to the opposite of Peter De Vries as they came. At age twenty-five, she was an up-and-coming journalist with a crystal-clear vision of where she wanted her career to take her. Sadler would be an international correspondent for a reputable network one day. She knew this to be inevitable, as if painted in the stars. Nothing and no one would stop her.

As far as female TV news talent went, Sadler had it all going on. Tall, leggy, glowing teeth with a warm smile, and straightish shoulder-length blonde hair. But not your classic beach-girl blonde, her round face more pleasant than stunning. She was intelligent, a sponge for facts and knowledge, feisty, tenacious, and never one to shirk from a verbal tussle. A journalist most politicians would prefer to avoid, but rarely could.

Cash half-nodded in her direction—barely able to acknowledge her presence, let alone her explanation.

Sabatini asked Sadler and the TV camera/sound operator, Bruce Wardlaw, to follow him into another room to get their flight gear.

"That bastard at the network will pay for this!" Cash snarled. "If that little cow does or says *one* thing out of step, I'll get her bloody catapulted right off the ship. You mark my words."

"I know, I know," Rouse said. "I'll do what I can, but she's no tame little filly, that one."

"I don't give a toss. It's your job to control her. Use a cattle prod for all I care."

"I'll brief her once we get there. It'll be okay."

"Make sure of it."

Sadler and Wardlaw returned five minutes later. They too had been kitted-out in jumpsuits and life vests with helmets and goggles in hand.

"Okay, folks, time to go flying," Sabatini said. "Please follow me outside. Keep your cranial off for now. I'll brief you some more before we get y'all on board."

The four passengers followed him onto the corporate aviation ramp.

Flying had never fazed Cash. He liked aeroplanes, so he was happy to travel in whatever the U.S. Navy provided that day.

"There's our trusty steed," Sabatini quipped, pointing towards a plane with two eight-blade propellers mounted on stubby wings. The wide tail section sported four vertical fins and a rear-facing loading ramp lowered to the ground below. Its thick fuselage ended with a nose that was bulbous and swollen, as if the aircraft designer had made the fuselage too narrow for the cockpit and then stretched it outwards as an afterthought.

"What the hell is that thing?" Wardlaw asked. "Looks like an antique."

"A C-2A Greyhound," Sabatini replied, looking somewhat offended. "It delivers freight, people, mail, parts, weapons … all that kind'a gear. The strike group would be lost without these old girls."

"Why's it called a Greyhound?" Rouse asked.

"Good question. I don't know. It doesn't go very fast. And it's not exactly a sleek little thing either."

"Old girls? How old?" Wardlaw asked. The look of concern on his face had deepened.

"Oh, this design first came into service way back in the 1960s. This girl is about twenty-five years old. She's getting retired to the boneyard straight after this cruise. Last of this breed, ya know."

Bruce Wardlaw had turned a shade of green.

Another member of the flight crew, who'd been checking things around the plane, ambled over to the group. He looked in his early to mid-twenties. "Howdy folks," he said in a twangy Kentucky accent. "I'm Lieutenant Mitcham, Commanding Officer for our flight today."

Cash had incorrectly sized up the man as another rear crewman. He turned his own shade of green—not as green as Wardlaw, but getting there. "I'm Matthew Cash, Deputy Premier," he said as he shook the pilot's hand.

"Good to have y'all with us, sir. I'm sure the captain is looking forward to your visit. We loaded up your freight boxes earlier ... it all looked mighty nice."

"That's our pleasure. We hope all on the ship will enjoy some of our fine Tasmanian produce."

"Hell, yeah. Looking forward to it! Now, we'll be hittin' the sky in about ten minutes, so I'll go get strapped in. Just wanna let you know ... weather's a bit interesting off your west coast. Sure knows how to blow hard out there. Sea's up too. We can expect a few bumps. Landing might be a little interesting. But nothin' at all to worry about."

Shades of green grew greener. Hard gulps all around. Except for Steph Sadler, who was busy snapping images for her Instagram feed.

*　*　*　*

First class? No way. Business Class? Nah. Economy class? Not even close. The navy-blue passenger seat Matthew Cash crammed himself into was padded alright, but that was the extent of comforts on board. Cramped leg space, no air-conditioning, and no seat-back entertainment. He couldn't even scroll through messages or listen to music on his phone thanks to the sound-gobbling cranial and the goggles encasing his head.

Cash, Rouse, Sadler, Wardlaw and Sabatini sat among sixteen rear-facing seats arranged in four rows at the rear of the aeroplane. A wire cage separated the passenger seats from the cargo area.

The only consolation for Cash was being seated next to the one-and-only passenger window on his side of the plane. If he leaned forward and twisted he could just see outside, but it was a struggle against the safety harness and the weight of the cranial.

Everything—the pipes, wires, cables, and hardware—inside the plane were laid as bare as the internals of a patient on a CT scan. Everything was either scratched, dented, or worn—or all three. And a strange placard had been taped on the retracted cargo door: IN COD WE TRUST.

This must be like flying on Aeroflot last century? Cash wondered to himself, *And who is this Cod bloke?*

Sabatini sat next to Cash to provide reassuring in-flight commentary. Cash guessed it must be the protocol given he was the top-dog guest on the flight. If the young man yelled at the top of his voice, Cash could hear him over the engine noise—sometimes.

Cash sensed the plane turn at the far end of the runway. The engine noise and cabin vibration were already extreme, but it was nothing compared to the next stage of the flight. The deep turboprop engine growl and the throbbing harmonic song of the propellers went to a level of cacophony Cash could scarce believe was mechanically possible.

"Here we go!" Sabatini yelled.

The entire plane began to shake, vibrate, rattle, and complain bitterly. The passenger cabin felt like it would shake to pieces. Then Cash was abruptly shoved into his rear-facing seat as the C-2A Greyhound sprung from its starting position and hurtled down the runway.

Cash clenched his fists and closed his eyes. For a moment, he was tempted to pray. But it had been too many years since Sunday School in Branxholm. He might have prayed to the mysterious Cod if he'd known who the hell that deity was.

Cash wrestled with his thoughts instead. *Why the hell did I volunteer for this? I could bloody cark it in this shit-can!* But he hadn't complained when the U.S. Navy had suggested he, one of his staff, and a TV news crew be flown out to the carrier the day before it was due into Hobart. He was the best choice, given he had initiated the visit on behalf of the Tasmanian government and moved heaven and hell to make it happen. And the public relations benefits were too big to ignore—or so Rouse had promised.

As the plane at last pitched upwards and left the ground, the vibration and noise reduced. Sabatini resumed his in-flight commentary but still yelling to be heard. "Pretty wicked, huh? But that's nothing. When we get shot off the carrier, man ... *that's* somethin' else."

Cash nodded to feign appreciation, but he badly wanted to cave in the commentator's cranial in that moment. He glanced past the aircrewman and eyed Bruce Wardlaw seated on the opposite side of the plane. His body was erect to the point of backwards contortion, his fingers buried deep into his seat in a terrifying death grip. One thing was for sure—if the plane crashed, they would find Wardlaw's hands still holding that seat cushion.

*   *   *   *

Overhead the Tasmanian central highlands
1528 hours

The Greyhound had levelled out at 12,000 feet, twenty minutes into the forty-five-minute trip. The vibration and noise had settled back further. But then, to Cash's anguish, they flew into a stiff blustery south-westerly wind throwing turbulence into the atmosphere as it slammed into the rugged peaks of Tasmania's remote south-west ranges.

The Greyhound could handle turbulence alright. But passenger comfort had not been a design consideration. Its ungainly wings and thick fuselage barrelled through the air with limited flexibility. The only real flex was in the passenger seat cushioning and the rumps of the passengers sitting in those seats.

And didn't Matthew Cash know it. Each gust resulted in a violent thump downwards or a swift ballooning upwards. A downward movement would give the powerful illusion of the seat slamming up through Cash's abdomen, and was often followed by a distinct cracking sound as the airframe absorbed the sudden change in wind direction and velocity. An upwards movement would induce the terror of plunging down a loop on a rollercoaster, followed by the nauseating sensation of his stomach merging with his chest as the force of gravity abruptly morphed from the negative to the positive.

After a further ten minutes of the airborne washing machine experience, the spin cycle was winding down. The Greyhound had crossed the west coast near Strahan and tracked towards the carrier twenty miles out to sea. Cash could sense the aeroplane still descending, then entering a steep left-hand turn.

Sabatini leaned over and peered through the window. He motioned for Cash to look. Cash took in a desolate seascape of deep greys and blacks under a menacing overcast sky. The rolling swells were visibly high, even from an altitude of five hundred feet. Angry white caps broke on the surface, their foamy extrusions decapitated by the howling wind and vaporised to nothing.

And there, above the bottom edge of the window, a large object in the ocean caught his eye. The object's many shades of grey camouflaged its bulk against the sea, but the frothy long wake of USS *John F. Kennedy* pointed to its position with no mistake.

"There's Mom!" Sabatini yelled.

Yep, he enjoys his job just a bit too much.

The left turn kept going, which kept "Mom" just within Cash's field of view. The ship looked increasingly large, yet somehow small in the expanse of the surrounding sea.

Turbulence returned as they descended towards the surface, although it was different this time—frequent short, jarring thumps. The equivalent of driving too fast down a corrugated bush track in an old car with worn-out suspension.

The landing area on the flight deck, marked with bright white lines and dashes, looked incredibly small. *Must be the angle we're on,* Cash thought in a valiant attempt to reassure himself.

The carrier slipped out of sight as the pilot banked the plane onto final approach. Cash resumed the Bruce Wardlaw death grip on either side of his seat cushion.

*   *   *   *

Up front in the Greyhound's cockpit, Lieutenant Mitcham was all eyes, hands, and feet. He worked the control yoke and column in his left hand like a coal miner with a blunt drill. His constant control inputs adjusted the plane's attitude to the horizon—*forward, then back a touch, forward again, hold it, trim it out*—while simultaneously managing the bank angle of his turn with short sharp jabs of the control wheel—*left, centre it, right, right a touch more, centre it, hold it now.* His right hand gripped and worked the two engine thrust levers—*forward a touch, back, stable, back again, forward.* His feet pummelled the rudder pedals left and right, punching the nose-direction of the plane into submission and fighting the wind gusts to stay aligned with the centreline on the carrier's landing area.

His co-pilot could only sit rigidly in her seat and trust the procedures and systems to do their thing. Her job was done, and she was glad not to be the pilot flying this sector. It was all up to the CO.

On final approach, at less than a mile from the carrier, she reported in on the radio: "Six-eighty-three, Greyhound, ball, three-point-four."

Mitcham had the vertical guidance lights in his view—the *meatball,* or just *the ball,* as it was called. The ball—a bright yellow light—moved up and down relative to a horizontal line, or datum, of green lights. If the ball appeared above the datum, the plane was too high. If the ball appeared below the datum, they were too low. If it was on the datum, the plane was right where he wanted it—on the correct vertical slope to touchdown and with a reasonable chance of hooking one of the three arresting wires in the landing area.

The landing signals officer, standing on a small platform off the flight deck next to the arresting wires, acknowledged the radio call: "Roger ball."

The LSO—an experienced C-2A pilot—would monitor the approach. He'd use all his experience and the video technology on the flight deck to help guide his colleague down to a safe arrested landing—or *trap*, as they called it—providing him with verbal feedback over the radio as needed. He knew where the aeroplane needed to be at every second of the final approach phase.

"You're high," the LSO said, deadpan.

The carrier pitched up and down as it wallowed through each swell in the heavy sea. The deck angled up, then down, rotating through a range of ten degrees away from the level, and it moved away from the aeroplane at a speed of fifteen knots. The only constant was the size of the landing area itself—ninety feet wide and five hundred feet long. More like a fast, floating postage stamp than a runway.

Mitcham had already sensed they were high. He pulled back the thrust levers and lowered the nose a touch. His eyes darted between the meatball and the white centreline on the carrier, and the primary flight display in the cockpit instrument panel. He noted every variation of aircraft speed, attitude, and vertical speed on the display. He felt it all too in his gut and in his butt. His hands and feet reacted to each variation without conscious thought, adjusting, trimming, tweaking, correcting.

Every parameter had to be spot on for landing. Changes in forward speed, vertical speed, and directional control had to stay within tight tolerances to make a successful trap. No second chances. Mitcham understood mistakes in this job rarely end well.

With three hundred yards to go, Mitcham was fully in the groove. To an untrained eye, he'd appear to be performing a bizarre dance at the controls. A dance so reliant on technical precision, yet so contingent on intuition and gut feel. A dance learned from thousands of hours of training and experience, and many hundreds of circuits and landings.

Few of those landings, however, had been in these conditions. This was about as bad as things got—not counting night carrier landings.

"A little power," the LSO said. Insistent, yet calm.

The aeroplane had not descended below the glideslope. But the stern of the ship and therefore the flight deck had moved upwards on a swell, shifting up six degrees in three seconds. Mitcham chased the pitching deck. He struggled with every ounce of his being to keep the plane lined up and within tolerances for the trap.

"Power. *Power—*"

The rear edge of the carrier flight deck was now only fifty feet ahead and slipping under the nose. The deck continued to rise towards the plane and Mitcham realised the dreaded wave-off command from the LSO might come soon, obliging him to abort the landing and fly around for another attempt.

He continued the fight, dancing with rapid control inputs, straining for the landing. Then they'd come to the point where touchdown was inevitable. Only time would tell whether the Greyhound's arrestor hook would grab one of the three arresting wires and bring the plane to a halt. About one-quarter of a second of time, to be precise.

*   *   *   *

Back in the passenger cabin, Matthew Cash could sense every change in the pitch, yaw, and roll of the plane as the pilot wrestled it towards the carrier. He could hear and feel the engine thrust surging and falling.

The sudden jarring compression of touchdown was a bone-shuddering shock. To Cash, the experience felt like the plane had smashed into the ship's deck. And it had. For a carrier landing is more of a controlled crash and not so much a landing.

But more surprises were in store. The engines went to full power and Cash sensed the plane surge forward. He chanced a sideways glance out the window. The port-side edge of the flight deck and two crew members in coloured shirts flashed past his view. And then, only the open and angry sea.

* * * *

"Bolter, bolter!" the LSO called over the radio.

Mitcham was doing a bolter alright. The Greyhound's arresting hook had missed all the wires. There was no real danger, however. With the engines already back to maximum thrust, the aeroplane lifted off at the far end of the flight deck and took to the sky. They'd do a circuit, come back around, and have another go.

No one wanted a bolter, but such things were a fact of life and all in a day's work.

* * * *

Sabatini sensed Cash's ratcheting anxiety. "Don't worry," he yelled. "Happens all the time. We'll come back around and trap the next one for sure."

Three minutes later, a trap was precisely what occurred. The arresting hook grabbed the number two arresting wire. Cash felt the sudden deceleration from one hundred and ten knots airspeed to nothing in two seconds. The sensation of being yanked forward into his harness by the g-force was pure ecstasy compared to the dreaded feeling of anticipating a fatal crash.

As the plane turned off the landing area and taxied to the side, Cash could finally let go of his seat cushion. He attempted to breathe normally, but it would take a while.

The Greyhound's rear cargo ramp lowered to the flight deck, ending its slow hydraulic journey with a firm *dong* as metal met metal. The daylight streaking in from outside, together with rushes of cool air, were a welcome contrast to the dim cramped passenger cabin.

Sabatini was already out of his seat and preparing for the

disembarkation. He signalled to the passengers to release their harnesses and make their way to the rear of the plane.

Sadler and Rouse were first up. They seemed none the worse for wear, as if they'd enjoyed the ride.

Cash wasn't rushing things. His sustained adrenaline spike was only just subsiding. He struggled out of his seat and made his way to the exit, supporting his wobbly legs by gripping the headrests of the remaining seat rows.

Wardlaw sat staring ahead at the headrest before him, his fingers still buried in his seat cushion.

"Bruce. Hey Bruce!" Steph yelled. "You okay, old mate?"

He slowly looked at her, his neck muscles jerking with the consistency of a mechanical clown turning its head from side to side at sideshow alley. His wits were returning, but he could not get his brain and mouth to work together. And he was becoming uneasily aware of a dampness in the seat of his pants. Whether it was fluid, or solid, or both, he wasn't sure.

Sabatini made his way back to help Wardlaw out of his harness and onto his feet.

The poor cameraman no longer looked green once he was outside. He'd improved to ghostly white. The small damp spot in the back of his khaki jumpsuit was not that noticeable. The orange and green blend of fluids and small solids sprayed across his chest like a carbonated smoothie gone wrong was, however, unmistakable.

Cash relished being safely on the "ground"—until the horizon disappeared below the edge of the flight deck. A stark reminder he was on a ship and well out to sea.

There was little else, though, to indicate he'd stepped onto a ship. The flight deck was much bigger than he'd expected. The place crawled with what looked like aliens in coloured tops: white, green, red, yellow, blue, brown, and purple. And they all had globular heads with oversized black eyes. These aliens—the crew—obviously had to wear the goddamn cranials and goggles too.

"This flight deck is the most dangerous place you will ever visit," one of the crew members with a white top yelled at Cash, Rouse, Sadler, and Wardlaw from short range, struggling to be heard. "Follow me close in single file. Keep your head on a swivel. Look left, right, up, and down. Watch your step. Your eyes will keep you alive. Got it?"

They nodded in awestruck unison.

Cash heard a colossal thump and a deep rumble from behind him. His head swivelled, just as instructed, just in time to see a fighter jet come to a straining halt with its captured arrestor wire in tow. The tip of its nearest wing, he estimated, was about ten metres away. An intoxicating wave of heat and the pungent odour of jet fuel swamped his senses as the wash from the plane's jet engines swept across the deck. The sensation was a nauseating, unrefreshing change from the cold Southern Ocean wind.

Once they'd unhooked the plane, people were running everywhere and doing all sorts of things. The flight deck was alive with a silent language of hand signals. To Cash, it looked like utter chaos. But everyone seemed to understand the meaning of the particular colour of their shirt, and they carried out their tasks accordingly.

The white-shirted man didn't seem to mind the four visitors watching the newly arrived jet for a few seconds. It was then he noticed something wasn't right with Wardlaw.

Rouse noted the crewman's puzzled expression. He moved closer to shout into the side of the man's cranial: "He did a Technicolor yawn."

"A what?" the crewman asked.

"You know ... he laughed at the floor ... hurled his guts."

The crewman nodded, then led them on a weaving path between parked aircraft, vehicles, and trolleys stacked with bombs and missiles. They stepped over hoses and wires. They contorted themselves, as instructed, to avoid hitting their cranials on protruding bits of parked aircraft.

The obstacle course ended at the towering superstructure of the carrier's island. The group passed through a steel hatchway and emerged into another foreign world. The internal world of USS *John F. Kennedy*.

CHAPTER TWENTY-TWO

*I am not bound to win, but I am bound to be true. I am
not bound to succeed, but I am bound to live up to what
light I have.*

—Abraham Lincoln

USS John F. Kennedy, twenty-three miles west of Tasmania
12 August 2023, 1620 hours

"Hey, Bruce. Feeling any better?" Sadler asked.

"Yes, um, a bit," he replied. "Although if I hit my head on any more of these hatchways, I may have to revise that status."

Wardlaw had cleaned himself up, and all four visitors were back in civilian clothes. They'd been on board less than an hour, with each beginning to comprehend the extraordinary world below the flight deck. All were learning—the hard way—how to duck under and step over a knee-knocker door hatch in one movement, while compensating for the constant motion of the ship on the sea.

The ladders were also a challenge. They looked like narrow stairwells with handrails, but the navy term turned out to be a better description. Going up a ladder was one thing. Coming down at any reasonable speed was something else. Sadler had already been reprimanded for half-sliding down a handrail.

Wardlaw and Cash were often falling behind, then having to rush along the corridor to re-join their group. The ensign escorting them appeared to have a limited appreciation of the inexperience of his entourage.

Other members of the crew seemed more attentive. They would often step aside in the corridors and doorways to make way for the visitors. They'd give a "you're welcome" or a "ma'am" or a "sir," along with a nod or a pleasant smile.

Cash felt older with every crew encounter. Almost everyone he passed by seemed less than half his age.

The long march ended at a meeting room within the public relations office. The ensign knocked on the door.

"Come."

Two officers—a middle-aged man and a woman in her mid-thirties—were sitting beside a desk. They stood as the group entered.

The man thrust a hand at Cash. "I'm Captain Thomas Vanbeck, Executive Officer of the *John F. Kennedy*."

"Hello. I'm Matthew Cash. Tasmanian Deputy Premier."

"Welcome to you all. This is Lieutenant Emiko Nomura, our Senior Public Relations Officer."

Cash shook her hand. "Hello, Lieutenant," he said. She had a welcoming smile, but there was an unmistakable sternness behind it.

"Most people call me Emily," she said.

Cash introduced the group. Handshakes and smiles all around.

"Please, everyone take a seat," Vanbeck said. "Lieutenant Nomura and I will be with you for much of your visit. It'll be our pleasure to introduce you to the ship, the personnel, and how we do things around here."

"Thanks, I—" Sadler began.

Cash cut her off with elevated volume: "Yes, thank you. We are honoured and excited to be here, Captain."

Sadler glared at Cash, then at Rouse, who gave her a return glare that all but said "Shut the hell up," and she seemed to get the message.

Cash, Vanbeck, and Nomura talked through the pleasantries of the visit, including the arrival into Hobart and their time in port. Both parties seemed to be well in sync with the public relations arrangements and well aware of the sensitivities.

"I guess we should discuss the live interview," Nomura said, looking at Sadler. "It's scheduled for 6:00 PM, yes?"

"Yes, 6:00 PM is—" Rouse attempted to interject, but it was Sadler's turn to run an intercept.

"Thanks Brad, I'll handle this," she said with a smile, and satisfied in the knowledge he hated being called that. "The live cross will go to air at 6:02. It'll be part of the lead news story, following a brief introduction to the carrier and the visit. We'll be using some of your file footage, thank you, plus we need to get some grabs around the ship after this meeting."

"Yes, very good," Nomura replied. "The ensign and I will escort you around. We'll have approximately one hour. Will that give you enough time?"

"It will be tight but, yeah, should be fine. It's important we get fresh footage to amp up the story."

Wardlaw imagined the story editor back at the Network-8 studio cursing as he received raw video footage over the satellite link with half an hour before the story was to go to air. They both knew the importance of getting it right. Network-8 had been given the scoop. They would blitz the story ahead of rival networks, which had been given only generic media releases about the carrier visit hours earlier and would have to cobble their stories together using old file footage and sparse facts.

"Very good," Vanbeck said. "I'm afraid it'll be too rough outside to do your field report on the flight deck. We've rescheduled it to be in Pri-Fly instead. Still good views from there, but without the damn wind."

"That's a relief," Wardlaw commented. He wasn't inclined to manage video and sound in such awful conditions.

"Um, so, what is Pri-Fly?" Sadler asked.

Nomura grinned. "Oh, navy talk, sorry. It's primary flight control. It's our equivalent of an airport control tower and located one level up from the bridge."

"So, we'll meet the captain there?" Rouse asked.

"I'm the officer you'll be interviewing," Vanbeck said. "Captain Collins is not available."

"Oh. No problem," Rouse said with a weak smile.

"You'll meet Captain Collins later this evening, once he's off-watch."

* * * *

Melbourne, 4:50 PM

The chief flying instructor, Harvey Walters, examined the medical certificate without a flinch. He'd seen it all before. "Is there anything further you'd like to tell us, Ben?"

"No."

Walters said nothing and looked Ben in the eye.

Ben had no choice but to say something further. "Ah ... the doctor I have been seeing says I need a short break. To get better."

Ben had not seen or met the doctor. He'd picked up the certificate from Doctor Huang's surgery in South Melbourne, as per the mission brief.

Walters handed the certificate back with a passive grunt. "You've been doing so well. You could go places with your flying career, Ben."

"But I will be back. The certificate is only for two weeks."

"Hmm. But often students who need 'a break' don't come back at all. They chuck in the towel. Waste all they've done."

"I definitely plan to return."

"Okay. Well ... I'll let the other staff know about your time off."

Ben nodded.

Walters paused and continued his rock-steady gaze. "Look after yourself, young fella."

"Thank you, Mr Walters. I will."

* * * *

USS John F. Kennedy, 1735 hours

The hour following the meeting in the public relations office had been frenetic. Of all the thousands of humans aboard the carrier, Steph

Sadler was the person most definitely on a mission. Bruce Wardlaw did his best to keep up with a bulky video camera perched on one shoulder, his sound gear in a heavy bag slung over the other, and a small floodlight on a boom. They had traversed the decks and hangars below to grab whatever preliminary footage they could of life and work aboard the carrier. Nomura and the ensign guided Sadler through places she could go and steered her away from places she could not.

They made it back to the visitors' meeting room exhausted. With no time to rest, Wardlaw had the video files running through the satellite uplink five minutes later. He did his best not to think of the editor back at the studio. The poor guy would be fuming by then, but such was life in the news business.

Sadler and the ensign were back in the corridor and heading at a rapid pace towards Pri-Fly. Wardlaw grabbed his gear and did his best to catch up. "Bloody talent," he cursed. "No respect."

*　*　*　*

Things would be quiet in Pri-Fly for the evening as the carrier made its way south. Flight operations had mostly ceased for the day, except for E-2 Hawkeyes taking turns to conduct early warning surveillance high up in the skies above the carrier, and pairs of F/A-18s taking turns to conduct air patrols in wide circles around the carrier's position. Catapult launches—or "cats"—and traps on the flight deck had been scheduled to occur during the live cross for dramatic effect.

Wardlaw kept busy as he prepared his camera, sound gear, and the satellite communications equipment. He'd read the Assistant Air Officer's grunt and glare towards him as being none too cooperative and attempted to be as unobtrusive as possible.

The mini-boss, as they called him on the ship, had more important work to do. A TV news crew was an unwelcome distraction from the business of safe flight operations. And he was none too happy about having to coordinate a trap and a cat to fit in with *their* schedule.

But with Vanbeck, a high-ranking superior officer, also in Pri-Fly for the interview, the mini-boss would keep any complaints to himself.

Sadler had finished a preliminary walk-through of the live cross with Nomura and Vanbeck. She was busy scribbling notes when Rouse, who had tagged along uninvited, sidled up close to her. *You slimy creep*, she thought while doing her utmost to ignore his presence.

"All good to go, Steph?" he asked at close to a whisper.

"Yep."

"I trust you're across all the parameters for this one?"

"Yep," Sadler replied. "We cross live at 6:02, for a minute and thirty seconds."

"You know that's not what I mean."

"Do I?"

"C'mon, Steph. This is important."

"What, you think I don't know that?"

"It's just ... I've had no chance to brief you for this assignment."

"Peter gave me the low-down before he went off sick, plus our news editor read me your riot act. I think I'm briefed plenty, thanks all the same."

"My riot act?"

"C'mon, Rouse. Don't act the innocent."

She had him there. Rouse's influence with certain journalists was better known than even he understood.

"Just work with us, Steph. *Please.* This is important for a lot of reasons, maybe more than you realise."

"Yeah. So important for Tassie, blah, blah, blah. I got it."

"Important for your career, too, Steph."

And he had her there.

"Whatever," she said, as she half-turned away. "Now piss off and let me prepare."

*   *   *   *

1802 hours

Video of life on board the carrier, plus snippets of flight operations, were flowing through the broadcast feed as the newsreader finished reading her lines off the teleprompter:

"... and with the *John F. Kennedy* expected in Hobart in coming days, we cross now for an exclusive report from our correspondent, Steph Sadler, who is on board the carrier."

Sadler appeared on screen, Network-8 microphone in hand, with the windows of Pri-Fly behind her. There was just enough light remaining in the western sky to illuminate the sea beyond the ship. Floodlights on the island lit up the flight deck and rows of parked aircraft to create a pleasing foreground.

"Steph, how's life at sea on a U.S. Navy aircraft carrier?"

"Thanks, Lucy. It's amazing to find myself on this floating city out here on the high seas. The flight here was interesting in our Tassie weather, I must say, and landing on the carrier was an experience I'll never forget," she said with a slight giggle. "But it's incredible now we're on board. We've been warmly welcomed here by the officers and crew."

"Sounds tremendous. And what are your first impressions of life on the ship?"

"Oh. It's much bigger than I imagined. There are so many decks and spaces here, and thousands of people at work. This truly is an incredible place."

In the background, an E-2 Hawkeye landed on the flight deck with a thump and a distant roar. Right on time.

"And where is the carrier now, Steph?"

"We are off Tasmania's west coast and making our way down towards Maatsuyker Island. The ship will come up the Derwent and into Hobart sometime tomorrow, we believe."

"And I understand the carrier will be here for an extended stay?" the newsreader asked, carrying on with the script.

Sadler took two steps to her right, and Wardlaw panned the camera to follow. "Yes, that's right, Lucy. And with me now is the Executive

Officer of the ship, Captain Thomas Vanbeck."

Vanbeck, wearing his service dress blue uniform, came into the shot as the camera panned.

"Captain Vanbeck, welcome to Tasmania. We understand the carrier will be in Hobart for a week?"

"Thank you, Ms Sadler. Yes. All of our officers and crew are looking forward to visiting Hobart and Tasmania. It's important for our people to get a break after working so hard at sea for the past six months, and equally important for us to visit our friends and say hi from time to time."

"It's been twenty years since a U.S. carrier has visited Hobart. Why now?"

"Oh, that's just the way schedules and deployments work out. The Fleet Commander tells us where and when to go, and we follow our orders. But Australia is always high on our list, you know."

"I see. And what do you have planned for the crew in Hobart during the visit?"

"Many of our folks will get to enjoy some liberty to explore your beautiful island, and no doubt some of your famous food, beer, and wine. And there's community events and projects we'll take part in."

"So not all play while you're here, then?"

"No, but we're all looking forward to it, I'm sure."

"Fantastic. And will you be going back to the Middle East after Hobart?"

"Ah, no. We'll be heading home."

"You mentioned you've all been working hard. Has it been tough being stationed in the Middle East?"

Vanbeck shifted his standing position. "It's always interesting there. Lots of influences in the one place ... they can create tension sometimes. But that's why this aircraft carrier and our strike group exists. We project freedom and stability. We're pleased to sail into those regions and support those who support freedom."

"And those who *don't* support freedom?"

Behind Vanbeck, an F/A-18 fighter had been catapulted into the night sky, roaring away with its twin plumes of sharpened blue afterburner illuminating all behind it.

"Well, let's just say … our presence helps those folks direct their intentions."

"I'm guessing all those aircraft out on the deck help with that?"

"Yes. This is a warship."

A half-second of silence followed. Sadler was still processing his comment and framing her next question.

Behind the camera, Nomura looked ashen. She mimed slashing her throat to Vanbeck.

He appeared to get her meaning. "However," he continued before Sadler could ask her next question, "we're not in the Middle East now. We're right here in sunny Australia—one of our key allies and closest friends. We're glad to park our planes for a good while and enjoy your great country, and this beautiful state we hear so many good things about."

"Thank you, Captain Vanbeck. We hope you enjoy your stay."

"I'm sure I will. And thank you."

Sadler faced the camera. "And I'm about to enjoy some U.S. navy cooking with the crew, Lucy. So, from Steph Sadler, aboard the USS *John F. Kennedy* … the freedom boat … it's back to you in the studio …"

Sadler continued to smile at the camera, holding her pose for three seconds.

"We're out," Wardlaw announced.

Vanbeck said nothing further and marched out of Pri-Fly, followed by Rouse.

Nomura stepped forward to lock eyes with Steph. "The freedom boat, huh?" she almost hissed.

"Yup. That's what he said."

"Actually, that's what *you* said."

"I guess we're in agreement, then."

*   *   *   *

USS John F. Kennedy, the captain's cabin

2145 hours

"Thank you for your time, Captain Collins. We're very pleased to be here," Cash said with an oleaginous grin.

"You're welcome," Collins replied, while secretly wishing his sixteen-hour workday could end in any other way. Meetings with politicians, for Collins, was the equivalent of swimming with alligators in the dark.

"And this is my Chief of Staff, Bradfurd Rouse," Cash continued.

"Captain," was all Rouse could manage as Collins shook his hand.

"Gentleman ... please take a seat."

Cash felt an overwhelming urge to salute and say, "Sir, yes, sir," but managed to suppress it.

Collins wasted no time with small talk. "Vice Admiral Garrison tells me you folks are all set."

"Yes. Much work has gone into the planning. Everything is as prepared and ready as it can be."

"Good. That's what I like to hear. And good to know you've found us a better anchorage, nice'n close to the city."

"Our pleasure, Captain. We hope this will make things easier for you and the crew."

"And maybe next time we could go right into the pier. Save us all those damn boat rides."

Cash laughed at the joke, with Rouse chuckling insincerely. But Collins was unmoved.

After five awkward seconds, Collins got back to business: "Let's go ahead and discuss your preparations. Make sure we're all on the same page."

The three men talked through the key aspects of the visit including the official engagements, social activities, community events, crew transportation, and ship security. Cash then realised, to his regret, it was time to discuss the possibility of protestors and how they were to be handled. "Bradfurd," Cash said, motioning towards the carry-bag beside him.

Rouse rummaged inside the bag. He withdrew a bottle of whisky—beautifully presented in a dark brown heritage box with exquisite red lettering. "For you, Captain," Rouse effused. "A gift to say welcome from the Tasmanian government."

"Oh my," Collins said, taking the box. "Well, thank you. Thank you very much."

He examined the lettering. This was, he discovered, a bottle of limited release single malt whisky from the Lark Distillery in Hobart. "I recognise this brand, but I haven't had the pleasure of tasting it yet."

"Ah, well, that bottle is for you captain, and *this one*—" Rouse said, pulling another bottle out of his bag— "is for us to share this evening. Do you have some glasses we could use?"

Rouse had uncorked the bottle before Collins had a chance to reply.

"No whisky glasses. I'm afraid we have a no-alcohol policy aboard the ship."

"Oh, I'm sorry," Cash said. "But perhaps just one drink to celebrate your arrival?"

"Yeah, I'm sorry too. But rules are rules," Collins said. "No alcohol."

But Rouse, ever the schmoozer, would not back down. "Perhaps not all the rules apply to you so strictly ... being the captain and all?"

Collins shifted in his chair to face Rouse. His left eye twitched as he exhaled through his nostrils. "We have a saying in the United States Navy, Mr Rouse. It's 'loyalty up and loyalty down'. You ever heard that?"

"Ah ... no, no ... I haven't."

"I figured as much. The saying was coined by one of our most respected admirals. He understood the rules, behaviour, ethics—all of it—are as important at the top as they are at the bottom."

Rouse shifted in his chair and his cheeks reddened.

Collins did not let up. "There is nothing, Mr Rouse, that I would expect the men and women on this ship to do and not also do myself. *Nothing.*"

A myriad of potential clever responses flooded Rouse's brain. But what to say?

"I just thought, maybe you could bend the rules, you know … just this once," Rouse blurted out, giving a wink as he did. "We won't say a word."

Collins was having none of it. "My integrity is what counts. Not my rank, or what you might or might not tell others. I will not say one thing and then do another. Do we understand each other, Mr Rouse?"

Rouse was certain he understood. *Of course I understand ethics,* he thought. *I've been dancing 'round them my whole bloody career!* He tried his utmost not to flinch as he struggled for his next words.

But he needn't have bothered. "Ensign!" Collins called, not moving a muscle or breaking his steady glare at Rouse. His left eye twitched again.

"Sir," the ensign snapped as he entered the room.

"Escort Mr Rouse to his quarters. He's calling it a night while I continue discussions with Mr Cash."

"Yes, sir."

Rouse spun his head around to look at Cash, dumbfounded. But he saw no sympathy there.

"This way, Mr Rouse," the ensign said.

"I appreciate your hospitality and the kind gift, Mr Cash," Collins said as the door closed behind them. "But please see to it your Mr Rouse does not attend any further meetings or events where I am present."

"Yes, sir."

CHAPTER TWENTY-THREE

*It will be difficult to describe my feelings at the sight of
this solitary harbour situated at the extremities of the
globe, so perfectly enclosed that one feels separated
from the rest of the universe.*
　　　　—Admiral Bruni d'Entrecasteaux, *Ship's Log 1793*

*USS John F. Kennedy, three miles south-west
of Maatsuyker Island
13 August 2023, 0642 hours*

It was still murky outside in the pre-dawn light. Visibility at sea level was a half-mile at best, given the patchy fog and low clouds of spray hanging in the ocean air. Just ahead, a beam of white light was barely discernible through the greyish murk.

A white flash.

7.5 seconds.

Another white flash.

7.5 seconds.

A third white flash.

Then nothing, for a time.

Captain William A. Collins lowered his binoculars and turned his attention to the nautical chart half-rolled out on the bench beside the captain's chair. He had digital navigation displays he could consult nearby, but Collins preferred to do some things the old way. A pair of eyes, a watch, a compass, and a trustworthy sea chart.

The chart symbology "Fl. W. 7.5 (3) in 30" confirmed what he knew to be there—the lighthouse of Maatsuyker Island casting its tell-tale flashes of brilliant white across the Southern Ocean. "Confirming Maatsuyker Island light," he said.

"Yes, Captain," the navigator replied. "GPS correlates. We are three miles south-west of the light, bearing zero-four-eight."

"Very well."

There was still a good half-hour before the sun would break the horizon to the east. The hint of dawn was still too feeble to illuminate features of the coastline to their north and east. But the light of the Maatsuyker lighthouse was the first actual evidence of the near presence of the main island—Tasmania—four miles further north of Maatsuyker.

Collins maintained a steady watch on the flashes of light as he waited for the ship to pass beyond the southern tip of Maatsuyker Island and away to the east. "What's our ETA for the turn into the Derwent?" he asked.

"ETA at our current speed of fifteen knots is … 0920 hours, Captain. That's seventy minutes ahead of planned ETA."

This was not a day to be early—or late. "Quartermaster, re-plot a course to come north, then east to follow the coast at close quarters, keeping us deep."

"Aye, Captain. North, then east. Follow the coast, staying deep," the ship's chief navigator confirmed. He'd come on watch for the challenging arrival into port.

"Officer of the deck. Reduce RPM to maintain ten knots."

"Reduce RPM, maintain ten knots, aye, Captain," the officer confirmed.

Collins waited for her to relay the required commands to the conning officer manning the engine controls. "You have the deck. I'll be outside for five mikes."

"Aye, Captain. I have the deck."

*   *   *   *

Vulture's Row, as it was affectionately known, was an exposed walkway mounted high up on the carrier's superstructure and a favourite place for naval aviators to watch flight operations. Collins had spent many hours there earlier in his career, back when he flew the F-14 Tomcat.

He pulled his cap down low, zipped up his bomber jacket, and flipped the lambswool collar upwards. They were no real match, though, for the biting cold air of the Southern Ocean as it whipped across the carrier's deck. The air was delivered direct from Antarctica courtesy of a deep low-pressure system centred two hundred miles to the south-west. Very little of the bone-shivering cold was lost as it travelled from the great white ice continent at the bottom of the earth.

There were no flight operations to watch from Vulture's Row that morning. The row and the flight deck were deserted, except for an officer standing halfway along the walkway and peering at the view off the ship's port side.

"Mornin'," Collins said as he leaned on the railing a few yards from where she stood.

She seemed startled at first, and even more so when she turned to reply, "Oh, Captain. Um, mornin', sir," she managed.

They stood in silence for a time, each peering into the thinning fog.

"Land ahoy," Collins said.

A mile and a half ahead of the carrier, a looming black mass was being revealed, its features materialising in the ghostly light. A sizable promontory, towering much higher than the ship, came into view.

"Yes, I see it now. Land it is," she said.

The sea churned and thrashed at its base. Plumes of white spray shot upwards and hung in the air. They could hear a thumping crash as each wave met its abrupt end on the vertical granite cliff-face, even over the blustering wind. And above, where the headland curved and disappeared into the landmass behind, slow-moving rivers of fog arced over the edge and down towards the sea, disappearing imperceptibly as the heavy condensation leeched from the air.

"This place," Collins said, still staring at the coast, "it's like no other."

They continued to gaze in silence. The female officer didn't need to reply or comment. The scene before them seemed beyond the bounds of language, something greater than humanity could conceive or express. This was even greater than the technological marvel they stood upon. The greatest work of humankind seemed a mere transient stain on the beauty and power of the natural world in all her ghostly morning glory.

As the ship turned further east and tracked along the coastline, the mass of the promontory disappeared off the port stern. The scene gave way to a remote ocean beach within a sharp curving bay, hemmed by rolling hills covered in dense green vegetation. They could see no hint of human presence, just an empty bay. A desolate beach, untouched hills, and thick virgin coastal forest.

"It's an ancient place, this," Collins said.

"Yeah. It's like no one has been here before. Like we're seeing it for the first time."

"One of the few places in the world like it," Collins reflected. "I love it here."

"You've been here before, sir?"

"Yeah. Twice, actually. The first time was many years back when I was a pilot on the *Stennis*. I fell for the place then and swore to God I'd come back to see it in my own time. We finally got to do that five years ago. Spent a few weeks in Tasmania, including one week right there," he said, nodding towards the coast.

"Oh. But it looks so remote along there?"

"Yeah. It's absolutely remote. And wild. But there's a hiking trail called the South Coast Track. You can't see it unless you're right on it, but it goes all the way along this coast and into Bathurst Harbour out west. Hikers use it in the warmer months."

"That must be quite somethin'."

"Hmm. Yep. Sure is. No one around for miles and miles. No roads, vehicles, phones, civilisation ... nothing."

"Wow," she said softly.

"Places like this, they do you good, you know. Kinda restore your soul, so to speak."

She nodded again, as if appreciating his wisdom. They continued to watch the unfolding landscape as it slipped by, standing in reverent awe.

Collins sensed it was time he returned to the bridge. As he turned, he caught a better glimpse of the officer standing beside him. She continued to look over the port side of the ship with her head tilted to her right. A few wisps of her brown hair had escaped the grip of her hair tie and were dancing in the breeze.

Collins shot out a hand and grasped the railing to steady himself. His knees went loose while his chest tightened. His peripheral vision blurred away.

She looked towards him. His face was ashen, which was no surprise given the temperature of the morning air, but his eyes betrayed a level of distress. "Are you okay, sir?" she asked.

He didn't reply. His eyes remained fixated on her, yet also fixed on somewhere else. On a woman who would sometimes admire the world with an identical look, her wisps of brown hair blowing in the wind.

"Sir?"

"Oh. Sorry, I was just light-headed there for a second."

"All good, sir."

He grabbed the hatchway handle, but stopped before going in. "Lieutenant Commander ... Sorry, I didn't get your name?"

"That's okay, sir. It's Marlowe."

"Just Marlowe?"

She chuckled. "Katherine, sir. Katherine Marlowe."

"Well, Katherine, not many people get to enjoy this place for what it really is. Make some time to get out of the city while you're here. Take a look around."

"Thank you, sir ... Was that an order, sir?" she asked with a glint in her eye.

Collins laughed. "Yeah, why not. This place will be good for you." He opened the hatch and disappeared inside.

Katherine looked back at the coast. The scene became brighter and clearer by the second, with the first hints of direct sunlight glancing off the fog in the distance.

Maybe he's right, she thought. *Maybe I'll do just that.*

*   *   *   *

1056 hours

"Approaching the turn, Captain," the chief navigator said.

"Very well," Collins replied.

They were still ahead of their ETA of 1100 hours, but only by a few minutes. Time to turn north-east and begin the complex track up the River Derwent to their anchorage point near Hobart, sixty miles upstream.

The ship's bridge buzzed with focused activity. The chief navigator had control of the ship, supported by the officer of the deck, his junior officer, as well as navigation, communications, and conning officers in various stations. Extra lookouts had been posted to monitor the fore, aft, port, and starboard sides of the ship.

Collins sat in the Captain's chair. He watched and listened intently and he tracked other nautical traffic through his binoculars. He kept a careful eye and ear on every station on the bridge, and every command and corresponding response from the officers and crew. He appeared to be a passive observer, but he was leaving nothing to chance. Everything would be done with precision and as ordered. There would be no mistakes on this watch.

He'd addressed the officers and crew over the 1MC earlier that morning. Collins left them in no doubt of the standard of conduct expected while ashore in Hobart. They were to enjoy themselves, yes, but absolutely not at the expense of the reputation of the United States Navy.

Collins had politely asked the TV news journalist and cameraman to leave the bridge before they made the turn. There could be no distractions. And from that point on there would be no information transmitted from the ship unless first approved by him.

Each minute and change of course had been carefully planned and would be executed without forewarning. Which was the way things had to be.

*   *   *   *

USS Columbia, Tasman Sea,
five miles east of the River Derwent entrance

"Conn. Sonar. Confirm aspect change on Sierra-Fourteen, their track now zero-one-five. They've entered the Derwent as expected, sir."

"Sonar. Conn. Aye." Captain Samuel Carter, Executive Officer of the Los Angeles–class fast-attack submarine, had acknowledged the report he'd been expecting from the sonar operator. USS *John F. Kennedy* had made the turn and was heading upriver to its designated anchorage.

Carter returned to the plotting table. He stooped down to examine the digital charts, bending awkwardly at his hips as he often did. His strong frame and his six-foot-two stature were not well suited to the cramped world of a submarine. The navy had almost laughed him out of contention when he first volunteered for the submarine service. But as an African American man from the country who'd earned an engineering degree from Georgia Tech, he'd learned to ignore the nonsense that he didn't need to hear. He blitzed his course at Officer Candidate School, then took to the world of the submariner with confidence, advancing through the officer ranks to be Executive Officer—second in command—by age thirty-eight, and earning the affectionate nickname of "Stoop" along the way.

Carter examined a chart depicting the expansive mouth of the River Derwent where it met the open Tasman Sea. The area was bounded to the south by South East Cape and the long narrow landform known as Bruny Island. To the north, Cape Pillar and Tasman Island guarded the river entrance.

He scratched his chin as he studied the depth contours of the river and the sea floor. The depth shifted between one hundred and fifty to three hundred feet, with a few shallower areas only fifty feet from the surface. Their high-definition charts and the high-accuracy position monitoring systems on the submarine would allow them to move through the shallows with reasonable confidence.

But this was still no place for a submarine. The shallow bottom and the nearby islands and rugged coastlines rendered much of their sonar equipment largely ineffective—much the same as the conditions around the Dampier Peninsula had hindered them during the Talisman Sabre exercise two weeks earlier. The volume of commercial, fishing, and pleasure vessels on the surface were a further acoustic hindrance to their sonar. And to add to the challenge, the Los Angeles–class submarine measured sixty-five feet from the bottom of the hull to the top of the sail, creating significant hazards with surface vessels going overhead in the shallows.

Even worse, though, were the trawlers and long-line fishing vessels operating out of Hobart. Fishing nets and lines towed in the depths are not on the list of a submarine commander's favourite things. They were to be given a very wide berth, and USS *Columbia* would not be playing in these shallows.

"Navigator, are we ready for the first patrol pattern?" Carter asked.

"Yes, XO. The first is a racetrack pattern, twenty-mile legs with five-mile radius turns."

"Very well. Chief, track to intercept the first leg on the plot, then maintain the pattern. Make your depth three hundred feet when able. Turns for eight knots."

The Chief of the Boat stood watch as Officer of the Deck and replied curtly: "Aye, sir. Intercept the first leg as plotted and maintain the pattern. Make our depth three hundred feet when able. Turns for eight knots." He issued commands to the dive officer to make it so, who then supervised the inputs made by the helmsman and planesman at their control stations.

Turns to commanded headings were made by shifting the submarine's single rudder. The submarine's stern planes were adjusted to set the deck angle and descend to the desired depth, with the bow planes used for fine adjustments. The Chief managed the movement of ballast between water tanks fore and aft to trim the deck angle and maintain the required buoyancy. Commanded speeds were managed by adjusting power to the single screw, which was driven by two steam-turbine electric plants powered by the nuclear reactor.

There would be many more commands given and control inputs made over the seven days to follow. The *Columbia* would patrol off Tasmania's south-east coast while the carrier was in port. The submarine would stay in a designated box for their patrol—an elliptical-shaped area centred forty miles from the mouth of the Derwent. The box extended thirty miles to the north-west and south-east, and sixty miles either side to the south-west and north-east.

Much further out into the Tasman Sea, a second submarine—the new Virginia-class USS *Oregon*—had also taken up station. Their patrol box was wider and deeper, with the closest edge of their patrol being one hundred miles from the Tasmanian coast. Both submarines would stay hidden below the surface, listening, watching, and tracking every vessel they could detect near and far. They would be the front line of warning and defence against any vessels that posed a threat to the carrier—including other submarines.

* * * *

USS John F. Kennedy, fifty-five miles south of Hobart

With the ship established on its initial inbound course, Collins took a moment to examine his surroundings. He raised his binoculars towards the Tasmanian coastline on the port side.

As he adjusted the focus ring, a small but wide bay came into view. Two narrow points of land bordered the entrance. Their shallow watery edges gleamed with a teal-green hue in patches of bright sunlight, contrasting with the brilliant white sand on their shores.

He could see, beyond the small entrance, the flat blue waters of the bay that looked as much like glass as a sea-facing bay could be. It was completely still thanks to the density of the tall trees and the topography that protected it from the prevailing winds. The undisturbed surface reflected both the white and blue of the sky and the dense green eucalypt forests on the shoreline. Recherche Bay was much as Collins had remembered it.

He lowered the binoculars and took in the landscape from a distance, contemplating how life might have been for the Indigenous people, the palawa, who had lived in and around the bay for millennia; and about the first European explorers to sail into the bay, and how this place must have seemed to them.

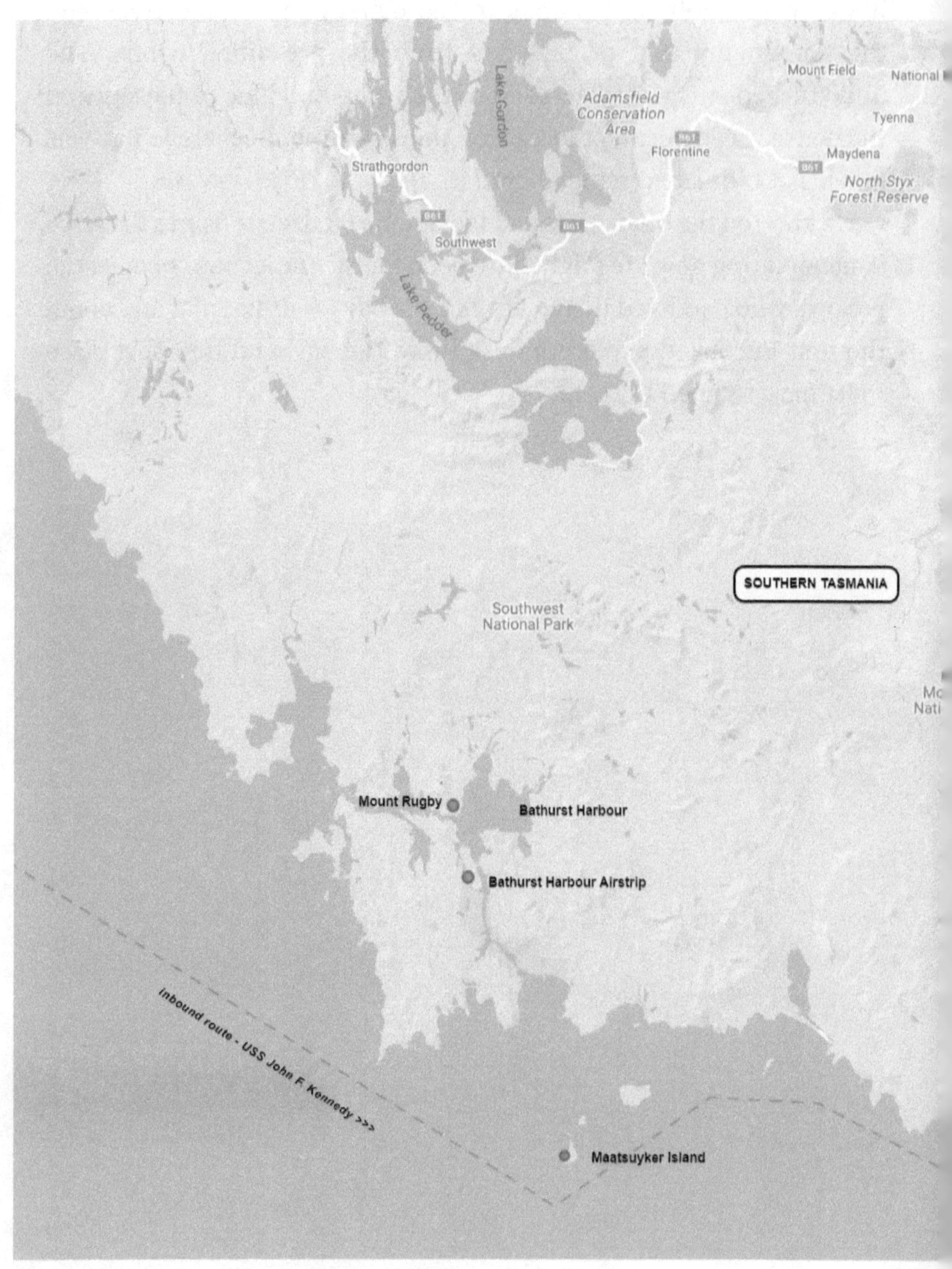

Lake Gordon
Adamsfield Conservation Area
Mount Field
National
Tyenna
Florentine
Maydena
North Styx Forest Reserve
Strathgordon
B61
Southwest
B61
B61
Lake Pedder
SOUTHERN TASMANIA
Southwest National Park
Mo
Nati
Mount Rugby
Bathurst Harbour
Bathurst Harbour Airstrip
Inbound route - USS John F. Kennedy >>>
Maatsuyker Island

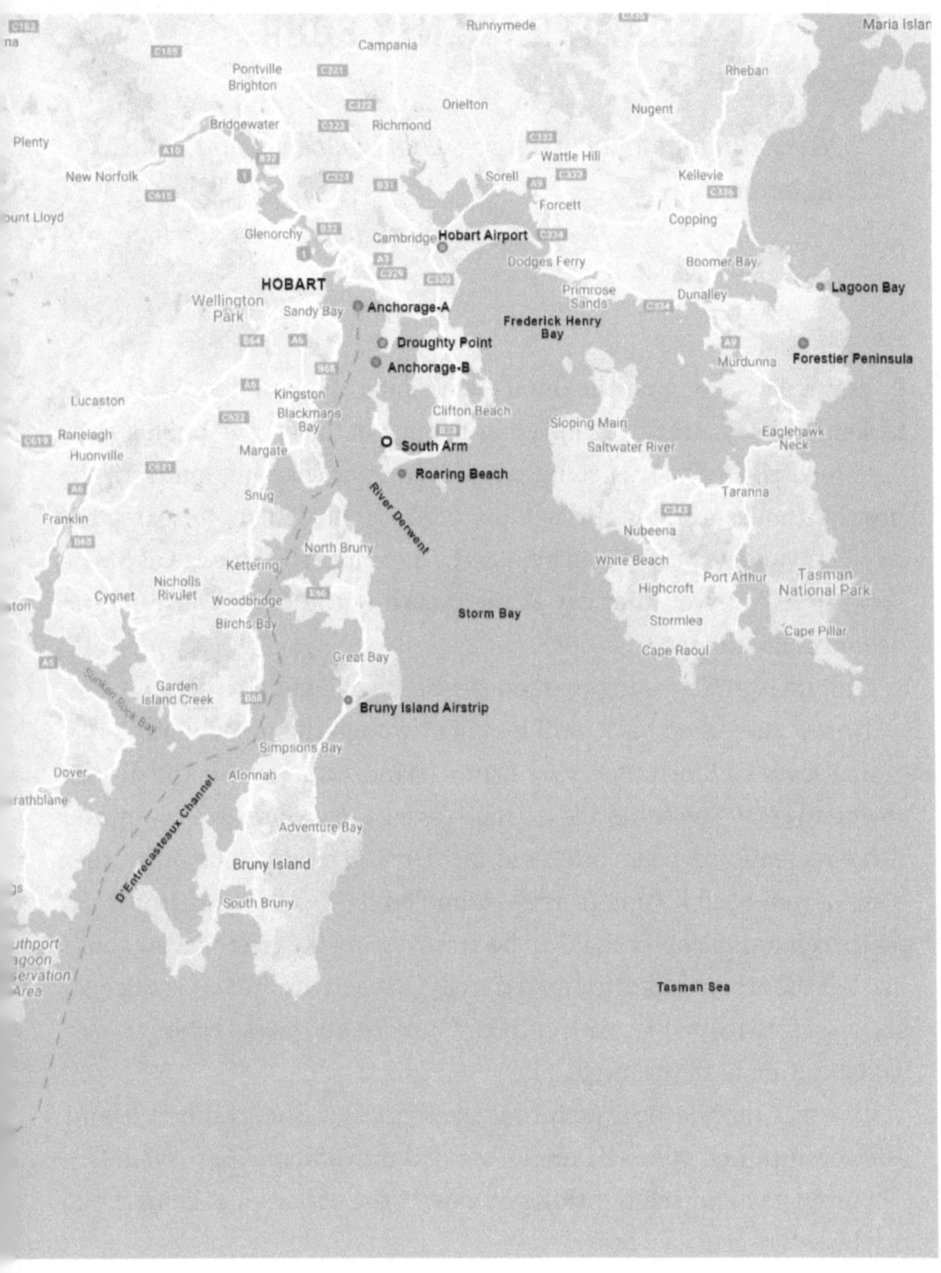

Maria Island
Runnymede
Campania
Pontville
Brighton
Rheban
C221
C222
Orielton
Nugent
Bridgewater
C223
Richmond
Plenty
A10
C332
New Norfolk
B32
Wattle Hill
1
C324
Sorell
C333
Kellevie
C618
B31
A3
C336
Forcett
ount Lloyd
Copping
Glenorchy
B32
Cambridge
Hobart Airport
C334
Dodges Ferry
Boomer Bay
1
A3
Primrose
Sands
Dunalley
Lagoon Bay
HOBART
C329
C330
Wellington
Park
Sandy Bay
Anchorage-A
Frederick Henry
Bay
C334
B64
A6
Droughty Point
A9
Forestier Peninsula
B68
Anchorage-B
Murdunna
A6
Kingston
Clifton Beach
Sloping Main
Lucaston
C622
Blackmans
Bay
Eaglehawk
Neck
C619
Ranelagh
B33
South Arm
Saltwater River
Huonville
Margate
Roaring Beach
C621
Taranna
A6
Snug
River Derwent
C343
Franklin
Nubeena
B68
North Bruny
White Beach
Kettering
Port Arthur
Tasman
National Park
Nicholls
Rivulet
Highcroft
Cygnet
Woodbridge
B66
Birchs Bay
Storm Bay
Stormlea
Cape Pillar
Great Bay
Cape Raoul
A6
Sunken Rock Bay
Garden
Island Creek
B68
Bruny Island Airstrip
Simpsons Bay
Dover
Alonnah
rathblane
D'Entrecasteaux Channel
Adventure Bay
Bruny Island
South Bruny
uthport
agoon
servation
Area
Tasman Sea

CHAPTER TWENTY-FOUR

*Never attempt to win by force what can be won by
deception.*

—Niccolò Machiavelli, The Prince

1:10 PM

Lauren Jack stood on the dune overlooking the deserted beach. Her
long locks of scraggly blonde hair flapped in the breeze, but her body
remained rigid. She was going cross-eyed after spending much of the
previous hour straining through her dad's old binoculars to search the
bay. Her vantage point, Roaring Beach, lined a northern edge of Storm
Bay—an expansive waterway at the mouth of the River Derwent and
opening onto the sea.

"Still no sign?" a young man on the beach called up to her.

"Nope," she yelled back, still looking through the binoculars.

She scanned Storm Bay, past Bruny Island, and towards the distant
river entrance. She could see a police vessel a few kilometres away and
three recreational boats scattered farther to the west. The only other
boat—a well-aged fishing trawler—trundled its way towards Hobart. A
police rescue helicopter that had been traversing the river farther south
had left the area, headed towards the city. Beyond the breakers, a fleet of
six kayaks, two dinghies with outboard motors, and an old cabin-cruiser
sat lolling about in the swell.

Lauren's mobile buzzed in her back pocket. She grabbed it and
answered in one smooth, single-handed movement. "Yep, what?"

"Surely you can see the thing by now?" the caller—a colleague out
on the cabin-cruiser—asked.

"If I'd *seen* the frickin' thing, Matt, I woulda called you by now."

"Something's not right, I reckon. It was spotted off South East Cape nearly two hours ago, headed for Storm Bay. Should've gone past here already."

Lauren lowered her binoculars. "Hold on. I'll call you back."

She was, like her colleague, experiencing a sinking feeling. The group of twenty-three activists she had hastily drawn together the night before had left Hobart at dawn and made their way to the South Arm Peninsula. They'd been secretly told a U.S. Navy ship was expected in Hobart in the coming weeks, but like almost everyone else in Hobart, they had only found out about the aircraft carrier's imminent arrival from the Network-8 news story on television the night before.

The group had first arrived at South Arm Beach, which faces west along a narrow stretch of the River Derwent. The beach was the ideal place to launch their boats and intercept the carrier as it travelled to its likely anchorage point a few kilometres from there. They would make their protests known: unfurling their anti-nuclear and anti-war banners, banging their drums, blowing their horns, and making as much of a nuisance of themselves as nautically possible. Which was why a squad of police officers and a patrol boat had been at South Arm Beach when they'd arrived.

The protest group retreated and headed for Roaring Beach a few kilometres away. Not as ideal, but it would do. They'd see the ship from a distance as they looked south from the beach, then launch their boats, go around the Iron Pot lighthouse on the point, and intercept the carrier's path in the river. This tactic would be more time consuming, but they were confident it'd work just the same.

Lauren lowered the binoculars and started scrolling through her phone. Seconds later, she stared in disbelief at an image on her phone, dropped the binoculars to the sand, and shrieked in abject fury. "*Shit!*"

* * * *

USS John F. Kennedy

The chief navigator had been snapping out rapid steering and speed changes for the past hour and a half, and there were even more to come. "Helm, come left heading three-zero-five on my mark ... five ... four ... three ... two ... one ... *mark*."

"Aye, sir. Left heading three-zero-five."

The carrier had emerged through the narrow strait between Dennes Point on the northern tip of Bruny Island, and Piersone Point on the Tasmanian mainland just to the west. She turned hard to port, preparing to track up the remaining waterway towards Hobart nine miles farther north. The ship was being kept to the west in the deeper channel and as far away from the South Arm side as possible.

Two police vessels had come alongside the carrier to patrol the one-hundred metre exclusion zone that had come into force that morning. Collins trained his binoculars to the starboard side and looked south-east towards the South Arm Peninsula. He could see scattered pleasure craft a few miles down the river. Most likely media boats and sight-seers, but no protestors in sight.

Collins had invited Matthew Cash to the bridge to witness the carrier's journey to its anchorage. He eyed Cash standing at the rear of the bridge and gave him a small nod.

Cash returned the gesture with a wry smile.

Their plan had worked.

*　　*　　*　　*

Roaring Beach

"What is it?" the man yelled.

"You're not gonna believe this."

"Not gonna believe what?"

But Lauren didn't answer him and continued to stare wide-eyed at the image on her phone—a U.S. Navy aircraft carrier posted to Instagram ten minutes earlier. The caption read: *Not every day you see this!* A Bruny Island resident had snapped the image from the car ferry as it crossed the D'Entrecasteaux Channel between Kettering and the island, then posted it online for all to see.

In the meantime, the young man on the beach had sprinted up the dune to get his question answered. He snatched Lauren's phone to see the source of the fuss. His mouth dropped open as he struggled to comprehend the image.

USS *John F. Kennedy* had not made the journey up the Derwent along the usual route—to the east of Bruny Island, across Storm Bay, past the Iron Pot and South Arm, and then upriver. Instead, the ship went to the west of Bruny Island after passing Recherche Bay.

"They've taken it through the D'Entrecasteaux Channel," he groaned. "How the hell did they manage that?"

But thanks to detailed charts, expert navigation, careful planning, and a timely high tide, the D'Entrecasteaux Channel was indeed navigable. Tight and shallow in places for a ship of that size, but navigable.

"C'mon Lauren," he pleaded, "we gotta get our boats moving!"

"Don't bother," she said as she took her phone back. "It's too late now. That nuclear fucking ship has long since sailed."

His energy and enthusiasm seemed to evaporate as he sank to the sand, head in hands.

"Don't worry," Lauren said as she forced a smirk. "There are other things at play now. Those smart-arse Americans won't be able to side-step *all* our plans."

* * * *

USS John F. Kennedy

"For God's sake, Bruce, get a move on, old mate!" Steph Sadler said as she hurried down the never-ending corridor on the O-1 level, traversing each hatchway with consummate ease.

"Slow down! I'm lugging all this bloody gear and not as young as I used to be!"

"I know, I know. But there's only fifteen minutes till we get to the anchorage. We gotta milk this time for all its worth."

Bruce Wardlaw knew she was right, and wrong. They'd been up and about since 7:00 AM, filming more activity around the ship and conducting pre-organised interviews with selected officers. Lieutenant Emiko Nomura had been with them every step of the way, keeping Sadler within the boundaries of U.S. Navy public relations protocols and the interviews on-message.

For Sadler, it had been like a never-ending ride at a rodeo where she was the bull and Nomura was the cowgirl. And when Nomura was called away to a briefing thirty minutes before the ship was to anchor, Sadler saw her opportunity.

Wardlaw had tried to reason with her, but she got through the door from the Public Relations Office while he was still mid-sentence. And with no hovering ensign at the door to stop them, USS *John F. Kennedy* and its unsuspecting crew were there for Sadler's taking.

Some crew members declined to be on camera, but Sadler still managed to interview five of them in quick succession. The unscripted comments and answers they provided were journalism gold. Sadler could feel the rush of a good story racing through her veins. But she wanted more.

"Here we go, Bruce. This way ... here's one of the hangars." Sadler had remembered where the aircraft were stored below deck, and where the people in the red shirts—the crew who handled the bombs, missiles, and bullets—were in plentiful supply. As she raced through the doorway and into the vast open space of Hangar Bay Two, she spotted plenty of targets. Red shirts were everywhere. She sighted two of them moving an ordnance rack and went straight in for the kill.

Steph Sadler wanted answers about the who, what, how, when, and why of the things on the ship which go bang. And no one would stop her.

*　　*　　*　　*

Collins caught Cash's attention and motioned him to the captain's chair, then handed him the binoculars. "Take a look at the hillside ahead."

Cash raised the binoculars and struggled to get the hill into view, then into focus. The hill above Droughty Point was rounded and denuded of trees. The ground was covered in low tussock grass with a few scattered bushes near the shoreline. An oversized grassy knoll.

"Your people have a strange way of saying welcome, huh?" Collins asked.

Cash gulped as he took in the scene. There, on the top of the hill, a group of bright white objects had been arranged among the grasses into clear patterns. The patterns were letters. The letters formed words. The words formed a single sentence:

USS JFK — KEEP YOUR FREEDOM

The hillside message had been placed in a position facing Anchorage B, where the protestors assumed the carrier would be stationed.

Cash handed the binoculars back to Collins. He, unlike the hill ahead, could not generate a sentence. Not even a word.

*　　*　　*　　*

Vulture's Row was packed with naval aviators and officers. Katherine managed to squeeze into a spot near the railing. The noisy, cramped space was a stark contrast to the serene atmosphere she'd experienced there earlier that morning.

She could sense a rising level of joy and eager expectation throughout the ship. An eagerness to experience new places, see new things, and meet new people. To leave the ship and plant their feet on solid ground, and to reacquaint their taste buds to the delights of alcohol and food beyond the monotony of the ship's mess.

And the U.S. Navy had turned out in style, as was their tradition on entering port. Hundreds of sailors were assembled around the fore, port, aft, and starboard sides, and all wearing their service dress blues. Each stood facing outward, "manning the rails." They were evenly spaced at an arm's length to the sailor either side, and each stood perfectly still.

Katherine was not the type to jump to attention every time she saw the flag, but as she looked at her colleagues standing motionless around the perimeter of the flight deck, she felt a surge of admiration and a deeper pride than she could remember.

Another group of sailors near the centre of the flight deck were assembled into small rows in various directions. They formed patterns. The patterns were letters. The letters formed two large words along the deck:

G'DAY HOBART!

Katherine did not see the reciprocal greeting from the protestors spelt out on the hill over Droughty Point, as it was obscured by the carrier's superstructure, but a minority of sailors positioned on the fore and starboard sides of the deck could not avoid reading the message as the carrier slipped past.

*   *   *   *

Hobart

Given it was a Sunday and the weather clear and mild, the residents of Hobart came out in their thousands to see the ship. Many of the shorelines and vantage points along the Derwent had swelled with groups of residents. Commercial vessels, recreational boats, and ferries packed with sightseers spilled out onto the river to greet the ship while staying outside the exclusion zone enforced by the police vessels.

Two helicopters and a light aircraft buzzed overhead. News cameramen on board the aircraft filmed the spectacle while press photographers snapped away. Their shots of G'DAY HOBART! on the flight deck went viral on social media in minutes.

Many of the residents seemed delighted to see the ship come to anchor much closer to the city than expected. The ship sat mid-river between the inner suburbs of Howrah and Sandy Bay, and less than a mile from the centre of Hobart.

*   *   *   *

Michael Cahill, head of Tasmania's State Emergency Service and chair of the Nuclear-Powered Ships Visits Committee, slammed the blinds on his living room windows shut. He didn't want to be reminded of the object then sitting in the river, just two kilometres from his home on Hobart's Bellerive foreshore.

"Anchorage A," he muttered to himself, still staring into the blinds. "Anchorage *fucking* A!"

*   *   *   *

Alix Zhao stood motionless, taking in the scene before her. The historic Mount Nelson Signal Station on the western ridge above Hobart was the perfect vantage point with an uninterrupted view looking east over Sandy Bay and the river, and across Hobart's eastern-shore suburbs in the distance.

She pressed the camera icon on her phone and framed the perfect shot. She reviewed the image—the Derwent, the landscape beyond, and an aircraft carrier moored in the middle of the river.

She needed to post the photo as soon as possible. But not to a social media account. It would be uploaded to a secure military server somewhere in the People's Republic of China.

CHAPTER TWENTY-FIVE

Speak the truth, but leave immediately after.

—Slovenian proverb

Melbourne

13 August 2023, 2:50 PM

"My ride will be here soon," Ben said. "I'll be leaving now."

Justin looked up from his textbook. "Okay. Gonna miss you around here, Benny Boy. But have a good break, ay?"

"Thanks. I will. And keep the blue side up."

*　　*　　*　　*

Ben cupped a hand around his phone to shade it from the bright afternoon glare outside. He watched the tiny car icon on the Uber app as it approached Moorabbin Airport and the arrival time counting down from its prediction of three minutes and twenty seconds.

A travel bag sat next to Ben's leg. He'd brought only what he needed and he'd left half of his clothes and belongings in his room. He'd also left his textbooks and study materials. The illusion of his imminent return was vital.

Ben had taken the further precaution of replacing his laptop's two solid-state drives with one new drive and a freshly installed operating system. He'd pulverised the old drives and flushed the silicon chips down a toilet.

"Ben!"

He recognised the voice. He looked to the sky for a second, shook his head, then turned toward her. "Yes?" he replied.

"Are you going somewhere?" Jia Jeong asked.

Ben glared at her as she approached. Her dark eyes and hair were a striking contrast to the perfect white of her student pilot uniform. And there was her neck again—so graceful with perfect skin. "Ah ... yes."

"Oh? Not for *too* long I hope?"

"Just a week or two."

"Are you travelling back to Hong Kong?" she asked.

"No."

"Oh. Sorry. I assumed you might be."

"I am taking a quick break ... within Australia," Ben said.

"Lucky you. Where are you going?"

"Ah ... not sure. A friend is arranging the itinerary. I am along for the ride."

"Oh."

Ben checked the app again: *forty seconds and counting ... hurry up!*

"Actually, I was hoping to speak with you," Jia said. "I think there's some information you could help me with, if you don't mind?"

Ben felt a surge of relief as a blue Honda Jazz pulled up at the kerb. His ride had arrived thirty seconds earlier than predicted. "I must leave now. We can talk on my return," Ben said as he swung open the rear passenger door and threw in his travel bag.

"Ah—"

"Bye," he said.

Ben slammed the door shut and the car sped off.

"See you then," Jia Jeong said as the car disappeared around the corner.

* * * *

USS John F. Kennedy , 3:25 PM

Bruce Wardlaw watched the small boat approach the stern of the ship from the rear edge of the flight deck, his video camera poised on his shoulder. This would be his final task before he left the ship later that afternoon. He would depart on a boat, though, and most definitely not on a C-2A Greyhound plane.

He began filming as the motor launch pulled alongside the ship, with the carrier dwarfing the small vessel in every sense of the word. The launch came to a stop near a temporary floating deck moored to the carrier's stern. After careful manoeuvring by the coxswain, the fore-and-aft lines of the launch were finally secured to the deck.

Two enlisted sailors waited at the railing to help the visitors aboard. They emerged in order of importance—the Governor of Tasmania followed by the Mayors of Hobart, Clarence, and Glenorchy, each of the latter dressed in their respective mayoral garbs, complete with heavy chains of office draped around their shoulders.

Captain Collins, standing with the receiving line on the ship's fantail, tilted his head toward Lieutenant Emiko Nomura. "I hope you've got the dive team on standby," he whispered.

"I'm sorry, sir?" Nomura asked.

"If that one falls into the river," he said as he watched the Mayor of Hobart struggle aboard, "that chain she's wearing will send her straight to the bottom."

"Sir," Nomura responded as she tried to repress a grin and failed.

Eventually the dignitaries and their entourages had clambered aboard, made their way up the stairs to the fantail, and worked their way along the receiving line of senior officers. Above the proceedings, on the flight deck, the ship's band struck up "The Star-Spangled Banner" followed by "Advance Australia Fair." This was capped with a twenty-one-gun salute by a squad of Marines. The visitors were then ushered inside the ship and up to the Admiral's Stateroom for an official reception.

Collins was dreading the many grip-and-grin events he'd have to endure over the following days, but he was resigned to take the good with the bad. As the last of the ship's officers made their way inside, Collins took a fleeting look at the River Derwent.

Lord, give me strength, he thought.

*   *   *   *

Melbourne, 6:40 PM

Ben stood on the starboard railing of the *Spirit of Tasmania II*—one of two large passenger/car ferries that ply the Bass Strait between Victoria and Tasmania each day and night.

He'd boarded an hour beforehand as a single passenger with no vehicle. He had a different passport now, with another name, having left his other passport, identity documents, and phone in a sealed case with the receptionist at Doctor Huang's surgery in South Melbourne. A replacement mobile phone was waiting for him there.

The ship had reversed from the pier and manoeuvred into Port Phillip Bay. The journey would take eleven hours and Ben was keen to get to his cabin before the infamous waves and swell of Bass Strait became a factor. He swallowed two sea-sickness tablets and a sleeping tablet with a swig of cola, then turned to go inside. As he reached for the door, a shape caught his eye in the reflection on the window.

Ben faced the railing for a better look. They were slipping by another large vessel moored at an adjoining pier. A U.S. Navy ship, with its distinctive low hull and imposing mast silhouetted against the sky— and a large red, white, and blue flag at its stern fluttering in the dusk.

*   *   *   *

Hobart

The evening had been long, yet Collins had enjoyed himself more than he'd expected. The Governor of Tasmania had invited Collins, the Air Wing Commander, and a sizeable group of senior officers to a state reception at Government House. They had been the first to disembark the ship at six o'clock that evening.

The who's-who of Hobart society had come to greet them at His Excellency the Governor of Tasmania's pleasure. The Premier, Deputy Premier, three cabinet ministers, the Leader of the Opposition, Mayors and Deputy Mayors from the southern region, a selection of socialites and business leaders and their partners had all packed the Government House Ball Room for the occasion.

Events like these were a long-standing tradition in Tasmania. The officers and crews of significant ships had enjoyed similar hospitality since the early decades of the nineteenth century. Maritime links to the outside world were to be encouraged and celebrated at the highest levels in the interests of the growth and prosperity of the island known as Van Diemen's Land, and later named Tasmania.

The sea had been, and still was to an extent, the lifeblood of the island it surrounded. Infamous maritime characters of the nineteenth and early twentieth centuries such as Bligh, d'Urville, Clark Ross, Crozier, Wilkes, Scott, Amundsen, Shackleton, and Mawson had all visited Hobart or embarked on their journeys of discovery from there.

In 1925 the United States Navy had chosen Hobart as one of its three ports of call on Australia's east coast. Many U.S. Navy ships and submarines had visited over the years including USS *Missouri*, USS *Enterprise*, USS *Kitty Hawk*, and USS *John C. Stennis*, to name a few. There was never a question USS *John F. Kennedy* would be given a welcome in similar grand style.

The dinner had been quite something—a celebration of the best of Tasmanian food and wine, together with ingredients from the kitchen garden at Government House. The guests had first enjoyed garden vegetable soup with chive oil, biscuits made with aged Tasmanian cheddar, and cold-smoked Atlantic salmon. A main course of oven-roasted blue-eye trevalla was served with a warm orange and wattle seed hollandaise, followed by a dessert of pressed apple terrine.

Several speeches were made after dinner, and digestif beverages served. With the formalities over, it would still be midnight before the guests began to leave.

The warm hospitality had softened the four hours of social duties for Collins. The relentless hand-shaking, smiling, and small talk had been bearable. But by the time the antique clock struck eleven, he was repressing an unappeasable desire to get away from it all, even for a few minutes.

Collins took the first opportunity to slip out of the ball room and into the garden, where the grounds were mercifully empty and silent. He took a sip of his liqueur, a smooth, aromatic Sullivan's Cove Brandy that went straight to his head. It was his fourth drink of the night after six months of sobriety, and his body reeled delightfully. *Better make this the last one,* he thought.

Collins turned to take in the building behind him. Government House was painted in soft floodlight from across the lawn, its Victorian sandstone features and neo-Gothic design standing proud in the cool Tasmanian night. Golden light poured from the many windows facing him, and he could hear the happy throng inside. The clink of glasses, the rise and fall of laughter, and the charming notes of a string quartet.

It had surprised Collins how welcome he felt. Not quite at home, but welcome. Perhaps it was the alcohol, or his earlier visits to the state. Or the rich maritime history that ran through the veins of this grand house and its gardens by the river. He imagined how things would have been for the captain of a visiting sailing ship in the mid-nineteenth century. His ship—most likely a barque or a brigantine—would have anchored in nearby Ross Bay, just a stone's throw from the grounds of Government House.

"May I join you?"

Collins turned to see a tall woman with undulating shoulder-length red hair. She was dressed in an elegant pastel emerald evening gown and her diamond necklace glinted in the garden lights.

Collins hid his surprise. "Certainly."

"Thank you."

The woman blew a cloud of cigarette smoke into the darkness, then dropped the butt to the ground. She snuffed it out with her foot with the confidence of extensive prior experience.

"Captain William Collins," he said with a nod. "But my friends call me Bill."

"Suzannah Denholm," she replied, shaking his hand. "My friends don't call me often enough."

Collins chuckled. "You and me both."

"I'm guessing you came out here for some peace and quiet, so, um ... sorry about that."

"No problem. I don't mind the company."

"Great, shall I call everyone else out?"

"I can't see your face that well, you know," he said with another chuckle. "How am I supposed to know when you're pulling my leg?"

"Oh, believe me, you'll know."

"Um ... so, what do you do, Ms Denholm?"

"You mean, apart from standing in dark gardens talking to handsome men in uniform? I'm the Crown Solicitor. And please call me Suze."

"That's a great name for a lawyer."

"Oh, *ha, ha*. Is that a lame-arse dad joke?"

"Lame, maybe, but I don't have kids."

"I suppose that makes it easier, being away from home as long as you are?" Suze asked.

"Yeah. I guess."

"Still, there must be others you miss?"

Collins crossed his arms. "Well, my job is all-consuming, there's no time to miss anyone much."

"So the big boat out there is your only darling then?"

"Hmm. Yeah, I gotta admit ... sometimes I wonder if that's the truth of it."

She brushed strands of hair from her face. "Do you have much planned while you're here?"

"It's quite a packed itinerary, yeah. I've got a few days to myself, though, and looking forward to that."

"If you would like some company, I'd be happy to show you around. I know this place better than most."

"Thanks."

"Well, don't overdo the enthusiasm, Captain."

"Sorry, I, uh … I just wouldn't be great company right now."

"You're doing fine so far."

"Thanks."

"See, there's that enthusiasm again."

Collins laughed awkwardly. "It's been a while, is all."

"Long cruise, sailor?"

"Yeah … no … I mean, longer than that."

She didn't reply, gazing at him in the dim light.

"It's just … my wife," he mumbled.

"Oh? You miss her, obviously. I can respect that."

Collins closed his eyes and exhaled. "It's complicated," he said.

"It usually is. Look, I'll be blunt. I'm brilliant company, and I'd show you a great time. But that would be it. There would be no harm done to your wife. The offer is yours if you want to take it. If you don't, no worries, I'll live."

"I'll be blunt too," Collins said. "My wife passed away almost two years ago."

"Oh no. I'm so sorry—"

"A brain tumour. She was diagnosed late, then gone within two months."

"Oh my god, Bill. That's awful."

"Thank you. Like I said, I wouldn't be great company right now." Collins took a step away. "Now if you'll excuse me, I'd better get back to the folks inside."

Suzannah Denholm lit another cigarette as the captain strode toward the house. "Really good, Suze," she muttered to herself. "Really good."

CHAPTER TWENTY-SIX

*Things are not always what they seem; the first
appearance deceives many; the intelligence of a few
perceives what has been carefully hidden.*

—Plato, *The Phaedrus*

Devonport, Tasmania
14 August 2023, 7:40 AM

A single night on the high seas of Bass Strait had been more than enough. The infamous Roaring Forties—the westerly winds that howl between the fortieth and fiftieth parallels—had again paid their regular visit to the exposed stretch of ocean between the Australian mainland and Tasmania.

Ben was among the first of the queasy passengers to wobble off the *Spirit of Tasmania II*, his legs destabilised after eleven hours on a heavy swell. He contemplated his travel choices as he left the ferry gangway and headed for the car hire office.

"Ow ya goin?" a voice asked when he opened the door.

The strange utterance came from a balding man at the back of the room. He sat in an office chair that was mostly hidden by his middle-aged bulk. It squeaked in sharp protest as he leaned on the wooden desk before him.

"Pardon?" Ben asked.

"I said ... *ow-ya-go-in*, mate?"

"Oh. I am going well."

"Good-o. What can we do for ya?"

"I want to hire a car. For a week."

"No worries. Any preference on the type?"

"A small car is okay."

"We only got a small Hyundai left. It's getting on a bit, but goes alright."

"Okay."

"I can do you a good deal on it, like thirty bucks a day, plus insurance. How's that sound?"

"Yes. That is fine. And I will not need insurance."

"Is that right?" the man asked.

Ben stared at him, still as a statue.

"On one condition then, young fella. You've got to promise me—stay on sealed roads only, and drive with extra care. It'll cost you a lot if you don't!"

Ben took out his wallet. He held it at an angle and tapped the bottom corner on the desk.

"I've had *way* too many of your type crashing my cars this year," the man said.

Ben gave the man a slight and sharp nod as he continued tapping his wallet against the desk.

"It's bloody nuts," the man went on. "Chinese drivers seem to enjoy writing off Korean-built cars. What's with that, ay?"

The man could see a storm building in the face of his customer and sensed he should speak nothing further of his concerns for his aged Hyundai. There was something in the menacing stare of this young man and the rippling tension in his lean muscular arms that sent a cool shiver deep into the man's innards.

I better just get his money and get him out of here ...

*   *   *   *

Hobart

Katherine sensed the rhythm of the engines building. They'd been put into reverse for a few seconds to halt the forward motion of the vessel. A solid thump followed as the river ferry contacted the rubber fenders lining the pier.

Katherine was one of the first of the eighty-two U.S. Navy officers and sailors to disembark. After six months at sea, with only a few days break on terra firma, she was eager to feel the inert confidence of solid ground beneath her boots. The swarm of passengers flowed across the pier and into the bright interior of the cruise ship terminal to join hundreds of their colleagues. Scattered video displays played footage of iconic Tasmanian locations while government and tourism staff milled around like worker ants. A jazz band played at the far end of the terminal with a little too much enthusiasm for 8:00 AM.

Katherine spotted the main exit. She was slicing through the crowd toward it when a young woman armed with a clipboard and a broad smile interrupted her path.

"Hi. Welcome to Tasmania. How are you?"

"Just fine, thanks," Katherine replied.

"How many days do you have off the ship?"

"Three days."

"Fantastic. We've got heaps you can do." The woman handed Katherine a glossy brochure. "Can I interest you in a guided tour into our convict past? We've got historic sites, great scenery, even Tasmanian devils and wallabies for you to see and touch."

"Ah, thanks, but I'm all set," Katherine said, resuming her bee-line for the exit.

"Oh, okay. Enjoy your stay."

Once outside and past the security fence, Katherine spotted a bench near the far end of the building, close to the side of the pier. She dropped her bag and took a seat, breathing in the crisp air and the sudden silence. The port district surrounding her was still to fully wake from its morning slumber. A few cars and taxis drove past at a slow pace. A smattering of workers with coffee cups in hand were making their way towards their daily grinds. A group of women clad in active wear jogged and shuffled along a waterfront pier in the distance.

A marina—beyond a long timber-clad hotel building to Katherine's left—was lined with yachts and fishing vessels. Beyond the hotel, she could see a gathering of mid-rise city buildings with suburban hills and an imposing mountain in the background. A collection of port buildings and warehouses stood to her right. Many had been reborn as hotels, bars, and restaurants, but all retained a quaint historic and English charm.

The toot of a car horn brought Katherine's attention to a vehicle pulling up to the kerb. The four-wheel-drive's roof rack was stacked with rolls of gear and it sported bulbous tyres primed for off-road action. Its purpose was confirmed by the lettering on the passenger side door: WILD TASMANIA TOURING ADVENTURES.

A tall man with a tight-cropped beard and scraggly dark hair emerged from the driver's side. He appeared to be in his early thirties and seemed to fit the appearance of a man from the bush. "G'day," he said, his tone deep.

He was seven minutes late, but Katherine would let it slide. "Hi."

He picked up Katherine's bag and placed it into the rear of the vehicle. "Hop in," he said.

"I'm Katherine Marlowe," she said as she put on her seat belt.

"Yeah, I know. I'm Martin. Martin Brady."

"How'd you know it was me?"

"You were the only chick waiting there. Figured it must'a been you."

Brady drove out of the port district and into the city without a further word.

She'd found Brady's business during an online search of things to do in Tasmania, and his tours had received glowing reviews. Package tourism for sailors was not her style. No, she'd go her own way. And she wanted to get well away from the city and see the wilderness of the island.

But as they drove toward the city, she wasn't so sure she'd made a good choice. If first impressions were everything, it seemed a miracle this guy was still in business.

"So," Katherine broke the silence, "how many others are on the tour?"

"Hang tight," Brady said as he pulled the vehicle into a hotel forecourt.

"I'll just go get 'em." He left the engine running and disappeared into the lobby.

Brady re-emerged with a middle-aged couple in tow, each carrying a camera, thick coat, and a broad hat. Both were short in stature and of Asian appearance. Brady squeezed their bags into the back of the vehicle as they climbed up into the rear seats.

"Meet Mr and Mrs Wu," Brady mumbled as he clambered in.

Katherine turned to greet them. "Hi there. I'm Katherine."

The man and woman nodded and smiled but didn't say a word.

"They come from Shanghai," Brady said.

"Oh, okay."

"Can't speak a bloody word of English," he said. "That's gonna make my life fun for the next two days."

"I hope you can handle American then?"

Brady grunted.

"Just the four of us?" Katherine asked.

"That's good," he said.

"What's good?"

"You can count."

Katherine crossed her arms, looked out the passenger window, and shook her head.

*   *   *   *

"We do not confirm or deny whether there are nuclear weapons on board this ship. This is standard U.S. Navy policy."

The text superimposed on the vision confirmed the speaker to be Petty Officer Third Class Alvaro Sanchez. He appeared to be caught off-guard as he spoke, standing flat-footed in the middle of Hangar Bay Two on board USS *John F. Kennedy*. Rows of ordnance racks were visible behind him and each was stacked with an assortment of air-to-ground missiles and bombs.

The vision cut to an aerial shot of a sentence formed atop Droughty

Point hill: USS JFK — KEEP YOUR FREEDOM, then to a mob of protestors near the Hobart cruise ship terminal. They were shouting angrily, chanting, and waving placards: NO NUKES; WILDERNESS NOT WAR; THIS IS TASSIE NOT IRAN; and GO EAT YOUR YELLOWCAKE.

"It's plain to see," Steph Sadler said as the vision cut to her standing near the protest group, "there are locals who are not thrilled with the arrival of a nuclear-powered warship, which, we can only assume may also carry nuclear weapons. The protestors you can see behind me have been making their voices heard since last night, and I'm told they intend to keep a protest presence here right throughout the carrier's visit."

Network-8's chief news editor, Stewart McLellan, or Mac as most called him, twisted in his chair as he watched the vision. He tried to hide any visible grimace on his face, but he understood Steph—seated beside him in the dim Network-8 editing studio—would probably read him like a book. "Geez, Steph," he said, "this is... edgy stuff."

The vision cut back to the ship. "Look. We're here to do a job. We're not politicians. We just, like … we do as we're ordered to." Seaman Hannah Berkovich shrugged as she offered up her words to the camera. "And yeah, sometimes I wonder if we're doing any good out there. Whether we're making a difference. It worries me sometimes. But … you know …?"

McLellan leant back in his chair. He looked up from the main review monitor as if requesting help from the great television gods beyond the ceiling. "This is excellent work, Steph. You and Bruce got some top material here—"

"And … ?" Sadler asked.

"And, well … it's pretty full-on."

"Yep. *Full-on* equals national audience ratings."

McLellan sensed he was getting nowhere with his fake attempt at diplomacy. Sadler was too much of a straight-shooter. He resorted to his usual communication style and his not-so-subtle Scottish accent made a sudden resurgence. "Okay, whatever then, but did you have to ask about all that foockin' nuclear stuff?"

"Yeah, of course. Look at all the angles, get all the grabs, see what shakes out."

"Aye, but there's so much else you could have focused on."

"I focused on the public interest and what was running hot. Some navy cook rustling up eggs in a ship's galley will put our viewers to sleep. If we wanted that bullshit, the U.S. Navy could have supplied it from their P.R. library."

"Our brief was to show life on the ship, how stuff works, all that bollocks—"

"Which is *exactly* what we've done," Sadler said as she grabbed the trackball, driving the video editing software back through the earlier scenes of the story. "See. All the establishing material about the visit, the ship, the crew doing their jobs, pretty vision of the ship at sea and planes flying, all that. *It's all there*, Mac."

"I can *foockin'* see that!"

"So, what's your problem?"

"Problem isn't mine."

"Who's is it, then?"

"The government'll have a fit when they see this. *Damn*, lassie. You know that, don't you?"

"Yeah? And? What's your point?"

"They gave us this story … as an exclusive."

"So, you're saying we owe them? Like, you scratch our back and we'll suck your—?"

"I'm not saying that!"

"So, what then?"

McLellan returned his gaze to the editing monitors before him, then spun his chair to look Sadler in the eye. "This is a great piece. I'm just asking you to tone it down a wee bit. Take a few of those nasty edges off. That's all. It'd be nice to welcome all these visitors and not just criticise what they do. It's not our job to piss up their kilts."

"Oh, *be nice*, huh? We're *journalists* last time I looked, Mac. Since when the hell are journalists 'nice'?" Sadler asked, making scare quotes with her fingers.

"Look. We've got some time to review this further. The story's set to be syndicated on *Affairs of the State* tomorrow night. We're expecting our network stations in other states to run it. Let's think about it some more, then meet tomorrow at one o'clock to finish the final edit. Fresh eyes will do this the world of good."

Sadler grabbed her things and made for the door, mumbling as she went.

McLellan didn't hear what she said, nor did he wish to.

As the door closed behind her with a thump, McLellan grabbed his mobile. He looked up a contact and tapped the number in record time.

After what seemed like too many calling tones, a familiar voice answered. "Bradfurd Rouse."

"It's McLellan. We've got a problem—"

*　　*　　*　　*

Lunch had been good. Tasmanian smoked salmon with lemon and capers in a sourdough baguette, crackers with Tasmanian double cream brie and local olives, and a platter of local fruits, all helped down with a glass of Tasmanian sparking apple cider.

The location for lunch was stunning. Arriving there had taken an hour's drive west of Hobart—out through the Derwent Valley, winding their way through hop fields, berry fields, and rustic townships. And then into the first hints of wilderness—the deep green, mutely lit stillness of Mount Field National Park. They'd walked through fern glades, gazed up at the endless eucalypt trees, then stood in silent admiration of the tumbling white effervescence of Russell Falls.

After they were done eating, Martin Brady turned the four-wheel-drive onto the Gordon River Road and headed west. Sharp hills rose in the distance, yet dwarfed by the tops of Mount Mawson, Florentine Peak, and Mount Field West towering over the road.

Brady had been giving his tour group morsels of information as they went: the history, ecology, and geology of the region. He seemed to know his stuff. And he had the good sense to fall silent for long periods and let the environment settle through the senses of each member of the group.

He'd given the Chinese couple an iPad and a pair of wireless headsets. As he spoke, a small microphone attached to his collar transmitted his words to their iPad, where they were translated into Shanghainese in real time.

Mr and Mrs Wu had thought this was wonderful. They thanked Brady profusely in their native tongue, not realising at first that the system couldn't transmit in the other direction.

Katherine took a brief glance at the man beside her. He was gruff sometimes and seemed moody, but the day had been good so far. Brady seemed to have an uncanny affinity for information technology for a man from the bush, and his deep knowledge of the area and the way he expressed it hinted at a man who might be at odds with a person's first impression of him.

"We're in the forests of the Upper Florentine," Brady began as they took a diversion down a narrow gravel road. "The trees you can see are old-growth forests. Mostly myrtle, sassafras, and giant eucalypts. And those are giant man ferns across the bush floor."

The three tourists gazed up and out, heads craning to take it all in.

"The mountains around here all have world heritage status, but not this valley. It's been logged a fair bit. This is one of the few untouched parts of the valley, I can take you where you won't see forestry coups and clear-felled areas."

There seemed to be an uncertain emotion to his tone and a measured guardedness that Katherine could not read.

"It's weird," Katherine said. "From the road you'd never know that they're logging up here."

"Yep. It's not that weird though. That's how it's designed to look."

As they drove on, the stands of tall trees and dense ferns gave way to a flatter, more open landscape. Scattered farmhouses became less scattered as a small township emerged.

"This is Maydena," Brady said. "Last stop for a long while, and the last bit of civilisation we'll see for a few days. I'll stop at the shop if you want to pick up something. And the public loos are back over there."

Katherine, needing some water, thought she'd take her chances. She entered the store, noting a faded FOR SALE sign hanging lopsided near the door. The store's shelves were mostly bare, and there was a lunch counter with a flat-top griddle behind it.

A tubby silver-haired woman waddled out to the counter. "G'day, luv."

"Hi there."

"Just the water?"

"Yes, thank you, ma'am."

The woman chuckled and coughed. "Long time since anyone called me ma'am! You're not from 'round here, ay?"

"No. I'm from the United States ... just visiting," Katherine replied, smiling.

"Oh, rightio. Did you come in on that big bloody boat?"

"The aircraft carrier? Yeah, that's me."

"First time here?"

"You bet."

"What you reckon so far?"

"Oh, I love it. I've been admiring your huge trees. Amazing ... the old growth forest."

The woman acknowledged Katherine with a muted smile and an unintelligible sound.

"It's a shame so many have been cut down," Katherine remarked.

The smile vanished from the woman's face. "People 'round here gotta make a living. No forestry means no jobs, no money, and no town. Something those bloody greenies just don't get!"

The woman slapped Katherine's change on the counter and waddled off.

Katherine let out a quiet "Phew!" as she got back into the vehicle.

"You okay?" Brady asked.

"Yeah. Note to self, though ... don't mention the trees."

"Oh bugger," he chuckled. "We better get outta here before the lynch mob arrives."

He checked Mr and Mrs Wu were on board. "One, two, three, four. All present and ready to go."

"That's good," Katherine said as their vehicle re-joined the main road and headed out of town.

"What's good?"

"You can count."

*　　*　　*　　*

Hobart

"What don't you understand about the word *fix*?" Cash snarled.

"I'm doing everything I can, believe me," Rouse protested.

Cash slammed his fists on the desk, then levered himself to a standing position in one smooth, gymnastic movement. He scowled at Rouse before stomping a few steps toward his office window. He faced the Port of Hobart with his back to Rouse. "If that bloody story goes to air like it is, the only future interaction we'll have with the U.S. Navy is a Tomahawk cruise missile right up the arse!"

"My contact at Network-8 is onto this. He *will* fix it, don't you worry."

"Don't worry, you say. Oh, don't you worry!" Cash's voice lowered into a growl. "He'd better friggin' fix this. There's *a lot* riding on this for everyone. Including me—*and you*."

"I get it, I get it. And look, I'm pulling out all the stops with our other channels. I've fed some juicy bits to the other networks and my contact at the paper is running a feature-spread on the carrier visit soon. I got people writing glowing letters to the editor—under other names, of course. And we've got social media support cranked right up."

"What, you posting pretty pictures on Faceygram or something?"

Rouse ignored the pointed sarcasm. "No, not exactly. And we can't use direct marketing. That would be too obvious. I've got our P.R. firm using all their social media accounts—Insta, Facey, Twitter, the lot—hundreds of members of the public saying how good this visit is for Tassie, how great the crew is—"

"Hmm. And the forum at the university? I got a bad feeling about that."

"It's pretty well set up, though. I think we'll be okay."

Cash eyed USS *John F. Kennedy*, which sat at anchor less than a mile away—right in the centre of his office window. "If you stuff this up, you better start looking for other work. And you won't find any on this island, I can guarantee that."

Bradfurd Rouse picked up his papers and walked out with barely a sound. He left Cash's office door wide open.

CHAPTER TWENTY-SEVEN

Be patient and calm—for no one can catch fish in anger.
—Herbert Hoover

USS Columbia, Tasman Sea
15 August 2023, 1305 hours

"Sonar, Conn, report all surface contacts within twenty thousand yards."

The order had come from Captain Samuel Carter, Executive Officer of the Los Angeles–class fast-attack submarine. He'd been on watch in the control room for an hour, in command of the submarine. The captain and the earlier watch had finished their handover and left to get some grub, some rest, and maybe some sleep.

"Conn, Sonar, aye. I hold two contacts on broadband. Sierra-Eleven is a fishing vessel bearing one-nine-eight, twelve thousand yards, tracking east out to sea at twelve knots. Sierra-Fourteen is a commercial tanker, the *Kingbird Arrow*, bearing one-three-three, sixteen thousand yards, tracking zero-two-five into the River Derwent. No other contacts, surfaced or submerged."

"Sonar, Conn, aye." Carter clipped the closed-circuit microphone back into its cradle. "Chief, stand by to come to periscope depth at 1315 hours. We're closer to the coast after our next turn, so I'll take a look around and make sure we've got no other company."

"Aye, sir," the chief replied.

Carter knew—with close to one hundred percent certainty—there were no other vessels on the surface nearby. But going to periscope depth and raising the periscope was sometimes performed just to keep the crew focused and alert. It helped break the boredom of conducting endless track patterns below the surface on a tedious patrol. And it would provide Carter with a welcome peek at the outside world in daylight, a luxury when all the usual rhythms of life above the surface were often closed to them for months on end.

*   *   *   *

Hobart

"Okay. Good job. That wraps this one up." Stewart McLellan saved the video project in the editing suite software, then closed it.

Steph Sadler stared at the blank review monitor, her face white and drawn as if she'd watched the most troubling horror movie of her life.

"Thanks for keepin' yer head, Steph. I'm sure you'll agree, it's an even better product now we've completed those edits. This segment will rate its socks off tonight and you'll get the cred."

"An even better product for who?" she asked, almost whispering.

"Better all round. This version gets the balance right."

"If you say so."

"Look, sometimes things happen above us, well above our pay grades. It's just the way of the world. You'll go far, lass, but remember to look after those who make the decisions, yeah? Survival of the smartest, I call it." McLellan stood and stretched. "Time for a wee spot a lunch. My shout?"

"No thanks. I feel sick," Sadler said.

*   *   *   *

Tasman Sea, eight miles south-east of the Tasman Peninsula
1:12 PM

The afternoon was clear and unseasonably mild at twenty degrees Celsius. With a low swell and little wind, the game-fishing boat rocked in the sloppy sea. Its substantial outboard motor sat silent as the craft drifted out to sea on the current.

Two fishing rods stood erect in the breeze, latched into mounts at the rear of the boat. A large steel tackle box lay at an angle across the rear left corner, held in by the opposing railings.

But a fisherman was nowhere to be seen.

Lee Todd was there, though. His stumpy, beer-bellied physique slumped low on a rear-facing seat, with his head propped against the driver's seat. He exhaled a rhythmic low vibrating snore in time with the boat's rocking motion.

This wasn't the first time Todd had fallen asleep at sea. He'd drifted off many times before, and today he was close to breaking his record of two and a half hours adrift in the land of nod—an unsurprising result of the eleven stubbies of beer and four shots of vodka he'd consumed since last evening. Even less surprising given the two pipe-loads of hard rock, or crack cocaine, he'd smoked on the boat earlier.

Todd ran a small construction firm in Hobart that generated a reasonable income stream. He operated mostly on cash transactions with little heed for his accountant or the tax authorities. The business survived, but only through the efforts of two employees who held it together.

Todd would often take a day off unannounced and abscond to the bush or sea. His four-wheel-drive and boating exploits were legendary, having bogged and crashed his Landcruiser more times than his insurance company could fathom, and creating havoc at local boat ramps with his bizarre attempts at solo boat launching and retrieval.

And fishing was not one of his finest skills. He didn't enjoy the hobby much at all and he hated the taste and texture of fish. For him, it was about the gear and being seen with the gear. And so, when one of his latched fishing rods bent into a semi-circle and the nylon line paid out with a scream as the reel refused to cope with the sudden load of a heavy running catch, Lee Todd resented the sudden commotion on his boat.

*　*　*　*

USS Columbia, eight miles south-east of the Tasman Peninsula
1315 hours
Petty officer Scott O'Neil had been on watch for two hours in the sonar

shack—a small, dim room not much larger than a cupboard that was stacked with electronic equipment and displays.

It had been a slow few days since they'd taken up patrol in the Tasman Sea south-east of Hobart. The current watch was looking no more exciting, with only two surface contacts to track in the patrol box and little else to do.

He thought about running diagnostics on the sonar arrays to keep his mind engaged, but decided against it. He'd ride the patrol pattern, do the basics of his job, and look forward to the end of the watch. Just like every other day.

*   *   *   *

Lee Todd had prised one eye open. The hubbub surrounding the fishing rod became clear as his vision adjusted to the sharp glare. He looked left to spot the horizon but couldn't see a coastline anywhere, then forced himself to a seated position.

As Todd's consciousness returned, he could feel a hammer pounding away inside his head. He gripped his howling stomach and returned his attention to the commotion on the stern. The rod, or if not the line, was about to snap in two. Maybe both. *Must be a bloody big fish ... maybe a bluefin!*

Somehow, Todd launched himself forward on his numb feet. He lunged at the offending fishing rod to rip it from the latched holder and into his eager hands. Instead he crashed sideways and crunched his shoulder hard against the fibreglass side of his boat. He let out a shrill gurgle as his head wobbled in recoil and messages of pain flooded his brain.

If there *was* a Poseidon—the great God of the sea—he was not finished with Lee Todd yet.

As Todd forced his other eye open, he heard an unexpected motion behind him. The sound was smooth and slow at first, but then gathered in pace and pitch—the harsh grind of steel gliding across aluminium.

And then as quickly as it had begun, the sound stopped.

Silence … although, not for long.

A thunderous splash splintered the tranquillity as steel met ocean.

Todd half-turned and half-stood. He stared at the offending piece of sea. The mass of white bubbles only confirmed what he didn't want to know. His beloved steel tackle box—the biggest and the best and the heaviest there was, and his thousands of dollars of the best fishing gear money could buy—were descending to the bottom of the Tasman Sea with all the grace of a miniature *Titanic*.

Todd turned to the heavens and screamed an elongated "*FUUUUUUCK!*" perhaps hoping Poseidon would respond to his anguish.

After a few further seconds staring in disbelief at the spot, he heard the bent-over fishing rod whip backwards and into its former erect position. The line had snapped.

Todd stomped to the driver's seat, threw himself down, and hit the engine starter. He shoved the throttle control to full before the engine had a chance to even idle.

*   *   *   *

USS Columbia

The sudden noise in O'Neill's sonar headset assaulted his brain with the power of an electric shock. He jumped in his seat and grabbed both his headset pads with his hands, straining to hear more. His eyes looked ready to leave his head as a surge of adrenaline sped through him. *So much for another boring watch!*

O'Neill shot a glance at the sonar waterfall displays. There it was: a sudden spike in sea noise at a bearing of zero-eight-zero degrees relative to the submarine's bow, and at short range. The sound frequencies on the display were chaotic and confused, confirming something heavy had gone through the surface of the sea.

His mind scrambled. Perhaps a biologic breaching the surface? But O'Neill hadn't heard any whale sounds in their vicinity.

He went to key the communication circuit to alert the control room when another sound stopped him mid-movement.

A sudden propeller noise, which went from idle to high power in a second, screeched in his headset. His sonar display confirmed the propeller noise was from the same bearing.

"Holy mother of—!"

* * * *

Lee Todd leaned forward, bracing himself as the boat punched through each swell at high speed. He continued to mutter and swear to himself: cursing the sea, cursing fishing, cursing tackle boxes, cursing Poseidon, cursing the unfairness of being alive. He adjusted the boat's heading to track due west. The Tasmanian coastline would be out there somewhere. This fishing trip was over.

* * * *

USS Columbia

"Conn. Sonar. New contact. Possible torpedo in the water bearing zero-eight-zero. It's almost right above us!"

Carter made it from the navigation plot table to the communication circuit in a single swift movement. *What the?* He keyed the mic. "Sonar. Conn. Confirm torpedo in the water?"

"Conn. Sonar, yes, sir. I got a heavy surface splash, then a single high-frequency propeller noise on the same bearing. Yet to identify. But sounds like a torpedo screw. Headed straight for us."

Carter shot a look at the control room ceiling on instinct—as if he could see the torpedo approaching from above. He could hear it, though, with its screw getting louder and higher in pitch by the second.

Carter dropped the microphone and swung to face the other side of the control room. He bypassed the chief and the diving officer, giving orders directly to the helmsman and planesman. "Helm, all ahead flank, right full rudder, steady course one-two-zero."

The helmsman swung into action at the controls and confirmed his orders.

"Chief, man battle stations. Prepare countermeasures."

The submarine came alive with the sound of the repeating claxon and crew members scurrying every which way.

"What's our sounding?" Carter barked.

"Depth sounding five-nine-zero feet, sir."

"Planesman, make your depth five hundred feet, maximum down bubble. *Expedite!*"

Everyone in the control room grabbed whatever they could on the panels and bulkheads to brace themselves as the submarine rolled hard right and pitched down sharply. The outer steel casing groaned with the sudden shift in inertia, sending an eerie vibration through the control room.

As the submarine rolled level on its new heading, O'Neill came back on the communication circuit. "Conn. Sonar. Range three hundred yards and closing fast. We're running straight at it!"

"Sonar. Affirmative. Hold steady," Carter said, expressionless.

The older hands in the control room were already contemplating the tactic Carter was using. He was running straight at the torpedo to pass underneath before its onboard sonar could lock on the submarine. And if Lady Luck was on their side, or even Poseidon, they might just descend through a temperature inversion layer to further throw the torpedo's sonar off their auditory scent.

The sound of the propeller grew ever louder as it approached.

"Sound the collision alarm!"

Carter was still gripping an overhead panel with both hands to prevent his body toppling forward as USS *Columbia* plummeted downwards. He squinted and thought hard … something was not quite adding up. "Sonar. Conn. Has the torpedo gone active?"

"Conn. Sonar. Negative. No active pings." As Scott O'Neill said the words, the likely reality of the situation hit him hard. He clenched his fists, threw himself backwards on his chair, and shook his head in abject capitulation. *Oh shit, no …*

The sound built to an ear-wrenching climax as it approached above the submarine, and just as quickly subsided as it passed overhead and away.

"Any change in its track?" Carter asked.

"Negative. It's on the same track with no aspect change. Now bearing one-eight-five and doppler reducing. Still no active pings."

Carter hitched the microphone and paused.

The deck angle pitched upwards and levelled out.

"My depth now five hundred feet," the planesman reported.

"Very well. Chief, all stop," Carter ordered. "Secure from battle stations and take us up to periscope depth."

*   *   *   *

1324 hours

Captain Samuel Carter leaned back on the edge of the equipment rack. He took a moment to scratch his nose.

Beside him, Petty Officer Scott O'Neill remained at his sonar station, still tracking the contact heading away from them towards the Tasmanian coast. His strained face and still-dilated eyes conveyed his disbelief and a growing sense of foreboding.

"Well, you sure know how to get the control room's attention," Carter said. "And how to get the Captain out 'a his rack in record time."

O'Neill looked at Carter as he tried to deduce the level of menace in the XO's words. He was certain this was the end of his career as a submarine sonar technician. But he was both relieved and confused to see Carter grinning.

"I'm sorry, sir, I, uh, I heard—"

"Easy, sailor. Take a breath. Just tell me what you saw and heard, and take it nice'n slow."

"All was quiet, sir, definitely no surface contacts above us, and no airborne contacts anywhere near us. But then this sudden heavy splash. Then the single screw going straight to high revs. It had all the marks of a torpedo being dropped, and starting up, and—"

"Okay. But did it sound like a torpedo screw?"

"To be honest, sir, yes, it did. I had no time to identify it though. It was so damn close and heading straight at us. I had to make a snap decision."

"Yup."

"May I ask, sir, what you observed on the periscope?"

"Oh, I really don't think you want to know that, O'Neill."

"Sorry, sir. It's just that everyone in the boat will be talking about this. I'll never live this down!"

"Easy there. You did nothing wrong." Carter took a few seconds to compose his next sentence, looking down to inspect his fingernails as he did. "I'd much rather be embarrassed than dead. You made the right call with the information you had. There's nothing else to be said. The log and my report to the captain will say exactly that."

"Thank you, sir."

"Not needed, son. Just keep doing your job, and do it well. And learn from today, yeah?"

"Yes, sir. I will."

Carter turned to the doorway, then stopped. "And one more thing, O'Neill."

"Sir?"

"You might find your nickname around here has been... adjusted."

"Yes, sir," O'Neill replied, doing his best to sound positive.

Carter stepped through the doorway, making one last comment as he left: "Carry on, Speedboat."

* * * *

It had taken Lee Todd a good half-hour to get his boat out of the water. A torrent of cursing, swearing, and grumbling had coaxed the wretched machine onto the trailer.

He spent the first ten minutes ashore informing another boat owner about his grand adventures for the day. He bragged about the massive bluefin tuna that he'd expertly snagged, only to be let down by his damned fishing equipment. The one that got away, if ever there was one.

Todd would never tell the story of the true catch that got away from him that day. For a few seconds he'd caught a three hundred and sixty-two–foot, seven thousand–ton black shark of the deep.

But he'd never tell because he never knew.

*   *   *   *

Hobart

Steph Sadler sat entranced by her laptop screen, sifting through social media posts. She shot out a hand to grab the desk phone receiver without looking or thinking. "Yep."

"Steph, the network in Sydney needs the final cut of your aircraft carrier story, and pronto. Mac hasn't sent the file package through yet and I can't reach him. Can you send them?"

"Yeah. No probs. I'll do it now."

"Great. Be quick, though. They need them in Sydney by three o'clock."

It's ironic, Sadler thought as she plonked herself into a chair in the edit suite. *Shouldn't be me doing the final transfer of this piece of crap.*

She located the project folder for the story, selected it, then hovered the cursor over the Export function. This would be the last step in the process to send the files to the studios in Sydney. The next thing she'd see would be the story as it went to air on *Affairs of the State* that evening.

Sadler paused. The cursor still hovered, waiting for her next command. There were two project folders: one contained the edit she and Wardlaw had assembled, and the other held the neutered version that snake Stewart McLellan demanded.

It's technically wrong, I suppose, but feels like the right thing to do.

But what about my career?
Those slimy pricks deserve it, though!
Sadler grabbed the mouse.

CHAPTER TWENTY-EIGHT

*When you go out there, you don't get away from it
all, you get back to it all. You come home to what's
important. You come home to yourself.*

—Peter Dombrovskis

15 August 2023

To Katherine, it felt like she'd already been away for a week.
USS *John F. Kennedy* and all those serving on it seemed distant
and hazy after just two days. Perhaps it was the relative solitude. There
were only three other people in her tour group, and they were quieter
types who were happy to converse, but not for the sake of it. And after
leaving Maydena and driving a long distance west, they hadn't seen a
single other human being.

Or perhaps it was the place? Katherine was starting to understand
Captain Collins' dreamlike description of Tasmania's south-west. This
was, as he'd put it, "A place like no other." A landscape hardly touched
by humanity. A unique and delicate blend of terrain, waterscapes, and
vegetation. And a subtle yet pervasive impression of an ancient world
seemed to lie within the rocks, seep through the soil, and trickle in
the water. As if the previous ages—some millennia long since forgotten,
and many never inhabited by humans—were somehow still present.
But it couldn't be explained. Only felt. Only enjoyed.

Katherine took in another long breath of the cool air, not doubting
Brady's boast this was the cleanest air in the world.

"We'd better be heading back," Brady said. "Our Chinese friends
might think we got lost."

But as they traipsed through the low scrub, Katherine felt anything
but lost. Martin Brady led the way as he picked through the button

271

grass and melaleucas. As a helicopter commander, Katherine was used to being in command and it was unnerving, but somehow liberating, to traverse a foreign environment under the direction of someone who seemed to rely on only his senses, memory, and instincts.

They'd spent the previous night in a tiny clearing in the wilderness, setting up camp in the late afternoon and preparing for the chilly night ahead. Brady had explained that they would usually stay in a cabin in Tasmania's central highlands, but a window of clear weather with little wind had opened the opportunity for a more authentic experience. "It'll be bloody cold," he'd said, "but worth it. Believe me."

Brady had all the right gear to manage the elements and the tents and sleeping gear were suitable for the Antarctic. The campfire he constructed brought a welcome warmth and burned long into the night. He could cook too. The bush tucker, as he called it, was hearty and tasty with touches of finesse. They enjoyed smoked wallaby garnished with wild pepperberry, a salad with kunzea leaves, water ribbon root and wattle seed, pickled pigface, and pink-eye potatoes with rosemary.

And around them that evening the place came alive. It was unnerving at first to hear a tree or a bush rustling with some passing creature, or the screaming snarls of Tasmanian devils undemocratically carving up an animal carcass in the distance. And their eyes were there too. Tiny bright pairs piercing the black of night as potoroos and wallabies cased the campfire from the edge of the clearing.

Mr and Mrs Wu had taken a good hour to relax into the environment. But this was the experience they'd requested and paid for and they seemed happy to be receiving it in spades. They went to bed around eight, leaving Katherine and Brady alone at the campfire.

At first the pair's conversation came in awkward spurts between long silences spent staring into the fire. Katherine was tempted to make for her tent. But she stayed—the warmth of the fire holding her in an indecisive trance.

Brady pointed out a gathering of stars above the horizon. "It's the Southern Cross," he said in a near whisper. "It points due south."

The silence resumed as they gazed southward.

"Well, I'll be," Brady said. "I think the lady is going to dance."

"Excuse me?"

"Not you," he chuckled. "The Aurora Australis. You want to see?"

"Hell, yeah."

"Follow me."

They made their way by flashlight to another clearing with a better view to the south.

Brady flicked off the flashlight. "Okay, you gotta be patient. Let your eyes adjust to the dark. It'll take maybe five minutes."

Katherine could see nothing at first. Their surroundings were blacker than she'd ever experienced, and to a degree that felt unsettling. Then she shifted her gaze upward and her eyes adjusted to vast constellations of stars in the heavens—some faint, but many bright and pinpoint sharp.

"Wow."

"No light pollution," Brady said. "This is as clear a sky as you'll see anywhere on the planet."

A subtle wispy haze began to materialise in the southern sky. The haze moved low to the horizon and seemed to shift and flow like waves in slow motion.

"I can see something," Katherine said. "It's kinda grey. Is that it?"

"Yep, you got it. But keep looking. You ain't seen nothing yet."

Katherine did as he suggested. Grey would *not* do it for her. She needed to see the colours she'd seen in photos of the Northern Lights. As minutes passed, the churning grey haze morphed into a green hue as her eyes further adjusted to the light. Its folds of colour shifted as if translucent sheets of light were being shaken by the gods in ultra–slow motion across the sky. And then brighter beams of intense purple light shot up from the horizon, some so short and fleeting they would be missed in a blink, others longer and higher, yet also gone a few seconds later.

The two strangers stood in silence as they watched the lady dance.

She twirled, pirouetted, and swayed for a good fifteen minutes before her ephemeral time on the universal stage was to be over. She retired to more southern latitudes, as if overcome with shyness.

As they settled back at the campfire, Katherine tried to find the words. "That, um, wow. I've never seen anything like it."

"It's hard to put into words, ay?" Brady said. "My advice—don't try. Just lock it in your memory and enjoy it." He smiled as he spoke.

Katherine wasn't sure whether it was the reflected light of the campfire in his eyes, but for the first time she could detect a warm soul there. Maybe the lady in the sky had softened him some—much like the opposite effect of seeing a ghost.

And then he surprised her. "So, tell me. Who is Lieutenant Commander Katherine Marlowe?"

Katherine pushed down her natural propensity to keep to herself. The lady's effect seemed to have touched her too. She talked about her life, her family, the navy, and flying. Brady listened at first, taking it all in, before the focus of the conversation naturally turned to him. He spoke of his upbringing in Tasmania, his parents, friends, and exploits in his younger years. Katherine was fascinated by his knowledge of the wilderness on this island—his home. She was surprised to learn he had lived in the United States for four years, although he seemed reluctant to talk about that much.

Katherine curled up in her sleeping bag later that night, satisfied as she reflected on her first instincts. She'd been right to think there was more to this man than he revealed at first glance.

*   *   *   *

Hobart

The scene was not unlike home. From Ben's position on the Tranmere shoreline, the wide expanse of the River Derwent before him was similar in width to Hong Kong's Victoria Harbour when viewed from Kowloon. Interlocked hill-lines rose behind the city on the opposite shore, with buildings and suburbs snaking along the water's edge. And behind, a significant mountain loomed over all as if guarding the city. kunanyi/Mount Wellington was much taller, but the presence of Victoria Peak above Hong Kong Island had much the same effect.

Both cities had a strong British look and feel in places, and a certain stoic politeness imbued from the old home country. Both had been under British rule and both had been peacefully handed to local governments.

But there the similarities ended. Hong Kong had been returned to China in 1997 after more than a century of British rule. The region had been "leased" to the British government after the Chinese lost the Opium Wars of the nineteenth century—a harsh punishment for the Chinese who had dared to stop British companies from flooding their population with drugs for capitalist profit.

And Hobart had none of the hundreds of glittering high-rise wonders of Hong Kong. Its population, at one-thirtieth the size of the Asian giant, was insulated from the rest of the planet and mostly white European in heritage.

Ben also recognised how different the place was from Melbourne. Still Australian, yes, but distinct too. The people had an unassuming, charming character of their own, and the look and feel of the place was not at all what he'd expected.

But this was no time for history, or tourism, or thinking of home.

Ben chose a large rock near the water's edge and took a seat. He retrieved his mobile and attachments from his backpack. He had work to do.

*   *   *   *

"Nearly there," Brady said, panting hard.

Katherine plodded on behind him, willing their destination back into view. The temperature had been falling and the cold burned in her chest with every breath.

Their destination—a lookout on a prominent hill near Lake Pedder—revealed itself soon enough. They'd left the Wus there an hour earlier. The couple had been content to stay and enjoy the view while Brady and Katherine went off to explore a tarn—a small mountain lake nearby.

Mr Wu seemed glad to see them. His face shone as he pointed across the vista before them. To the west, expansive lakes wound between rounded grassy hills. To the south, button grass plains and scattered trees gave way to an endless line of snow-covered mountain peaks, and in the far distance, a blue lake glistened in the late afternoon sun. All around them, craggy peaks and sharp ridges criss-crossed the horizon, too many to contemplate.

"Happy. *Happy!*" Mr Wu effused, using one of the few English words he knew.

Mrs Wu was less exuberant. She sat by herself a distance away to take in her own version of the view.

Katherine sensed something amiss. As she approached, Katherine could see tears streaming down the woman's face.

Katherine, not knowing any Chinese, had no words to say. She squatted next to Mrs Wu, put an arm around her shoulders, and offered a few words of comfort in English.

"Okay. Okay," Mrs Wu struggled to say, placing an open palm over her chest and clearing her throat. She nodded, tried to smile, then pointed to herself. "Okay ... okay."

Katherine looked up at Brady, confused.

"Don't worry," he said. "People react in different ways, and this is one of them."

"I'm not sure what's happening," Katherine said.

"Imagine you've been living your entire life in a mega-city like Shanghai. Even in the regional areas, every square inch is taken up by dwellings, infrastructure, and agriculture. And people *everywhere.* You've never been truly alone there, not in your entire life."

"Oh, I see," Katherine said as she stood. "It's a lot to take in, I guess."

Mrs Wu followed her lead, taking her husband's hand to help her up. She wiped away the last of her tears, looked at Brady and nodded once more. He nodded back. They each seemed to understand the other.

"Right-o. Let's make our way back to the vehicle. The weather's gonna change and come in pretty quick."

The three tourists picked up their things and followed Brady as he began the descent.

Each of the three stole one last look at the ancient world behind them before it slipped below the hill line and out of their view.

*   *   *   *

Hobart

Ben kept his mobile hidden in his lap. He had the screen tilted upward to see the video as it streamed in. A small black cylinder, perched on a large rock next to him, pointed across the river.

He manipulated the app's controls to zoom in on the video image feeding in via Bluetooth from the miniature zoom lens. He adjusted the focus and began recording.

Ben had positioned himself less than a mile from the object. The lens provided clear high-definition images and to his surprise he could make out the faces of crew members standing on a suspended walkway below the flight deck. Up above, parked fighter jets appeared in pristine detail as he panned the view. He could even see human figures and display screens in levels of the tower at the rear of the flight deck.

He'd chosen this position on Hobart's eastern shore to match the current orientation of USS *John F. Kennedy*. The ship was aligned north-east as it pointed into the wind. His final briefing would depend on this view.

This location was also happily devoid of people. A small, quiet suburb snaked behind the shoreline, and the walking path nearby had been unoccupied when he'd parked his car. The houses were about a hundred metres back and out of sight, and a line of grasses and rocks provided further privacy. A perfect place for the task at hand.

"Pretty impressive, isn't she?"

Ben jumped at the voice behind him, and caught his phone just before it crashed from his lap. He whipped around to see a man standing about ten metres away and above him near the edge of the grassed area. The old man was stooped over a walking frame, his body twisted to one side with his head at an odd angle.

"Ah …" was all Ben could manage. He was still in shock and cursing himself for losing situational awareness, but relieved to see the owner of the voice presented no immediate threat.

"Bloody amazing things, these American carriers. We got the best view in the house from 'ere."

Ben nodded and forced a grin. He extended his right hand as if to lean on the rock beside him—to cover the zoom lens.

"You from China? Korea? What?"

"Ah. So-rry. No En-grish," Ben said, laying on the thickest accent he could muster.

"Oh, right."

Ben faced the river again, hoping the man would take the cue and leave.

"I bet you don't even know this place you're sitting in," the man continued. "It's called Chinaman's Bay. Hundreds of you Asians wound up here a long time ago. You should look it up, interesting reading that."

Ben half-turned back towards the man. He feigned an ignorant half-smile and a subservient nod.

"You look Korean to me, young fella. I've seen lots 'a you little buggers before. Running around the hills near Pyongyang and Kujin. All trying to shoot me and my mates dead. Our 3RAR battalion stuck it right up youse back then."

Ben gripped the zoom lens hard. He steadied himself with his other hand and forced himself to breathe easy.

"Anyway, you just keep your distance from those Yanks out there, cobber. Mind your own bloody business. You best go back to where you came from—"

Ben's mind ran through his options and prioritised his best course of action. He started to stand up, but then heard another voice.

"Oh, *there* you are, Henry!" A much younger man appeared beside the old man.

He was followed a few seconds later by an elderly woman. "Henry! You have to stop wandering off like this. How many times have I told you?"

The young man was helping Henry turn around when he saw Ben sitting below them. "Oh. Hi, there. Don't worry, the old fella here is a bit unwell."

The three made their way off with Henry muttering and gesticulating as they went.

Ben gathered his things and headed for his car, keeping below the line of sight of the houses for as long as he could. He'd have to find another place and he'd be much more selective this time.

Will they tell the authorities about me? Ben thought the risk was low. He couldn't be certain, but it wasn't something he could control. He could only be more careful from that point forward.

*   *   *   *

It had only been a short walk from the river's edge back to Henry and Deirdre's house, but it took them ten minutes to return.

The carer settled Henry into his recliner chair. "Geez, mate, you had us all worried."

"The Chinese. They're coming," Henry said, his eyes like plates.

"Come on now, dear, it's time to settle yourself down," Dierdre said.

"Those little Korean yellow-bellies. We can't trust 'em either, you know!"

"Easy, Henry, he was just a tourist."

"No! You gotta tell command. They want that ship!"

The young carer took Dierdre's cue and followed her into the kitchen.

"I'm so sorry," she said. "I think he's getting worse again."

"Don't be. When I get back to the centre, I'll speak to the doctor. I think he needs to come out and review Henry again. We might need to adjust his medication."

"I don't want to lose him."

"I know. And we'll do everything we can to keep him at home as long as we can."

"He carries on about his past so much now … his teenage years, his parents, the Korean War. He can't remember how to stir a cup of tea, but he can remember his early life in such detail."

Henry's thin raspy voice boomed from the living room: "You've got to get a message to command! The brigadier must be informed!"

"It's just the dementia," the carer said. "It goes like this for many of our patients."

CHAPTER TWENTY-NINE

I always wanted to be some kind of writer or newspaper reporter. But after college ... I did other things.
                    —Jacqueline Kennedy Onassis

Hobart

15 August 2023, 6:41 PM

Ben had been halfway through his takeaway meal of fish and chips—a Tasmanian dish he felt compelled to try. It was impossible to cook in the small room he'd rented on a rural property south-east of Hobart. The kitchen was empty but for an old plastic kettle, a mug, a glass, two spoons, and tea that tasted like dust.

But the room was quiet and out of the way, and there was no CCTV anywhere on the property. Ben had gone out a few times to conduct surveillance and buy food. For the rest of the time, the room was an ideal place to stay undetected.

Ben had grown tired of other takeaway. The quality of the local Asian food was reasonable, but presented with an obvious Western bent. A poor comparison to the cuisine from his homelands and well below the quality of his mother's cooking.

The thought evoked unbidden emotions and feelings of place. The streets of Hong Kong, the faces of his parents, the smells and sounds of sharing a meal in their apartment ... *home.* Ben struggled to intercept them before they took hold. He was getting worse at this, not better, and it frustrated him no end.

He tossed what remained of the fish and chips to the floor. Too bland, oily, and salty.

Ben had flicked on the television and watched the local evening news. Most of it didn't interest him, although he had nodded to himself at the story about joint military exercises between China, Russia, and North Korea. The footage was well out of date and out of context, but there was a clear tone of heightened concern throughout.

"Things are coming together," he murmured.

The next program—a national current affairs show—featured a story set right here in Hobart. The circling aerial vision of the aircraft carrier had him sitting upright at the end of the bed. He watched, fascinated by the footage of flight operations above deck and the scale and complexity of life in the many decks below. He drank in the scenes, grateful for a rare glimpse inside a new Ford-class aircraft carrier at sea.

But it was the people on board who held his interest. The journalist had pieced together a collage of comments from officers and crew throughout the ship. She simply posed the question: "How do you feel about this deployment and about going home?"

A pilot sat alone in a squadron ready room, his arms folded, leaning forward. "It's been great, but … yeah, it's time to go home."

A woman in her early thirties and kitted out in a bright yellow jersey stood on the flight deck with goggles raised. "I left my little boy with my parents back in Arkansas," she said. "It's been a year now since I've seen him."

"I wanna go home and see everyone again," said a petty officer seated at his desk. "Give 'em all the biggest hug I can."

"The chow here is okay," said a man sitting in a mess hall. His green jersey and face were smeared with streaks of black grease. "But I miss my mom's cooking. What I wouldn't give for a plate of her grits right now."

Ben closed his eyes. He understood how it was to pine for his mother's cooking. He could almost smell her handmade pork and shrimp wontons, and her delicate egg tarts. Ben didn't understand what grits were, but that was beside the point. The home-cooked food both men craved was different, but for the briefest of moments Ben understood this young American.

*   *   *   *

6:42 PM

"Begging your pardon, ma'am, but we don't decide where these munitions go, or why. We make sure they're ready for each mission as our orders tell us. We get 'em up the weapons elevators and our people up on deck get 'em hooked up to the airplanes and armed. The pilots do the rest."

"So that's it, then?" Steph Sadler asked. "It's the *pilots* who do the killing, but it has nothing to do with your role on the ship?" She stood behind the camera and out of the frame.

Deep furrows emerged on Petty Officer Third Class Alvaro Sanchez's forehead. "That's not what I'm saying," he managed. "We're a team. Ain't nobody can carry out a mission unless we all do our bit. The pilots are at the end of the chain. Our commanders, they're like … at the start."

"So, you just do what you're told then? You never think about who that bomb beside you there will fall on, or what it will do when it hits the target?"

"They're called orders, ma'am. Somethin' I don't expect you can understand."

"Really. How so?"

"What we do protects our way of life. Our liberties. It keeps our people safe." Sanchez paused and shuffled on his feet, seemingly conflicted. "I don't doubt for a second why I'm here," he added as he folded his arms tight. "I trust my orders and those who give them."

Deputy Premier Matthew Cash screwed up his face as he watched the exchange between the ordnanceman and the journalist on the television. Bradfurd Rouse had assured him that he'd fixed the issue with this muckraker journalist. And for the first few minutes of the story, all had seemed fine. Life onboard the carrier, benign but interesting personal comments from a few officers and crew, and a reasonable synopsis of the history of the ship and its first deployment.

But decades of experience in politics had taught Cash the only genuine rule in the game that had no rules: *never put absolute trust in anyone or anything.*

* * * *

6:43 PM

Stewart McLellan sat stiff as a corpse with his head pushed over the armchair's top, staring up at the ceiling as if waiting for an executioner's axe to fall. His mobile buzzed and chirped on the couch beside him. There was no need to look at the screen. It would be Rouse, that was for sure.

No sense either in calling the national studio in Sydney. By the time he spoke with someone in the control room, the five-minute story would be as good as broadcast.

* * * *

6:44 PM

Cash's mouth dropped wider as he watched the vision of himself, Captain Collins, and three officers disembarking from the ferry at Hobart's cruise ship terminal. Then a sudden cut to the protestors shouting, singing, and carrying on like the whingeing, demented, anti-everything interlopers they were.

In reality, there'd only been a handful of protestors around when he disembarked. But a clever piece of editing had brought the two factions together and melded them into one piece of believable half-fiction. And where was his interview recorded back on the ship and his carefully crafted messaging?

And then things got worse. *"Bugger it,"* Cash muttered to himself as the hard countenance of a thin silver-haired woman appeared on his screen.

"Our government has deceived us! They're putting us at risk!" she thundered.

The caption at the bottom of the screen told the national television audience what he already knew: JESSIE COCKERILL: *SAVE THE PLANET PARTY* LEADER.

He always cringed when he saw her far too familiar face. Whether from across the floor of parliament, or at a political function, or when they passed in the corridors of the parliamentary office complex, the effect was always the same.

"Here we have the Deputy Premier, Mr Cash, swanning around telling us what a wonderful thing it is to have nuclear-powered warships parked in our harbour. But it's what he's *not* telling us, *that's* what we need to be most concerned about!"

"And what would that be?" Steph Sadler asked.

"He's breached government policies that are there to protect our citizens. If *anything* goes wrong with that ship's nuclear reactors, the people of Hobart are at direct risk of immediate radiation poisoning."

"Do you know that for sure, or is it just your opinion as a politician on the opposite side of the fence?"

Cockerill scowled. "Yes. *Absolutely*, yes, I know it for sure." She lifted a copy of a government document into the frame as she continued. "This is the port safety plan for the visit of nuclear ships to Hobart. All the experts say this ship should be parked *way* down the river and well away from our city. But Mr Cash has let it anchor right here among us. The risks are enormous!"

Cash's mobile buzzed and chirped on the armchair beside him. There was no need to look at the screen. It would be the Premier, that was for sure.

*   *   *   *

6:45 PM

Ben bent down to grab the last piece of fish as he continued to watch the television.

"We have an obligation and a duty to our people, our allies, and all the free nations of the world," the woman said, dressed in her navy blues.

Ben glanced at the bottom of the screen to get the officer's name: LIEUTENANT EMIKO NOMURA: SENIOR PUBLIC AFFAIRS OFFICER, USS JOHN F. KENNEDY. "They have a jjokbari pig to speak for them now!" he sneered to himself.

"Our carrier strike groups bring a powerful message as they move through the world's oceans," she continued. "It's a message of liberty, freedom, and equality … the values we cherish in our democracies. It's a message to all nations: the United States will protect those values in any part of the globe as we see the need."

Ben spat his half-chewed mouthful of fried flounder to the floor. He wanted to scream at the arrogance of this Japanese bastard, but his training engaged before his rage fully surfaced. Instead, he whispered as he stared hard at the screen, "And we will soon have a message for *you*, you damned pig."

*   *   *   *

7:28 PM

Brady pulled the four-wheel-drive to a stop outside a heritage-style cottage in the hillside suburb of West Hobart. He fetched Katherine's bag from the back of the vehicle as she made her way to the front gate.

She waited for him at the illuminated BED AND BREAKFAST sign, thinking about their trip. She'd experienced a pang of sadness when they said good-bye to the Wus at their hotel ten minutes earlier. Brady and Katherine had learned more from the Wus on their way home. They'd confided, as best they could with their phone's translator app, that their only son had dreamed of travelling to Tasmania to experience the wilderness, but was killed in an industrial accident two years ago. His parents had taken the trip in his honour, determined to experience the place on his posthumous behalf.

The depth of their emotions made more sense now. And it had

dawned on Katherine as she reflected that the Wus were about her parents' age.

"I guess that's it then, Lieutenant Commander Katherine Marlowe," Brady said, dropping her bag at her feet.

Katherine smiled, no longer put off by his gruffness. "I guess it is," she replied. She studied his face as best she could in the dim light provided by the sign. "Martin, thanks so much. The trip was more than I expected. I think it's done me a whole lot of good."

"Glad to hear it. Make sure you write that up in TripAdvisor, ay."

"Hmm. We'll see."

"Enjoy the rest of your stay, Katherine."

"Thanks."

Brady returned her smile, tilting his head a fraction. Maybe there were more words to say. Maybe there weren't. He headed for his vehicle. "See ya later."

*   *   *   *

8:02 PM

"I just got off a long call from one of the rear admiral's staffers."

"She's pissed, huh?"

"Yeah, you could say that. She's already getting questions from Garrison's office back home, and another journalist tried to contact her for comment."

"Mmm."

The phone conversation fell silent. If Lieutenant Nomura was expecting words of wisdom from Captain William A. Collins, or even guidance on what to do next, she'd be waiting a good while.

"Captain?"

"It is what it is."

"Well, yes. It's just, I think we need to decide what comes next."

"I don't think we need to do anything special. This is just one story. There's been some good media too, I'm guessing. I don't look at that stuff at all, but I trust you're doing your job. Best thing we can do is get on with things."

"Understood, sir. But shouldn't we try to counter it? Correct the mistruths? Make the facts clear?"

"Well, no. I don't think so."

Collins reached to the bedside table and retrieved a novel. He thumbed the pages with one hand to get to his place.

"Sir?"

"Yes."

"I thought you'd want me to draft a statement for the media?"

"From us? Hell, no. I don't waste my time with snotty-nosed, self-serving journalists. Never have, never will."

The line went silent again.

"No need to stoop to their level," Collins continued. "Wrestling with pigs only gets you dirty."

"Sir," Nomura replied, her tone deflated.

"Very well, Lieutenant. Carry on."

"Aye, sir."

Collins powered off his phone, tossed it on the bedside table, and returned his attention to his book. He'd be getting calls and texts for hours to come—from Rear Admiral Paterson, or Deputy Premier Cash, or whoever else thought they needed him, that would be for sure.

CHAPTER THIRTY

There is more time than life.
>   —Mexican proverb

Hobart, 16 August 2023

Katherine stretched out blindly, eyes still closed, eventually finding her phone on the floor. She managed to wake it from its overnight slumber, then find the source of the notification that had awakened her. 8:53 AM. *So much for my first real sleep for months.*

The need to be somewhere else and not let others down tugged at her mind. But she resisted the urge to jump out of her rack, throw on her uniform, and get the hell out of there and back on watch.

The bed was no rack. The king-size expanse felt like a giant marshmallow with thick cuddly sheets. And the bedroom was lavish—spacious, lit softly through lace curtains, and beautifully decorated in the mid-nineteenth-century style.

Katherine exhaled as the spike of anxiety drained away. She looked again at her phone with one eye open and forced herself to read the text message:

Hey. You like a drink?

She shook her head and allowed herself a small grin as her fingers flew across the virtual keyboard:

Oh no, you heard about my problem then? :(

Two minutes passed with no reciprocal message to quell her building dread. Katherine wondered whether her playful message had bamboozled Martin Brady, or worse. But his reply came, eventually:

No. I meant do you want to come out for a drink later?

Oh sorry, here I was thinking you had nailed my alcoholism issue

Yeah, already worked that out. That's why I'm going to ply you with the stuff. Pick you up at 4?

See you at 4 :) K

*　　*　　*　　*

The special feature in the local newspaper had been published as Bradfurd Rouse had expected—packed with positivity and optimism. The images were lively and bright. The stories about the aircraft carrier, its captain, its crew, and its role, were informative and the writing was passable.

Local businesses had offered their support with an array of special deals for sailors. Rouse smirked at the advertisement from the local Gentleman's Gallery establishment: "25% off all lap dances for U.S. sailors." Their offer was generous, but he wished the advertisement had been placed somewhere less prominent than page three.

"You'd have to be happy with this, then?" he asked, gesturing towards the paper.

Lieutenant Emiko Nomura sat next to Rouse on a bench seat facing the Elizabeth Street Pier. The spot he'd chosen was near the parliament buildings and bathed in the subtle warmth of the afternoon sun. Nomura sat rigid, her face grim, looking ahead at the sailing ship bobbing in the water alongside the pier. The old vessel strained every now and then on its mooring ropes, creating an elongated creaking sound like a door opening in a B-grade horror flick. "You think this is enough to undo the damage caused by the story last night?" she asked, still looking ahead.

"Not just that, no," Rouse said. "But there will be more good exposure. There's tangible goodwill developing between your people and ours. The media and socials are picking it up already and there's *much* more to come."

"You seem confident in yourself," Nomura remarked. "How do you know?"

"Because I make it happen."

"Is that right?"

"Of course. C'mon, Emily. You're a public relations officer, you know how this stuff works."

Nomura shifted in her seat. Perhaps her discomfort came from the uncomfortable truth of his words. Or his uninvited use of her first name. She'd dealt with his type many times before, but he had a presence she couldn't stomach. "I know how to spin and pull strings, if that's what you mean," she said.

"Yeah. And the rest," he said, faking a chuckle.

She turned to look at him. "I don't make stuff up."

"Neither do I … not really. I let the public create it for themselves. It takes some encouragement in the right direction sometimes. The media and the public—they do the rest."

"Really."

"Yep. If you want to galvanise the public about an enemy, you focus their attention on the threat. You drum up the fear. You dehumanise them. But if you want to create the opposite reaction, like in this situation, then you drum up the warm and fuzzy. And you humanise the people on the other side."

"Us, you mean?"

"Yeah. Everyone on the ship and Americans in general. That's what this article did. And that little smart-arse Steph Sadler? She's too stupid to realise it, but her human-interest clips about your crew have done the same thing."

Nomura changed tack. "This goodwill you mentioned, what are you hearing?"

"Lots. Thing is, Emily, us Taswegians are hospitable. The adopt-a-sailor program you guys suggested is going great. Over eight hundred of your crew are billeted in Hobart homes. They're enjoying family hospitality and home-cooked meals. Our people are loving it and we're getting more requests from our locals than we can fill.

"And the teams of crew members you've sent out on projects—going great-guns there. Your guys are playing our local basketball, rugby, and soccer teams, and it's getting great traction on social media. The schools and community groups your people are visiting are sending glowing reports. And—"

"I get the picture."

"Cool. We gotta give it some time. By tonight, the Network-8 story will be yesterday's news."

Nomura rolled her eyes and rose to her feet. "I'll see you at the forum tomorrow night. I'll be there at six and we can sync-up some more then."

"Sure, see you at six."

"I expect you've put the containment strategies in place, as we discussed?"

"Of course."

Nomura turned on her heel. She strode away toward the cruise terminal and a ferry to return to her world aboard USS *John F. Kennedy*. She'd have to traverse the line of protestors again—they had grown in size and volume since the TV story the night before. But their songs and chants were becoming only noise to her. Much like public relations.

*   *   *   *

PLAN submarine Shaanxi-2, Tasman Sea, four hundred and thirty-five miles east of Bass Strait
1920 hours

"Navigator. Do you have the revised ETA for Bravo-One?"

"One moment, Captain."

"I do not have the luxury of moments. *Move it!*"

"Sir."

Captain Zhang Yong glowered at his navigator as the man worked the digital plot table in the centre of the control room. His fingers flew across the expansive touch screen as he plotted alternative routes and calculated time and distance.

The plot table—large enough to be right at home in a suburban dining room—cast a faint blue-white light up onto the pale ceiling. Its light blended with those of the tactical, sonar, and weapons control consoles lining both sides of the control room to create a dim ambience of cool blue.

The console operators were also immersed in the blue. Their faces reflected the light of their digital displays and punctuated only by the white of their eyes ever focused on the visual information presented to them.

And an aroma hung in the air, as if the dim blue atmosphere had a smell all its own. The subtle blend of hydraulic fluid and diesel smells, mixed with the body odour of men who'd worked too many extended watches with too few breaks, pervaded the room. Those who'd managed to take a shower had only three minutes to perform the task, and of those three minutes the water could run for one minute only.

Zhang sat upright in the captain's chair, tapping his fingers to an invisible rhythm on an armrest. The captain's face was hard and devoid of any emotional hint. His head held vertical and steady on a sinewy neck.

The crew understood the captain's eyes were the only non-verbal giveaway of his demeanour and feelings. His pupils would sometimes transform to a deeper blackness—the first sign of potential trouble. And if his eyes should narrow, then actual trouble was assured. He'd never shout at the crew, but they could expect a withering assessment of their performance, that was for certain.

Zhang was ahead of their game, though. He always wore his PLAN submariner's cap outside his quarters. The cap was well-worn but smart, with a pixelated mottling of blue-green-grey khaki matching his operational uniform. He would pull it down tight and low. If a crew member was brave enough or stupid enough to try to read Zhang's eyes, he would need to work hard to do so.

"Captain, I have the plot solutions," the navigator said.

"Go ahead."

"At our current speed of six knots, we will reach the Bravo-One fix off Tasmania's north-east coast in approximately seventy-three hours. Our ETA to reach the Alpha-One mission rendezvous will then be 21 August at 0420 hours local time."

"This is unacceptable. What is your contingency?"

"Sir, if we increase to eight knots our time to Bravo-One is fifty-five hours, and our ETA for Alpha-One will be 20 August at 0200 hours."

"This is marginally acceptable, but our arrival can be no later than this. How confident are you of your revised ETA?"

"It will depend on the strength of the currents on Tasmania's east coast. The prevailing current runs south-east and this should help us stay within our ETA. But our weather modelling from the satellite is over two days old now. The actual winds and currents, I therefore regret, I cannot predict with accuracy."

"Modelling!" Zhang swivelled his chair away from the navigator and yelled a command over his left shoulder toward the pilot position: "Increase speed to eight knots."

"Eight knots, sir," the pilot confirmed.

As Zhang turned back in his chair, he saw a dark figure at the far end of the control room in his peripheral vision. A tall, wiry man leaned against a bulkhead—his plain black outfit blending into the shadows. The man's eyes were a bluish-white in the dim light of the control room and focused on the captain.

"Captain, what is your status?" the man asked, his voice deep and flat.

Zhang knew the man only by his Korean family name of Tak. The mission briefing described Tak as a mid-ranking commando in the Korean People's Army Special Operation Force, but Zhang did not know his actual rank or anything of substance about the man. Even lesser known was Tak's colleague, Ryeon, the second DRPK commando assigned to the mission. He was even more elusive than his senior officer, only venturing outside their designated zone in the forward torpedo room for exercise, hygiene needs, and food. Zhang had only heard Ryeon speak once when the two operatives had first boarded the submarine from the supply ship.

"Status normal," Zhang shot back as he turned away from Tak.

"Captain. The conversation with your navigator indicates otherwise."

Zhang tensed. He didn't know how long Tak had been lurking in the shadows of the control room. Zhang had insisted, earlier in the mission, that Tak ask permission to enter the sacred command sanctum of the submarine. Tak had complied on the first few occasions, before ignoring the requirement and making himself at home at will.

"Everything is proceeding according to plan," Zhang said.

"Then what is this concern about ETA and speed?"

"I command this submarine. I assure you we will arrive at the mission location as per mission requirements."

"Captain, as mission commander I must concern myself with how this happens. We have only one opportunity. If we are late, or if we are rushed in the final hours, the entire mission will be in jeopardy. We cannot allow this."

Zhang detested Tak's interchangeable use of "you" and "we" to suit his arguments. He was tempted to order the North Korean to get out of his control room, but wisdom and experience tempered his response. "We cannot always predict the sea. Our strategies must be as fluid as the condition of the sea itself. We have proceeded at a steady six knots. This is slow, but it is the optimum speed for avoiding detection and the best endurance speed when running on AIP."

Tak frowned, obviously perplexed by the acronym.

"AIP is our air-independent-power system. It uses a chemical reaction to produce steam, which drives electrical generators to charge our batteries. Our propulsion system is electric and takes its power from the batteries. This makes for the quietest propulsion there is."

Tak was still frowning, as if he needed to know more.

"AIP does not require outside air, so we do not have to surface every few days to run the system and charge our batteries. Our latest version of AIP is more advanced than any other in the world. We can stay submerged for up to twenty-five days at a time, and our adversaries have no idea we have this improved capability."

If Tak was impressed by all this, he had a strange way of expressing it. "Then why are we running behind schedule?"

"A deep low-pressure system in the Tasman Sea produced unfavourable currents."

"Is that all?"

"No. We've been coming to periscope depth every two days to update our position and communications. On day six we were advised an Australian submarine had departed their base at Jervis Bay and proceeded east into the Tasman Sea. We had to assume a certain patrol radius and this meant taking a more easterly course to avoid them. This cost us many extra miles. The diversion put us close to the New Zealand economic zone and one of their patrolling frigates. We spent a day dodging the frigate at low speed to ensure we never came to their attention."

"I see. And now?"

"We have increased speed to eight knots to make our required arrival time. This makes us more vulnerable to detection and will deplete our AIP chemical reserves faster than we want. We may need to run on our backup diesel-electric generators for part of the return journey."

"Understood. Keep me informed of any changes, and your progress."

Zhang nodded in Tak's general direction, then turned away. His eyes had darkened. And narrowed. He had no intention of complying with the man's insolent request.

*   *   *   *

Hobart

4:20 PM

"You're late," Katherine said as she slid into the passenger seat.

"Yep," Brady grunted.

"So where are we headed?"

Brady turned the four-wheel-drive around and headed back towards the centre of Hobart. "It's a surprise."

"I'm not into surprises much."

"That's surprising."

"Oh God, you're in fine form today."

"As are you, Lieutenant Commander."

"How's that?"

"You, ah, you look … good."

Katherine looked out the passenger window and did her best to hide the red blush creeping across her neck and face. Yes, she'd spent more time than usual on her hair, make-up, and choosing the right outfit. And yes, she'd been mildly happy with what she'd seen in the mirror a few minutes before. But she wasn't prepared for the compliment.

*   *   *   *

Katherine sat with her back at a shallow angle to the fireplace in the corner. She relished in the warmth, the soothing glow, and the rustic sound of flames licking at the wood. The pub was a timeworn two-storey building a half-hour south-west of Hobart that had appeared out of nowhere on a winding mountain road.

The place was quiet, with only a few old-timers perched at the bar. They each said little, content instead to stare at their beer, the Indian cricket match on the TV, or the girl polishing glasses behind the counter. Fifties-era music drifted down the staircase from the floor above.

The walls, the floor, the doors, the furniture, the bar, and even the ceiling in some rooms were all made of timber. Vertical boards of the darkest brown shade lined the walls. Each was caked in many layers of thick varnish and decorated with paintings and photographs of yesteryear. The faces of farmers, bushmen, and timbermen, and of wives and children and grandparents, who had all at one time identified with the old place.

Brady returned from his expedition to the bar and plonked two tall glasses of tannin-coloured beer on their table. "Here. Get that in ya."

"You do have a way with words," Katherine said.

"It's a local brew. Best drop around."

Katherine sensed a certain tension in her drinking companion in the seconds of silence that followed. "Do you come here often?" she asked as innocently as she could.

"Yeah, it's my local. But, ah … I haven't done this in a while."

"This?"

"You know …"

Katherine's eyes sparkled. "Been a while since you asked a girl out for a drink?"

"Yeah. You could say that."

"Well, I'm flattered." Katherine took a sip of beer. She didn't like the taste, but it had alcohol, and was exactly what she needed at the moment.

"I'm not usually this forward, you see," he went on. "It's just that your ship will leave in a few days."

"Yeah."

"I was worried if I contacted you the next day, straight after the tour, I might have come across like a creep, or something." Brady took a long swig of his beer.

"Martin, I was glad when your text came through."

He put the beer on the table, but held onto it like a lifebuoy. "Yeah?"

"You seemed like a bit of a dick at first, I gotta say, but your company kinda grew on me."

"What, like algae?"

"Nah. Slower. More like fungus, I think."

*　　*　　*　　*

Six o'clock had turned into seven o'clock and then eight. One beer had turned into two. Then a whisky. Two plates of slow-cooked marinated wallaby and vegetables had appeared, then disappeared. Time then for a short glass of brandy.

Brady and Katherine's conversation eased back to their respective histories, their present, their loves, and hates; the things they liked to do and would never do. The people they were and were most definitely not. But there were still expanses of shadow between them. Things unsaid, not yet explored.

"You mentioned you lived in the States for a few years," Katherine prompted.

Brady pursed his lips. "Ah ... on the West Coast. Around San Francisco."

"Oh yeah? How long?"

"Four years."

"That's a long holiday."

"A bloody long time."

"C'mon, now. Tell me more."

Brady leaned back in his chair. "You won't believe me."

"Probably not, but give it a try."

"I worked in a technology think tank. A joint thing between Australia, Britain, and the U.S., funded by our governments."

"So ... you all sat there and thought about computers?"

"Very funny," he said, shaking his head. "We invented stuff. Most of it's classified, so that's why I'm cagey about it."

"Yeah, but I work for the U.S. government, remember? You can tell me," Katherine said with an exaggerated smile while flicking her eyelids as if in a daytime soap.

Brady looked down, then to his left, then right. He did it without thinking—an old habit yet to leave him. "Artificial intelligence," he said in a hushed tone.

"No shit? Martin Brady, from the Tasmanian bush, developing A.I. in the Silicon Valley."

"I said you might not believe me."

"Convince me, then."

Brady let out a steady breath through pursed lips. "Thing is, I always loved the bush, but through school I became a bit of a whiz in IT. I did an honours degree at Melbourne where I developed some out-there A.I.

code that made waves internationally. To cut a long story short, this led to that, and two years later I found myself in the U.S."

"And then?"

"And then we got to work on the craziest stuff I ever saw."

"Yeah?"

"I can't say what, but let's just say the future is coming and it may not be too bright."

A roar boomed from the direction of the bar. "Oh, shit yeah!" The man jumping off his barstool with both hands raised in victory. His fellow barflies started clapping and cheering as if there was no tomorrow. The man stared with reverence at a screen mounted on the wall above him, riveted by what he saw. The Keno game result on the screen said it all:

WINNER—$2,000!

"Seems odd," Brady said, "discussing artificial intelligence in a place like this."

Katherine glanced at the commotion at the bar and smiled. "What sort of things did you work on?"

"My specialty is a thing called fuzzy-logic. It's about technology making smart decisions in high-stakes, volatile environments. I worked on A.I. which can learn and grow in those environments."

"Like, in defence?"

"Yep. That's one."

"I'm often on the end of A.I. these days. If we aren't being told what to do by a tactical controller who's saying what an A.I. system tells him to, then we're getting orders directly from the A.I. itself—by frickin' datalink."

"In the helicopter?"

"Yup. It's the networked battlefield of the future. Except it's now. More and more computers, less and less humans. They'll probably replace all us pilots too, someday."

"Wouldn't be surprised," Brady said. "But it's what's in the middle— between us and all the new technology—that's what got to me. Augmented humans, brain-to-computer connections, technology you can wear and integrate into your body, all that crazy sci-fi shit. It's coming, and it's coming fast. The definition of being human is going to change, I reckon."

"Did you work on those things too?"

"Nah, but some of my colleagues did. I got to hear about things and see some things no one would believe." Brady's face had taken on a sullen expression. "Our species … we're taking evolution into our own hands. We aren't ready for such a thing and our planet isn't either. Nowhere near it. That's why I got out. Figured I may as well enjoy the natural world while it's still what it is. And do what I can to delay the inevitable."

"Shit. You're starting to scare me now."

"Sorry. That's why I don't like discussing this stuff."

"So, the story is not so much how Martin Brady went from Tasmania to Silicon Valley. It's more why you *returned* to Tasmania from Silicon Valley."

"Yeah. Sounds about right. Funny how we can end up where we started." Brady shifted his attention to the fireplace. The flames were gone, but the coals were glowing a pulsating red.

Katherine took in his profile—the muted coals of the fireplace highlighting the rusty flecks of red in his dark beard. She could sense the lure of the great unknown, of new ground, much like the wilderness she'd tasted the day before. *But no need to rush*, her instinct whispered.

"Shall we change the subject?" she asked.

"Yes, please, that'd be good."

"Right. So, tell me again why this Jimmy Barnes of yours is better than our Bruce Springsteen?"

"Okay. Before I do, hang tight there for a sec …"

Brady made his way to an open area at the centre of the pub. He stopped near the upright piano and leaned forward to rest his hands either side of a large glass dome. He blew the dust away, pushed a few buttons, then fed the object a gold coin.

The stately jukebox jumped to life. The machine hadn't played a tune in years, it seemed, and took a few seconds to warm to the task. Martin looked surprised and delighted as it cranked into gear.

The melodic tones of Cold Chisel's "Flame Trees" radiated across the room. Some patrons nodded. Others tapped along in silent recognition of the stark raw philosophy of everyday Australian life, as sung by Jimmy Barnes. Others rose to the lyrics to add their own alcohol-inspired harmonies to the chorus. The song carried the deep guttural sounds of the streets, of the unpretentious Australian way of life, of a nation and a resilient people carved from a vast brown land at the bottom of the world.

Katherine could see Brady's boyish grin returning as he made his way back to their table. He seemed carried along by the music as an anthem of what he valued most. Martin Brady had not set the world on fire, or even his hometown. But one thing seemed for sure—he was home and right where he wanted to be.

CHAPTER THIRTY-ONE

Study the past, if you would divine the future.

—Confucius

University of Tasmania, Hobart

17 August 2023

A digital clock on the side wall flicked to 7:00 PM—the signal for the auditorium lights to dim to a reverent tranquillity. The noisy bubbling of the audience fell to a hush. Those still standing rushed to the few spare seats remaining, with the forum being fully booked.

"Ladies and gentlemen," Karina Idstrom began, "welcome to the University of Tasmania's State of Tasmania Forum 2023." Her voice, crisp and clear, carried across the shell-shaped, tiered auditorium by the amplification system.

Idstrom stood at the centre of the wide platform without notes or a teleprompter, a picture of confidence and calm. Her light blonde hair, radiant in the stage lighting, cascaded to her shoulders, and her eyes sparkled with expectation.

"It's a great delight to return to my home state to host this forum," she continued. "Twenty-six years ago, I would sit at the back of this venue and listen to one of my arts lecturers droning on. I was young, rather arrogant, thought I knew it all and didn't need to listen. I may have been hungover too, just once or twice!"

A tremor of laughter moved across the audience, seven hundred and forty strong.

"It wasn't until my third year when I realised I'd better pull my finger out and do some work. I managed to graduate with an arts degree, majoring in journalism. I found my feet as a journalist and the rest, as they say, is history. As you may know, I'm the host of ABC's Q&A

program. It's a show I love, and every week I count my blessings to be the host. But you know what?" she asked, pausing as she looked across the audience. "It's *so good* to be home."

If Idstrom had not already connected with the audience, she did in that moment. A thread of understanding wove between them.

"In a moment it will be my pleasure to introduce our special guests for this evening. Before I do, we have a few housekeeping items to attend to."

Idstrom took a few easy steps to her left, still talking as she went. "Our forum this evening will not be televised or recorded. This venue is using FreezeTech technology, which means in a few moments all electronic devices will lose connection to Wi-Fi and mobile networks, and their screens will freeze in their current state. We hope you enjoy the next ninety minutes of a distraction-free existence. So please, take a breath, relax, and just *be*. Let's enjoy our time together.

"Each of our four guests will have ten minutes to speak on their chosen subject. Our theme for this evening is "A better world." They have the freedom to explore this theme as they see fit. We'll have time then for discussion and debate across the panel, and some questions from the audience. I'll do my best to manage the traffic. I only ask we all be respectful of differing views. Disagree if you will, but please do not be personal or sensational. Thank you."

Most of the attendees were aware of Karina Idstrom's ability to manage a debate with assertive direction, clever insight, and incisive wit. She'd interviewed the best of the best, the worst of the worst, and many in between—prime ministers, presidents, CEOs, stars, criminals, politicians, and creatives. She could smell bullshit at long range and cut through spin, all while keeping her cool and her natural air of inquisitive discovery.

"Well, that's enough from me," Idstrom said. "Time for those who we really came to hear! Two of our speakers this evening are senior officers in the U.S. Navy who serve on USS *John F. Kennedy.*

"Our first speaker graduated from the navy's Officer Candidate

School before joining the nuclear program. She qualified as a naval reactors engineer and has served in various shore and surface positions throughout her twenty-five-year career. She's reached the rank of captain and is the reactor officer in command of nuclear propulsion aboard *John F. Kennedy*. Ladies and gentlemen, please welcome Captain Helen Turner."

Turner made her way to the podium to warm applause, her epaulettes and insignia glinting in the lights. She cleared her throat to begin. "Thank you very much. It's our great honour to speak at your forum this evening. We're so glad our visit could coincide with this event."

She looked down at her notes, eyes wide open, then cleared her throat a second time. "A better world," she began. "Wow! Now there's a subject. I'm sure we can all agree that a better world is something we could do with right now. And what would a naval officer have to say about that? And a nuclear engineer at that? I wouldn't blame you for wondering. And to be honest, I wondered what I could bring to this topic at first.

"But you know, I *do* have something to offer. Not all of you are going to agree with how I envision a better world. Some of you might go right ahead and hate it. It's okay, though. Just hear me out is all I ask.

"In our solar system, we have an amazing energy source at the centre ... a G-type main-sequence star we call our sun. It's incredible to think that, every ninety minutes, our earth receives enough solar energy from the sun to power all human activity for an entire year.

"So, is solar energy the answer to our world's energy needs? Can we make our world a better place by eliminating carbon-based energy and all its downsides, and replacing it with an endless energy source with low emissions? The answer is yes ... and no. We are limited by factors such as weather, how we convert and store the energy, physical space, and the cost of infrastructure.

"But wouldn't it be cool if we could have miniature suns right here on planet earth? Tiny sources of energy—safe, efficient, and clean. Miniature suns that meet all our energy needs and never run dry."

Turner could see faces in the front rows. Some looked concerned. Others confused. Some wanting more.

"You'll have to excuse me if I'm getting excited. I believe in what I do with *everything* I have. I have no doubt that my miniature suns can solve our world's energy problems for good. So, stick with me … *please!*" she pleaded, drawing a murmur of laughter from the audience.

"We all know that Tasmania has been a leader in renewable energy for many years. Your pioneering work in things like hydro-electric power are world class. But let's imagine that something goes terribly wrong and your power grid goes down."

"It's bloody happened before!" someone yelled from the back, eliciting laughter.

"And it could happen again, and anywhere in the world, at any time," Turner continued. "But let's pretend it happens at midnight tonight. Hmm, what to do?" she play-acted, looking to the ceiling for an answer.

"Plug us into your carrier!" a person yelled.

"I swear to god," Turner said, "I didn't bribe whoever made that suggestion. I'm happy to PayPal him later, though!

"But you know what? Our friend over there has just nailed it. If we ran an electric cable— a big one—from our carrier, tonight, we could supply you with more than enough electricity to keep your entire region going for as long as you need. And the *John F. Kennedy* wouldn't miss a beat."

The audience fell silent.

"Our ship can power half your island because we have two miniature suns on board. Two tiny concentrations of energy that produce stupendous amounts of heat, which we convert to an endless supply of electricity.

"Now I know some folks are concerned about nuclear power, and some of you might be dead-set against it. I get it. And please understand, I'm not here to discuss nuclear energy as a weapon, only as an energy source. But let me explain how we can harness this technology to help build a better world …"

Turner went on to explain how reactor safety, monitoring, and compliance was managed in the U.S. Navy, and their impeccable safety record. She outlined how the navy's work had paved the way for small commercial reactors that were safe, cost-effective, and produced fewer and less volatile amounts of nuclear waste.

"Think about a world that's free of fossil fuels, where every community and every nation has access to ample and affordable energy, where there is no fear of the fuel ever running out, and where we're not held hostage by the vagaries of weather, wind, and clouds. Imagine all the problems this would solve. Imagine *a better world.*"

Turner picked up her notes from the podium and smiled. "Thank you so much."

Most in the audience applauded, but some with less vigour than others.

"Thank you, Captain Turner," Idstrom said, returning to centre stage as she applauded. "I'm sure there will be many questions for you and we'll hold those until all our guests have spoken.

"Our second guest this evening hails all the way from Germany. He's working at the University of Tasmania as part of an international research fellowship, and I'm told he has taken to life here in our island state very well. He graduated from the University of Munich in 1986 before attaining a string of post-graduate degrees, including a PhD in anthropology. He is a distinguished scholar in his field and a well-known author and commentator, often cited and invited to speak on human evolution, human history, social change, and the future of the human race. Please join me in welcoming Professor Karl Hoffman from the University of Hamburg."

As Hoffman made his way to the podium, the audience took in a tall man of solid stature with thinning and dishevelled blonde hair. He seemed uncomfortable in a suit and tie. His reading glasses hung from his neck on a length of black elastic cord and as he raised them to his eyes, the classic appearance of a career academic seemed complete. For those in the audience who'd never heard of Professor Karl Hoffman, his appearance was a sign they could tune out and let their minds wander.

But then he spoke. "I have news for you," he said in a thick Germanic accent. "News which can change your view of the world as it is, your view of our history as humans, and of our future on this planet. If you walk out of this forum tonight and you have not changed ... if you are the same person with the same views who sat down a few moments ago, then either I have failed, or you are dead inside."

Hoffman took a few seconds to scan the audience. His face remained serious, solemn. A pin dropping to the auditorium floor would have been deafening.

"It appears I have your attention," he said, smiling. "This is good!" he exclaimed, thumping an open hand down onto the unsuspecting Perspex podium.

The audience chuckled, and the tension eased.

"I have but ten minutes to speak, so I will come straight to the point. What is a better world? A better world is a world where racism does not exist. And tonight, I declare, once and for all, racism is no more. It is gone. Terminated. Nada. Nil. Neín. Bye-bye. See you later."

He paused again, letting his words sink in.

"Racism is, by definition, prejudice, discrimination, or antagonism directed against someone of a distinct race, based on the belief one's own race is superior. For racism to exist, then, we must have at least *two* races of humans. One to be inferior, the other superior, in the racist's mind at least.

"Fine, you might say, Karl, this is true! We have many races across humanity. There are races of continental origin, such as Europeans, Asians, and Africans; races of colour, such as black, white, brown, and yellow; and races of social and economic position, such as Western, Eastern, and the developing world.

"But these groups are not races at all. Not one of them! These are loose social constructs developed to categorise us as human beings. These categories, these so-called races, have no scientific, biological, anthropological, physical, or genetic basis whatsoever. They are, to put this in non-academic terms, a *pile of steaming bullshit*. Ladies and gentlemen, we are but one race. One human race I say!" The small podium reeled again as Hoffman's hand slapped down in time with his point.

"I am sometimes asked, 'How can this be? Can I not see the differences between many human beings?' You may well have similar questions here this evening. To you, I say this ..."

Hoffman continued with enthusiasm, expounding the history of the species *Homo sapiens*. He described their evolutionary origin in east-central Africa as a species diverging from the other great apes. But they were not the only type of human to do so. *Homo erectus* had migrated to East Asia, and *Homo neanderthalensis* had migrated to Europe and Western Asia, and other species— *Homo rudolfensis*, *Homo rhodesiensis*, *Homo heidelbergensis*, and *Homo ergaster*, among others—had also left their mark on the fossil record. Hoffman emphasised they were all from the genus *Homo* and all shared defining characteristics with near-identical genetics. They were, therefore, all human beings.

"When *Homo sapiens* moved across and out of Africa," Hoffman continued, "they interacted with other humans such as the Neanderthals. Through interbreeding, and/or though acts of violence and genocide, *Homo sapiens* became the dominant type of human, and eventually the only surviving type of human."

Hoffman removed his glasses. "And so, thousands of years later, we arrive in the twentieth century. And what do we see? In my homeland, in Germany, we see a group of people emerging in the early 1900s who believed *Homo sapiens* were still a collection of different types of humans, or races. The group called themselves the Nazis. They believed gays, Jews, and the mentally ill were inferior types of humans who needed to be extirpated. They saw themselves as the superior race, the Aryans. The Nazis saw the task of making the Jews extinct as being identical to how *Homo sapiens* caused the Neanderthals to become extinct. The Holocaust was their way of giving evolution and natural selection a helping hand.

"The Nazis were, of course, completely misguided. There are *no* significant genetic differences between different lineages of human beings."

Hoffman looked back up at the audience.

"Am I ashamed of what the Nazis and the nation of Germany did? Yes, I am appalled. But I am equally appalled by how other groups of humans have done similar things. I am equally appalled by the White Australia Policy, parts of which survived here right up until 1973. I am equally appalled by white supremacy movements which flourish in countries such as the United States to this day."

Hoffman's volume and pace gathered, driving home his point. "And I am equally appalled by all the other genocides committed by humans in the past century ... in Cambodia, China, Rwanda, and Bosnia, to name only a few. And why is it I can say I am equally ashamed? Because all these acts were committed by *my* species ... by *Homo sapiens* ... that is why! These acts were committed by *us*. Not *them* ... us!"

The audience appeared to draw a collective breath, as did Hoffman. He moved back to the podium as if to look again at his notes, despite the fact he had none.

"One thing is common to all these examples. There is a fundamental belief in an *us*. And then inevitably a fundamental belief in a *them*. When you create *them* and *us*, when you create fear and division, then many things become justifiable, and we can then do unthinkable things to each other.

"And here we are in the year 2023. And where are we as a species? We still have nations, leaders, religions, and philosophies promoting and using this pitiful excuse of *them* and *us*. They seek to divide, differentiate, and create imagined social hierarchies to suit their selfish purposes. So I ask you, ladies and gentlemen, where is *them* and *us* in your nation, in your community, in your very thinking tonight?"

Hoffman let the question hang in the air as he made his way to the other side of the stage.

"Nations, regions, communities, families ... as humans we naturally organise ourselves into these units. And there's nothing wrong with this, you know. It's in those units we find our sense of belonging, where we find protection and care, and where our values make shared sense. But none of those units should be a place from which we dehumanise, attack, or exterminate other humans. A warped sense of belonging is no excuse for war or genocide.

"I began by telling you racism does not exist. I will conclude by repeating the same. Racism cannot exist because it requires at least two races. We are one race … we are *Homo sapiens*. There are not black humans, German humans, Asian humans, Western humans, brown humans … not even Australian humans. There are only *humans*."

His voice softened as he spoke his final words. "A better world, my friends, is a world where we cooperate, collaborate, and communicate on the understanding racism is a false construct. It, along with all its terrible effects, need not exist. A better world is a world where all eight billion of us understand we are all *Homo sapiens*. We are *one*."

Hoffman resumed his seat behind the long desk. He clasped his hands and stared at them. A wave of applause ensued, with most of the audience standing to thunder their approval.

"Thank you, thank you everyone," Idstrom said, motioning to the audience to resume their seats. "Professor Hoffman … thank you. My partner will tell you it's not often I am caught without words, but this is one of those occasions."

Hoffman looked up and nodded, managing a small grin. He appeared spent.

"I will say nothing further for now," Idstrom said, "other than to introduce our next guest."

CHAPTER THIRTY-TWO

Our mind is capable of passing beyond the dividing line
we have drawn for it. Beyond the pairs of opposites of
which the world consists, other, new insights begin.

—Hermann Hesse

University of Tasmania

17 August 2023

Lieutenant Nomura's relaxed posture had transformed to upright and alert. She was sitting in the front row and close to the centre. The perfect position, she'd thought, to watch and influence the main event.

She took the opportunity to look around the auditorium. A few of her colleagues sat to her left and right, and she could just make out the form of Deputy Premier Matthew Cash at the end of the front row. His face had all the emotion of a polished concrete floor. Meanwhile Cash's oily adviser, Bradfurd Rouse, had emerged from the shadows and perched himself against the sidewall.

"Thank you so much, Nicole," Karina Idstrom said. "Tremendous food for thought there! And now, for our last speaker, please join me in welcoming Captain William A. Collins."

Collins took his place at the podium. "Thank you so much. It's great to be here."

This was the moment Nomura had been waiting for. She'd spent hours crafting his speech to address the topic with an interesting slant, while balancing the intended outcomes and political boundaries of the U.S. Navy. She took a sharp breath as Collins unfolded his notes. *Her notes.*

"I have enjoyed my time in Tasmania so far," he began. "We've been warmly welcomed, and while this is a long way from home for us, this place feels like the next best thing. So, thank you. Thank you to Deputy Premier Cash, your government, and the Tasmanian people."

A little improvisation is fine, Nomura said to herself, *no problem*. But she took an even sharper breath as Collins refolded his notes and put them aside.

"You might be surprised to know that I've been here before. Once back in 1999 on USS *Carl Vinson*, and the second time in 2017 for a holiday. I walked your south-coast track, which nearly killed me," he said with a chuckle, "and I spent some days in your wilderness. It's something I look back on with fondness. And it's great to be back here again."

Nomura had crept almost off the edge of her chair.

"I've taken much interest in your fair state and its early history. It is a fascinating place for a sea captain. It's kinda interesting, I think, that your first governor had the surname Collins, just like me. Maybe we're related? My ancestors, settled in what would become America, back in the seventeenth century, and they migrated from the same part of England as Captain David Collins. So, you never know.

"I've studied the other well-known captains who've visited your shores too. Famous names like Bruni d'Entrecasteaux, Abel Tasman, and William Bligh. It's fascinating to compare the purpose of their missions and how they and their crews conducted themselves while they were here. Was it the thrill of scientific discovery that motivated them? Personal fame or wealth? An insatiable desire to colonise and subdue other races?"

Collins turned to Professor Hoffman. "And by *races*, I mean, in their flawed understanding of the term."

Professor Hoffman nodded.

"I was intrigued to learn how Captain David Collins went about setting up the colony here, long before it became the City of Hobart ..."

He went on to describe the abject conditions that the newly appointed Lieutenant-Governor Collins worked to overcome throughout his six-year leadership. He talked of the rising conflict between his men and the people of the Indigenous palawa tribes in the area as they clashed over access to hunting grounds and scarce food.

"The genocide of the Aboriginal people in the decades that followed, mainly after Collins's untimely death in 1810, is a matter of history. Some would say it's well known, others would say it isn't, and others may disagree it even happened."

Nomura could not resist looking back at Rouse. He was still perched against the wall. He too wanted to be able to capture Collins's attention if the captain wavered from their cleverly crafted script. But from the storm clouding Rouse's face, Nomura could only conclude he too was being ignored.

"But you might well ask me, what about your own country, Bill? And you'd have a darn good point there. I don't come to you with clean hands. History also tells how the American people have treated the Indigenous Peoples of our lands, and the slaves we imported there. And it seems the stains of that history are only widening the divisions we face today."

Collins paused for a few seconds. Nomura deflated into her seat.

"Yesterday I took a drive along the Midland Highway. I visited some of your historic towns and checked out the rural heart of the island. It was great, but the part that stuck out the most was a commemorative sculpture in a field near the township of Ross. At that sculpture, I stood on a line. My left foot stood in southern Tasmania and my right stood in northern Tasmania. Straight underneath me, running east to west, is the line known as the forty-second parallel.

"It's just a line on a map, yet it divides your state in half. Back when your state was two colonies—one based in Port Dalrymple up north, and the other based right here, in Hobart Town. The north was run by Lieutenant Colonel William Paterson of the British Army, and the south by Captain David Collins of the British Navy. The seeds of division were well-sown, it seems, and even when the administration of the northern colony was given over to the south in 1812, the memory of this division remained. I'm told it remains to this day. A guy from

Launceston told me all about it over a beer at the pub in Ross yesterday, and he wasn't pulling any punches!"

"Too bloody right, mate!" someone yelled from the upper level.

"Was the beer Boags or Cascade?" another hollered from the back.

Pockets of subdued laughter bubbled across the audience.

Collins chuckled. "Professor Hoffman's speech made me think. How easy it is for us humans to create these lines between us. Not real lines, but imaginary lines that end up meaning much more than they should. Where I come from, there's still this north-south, Yankee versus Confederate antipathy going on. And we have an urban versus rural divide that gets more bitter by the year. Black and white. Religious and secular. Rich and poor. The list goes on and on.

"I could talk for hours about these lines in the sand. They are everywhere and exist not just within countries, but between countries too. They're not just lines on a map, they're lines between cultures.

"But the fact is, I've got one minute left. So what's my take on a better world? What could the captain of a U.S. Navy aircraft carrier possibly have to say on this topic? Don't worry, folks, I get the irony of this. You could say the ship I command *creates* lines wherever it goes. Maybe it does. And sometimes those lines cut deep. But that's my job, and it's my commission to execute my orders without fear or favour. But I think of it like this ... sometimes you need a show of force, like the presence of an aircraft carrier, so the lines in our world don't cut our flesh apart. My mission, as I see it, is to help create a peace where people have the security to forget the lines that divide them, that bind them, that wound them."

He paused.

"The only way to *prevent* a war, I think, is to actively show you have the means to win a war. Now that comes with a heavy responsibility. And I'm not saying we always get things right. But if it's not us ... if it's not the United States and our allies doing this ... then who will?"

A hush had fallen over the audience as his question hung in the air.

Nomura looked to her left—Rouse was gone.

"A better world? For me, it's seeing these lines for what they are. They're fake. They've been made up over time and have taken on a life of their own. Much like the so-called races Professor Hoffman was telling us about before. Surmounting them takes recognition. It takes active thought. It takes a determination to change, starting at a personal level.

"Ladies and gentlemen, a better world is one where we put our minds, and our efforts, not to what divides us, but to what we share ... to all we have in common. Thank you." Collins collected his folded notes and returned to his seat.

*   *   *   *

"Ladies and gentlemen, our time together is at an end," Idstrom said.

Collins relaxed as a wave of relief swept over him. His thoughts had turned to his hotel room, a glass of whisky, and the remaining chapters of his book.

"... but we have time for one last question from ... Lauren Jack," Idstrom said, looking across the audience. "Lauren?"

Lauren Jack stood to her feet. Her long golden locks were more presentable than usual. She'd worn her best jeans and favourite hand-knit woollen jumper for the occasion. "Thank you, I have something here ..." she said as she reached under her jumper.

The surrounding audience gasped. Some braced sideways in surprise.

Idstrom strode toward Jack with a hand outstretched. "Please don't—"

"It's okay," Jack insisted with a grin. "It's all good." She withdrew a piece of folded cloth. "This is the banner I've been holding at our protests all week." She let the banner unfurl and presented to the stage: WE WANT PEACE, NOT WAR. "Captain Collins, these five words say everything I believe in. And what do you have to say about it?"

Collins waited a moment before leaning forward to make his reply. "Ms Jack ... I agree with you, one hundred percent."

CHAPTER THIRTY-THREE

*He is a friend indeed who proves himself a friend in
need.*

—Plautus

18 August 2023

Looks like her. Ben scanned the woman in the distance and the sparse surroundings of the Rosny Hill Lookout. The River Derwent ran straight and wide under the Tasman Bridge. A futuristic ferry painted in blue-grey camouflage passed under the bridge, heading north. Morning peak-hour traffic hummed in five lanes across the bridge and along the highway on the opposite shore. A thick meeting of stately trees covered the opposite riverbank. A sandstone mansion with castle turrets was the only building to interrupt the hillside forest. Behind the hill line a long trail of heavy low-lying fog snaked through the suburbs and disappeared from view to the north.

The Rosny Hill Lookout was quiet by contrast. Just three parked cars and a scattering of people enjoying the elevated view of the river, the bridge, and the city. A photographer stood thirty metres behind Ben at the southern end and fought a losing battle with a recalcitrant tripod. An older couple were taking in the view near their campervan. A young woman at the far end rested against the front of her car.

No close threats. No CCTV. All clear.

Ben stayed on high alert, given his close proximity to the port and the city. The mission brief had been clear: the place would be crawling with U.S. Navy shore patrols—and worse still, counterintelligence and counterterrorism officers of the Naval Criminal Investigative Service. The spooks would be in plain clothes, but the mission planners had briefed him well. NCIS officers often wore chino pants, plain polo

317

tops, and sunglasses. Their heads were always on swivels, watching everyone and everything. If Ben saw any sign of the "Chino Brigade" he was to leave that place immediately.

That's her, he confirmed to himself as he walked toward the woman. Ben could see she was of average height with long black hair. She wore faded jeans and a red hoodie. A blue clutch-purse sat next to her on the hood of her car.

"Good morning," he said.

The woman faced him. "Morning," she replied.

"It is cold here for this time of day."

"Yes. But not as cold as on top of kunanyi," she said, nodding at the mountain.

With their respective phrases spoken and accepted, their identities as clandestine operatives were mutually confirmed. Their names would not be spoken.

Ben motioned towards an open grassy area. They walked down the slope and away from the car park in silence. He checked their surrounds once more—alert to any change or any person out of place.

He turned to face her and removed his sunglasses. "It is good to meet you," he said.

The man's unflinching stare pulled an icy shiver from Alix Zhao's lower back. She looked down and was surprised to see his hand outstretched toward her. "And you," she said with a barely hidden gulp. As she shook his hand, Alix felt his fingers scoop up the USB memory stick she'd placed in her palm.

"When are you scheduled to go to work?" he asked. The cold, flat tone of his question matched his stare.

Alix took in a sharp breath. She had to recite her next words exactly as she had been told to. "I am told it is all as planned," she said. "I will be picked up at the meeting place this Sunday morning at ten o'clock. My co-workers said they will wait there and they will be on time."

"Very good."

Alix's mobile buzzed, and she took it out of her back pocket to silence it. The man snatched it from her grasp before she had a chance.

"What the hell are you doing?" he growled in Mandarin as he ripped off the battery cover. He jammed the battery in his pocket, then tossed the phone back at her. She missed the catch, and it fell lifeless to the frosty grass.

"Do you know nothing?" he continued in Mandarin, his words laced with venom.

"Sorry, I—"

"Fuck *sorry*, you stupid woman! Your foolishness will compromise this mission."

Alix noticed him grimace as he finished his sentence, as if he regretted what he'd just said.

"Mission?" she asked.

"Never mind."

They stood in silence. The *stupid woman* insult had hit its mark. Alix Zhao could tell the man despised her as a mere part-time local operative, and a poorly trained one at that. He was not to know she rarely undertook such tasks, and then only to protect her family in China. But she was not the type to be lectured and insulted by strangers, and not by this robotic man who looked more Korean than Chinese.

Her next words, once she'd conjured them, were in English and with an unmistakable Australian accent. Only two words, but with a newfound resolve: "What mission?" she asked.

His face remained devoid of emotion, yet his eyes appeared to have deepened beyond the darkest black.

As Alix returned his stare, a large object behind him in the distance caught her attention. It took only a small shift of her gaze to the right ... beyond his face, down over the trees, past the riverbank, and out into the middle of the river to recognise the object. *The aircraft carrier—* moored where she'd photographed it five days earlier.

Alix snapped her gaze back to his. The man's eyes constricted, just enough for Alix to understand that he'd recognised the moment when the object of the mission had crystallised in her mind.

He moved a step closer.

"You will forget this," he whispered, "or you will pay a very high price."

Alix Zhao watched him stride up the slope and out of sight.

The shiver came back as she bent down to pick up her phone. And the feeling would return to haunt her again and again that day, and in her dreams in the dead of night.

*   *   *   *

Southwest National Park, Tasmania

The thin white line—even at only five hundred metres long—looked like a stark scar on the plain. The white brilliance of the quartz-gravel surface of the narrow runway seemed to glow amongst the deep green button grass plains surrounding it.

"We're here," the pilot said.

Collins nodded. He understood exactly where they were, but appreciated the young pilot's narration. He'd been more than informative as the one-hour charter flight from Hobart-Cambridge Aerodrome progressed.

"Okay. Check your seat belt is done up nice'n tight. This'll probably be the smallest runway you've ever experienced. But you can relax, mate ... we do this all the time."

But Collins was relaxed. He relished how his body and mind had begun to unwind for the first time in months. And the young pilot, with barely three hundred hours in his logbook, had no way of knowing that the unassuming passenger seated beside him had fourteen thousand hours of flying experience, with most of his flights ending on an aircraft carrier flight deck even smaller than the runway of Bathurst Harbour Airstrip.

The Cessna-172 made its final approach with flaps extended, its nose high, and its airspeed pegged back at a conservative sixty-one knots. The contrasts were obvious as Collins recalled the sensations of guiding an F-14 Tomcat on final approach to a moving, pitching flight deck. And at one hundred and twenty-five knots to boot.

*   *   *   *

Within thirty minutes after landing, Collins was on board a small tourist boat as it grumbled along Melaleuca Creek at low speed. There were just two men aboard: Collins and Geoff Denman, the local guide steering the boat. For the next two days and nights he would be Collins's boat driver, camp director, cook, and walking guide.

And Denman was also beginning to relax. The tourism and bushwalking season was still months away, and this single-person experience would be a breeze compared to the groups of six or eight he often led. It had been four months since he'd been to the region. He'd missed the place, as he often did over the winter. The wilderness camp, hidden away in thick forest near the creek, was always a delight—a small oasis of rustic luxury with just enough comforts for even the most ardent city-dweller to feel at ease.

The dark tannin waters of Melaleuca Creek sparkled in the morning sun as the boat navigated its winding path. Out ahead, the creek's surface was a perfect mirror in the stillness. The surface reflected the dense shrubs and trees lining the banks, their emerald green shades juxtaposing the azure blue of the sky from above.

Denman recognised the distinctive form of Mount Rugby rising above the landscape, and knew the blue waters of Bathurst Harbour lay immediately at its feet. It would be good to see the harbour again.

Denman glanced at his lone passenger perched at the bow. The man held his face set to the breeze. His salt and pepper grey hair, still thick and ample for a man in his mid-fifties, flicked lazily in the slipstream. His face was calm, his body at ease. An image of peace.

Denman had seen it before—*that look*. When a person really took it in, this place would somehow seep into their being. As if ancient spirits of the wilderness would enter the person and purge the personal demons of their host, gently jettisoning their emotional baggage into the creek, the harbour, or the mud of the button grass plains.

The passenger looked towards the back of the boat. The two men caught each other's attention for a mere second, but long enough to recognise their common emotion in the moment.

*   *   *   *

Bellerive, Tasmania

Katherine relaxed in the winter sunshine streaming through the window and across their table. The sun had reached its peak and the people below on Hobart's eastern shore were out and about to enjoy the warmth. But a certain chill persisted in the air and it surged with a vengeance when a cloud passed in front of the sun, reminding the locals that summer was still a good few months away.

"Not bad, ay?" Martin asked.

"The fish? Yeah, fantastic. Kinda reminded me of home."

"Martin!" A woman had spotted Martin Brady from the bar. She made her way over with a man in tow.

"Leona … Daniel … g'day," Martin said, getting up from his seat.

Leona Manning giggled. "Fancy seeing you here. It's been, what, two weeks?"

"Oh, yeah … down at Cygnet," he replied. He gestured to his left. "This is Katherine."

The three said their hellos and shook hands.

"We've come to check on our new yacht. You must come and see!" Leona insisted.

"Thanks. Um, maybe another day," Martin managed.

"No, no, no. *Come on.* Follow me … it's not far."

Katherine noticed Martin's neck and face had taken on a crimson shade, but she couldn't read the cause of his uneasiness.

And Leona Manning was already at the restaurant door. *"Come on!"* she insisted. "And Daniel, hurry up, darling."

*   *   *   *

Katherine and Leona made themselves comfortable on the yacht's rear deck. They'd sent their male companions back to the yacht club to get drinks for the group.

"So, how did you guys meet?" Leona began.

The woman seemed friendly enough, but Katherine sensed her question was more than a simple conversation starter. "It was just this week," Katherine said. "I happened to choose a tour with Wild Tasmania Touring Adventures and, well, Martin was the guy."

"Ah, okay."

After seconds of silence, Katherine changed the subject. "This is a mighty fine boat."

"Thanks. Yeah. It's been a dream of Daniel's for years. Took weeks for it to get here from New South Wales. It was a relief to see it arrive at the marina last week."

"Awesome. I'm sure you'll enjoy sailing her. There's nothing like the wind and the sea."

"Yep." Leona folded her arms. "Is that an American accent, then?"

"You got it, yeah."

"I didn't want to assume. I made the mistake once, thinking a Canadian was from the United States."

Katherine laughed. "Oh, hell yeah. That can end real bad!"

"Can I assume you're here with the navy?"

"Right again."

"I see."

Katherine turned to the view beyond the yacht's starboard railing. She could see darkening clouds building beyond the hills on the western horizon. The clear weather and the warmth of the sun were about to come to an end.

"If you're on the ship all the time, how come you still like the sea so much?" Leona asked.

"On the carrier … yeah, maybe not so much. But sailing, real sailing, that's something else."

"And what do you do? Which part of the ship do you work in?"

"I'm not actually attached to the ship. I'm part of the air wing deployed to the carrier strike group."

"So, like … an administration role, or catering, or something?"

Katherine squinted. "It feels like lots of admin sometimes, yeah. But no. I'm a pilot … a helicopter commander."

From the look of disbelief written across Leona Manning's face, Katherine was glad the woman sat with her back against the railing. Without it, she may well have fallen overboard.

Further uneasy seconds followed before Leona changed the conversation's tack—and right back to where she'd begun. "Right. And … you guys are *friends* now?"

"Yeah. I guess so," Katherine managed.

"There we go!" Daniel and Martin had returned to the yacht. They passed beer bottles over the railing to Katherine and Leona. "Cheers!"

"Bit of a surprise packet, this one," Leona said as she waved a thumb towards Katherine.

"Great. I like surprises," Daniel replied.

"Yes. She also likes boats."

"Great!"

"Oh, and helicopters … and aircraft carriers."

"Is that right?" Daniel asked, turning to Katherine, who shrugged.

From the intensity of Leona's glare, it seemed she was attempting to communicate something. But Daniel didn't seem to have a clue. It wasn't until she flicked her eyes subtly toward Martin, and then toward Katherine, that things seemed to dawn on him.

"Um, okay. Wow." Daniel said. He looked at Martin. "Never picked you as one who'd go chasing sailors."

Martin took a long swig of his beer.

"We're just friends, is all," Katherine said.

"Just like us then," Daniel said, seemingly attempting a backtrack.

But Leona did not follow his lead. "Martin has lots of friends. Isn't that right, Martin?"

"I wouldn't say *lots*," he replied.

"You would have met some of them already, Katherine."

"Ah, no. I don't think so," Katherine replied.

"Yes you have, down at the pier. The protestors, people who love this state, who care about our planet. Lots of our friends are there every day making themselves heard. My friends. *Martin's* friends."

Silence reigned, except for the gentle slap of the river against the yacht's hull.

Martin Brady took another long swig of beer. Daniel mimicked his swig as if in sympathy.

"It's been great to meet you all," Katherine said as she stood, "but I must be going."

"So soon, Katherine?" Leona said, barely masking a smile.

"Yes, Leona. I better get back. Things to do."

Martin went to stand. "Katherine, I—"

"It's okay, Martin. Stay with your friends."

"Katherine, look, sorry," Daniel stammered. "We didn't mean to—"

"Leave it," Leona snapped. "She needs to get back to her ship. Maybe the world needs to be *saved* or something."

"Nope," Katherine said. "I need to do some paperwork and arrange dinner for the crew. We're having Chinese tonight."

Leona's smile evaporated.

Katherine stepped onto the pontoon and lowered her gaze toward Leona. "And Chinese is a cuisine you should get used to, Leona ... if my country's military isn't around to save your asses again, you know, like we did in World War Two."

CHAPTER THIRTY-FOUR

Man has only to sink beneath the surface and he is free.
—Jacques Yves Cousteau

PLAN submarine Shaanxi-2,
sixty-five miles north-east of Tasmania
19 August 2023, 0255 hours

The yellow triangular symbol—and its SX22 text designation—wobbled on the screen as it eased toward the centre of the display.

"*This one … what is that?*" he asked.

The tactical warfare officer flicked the trackball over the symbol and clicked. "Sir. It's a commercial ship, heading south."

Captain Zhang Yong snapped around to bark across the submarine's cramped control room, "Sonar, identify the designated target … Sierra X-Ray Two-Two."

"Sierra X-Ray Two-Two, yes, sir."

Zhang had appeared beside the sonar operator before the crewman had any real chance of following the captain's order. "And?" he demanded.

"Still identifying, sir."

Zhang watched as the operator checked the sonar system's visual and audio feeds. He rhythmically tapped his fingers on the back of the man's chair.

"It's a commercial vessel," the operator said. "Heavy tanker of some sort. Two screws."

"Tell me what I don't already know," Zhang grumbled.

The operator's hands flew even faster across his keyboard. "Sir. The system identifies it as the *Union Mark*. A bulk ore carrier."

"Destination?"

More furious key-clicks and trackball spins. "Tasmania, sir. Destination is the port of Hobart."

"Speed and course?"

"Twelve knots, tracking south … approximate heading: one-six-five. Range two thousand metres and closing."

"Any other close surface contacts?"

"None, sir."

Zhang spun to face the centre of the control room. "Pilot, steer left heading one-six-zero and come to periscope depth."

As the submarine pitched up and rolled left, Zhang instinctively grabbed a bulkhead handle above him. Just in time to see the ghostlike presence of the Korean special forces commando hovering again in the shadows.

"How does this damned Bangzi know when to appear?" Zhang grumbled to himself. The derogatory Chinese term *bangzi*, or "stick," seemed to fit the tall, lean Tak well. Zhang moved to the attack periscope in the centre of the control room and waited.

The call came thirty-five seconds later. "Now at periscope depth, Captain."

Zhang raised the scope, flipped down the handles, and bent down to peer into the eyepiece. He spun the scope through all three hundred and sixty degrees, following it around in his stooped position, much like a ballroom dancer with too many shots of baijiu in his bloodstream.

The world above was bathed in ghostly phosphorous green and white tones by the night-vision system. Heavy swells washed over his view, obscuring the horizon every few seconds. He continued to spin and stare until his periscope dance came to an abrupt stop.

There. The bright lights he'd been expecting and the blunt bow of a large ship coming head on through the swell. He flicked the stopwatch in his left hand to begin the count and noted the angle to the top of the ship's bow on the periscope readout. He watched unflinchingly as the ship's bow grew larger in the eyepiece.

Zhang stood back from the scope and clicked his stopwatch to stop the count. *Twenty-eight seconds.* From there it became a trigonometric exercise—a rapid mental calculation using two heights, two angles, and the seconds elapsed. A calculation he'd performed many times before. "Mark my range to target," he said. "Now one thousand six hundred metres. Relative bearing one-eight-zero, dead astern. My calculated speed: thirteen knots."

"I concur, Captain," the sonar operator said. "Target is designated Sierra X-Ray Two-Two. It's the *Union Mark.*"

"Very good. All stop!"

Zhang felt a shudder in the deck as the propulsion of the submarine faded to idle and its regular hum receded. He grabbed the handset from the overhead. "Engineering. Secure from AIP. Switch to standard propulsion. No delay."

Tak had emerged further into the dim blue light of the control room. "Captain. What is happening?" he asked.

"Silence!" Zhang snapped. He faced Tak and lowered his voice: "Not another word until I am ready. *Not one.*"

Tak bared his teeth and hissed a sharp breath, but slipped back into the shadows without a word.

The singing throb of the *Union Mark*'s screws grew in the sonar operator's headset and then in the control room itself.

Zhang snapped in the periscope's handles and sent it downwards. "Make your depth sixty metres. Maintain course. Speed steady five knots."

He looked up, imagining the bulk of the ship ploughing through the waters behind them. The ship's distinctive sound gained in pitch and strength. An eerie vibration of millions of tiny bubbles exploding in the wake of her screws, known in the trade as cavitation. The sound grew to a feverish pitch above them before sliding away.

"Sonar, any change?"

"Negative, sir. She's bearing zero-zero-two degrees, twelve knots steady."

"Very good. Pilot, increase speed to sixteen knots. Steady course."

Zhang's commands were confirmed back to him. He sensed the boat surge again as the propulsion returned with enthusiasm. "Sonar. Advise when we are approaching fifty metres astern of the ship."

"Fifty metres. Yes … sir," the crewman confirmed, his bewilderment at the captain's tactics well-evident.

Zhang dropped himself into his captain's chair and rested his chin on one hand. "Tak," he called.

He found Tak's re-appearance to be satisfying for a change, as if the Korean had obeyed his order. "You would not understand such things," Zhang began. "However, the sea conditions have continued to fight us. We were close to two hours past our estimated arrival time for the Bravo-One point. The only way to make our Alpha-One destination on schedule is to increase speed."

"I see."

"This speed brings risks. There are navigation risks in the shallow waters ahead, and detection risks as we run at higher speed. The northeast coast of Tasmania is not far off our bow, which means we are well within Australian waters."

"We cannot afford detection, Captain. This is unacceptable."

"Arriving late at the mission destination is also unacceptable. Which would you prefer, then?"

Tak eyed Zhang. "You are asking me? Are you not the captain?"

"Precisely." Zhang smirked. "And I have chosen a third option. We have caught a taxi. It'll get you there on time."

Zhang reached for the intercom control panel, flicked a switch, and turned up the sonar audio feed. "You hear that sound? That ship is an old and noisy cargo ship and she gets along at thirteen knots. If we keep tracking within her wake and match her speed, we get our high-speed taxi ride south."

*　　*　　*　　*

0527 hours

The crewman on the bridge of the *Union Mark* had every right to feel alone. His only company—a senior colleague in charge of their watch—snored as he lay curled in the captain's chair.

The ship rumbled on into the black nothingness of the last hours of night. Her thick bow thrashed through each swell, sending small clouds of spray aloft and churning the sea to white on either side. Light rain had been falling for hours with crazed sheets of moisture blowing up and around the bridge in the stiff wind.

The only sign of life—eighteen miles away on the Tasmanian coast—was the steady repeating flashes from the Eddystone Point lighthouse.

The crewman glanced at the surface radar and depth-sounding displays. Still nothing of interest.

He had no inkling of the company they were keeping. No clue a steel leech had latched below their vessel and behind their stern. The leech stayed hidden within the violence of the ship's own flow and cavitation noise, their depth-sounding sonar blind to its presence.

A long, black, and sticky Chinese leech the *Union Mark* crewman never knew existed.

CHAPTER THIRTY-FIVE

We may have all come on different ships, but we're in the same boat now.

—Martin Luther King Jr.

19 August 2023, 7:50 AM

The upper ramp descended to the pier, eventually meeting the bitumen with a distinct clang.

With only a handful of vehicles on the ferry's upper deck, Ben would be the second to disembark. He guided the car onto the ramp and glided down. He accelerated once he got onto the pier proper before driving away on the narrow road ahead.

The road meandered up a long hill. Dryish paddocks with patches of green and a scattering of gum trees spread on either side. No buildings or infrastructure, just open farmland as far as Ben could see. Which was just how the six hundred permanent residents of Bruny Island preferred to keep it.

*   *   *   *

Katherine's thumb hovered over her phone's answer icon. She paused, as if closing that inch between her thumb and the screen would somehow impact the rest of her life.

"Hi."

"G'day," came his reply.

Then a pause so pregnant its waters seemed sure to break.

"I, um," Martin Brady continued, "just wanted to see how you are?"

"I'm fine. Thanks."

"You sound a bit … tense?"

"Is that right?"

"Look. I didn't want to leave things like they were. But are you trying to punish me now or something?"

"No. But if I *were*, you'd damn well deserve it."

"I'm sorry. I didn't know Leona was gonna lose her shit like she did. She's not like that."

"What—not normally a sarcastic, jealous, racist, nasty son of a bitch, you mean?"

"Ah ... yeah, sorta."

"Good to know. I'll take your word for it, I guess."

"Could we ... talk, you know, face to face? I'm not good with these things on the phone."

Katherine sighed. "I'm working till early this afternoon. We can meet once I'm off. I'll send you a text."

"Okay. Sounds good."

*　*　*　*

Bruny Island, Tasmania

The hills gave way to open flatlands and the stands of tall gum trees thinned as Ben drove on. There were houses every now and then, but they seemed empty and lifeless. Patches of white sand among the flowing grasses and thick stands of coastal shrubs hinted at the island's eastern coastline nearby.

A tiny sign ahead, which depicted an aeroplane flying at a bizarre angle, informed Ben he was close to his destination. He parked the car off the road near the entrance to a walking track.

Ben checked his surroundings. There were no other vehicles in the parking area and no sign of human activity. Perfect. He stood by the car and paused. The bush was bizarre and enveloping. Insects buzzed and flew every which way. Strange bird calls and peculiar squawks. An underlying aroma of tea tree and eucalyptus. And a crispness to the air that felt freshly created.

Ben set off into the scrub. He picked his way through the low trees and shrubs, unsure of the other-worldly environment surrounding him, yet driven by what had to be done. Within a few minutes the scrub thinned and he crouched near a tree to survey the scene ahead. A long dirt runway ran to the east with six white cones and a taxiway at the near end. A small hangar sat behind it, the sign on the roof proclaiming SOUTHERN FLIGHT TOURS. SEE OUR ISLAND FROM THE SKY.

Two aeroplanes were parked outside the hangar, a Cessna-172, and a larger Cessna-206. A young man in a white shirt stood on one of the aeroplane's wing struts. He was refuelling the plane and staring into the distance as he held the nozzle.

Ben noted only a single vehicle in the car park next to the hangar. And none of the vehicles from the ferry were stopping. No great surprise, given the start of tourist season was months away.

And Bruny Island airstrip would, no doubt, be just as quiet at the same time the following day.

Perfect.

*   *   *   *

Southwest National Park

"Okay, mate. I'll be back at four o'clock to pick you up," Geoff Denman said.

"Thanks. See you then."

Denman gunned the throttle, sending the boat off the shallow sandbank and back into the blue waters of the harbour. He turned to give Collins a wave as he sped off towards Melaleuca Inlet and the Wilderness Camp.

Collins craned his head to look at his goal. Mount Rugby towered above him with all twenty-five hundred feet of its altitude. He'd tackled this mountain before, and he understood how demanding the walk and the final climb would be. But it wasn't the climb that dominated his thoughts. Monstrous voices were whispering to him, stirring terrible memories ever closer to the surface of his mind.

He closed his eyes, but the image of her remained. Her eyes dancing with anticipation. Her cheeks red in the cold air. Standing in the same spot five years earlier, and raring to go. "Come on, old man," she'd joked. "It can't be *that* hard. Let's climb this thing!"

Collins waited for the apparition to pass before opening his eyes. He half-opened the zipper on his daypack and slid a hand inside. He knew it would be there, but he had to check again, just to be sure. His fingers felt down past his drink bottle, through the folds of his rain jacket, and all the way to the bottom.

There.

Its presence sent a quiver through Collin's gut. He withdrew his hand and closed the zipper. It was time to silence the voices. Once and for all.

*   *   *   *

Hobart

Martin Brady yanked the buzzing phone from his pocket. He'd usually ignore it for a time before giving in to its annoying need for attention, but this day was different.

A text message:

Hey, meet you at the Hobart Regatta Grounds @ 2 x

He wasn't certain if he'd received an order, although the single kiss at the end seemed to soften it some.

*   *   *   *

Brady parked near the Regatta Grounds stadium and walked towards the river end. The structure sat on a corner of open land near the river's edge, close to the city and the docks. He was five minutes early—miraculously—and she was nowhere to be seen.

He could hear traffic humming along the nearby Tasman Highway and Tasman Bridge, disrupted only by the sounds of the city nearby. The odd car horn. A siren in the distance. The dull grind of machinery at a construction site.

And then … something else. A deep repetitive throb. Subtle at first, but then building in intensity. Not a sound, more of an unmistakable sensation in his feet and ears that emanated from the small valley where the Tasman Bridge connected with the eastern shore. The vibrating throb mutated into the distinct sound of blades beating the air at high speed, underwritten by the singing whine of turbine engines.

A helicopter emerged from the valley, sprinted past the Tasman Bridge, and flew towards the city. Brady couldn't tell much from its oncoming shape, only that it was on the large side and a light grey colour. He guessed it would fly over where he stood and he braced himself to watch the high-speed pass.

The noise was deafening as it roared past a hundred metres above. But instead of disappearing over the city as he'd expected, it wheeled around, flew a tight half-circle, and came to a low hover at the river's edge.

Brady glanced at his watch: 2:01 PM.

The machine slid over the helipad as it hovered, then settled to the ground. The rotor blades slowed, the turbine whine settled, and the side door slid open. Three officers in navy blues stepped out, spotted the car waiting for them nearby, and made their way over. The car left soon after.

As Brady returned his gaze to the helicopter, a navy crewman emerged, dressed in blue-grey khaki with a white helmet. "Mr Brady?" the man shouted as he approached, competing as best he could with the persistent helicopter noise.

"Uh, yeah."

"My commanding officer has requested that you join us to say a quick hello."

"Oh. Right. In that?" Brady asked, nodding at the helicopter.

The crewman laughed. "Yes, sir. In *that*."

In less than a minute, Brady was onboard, seated in the rear cabin, and strapped in. He'd donned a life vest and helmet as the crewman directed, but with building trepidation.

The crewman reached over, grabbed Brady's helmet communications cable, and plugged it into an intercom port near his seat. "Can you hear me, sir?"

"Yep. Yep, I can."

"Great. Welcome aboard. I'm Naval Air Crewman Emilio Perez, but just call me Perry."

"Right. Ah, g'day."

Another voice crackled through the headset in Brady's helmet. He couldn't see the woman speaking, but guessed she was one of the two pilots seated up front. And her voice seemed familiar, yet different. "Whattya got back there, Perry? Some feral you dragged outta the Tassie bush?"

Perez's laughter echoed through the intercom.

Brady sensed the rotors gaining speed. Engine vibrations pulsed with increasing rhythm through the seat and into his butt.

"Hold on tight there, Mr Brady," the female voice said through his headset.

Brady grabbed the sides of his seat as the machine lifted into the air. He'd barely taken in the sudden sensation of the take-off when he felt the nose dip low. He braced, hoping they wouldn't tumble over. He chanced a look into the front cabin—between the two faceless pilots with their dark visors down—and out through the front windshield. The ground looked close enough to touch. And then it moved under them, faster and faster, until it became a hysterical blur of green and grey.

Brady looked toward the open side door as the nose levelled out. Perez sat on the edge with his uniform and helmet cable fluttering in the slipstream. He looked, to Brady, like a man sitting on a jetty, waiting for a fish to bite.

The view outside raced by like a movie on fast-forward. Brady could make out buildings and landmarks in Hobart's city centre, and then the Wrest Point Casino tower, but they flashed by all too soon.

And Perez started waving. They were travelling south along the beaches bordering Sandy Bay and locals on the shore were politely waving back.

"And don't you *dare*, Perry," a man ordered over the intercom.

"Aw, c'mon, Mets. Just some fun for the good people of Hobart!"

Perez turned to Brady. "I have been known to, uh, moon the locals from time to time. But not today. We're on best behaviour. Captain's orders."

Brady could sense the helicopter gaining altitude. The suburb of Taroona passed his view, and then Kingston and Blackmans Bay in the distance. The helicopter banked hard left to fly a tight turn over the Iron Pot Lighthouse before levelling off to track back along the Derwent towards the city.

"You been on a helo before, Mr Brady?" Perez asked.

"No."

"Cool. How about an aircraft carrier?"

Brady craned his head to look through the forward windshield again. The looming shape of the aircraft carrier grew larger as they approached. They came to a hover beside the flight deck, and the helicopter settled onto its assigned landing spot.

"Say hi to Mom," Perez said, jabbing his thumb at the superstructure dominating their view.

It took a few minutes for the helicopter to quieten down. The pilots had already exited through the cockpit doors.

"Thanks," Brady managed as he followed Perez's directions to remove his gear and disembark onto the flight deck.

"You're welcome."

Brady squinted in the bright afternoon light. He could see the two pilots standing a short distance away—a man and a woman—their helmets held in their hands.

He didn't recognise her at first—the woman illuminated in the golden sunlight. Her flight suit and her dishevelled hair didn't quite register. Until she smiled.

"Welcome to my world, Mister Brady," Katherine said.

CHAPTER THIRTY-SIX

The worst of all fears is the fear of living.
        —Theodore Roosevelt, *Theodore Roosevelt: An*
                                        Autobiography

Southwest National Park

Low cloud had enveloped him for much of the two-hour climb—its sudden presence emerging from nowhere. One minute the sun had cast the peaks and saddles of the mountain in gold, and then it was gone. The daylight decaying to a sombre, damp dimness and the visibility dropping to a matter of metres.

A faint breeze had picked up when Collins stood on the last rise to the summit of Mount Rugby. The breeze ushered away the cloud, sending it tumbling down the mountain slopes to disappear as the condensation evaporated in warmer air. A few pockets of fog held on in the lee of the highest peaks.

Collins hiked the few remaining yards to the summit, dropped his daypack, tightened his jacket against the breeze, and looked to the horizon. The three-hundred-and-sixty-degree view of land and sea had emerged in all its late-afternoon glory around the summit, like a curtain had been lifted on a magnificent stage. The blue waters of Bathurst Harbour sat as a vast mirror below, reflecting the endless line of mountain ranges to the west. To the east, the distinct peaks and ridges of Mount Rugby and its close neighbours sat rendered in the golden afternoon light. And to the west—out to the vastness of the sea—the narrow waterway of Port Davey wound its way to where the waves crashed ashore. Its troubled path frustrated by twists and turns in the terrain, and then by lumpy but charming mounds of bright green and shale-grey in the bay—the Breaksea Islands dutifully performing the task their name so well implied.

Collins knelt and opened his pack. He braced himself for the cold sensation, yet still winced as his fingertips met its metal surface. It glinted and dazzled in the sunlight as he withdrew it. He caught his reflection on its perfect curve, reeling at first at his own image: a pathetic man lost against a vast blue sky. A mere speck on an ancient landscape. A man alone.

*　　*　　*　　*

USS John F. Kennedy

"Just through here," Moretti said as he motioned Brady to follow him into the squadron ready room. "Take a seat. Katherine has some paperwork to do. She'll be back in a few minutes."

"No worries," Brady replied as he lowered himself into a luxurious crew chair.

Moretti sensed how out of place their visitor seemed to feel. "You've had quite an unexpected adventure today, huh?"

"Yeah. Bloody oath. Wasn't expecting the little joy flight, or to end up out here ... on this."

Moretti chuckled. "It's a rare privilege, getting to visit a ship like this. Security is tight—it takes some arranging."

"Guess I must be special or something, although I got no idea why."

Moretti laughed again. "Well, maybe not special to the navy, but obviously special to a certain someone."

"She's done this before, for other people?"

"Not that I know of."

Brady shifted in his chair and cradled his chin.

Moretti took the cue and stood. "Okay, sit tight. Katherine won't be long."

"Thanks."

Moretti stopped as he got to the doorway. "She's talked a lot about you, you know. You guys must have hit it off pretty well."

Moretti wasn't sure why his next words spilled out, nor from where they came. Perhaps it was the comradeship he and Katherine had developed over the years—a deep yet unspoken devotion forged through the furnace of shared military service. Or perhaps it was the recent birth of his first child—a daughter born five weeks before and whom he was still to meet—that stirred a primeval urge of fatherly protection within him. Perhaps it was both.

"She's a special sort, our Katherine," Moretti said. "There's a tough shell on the outside, but there's a wonderful person within. Be good to her."

Brady nodded.

*   *   *   *

Southwest National Park

The voices were back and gaining in strength as Collins gripped the object's cold surface. His wife, Debra, was as alive as ever in his mind's eye—just as she'd been five years ago, here on this summit as their incredible time in the Tasmanian wilderness drew to a close. She had seemed more joyful and at peace with her world than Collins could ever recall. This was where they reflected on their years of moving slowly apart: Collins drifting away as duty persistently called, her becoming lost in a legal career. Their marriage still alive, but dangling by a dwindling thread. This was where the wilderness had worked its magic—stripping back the hurt, the disappointments, the many words unsaid.

Collins's hands shook as he eased a finger onto the metal lever. He closed his eyes and pictured her standing next to him. Her eyes delighting in the view, face beaming at the vast wilderness as if to convey her thankfulness for being alive at that very moment in time.

A sharp metallic sound punctured the silence.

As Collins opened his eyes, he caught the last plume of ashes as they spilled out and merged with the breeze in a graceful, twirling dance. He bent down. The earth was freezing and hard, yet he felt no pain as he dug a small hole with his hands. He placed the urn into the hole and covered it.

As he stood to leave, the brilliant white flash of a sea eagle winged its way around the lower hills, gliding without effort in the air currents as it headed along the waterway toward the open sea.

He had an urge to say something profound, but the words were not there. "Goodbye," he whispered, before exhaling a long warm breath into the cold air.

As Collins picked up his daypack and took his first steps down the slope, he experienced a first glimmer of peace. But it was a peculiar emotion. A sense of something missing, yet something restored.

And the voices were gone.

*　*　*　*

Battery Point, Hobart

"Hey, thanks for the tour. That ship of yours is quite something."

"You're welcome," Katherine said, her eyes glinting. "You did such a great job showing me your world, it was only right that I return the favour."

"Hmm. Seems like you went to a lot of trouble."

"Maybe, but it was worth it. The look on your face when we lifted off! Something I'll never forget!"

"Yeah. Good on you. I nearly crapped myself."

Brady took another sip of his beer and glanced out the window beside their table. The old pub in Battery Point was warm and cosy, but the temperature outside had plummeted and the daylight had gone with it. "So, tomorrow is your last full day here?"

"Yup. We weigh anchor first thing Monday morning."

"Do you have to work tomorrow?"

"Yeah, just a short watch though. I should be free by early afternoon."

Martin clasped his beer glass and held on tight. He looked into the head of froth. "It would be good to talk ... once you're off."

"Talk?"

"Yeah. You know, about where to from here."

Brady could sense Katherine scanning him. He resisted the urge to look up—if their eyes met, it would be all over.

He looked up.

"Martin," she said as she looked into his eyes, "what are you afraid of?"

He looked to the ceiling, then back towards her. "I'm afraid you'll just sail back to America. And, um, I won't ever see you again."

He could feel her holding his gaze. His eyes locked to hers.

"Yeah. Yeah, I know," she said.

"It's only been a week, but I feel like I've known you much longer. And I don't want this to be a one-week wonder. I reckon it's been too good for that."

Katherine prised his fingers from the beer glass, then held his hands in hers. "Me too," she whispered.

"Yeah?"

"Yeah," Katherine said, a smile dawning on her face. "Let's make it a date. Tomorrow night. I have no idea how we're going to make this work, but we're going to figure it out. You ain't seen the last of me, Martin Brady."

It was Brady's turn to smile, for a second. He watched the tiny drops of rain spattering on the window behind her and the first hints of fog forming on the street outside as his next sentence took shape. "So, I've told you what *I'm* afraid of. I think it's your turn now."

"Me?" Katherine laughed. "Are you kidding? You've seen what I can do. Nothing scares me, buddy."

"Bullshit. We've told each other a lot," he said. "I think you know more about the real me than anyone. But I reckon there's things you haven't told me. Things you keep secret that get to you. I can sense it, and I think it's time you told me some more."

"So, male intuition, huh?"

"Something like that."

*　　*　　*　　*

Bruny Island

Ben found the abandoned bush track near the airfield and parked the car in a clearing. Night had fallen quickly as rain clouds sliding in from the west extinguished the usual long twilight. The rain started light at first, then picked up in intensity—not heavy, but persistent. He watched the drops hit the windscreen and work their way down the glass.

Ben pulled the blanket closer around him to lessen his shivers. He could hear the peculiar sounds of the Tasmanian bush outside, even above the rain. All so foreign to Ben, so different. The streets of Hong Kong a complete world away.

But no thoughts of home, no.

The night ahead would be too long and sleep too hard to find.

*　　*　　*　　*

Battery Point, Hobart

Katherine did not believe in male intuition, but Brady had prodded right under her protective layer somehow.

"You don't speak about your family much," he'd pointed out. "When the topic comes up you skim right over it."

She'd started with her grandfather, describing her relationship with her closest relative, and the disturbing news of his recent diagnosis. How she dreaded the moment she might receive the news of his loss while away on deployment. The thought kept her awake at night.

And how she feared for her mother. Of how alone and aimless she seemed to be, and how much she needed the presence of her only child who only came home for a few weeks each year.

And her father. She wasn't afraid of him, or even for him. But she had a fear of time passing. Of opportunities that might be missed, of connections that might never be made.

"Seems to me," Brady said when Katherine's outpouring came to an end, "you want to go home. So, what's keeping you?"

Katherine looked into her empty wineglass as she ran a finger around its rim. "My job. The navy. All of it."

"In other words ... *you*."

Katherine looked up. "Are you my therapist or something?"

"Nah, heaven forbid. Let's just say I've been there, done that. I know what it's like to make a hard call between a career and home."

"I love what I do," she almost pleaded.

"I can see that."

"And it's important work ... important for our country, and what's happening in our world."

"No doubt. And I bet the person who replaces you will feel the same way."

"You're a bastard, you know that, right?"

They broke into laughter, snapping the tension. Katherine resumed her examination of her wineglass, but Brady held his grin—appreciating the softness emerging across her eyes.

Katherine resisted the urge to look up—if their eyes met, it would be all over.

She looked up.

"I think I'm worried life will pass me by. Time will get away. I think ... I'm scared I'll end up alone." The softness in her eyes had descended to the dampness of tears.

"Lonely ... even with all those thousands of people you work with on the ship?" he asked.

"Yeah. Even then."

His grin remained as she studied his face. He wasn't being smug. She could see only warmth in his eyes. And recognition.

Katherine looked away, out through the window and into the dark. The rain had stopped and the fog had begun to clear.

CHAPTER THIRTY-SEVEN

*Choose silence of all virtues, for by it you hear other
men's imperfections, and conceal your own.*
                                      —George Bernard Shaw

PLAN submarine Shaanxi-2

19 August 2023, 2025 hours

"Ahead slow. Steady course."

The submarine glided through the coastal shallows like a shark sensing its way through the dark. The muted black shape invisible in the light-starved waters, with not a hint of moonlight penetrating the shallows from the evening sky above.

Captain Zhang Yong turned his head, and sometimes his body, to monitor each crew station lining either side of the control room. Every crewman understood—from his regular unflinching glares in their direction—there were no margins and there were to be no errors.

They had left the sonar-obliterating safety of their unwitting host ship on the surface—the bulk ore carrier *Union Mark*—three hours earlier. Zhang had brought the submarine to a dead stop, then hovered for an hour at depth while the sonar and tactical officers constructed a detailed tactical picture of the area. They made a brief trip to periscope depth to update their position, send a final communications update, and run an electronic-measures sweep of the surface for hostile radar emissions. Once Zhang was satisfied there were no threats, they'd proceeded ultra-quiet at a miserly four knots to a position five miles off Tasmania's south-east coast.

Despite all external appearances, Zhang was not feeling his way. Navigating blind in shallow water was his specialty and a task his boat was well-designed for. He knew their precise position as he monitored the high-definition hydrography mapping of the ocean floor on the screen above him. He stood motionless, hands on hips, leaning forward, his eyes unblinking and hard.

"Engage the low-intensity depth-sounder. Give me a sounding every five seconds. All others stay silent."

The low-intensity sounder—only marginally more sophisticated than a high-end fish-finder used on pleasure boats—provided vital depth information in shallow waters. And to anyone listening for sonar emissions, they'd be just another boat looking for fish.

"Depth on the keel amidships now sixty metres," the sonar operator announced. "Sixty-three ... fifty-seven ... sixty-one ... sixty-five ..."

Zhang's eyes narrowed.

"... seventy-four ... eighty-nine ... one-zero-two ..."

Zhang looked at the hydrography contour map. *This is it.*

"... one-zero-eight ... one-zero-four ... one-zero-five ..."

"All stop. Secure to idle," Zhang snapped.

The submarine's slow creep quickly decayed to a stop.

Zhang was in no doubt he'd found it: a trench in the shallow ocean floor plunging to a hundred and twenty metres' depth and close to five hundred metres in diameter. A hole in the seabed—the perfect place to hide a submarine.

"Pilot, commence a slow dive to ninety metres, zero bubble."

The submarine stayed dead level on its keel, descending beyond the edges of the trench and into the deeper water below.

"Our depth is steady at ninety metres, Captain," a crewman reported. "Sounding is thirty-four metres under the keel."

"Very good. Engage the auto-hover. And monitor our position as if your life depends on it."

Keeping a submerged submarine in one position, and at the same depth, was a near impossible task for a human pilot in those conditions. A skilled submariner could manage it for a few minutes at a time before the constant adjustments to ballast, trim, heading, and thrust would overwhelm the human brain. The computer-controlled auto-hover system, however, could keep them motionless for days.

Zhang lifted the handset and pressed a button.

"Torpedo room," the officer replied.

"This is the captain," Zhang said. "We are in position. Commence preparations. Target-time for launch now 0100 hours."

*　*　*　*

2140 hours

Weapons Officer Lieutenant Li Wei's world was one of the most cramped spaces on the boat, with only minimal room for a handful of crew to manoeuvre between the floor-to-ceiling racks, equipment lockers, shelves, control panels, and weapons-delivery units. He never complained when his torpedo room was used as an overflow storage facility, or even an overflow accommodation facility. Submariners accept such facts of life without complaint.

The previous three weeks, however, had been close to unbearable—close, even, to his unflappable limits.

The first insult had been the absence of weapons. The mission called for no torpedos and none had been loaded.

The second insult followed the first: with no torpedos to manage, the two crewmen under his command were not required. They'd been left on the support ship in the middle of the Pacific.

The third insult followed the other two: with empty torpedo racks, the spaces had been used to store the mission payload. The long grey cylinders were shaped similar to torpedos, but appeared to be passive beasts with no propulsion of their own. He'd been given no information on their contents other than to "take extreme extra care." Which he did.

The fourth, and ultimate insult, were the areas then converted into sleeping and storage spaces. Not for him, or their crew, but for two imposters. Two commandos from North Korea had made *his* torpedo room their home.

And the two men were poor company, showing no manners and scant respect. Li had made the mistake of attempting a friendly conversation with Tak—the commanding officer—on the first day they'd put to sea. The man reciprocated with an icy stare. When Tak spoke to him—which was rare and only by pure necessity—he was gruff and used as few words as possible. The other man spoke only in Korean, and only ever conversed with Tak.

Li had decided his best strategy was to pretend they weren't there. This had been only partly successful, given the size of their shared space. Each time he'd left the torpedo room he would shut the hatchway and march off along the corridor mumbling a profanity in Mandarin, "cào nǐ mā." If they heard him, they'd be in no doubt about his view of them and their respective mothers.

There was no time to be territorial, though, or even for mumbled profanities. There was work to be done. The loose mission gear was to be moved from the torpedo room to the dry deck shelter—a special module mounted on top of the submarine where divers could launch while the submarine was submerged. This would be the first step before they could move the payload cylinders within the torpedo room.

"Ensign," Li ordered, "take the weight of the equipment case as it comes out."

The young ensign, who'd been conscripted from another part of the submarine, was strong enough for the task. The two DPRK commandos he assisted were stronger, and faster, and keen to get the mission moving.

"Careful now … easy," Li chided. His stomach gripped as he considered the complex task ahead. *So much to do, but with three untrained assistants … one young and inexperienced, another one arrogant, and the third can't even speak my language!*

Ryeon, the second commando, withdrew the stainless-steel case from the overhead rack.

The ensign waited below as the case slid out above him, its cool surface gliding over his extended fingers.

"*Ttangjang!*" Ryeon barked.

The ensign, surprised by the sudden instruction and not knowing a word of Korean, turned on instinct toward the man. The rear edge of the case slid off the rack. Seventy kilograms of weight fell through the ensign's hands, thumped against his chest, and crashed to the steel deck below.

*　*　*　*

USS Columbia

Petty Officer Scott O'Neil studied the characteristics of the sound spike: its replay sounding in his headset, and its unique acoustic shape dancing on his display. The sound had originated from a good distance away, and towards the Tasmanian coast. Perhaps not so unusual, given the pleasure and commercial vessels likely to be operating on the surface there. But he knew, at 8:30 PM local time, those local sources would be more limited.

He keyed the communications circuit. "Conn. Sonar. I'm analysing a recent transient, possibly submerged, may be of interest."

Transient sounds—unexpected, short-lived sounds in the underwater environment—were not unusual in shallow coastal areas and could be generated by humans, the environment, and biologics. O'Neill was used to detecting transient sounds on or near the surface. Submerged transients, though, were far less common.

Captain Samuel Carter was again on watch. "Sonar. Conn. This is the XO. What you got, Mister O'Neil?"

O'Neill was relieved to hear his surname. He'd had enough of the "Speedboat" tag in the past few days. "Captured it a few minutes ago, sir. About twenty-five thousand yards out and near the coast, our bow sensors picked up a distinct, isolated transient. High amplitude, but fairly low frequency. Has the characteristics of a heavy object hitting something, possibly metallic."

"And submerged, you say?"

"Affirm. From the way the sound attenuated, and the fall-off of the reverberation … has the hallmarks of a metallic source. And well submerged, I think."

"Understood. Any contacts near that range?"

"Negative. There's been some regular coastal traffic in the past few hours. Fishing vessels mostly."

"You got a bearing for me?"

"Approximate bearing … around three-one-zero true."

Carter stretched out the handset cord and stooped to the navigation table. He manipulated the touchscreen to zoom in on the Tasmania coastline on a bearing of three hundred and ten degrees at twenty-five thousand yards range.

"That's near the Forrestier Peninsula, right on the coast," Carter said. "Could be lobster fisherman, or abalone divers. But we'll take some time to be sure. Keep your ears on, O'Neill."

Carter brought the submarine around to track three hundred and ten degrees and reduced their speed to a crawl. They'd keep the submarine's highly sensitive bow sonar pointed at the source and listen.

*   *   *   *

PLAN submarine Shaanxi-2

Zhang didn't sprint down the lower-deck corridor, or even jog, yet his pace seemed super-human. He opened the torpedo room hatchway to a scene of pandemonium. The young ensign was half-lying and half-sitting on the floor, clutching at his ankle and screaming in agony. Li, Tak, and Ryeon were attempting to lift the equipment case off his leg but struggling with the load in the tight space.

Zhang took charge, directing the three to lever the case upward as he grabbed the ensign by the shoulders and pulled him clear. The young man's screaming sharpened as his body slid across the deck and was only muffled once Zhang got a hand over his mouth.

"Li, get the medical response team and a stretcher," Zhang commanded.

"Sir," Li managed as he clambered past and through the hatchway.

Tak folded his arms and looked down at Zhang. "His foot is inverted," Tak commented. "The ankle is smashed."

Zhang glared up at him. There was no sign of compassion in Tak's bedside manner, only facts. He ignored the frosty diagnosis and leaned forward to whisper near the ensign's ear: "Hush now. Help is coming. You must control yourself, for all our sakes."

Zhang released his hand from the young man's mouth. The ensign took in a sharp breath, closed his eyes, and let out a long guttural moan.

"Loud noises, in this business, bring detection," Zhang growled, looking again at Tak. "And detection often brings death."

"This is contained," Tak said.

"You cannot know this," Zhang snapped. "The fools who dropped that case may have cost us the mission. Maybe more."

*　　*　　*　　*

USS Columbia

2205 hours

"Sonar. Conn," came XO Carter's voice through Scott O'Neill's headset. "Anything further to report?"

"Conn. Sonar. Negative, sir. All's been quiet on that bearing."

"Understood. Probably just local fisherman. We'll resume standard ops, but keep a general watch and update me on any changes."

"Aye, sir."

CHAPTER THIRTY-EIGHT

I used to have nightmares about the Antichrist—what would happen, where it would come from, and who it would be.

—Marilyn Manson, *Beliefnet.com*

North Sea Fleet Headquarters, Qingdao

Rear Admiral Pengcheng Tao had resigned himself to a lounge chair as midnight passed. A lamp projected a single pool of light across his office desk at the far end of the room, and the tip of his cigarette shed a red glow on the ceiling.

He had not bothered to return to his apartment. Attempting to sleep would be a waste of time. In the hours before a mission his brain would go into overdrive and his body would become irrelevant. Prosaic needs such as sleep and food were irritations that could wait.

A simple sound—a minuscule solitary *ding*—punctured the silence. Pengcheng reached for his phone. He opened the PLAN secure messaging app and clicked the unread message from Lieutenant Colonel Li Guoliang:

S2 reported on station @ alpha-one. proceeding as planned. weps-free. etd 0100 local.

He sent back an acknowledgement, then settled back into his chair. *Weps-free* informed Pengcheng the submarine crew and the DPRK commandos were *weapons free*, meaning they were committed to execute the mission under their own command, commencing at 1:00 AM local time.

They're on their own now, Pengcheng told himself. *They are in the hands of destiny.*

*　*　*　*

PLAN submarine Shaanxi-2
20 August 2023, 0105 hours

Clad in a black wetsuit and scuba gear, Lieutenant Commander Tak waited as the diver spun the locking mechanism to open the dry deck shelter's outer hatch. The Chinese divers left the submarine with a few kicks of their flippers.

Tak sensed the surge of cold from the open sea, and familiar muffled echoes of life and movement beneath the waves enveloped his senses. *Finally, it begins. This is my time.*

Tak tapped Ryeon on the shoulder and made a sharp punching motion in the water between them—his gloved fist closed hard and tight.

Ryeon nodded. Hard and deliberate. This would be his time too.

The DPRK commandos and the Chinese submarine crew had practised their next actions so many times, the exercise had become second nature. They guided the swimmer delivery vehicle out of the flooded dry deck shelter on tracks. The Chinese divers signalled to Ryeon when the vessel was clear. He signalled back, opened the throttle, and guided the SDV to a safe distance ahead of the submarine.

Tak sat behind Ryeon in the SDV. They were still exposed to the water and remained in their scuba gear. The vessel—an electric-powered mini-submarine five metres long—would take them to the Alpha-Zero destination submerged and with scarcely a sound.

But for now, they could only hold position below the surface and wait.

*　*　*　*

0115 hours

The first identification signal on Ryeon's waterproof device came through right on time. The tiny white blip oscillated on the display. Ryeon motioned to Tak, then switched on the SDV's headlamp. They couldn't yet see anything ahead in the inky underwater gloom, but they knew a long cylinder had exited from one of *Shaanxi-2*'s forward torpedo tubes.

Tak and Ryeon had helped Li load the four cylinders into the torpedo tubes an hour earlier. Li was to complete a slow manual flooding of each tube before the launch, then manually eject each cylinder with a low-powered shot of compressed air into each tube. Not quite a torpedo launch, but somewhat satisfying for Li just the same.

Within two minutes, Ryeon had four active idents on his display. He edged the SDV forward … looking … searching, until …

There. All four cylinders, dead ahead.

LED identifier lights twinkled on the top and bottom of each cylinder as they sat suspended in the water. Chinese technicians had set the cylinder buoyancy to maintain a depth of ten metres. The cylinders would carry the heavy mission payload and neither sink nor surface.

The Chinese divers had waited for the launch, then followed the ident signals to locate the cylinders. Ryeon manoeuvred the SDV to the closest cylinder and turned the vehicle to a rear-facing position. The divers connected the cylinder's cable to the SDV, then the second cylinder's cable to the first. Within five minutes, a daisy chain of four cylinders had been connected to the vehicle.

Ryeon acknowledged the *go* signal from the divers, then opened up the throttle of the SDV. The cylinders followed on their cables like a miniature submerged train. Their destination: a deserted beach, three miles due west.

* * * *

Bruny Island

Her eyes floated before him in the darkness. Warm. Knowing.

"Hush now, my child. Hush now," she whispered.

"But, Mama. I saw them. They're *here*."

"Shh. There is no one here but us."

"They will kill us. The Americans are here. *They will murder us all!*" Ben pleaded as his tiny chest heaved.

"It is just a dream," she said. "Shh now ..."

"No, Mama. No! It's like Papa said."

Her voice stayed level and easy as she sat beside him on the bed, stroking his forehead. "Hush now, my child ... my silly child."

Ben's eyes flicked wide open as a screech cut through the night. His legs jammed hard against the car's steering wheel and his head slammed the headrest as his body jolted in the driver's seat. Two piercing orange eyes were still floating in the blackness before him.

Ben thumped the dashboard, and the possum leapt from the windscreen and disappeared into the overhanging tree.

But the sound of Liling's voice, and the sensation of her hand on his forehead, would stay with him until dawn.

*   *   *   *

0215 hours

The journey had taken longer than expected, but they were still within limits. They could keep a steady pace with no need to rush or panic.

Tak surfaced short of the breakers and held position, treading water. He lifted his facemask and brought the waterproof night-vision scope up to his left eye. Icy light rain spat from the sky as he examined the bay surrounding him.

A headland to the north, the flat white beach spanning the tightly curved bay, and a flat peninsula to the south ending in tiny island outcrops. And beyond the beach: no lights, no roads, and no structures. Just trees.

Tak lowered the scope and dropped his mask back into position. Before him lay Lagoon Bay on Tasmania's Forestier Peninsula. Ryeon's underwater navigation had been spot on.

*   *   *   *

0223 hours

Tak released the ballast from the last cylinder in the line, then switched off the LED indicator lights. The cylinder rose to the surface and bobbed in the gentle swell. He disconnected the towing cable from its nose and swam it onto the beach using the surge of the waves and rhythmic kicks from his oversized flippers. He repeated the process until all four cylinders lay beached in the lapping water.

Tak sat low on the waterline, combat weapon ready in one hand. He kept a careful scanning watch on the cylinders, out over the breakers, and along the length of the beach. He didn't expect any human movement, but he braced for it just the same.

Lagoon Bay was isolated and uninhabited. Bushwalkers and pleasure craft would sometimes visit in the summer months, but rarely, and the local farmer would sometimes visit the open pasture beyond the beach. But they expected no visitors in the dead of a Sunday morning in late winter. The place was as empty as the moon and almost as cold.

A shadow moved at the end of the beach. Tak crouched lower, flat on his stomach in the shallow water, then brought the night-vision scope to bear. He spotted Ryeon using the coastal scrub as background cover as he moved along the beach. He knew Ryeon had just hidden the SDV in a small rocky inlet at the southern end of the bay.

*   *   *   *

0540 hours

"Get some rest," Tak said. "I will take watch until sunrise."

Ryeon shimmied further into the bare corner of the room and closed his eyes. But both men understood he would not sleep. There'd been ample time for sleep on the submarine. Three weeks, in fact.

They had entered a small hut positioned in the coastal shrubs, fifty metres from the beach. The place was deserted, as expected, and the single door was not locked.

In the hours since they'd landed on the beach, Tak and Ryeon snapped open each of the four cylinders, then lifted out the smaller containers encased within. They ferried the containers up the beach and hid them in the low scrub near the hut. Each of the four payload cylinders were separated into smaller parts, carried to the southern end of the beach, and buried deep in the sand.

The first hint of dawn came as Tak peered out the window. A mile of flat grassland stretched toward high wooded hills in the distance to the west. A windsock hung flaccid above the long, narrow, and flat stretch of open ground in the foreground.

More waiting now, Tak told himself as he braced himself against the freezing air. *But soon.*

CHAPTER THIRTY-NINE

*Some people talk to animals. Not many listen though.
That's the problem.*

—A. A. Milne, *Winnie-the-Pooh*

USS John F. Kennedy
20 August 2023, 0720 hours

Moretti tossed the briefing sheet onto the empty crew chair beside him. "I could have sworn I joined the United States Navy. But here I am doing air taxi rides for foreigners."

"Yeah," Perez joined in, "and I'll bet those Aussie jerks don't even tip."

Katherine didn't look up from her paperwork. "We ferry the nuclear testing people from the ship out to Hobart Airport. We wait for the mail bags to arrive on the inbound flight at 1000 hours, then bring it back to the ship. Quick and easy."

"Oh, so we're the Postal Service too?" Moretti whined. "This is nuts. We hardly ever fly when we're in a foreign port."

"It's because we're moored in the river and not docked at the pier," Katherine said, still not looking up. "And anyway, that's our orders."

Moretti rolled his eyes. "Nobody likes a mouthy woman, Lieutenant Commander."

Katherine gave Moretti a death stare before returning to her fuel calculations.

"I dunno, Mets," Perez said. "Her Australian boyfriend says he really likes how she puts that mouth of hers to work!"

Perez laughed at his own joke, and Moretti couldn't resist joining in.

"Oh, grow up, you two. *Honestly!*" was the best Katherine could manage. "I'll be out at the helo," she said. "Try not to harass anyone

359

else while I'm gone." She summoned all her strength not to smile as she made for the door.

*   *   *   *

Lagoon Bay, Tasmania
0735 hours

Ryeon swung the door open and strode into the hut with clear military intent. He withdrew the black handgun from his pack, snapped in the magazine, and chambered the first round.

"All clear?" Tak asked, sensing things were anything but clear.

"Not yet," Ryeon said as he made for the door.

"Wait. What are you doing?"

"You asked me to make sure the airstrip is clear."

"With your handgun?"

Ryeon lowered the gun to his side. "Come," he said, "and see for yourself."

*   *   *   *

Bruny Island

The dull pain in Ben's hips and lower back was becoming harder to ignore. The night in the car had been tortuous. Bone-invading cold, screechy nocturnal wildlife, and his incessant thoughts of home had combined to deprive him of sleep. He'd drifted off before dawn—more from exhaustion—then woke with a start to a daylight scene.

Ben cursed as he looked at his watch: 7:58 AM. Later than he'd planned, but still enough time for the next step. He reached for the key and turned the ignition. He had a plane to catch.

*   *   *   *

Lagoon Bay

"See," Ryeon grunted as he pointed to the nearest creature, fifty metres away.

Tak frowned and peered along the length of the airstrip. He could see a pronounced brown-grey lump sitting in the grass and another five scattered farther down, each of them the size of a large pumpkin.

"What the hell are they?" Tak asked.

"I don't know," Ryeon replied, staring in bemusement at the small mob of wombats. "They weren't in our brief. I tried to frighten one away by clapping and yelling and it charged at me. So now I will kill and remove them all."

"Absolutely not," Tak said. "We cannot draw attention."

Ryeon shook his head.

"Go back to the hut and get the energy food from our packs," Tak ordered. "We will draw them away."

Ryeon trudged back to the hut, despondent. The special forces commando was trained to deal with each and every unexpected eventuality on a mission. But he would usually handle problems with a knife or a gun, and never before with trail mix.

*   *   *   *

Bruny Island

Jacob Sawyer sauntered towards the office from the hangar. He'd heard the doorbell chime, though he wasn't expecting his first customer for another half-hour.

Any other commercial pilot would curse an early morning booking on a Sunday, but not Sawyer. He'd rather have been out on his board catching early waves, certainly, but surfing didn't pay the bills. He was paid only by the flying hour and needed every minute in the air he could muster. His employer, Southern Flight Tours, was a two-bit scenic flying company with no genuine prospects and it had been his last and only resort for paid flying work. Other aviation businesses picked from the cream of the crop of newly trained pilots, or from the many laid-off airline pilots still looking for work. Few operators would waste their time on a twenty-one-year-old beach bum who'd only just scraped through to get his commercial pilot licence.

Sawyer entered the reception area to see a young Asian man standing at the counter. The man seemed serious and focused, as if more ready for a fight than a flight. "You're bright and early," Sawyer said.

"Yes. I prefer to be early."

"Fair enough. Anyway, I'm Jacob, your pilot for today."

"Hello. My name is … Eddy."

They exchanged nods as Jacob looked past him and out to the car park. "Where's the others? I've got four passengers listed for the nine o'clock booking?"

"It will only be me," Eddy said. "My friends have contracted food poisoning. Probably bad oysters, which I did not eat."

"Oh, right. Well, that's no shucking good!"

From the blank look on his customer's face, Sawyer deduced the man didn't understand the oystering terminology, or had no sense of humour, or both. "In that case we'll change to the smaller plane. It'll be cheaper."

"*No*," Eddy replied. "It must be the Cessna two-zero-six."

Sawyer took a moment to absorb the sharp reaction. "You know some things about planes, then?" he asked.

"Not really, no." Eddy smiled. "It's just … I am not used to small planes and I do not wish to go in the smaller one. Please use the bigger plane, as I have booked. The cost is not an issue."

"Okay, mate. Whatever you say. You're the customer."

"Thank you."

"No probs. Well, take a seat for a sec. I'll go finish checking the plane. We'll be on our way in about fifteen minutes."

*　*　*　*

USS John F. Kennedy, 0840 hours

Every now and then, as the Seahawk's rotor blades began to turn overhead and the turbine engine whine gathered pace, Katherine's mind would wander back to the early days of her flight training. She could almost hear old Mitch Parker's voice in her headset:

"If you take any longer with that checklist, I might fall asleep," he'd said.

"Sorry," Katherine said." I just don't want to miss anything."

"I get that. But what's the good of being so perfect here on the ground that we use up all our time? We're supposed to be going flying, you know. You need to be one with your machine, and less of a god-damn robot. Good pilots don't strap themselves into the machine. Good pilots, natural pilots ... they strap the machine to them. You're gonna be a good pilot someday. It'll just be you, and the plane, and the sky. You'll be one with it. And that's when you'll really fly."

That day old Mitch Parker had predicted arrived in the advanced stages of Katherine's helicopter flight training with the navy. On that day, it seemed the helicopter could read her thoughts—as if every movement, sound, and vibration of the machine were wired straight into her brain.

Katherine smiled as the rotor blades spun to a blur above her on the flight deck of USS *John F. Kennedy*. The transition was happening. The magical moment when she would transform from a ground-confined human being to a creature of the air and free to roam the open expanse of the sky. The moment when she and the machine would merge into one. When she would, without conscious thought or effort, *fly.*

*　　*　　*　　*

Bruny Island

Jacob Sawyer hit the transmit button: "Bruny Traffic, Cessna Two-Zero-Six Hotel November Lima, taxiing Runway One-Four for departure to the south. Bruny."

Ben tightened his harness in the right-hand seat as the plane trundled towards the end of the dirt runway. He'd kept a close eye on the young pilot and was appalled to see him use no checklists. The pilot seemed to do everything from memory. He had the key items covered, but he was sloppy and too casual for Ben's liking.

The only response to the pilot's departure call on the radio was a slight crackle in Ben's headset. Not that he'd expected a response. They were well outside controlled airspace, being twenty-two miles from the Hobart Airport airspace boundary, and eighteen thousand feet below the attention of Melbourne Centre's air traffic control radar. And it was early on a Sunday morning, with little if any other aviation traffic in the vicinity. They'd be on their own in the southern Tasmanian skies.

"Righty-o," Sawyer said on the intercom. "Let's go flying."

Ben tensed as the Cessna's turbocharged engine roared to a howling racket. Unfamiliar bumps and vibrations jarred him as they accelerated along the airstrip.

Sawyer sat lopsided in the left-hand seat, his left hand barely gripping the control yoke, his right hand resting on his knee. He looked forward out the windshield as the runway rushed beneath them, taking it all in with the unimpressed eyes of an office worker on a two-hour commute to work.

*　　*　　*　　*

Mobile phone coverage of the Forrestier Peninsula was patchy. At remote Lagoon Bay it would only work if a person stood in the right spot, and in clear weather. And at 9:15 AM that morning, it was non-existent.

The closest mobile phone towers at Boomer Bay and Dunalley had automatically shut down due to an apparent severe power spike in the area. Technicians at the remote monitoring facility in Melbourne had attempted to reset the towers, but there was no response on the comms links. A local on-call technician was dispatched from Hobart, but she was already on the job at another tower near the city that was also playing up, and it would be at least an hour before she could be on her way.

*   *   *   *

The view was inspiring from three thousand feet up. The gossamer blue breadth of Storm Bay stretched from its western boundary along the coastline of Bruny Island, out to the Tasmanian Peninsula on the eastern side. And beyond the bay, to the south, nothing but ocean as far as Ben could see.

The young pilot had been forthcoming with bright, chirpy commentary since they'd lifted off from the airstrip, turned right, and made their way along the coast. He pointed out key landmarks on The Neck connecting the north and south parts of the island, then Adventure Bay and the rugged coastline of Fluted Cape. He turned the plane to head across Storm Bay and had them tracking for Cape Pillar on the tip of the Tasman Peninsula, thirty miles away.

Ben watched the peninsula grow larger in the distance. He looked back at Bruny Island and could see they were close to the mid-point across the bay. He'd seen only a few recreational vessels near the coastlines below, and none out in the expanse. He chanced a look sideways at the pilot. Sawyer still sat off-centre, as if in his favourite recliner, and stared mindlessly at the sky ahead.

Look at your damn altimeter, Ben said to himself, knowing it had crept up to two hundred feet above their intended altitude.

It was then Ben caught another glimpse of the three small bars, the sunlight dazzling off their golden textures. The epaulettes on Sawyer's right shoulder signified his status as a commercial pilot. Not a good pilot, Ben already knew, but a qualified pilot, nonetheless.

For a moment, Ben's thoughts swung back to the academy in Melbourne. He hadn't intended to get caught up in that culture, but it had taken a certain hold on him. His classmates revered those golden epaulettes and dreamed of the day when they would clip on their own.

And one day, somewhere in the distant future, the three bars might become four—for a select few.

Ben snapped his gaze from Sawyer. He needed to stop the thoughts gripping in his gut. But as he attempted to focus on the view through his side window, the wrenching thoughts stayed with him.

He inhaled deeply as he released the strap on the hidden pouch strapped above his right ankle and felt for the handle.

The plane had reached the middle of Storm Bay. The time had come.

CHAPTER FORTY

You have to go on and be crazy. Craziness is like heaven.
—Jimi Hendrix

Hobart

Mia Gianopoulos lifted the receiver and pressed speed dial.

"Traffic Branch, Senior Constable John Randall," the man on the other end droned.

"John. Hi. It's Mia, from the traffic management centre."

"G'day, Mia. Shouldn't you be at home in bed reading the Sunday paper?"

"Yeah, I wish! Look, we got something weird happening."

"Yeah? This had better be good. I just got my brekky and I'm not in the mood to go driving this morning."

"The traffic lights on the Tasman Bridge. They've gone out."

The officer's voice switched from casual indifference to policing mode. "Okay. What's happening?"

"Well, about five minutes ago they went out. All the traffic lights. No red or green lights working on the approaches, or on the bridge itself. Nothing to tell drivers which lanes are running east or west. Drivers are sticking to the usual lanes for now, but I'm not sure how long that'll last."

"Can you fix it from there?" Randall asked.

"I'm trying, but I'm on my own this morning. I rebooted the control software, but no change. Then I tried manual control of the PLCs, but they aren't responding. It's like we've lost control of them or something."

"PLCs?"

"Sorry. The programmable logic controllers ... the mini-computers which control the signals."

"Right, well—"

"Hold on. Something's happening ..." Gianopoulos scanned the bank of CCTV screens blanketing the control room. Hobart's major roads, arterial routes, and intersections flashed across the screens as video feeds poured in from the many cameras mounted across the city. She focused on the screens showing the eastern and western approaches to the Tasman Bridge, and then on both ends of the bridge itself.

"Oh shit. *Oh no.*"

"What the hell's going on?" Randall demanded.

"The lights are back on, but they're all over the place. The lanes are all changed and cars are going ... *oh no!*"

"Right. I'm onto it. I'll get some officers out there right now."

"You'll need everyone you can get. And ambulances. I've just seen two head-on collisions already."

*　　*　　*　　*

Thirty-two hundred feet above Storm Bay, Tasmania

Ben couldn't look at him any longer. He'd seen enough. He grasped the control yoke to steady the plane and kept his face forward.

It was his third kill. He'd achieved the first via an overdose of anaesthetic stabbed into the man's neck. He'd delivered the second as an additive to the woman's drink—a tasteless nerve agent which transformed her cocktail from flirty to lethal.

But this one was different. Not another quick covert delivery followed by an equally quick disappearance. No. The knife, and all the blood now painting the cockpit, had been the only choice. And leaving the cockpit straight afterwards—out of the question.

Ben had expected blood, yes. But not *that* much blood. And he hadn't expected the pilot to grab the handle and try to pull the knife out of his chest. Or to turn and look at him as he took his last breath and the last spurts of blood throbbed out over his weakening hands. The abject disbelief and terror on Jacob Sawyer's face was then etched forever somewhere behind Ben's eyes.

With the pilot unmistakably dead, it was just Ben. He was in command of the aeroplane, and it felt good to be flying again. He banked the wings to turn the plane fifteen degrees to the left and head directly for his destination, on track, and on time.

But there was a problem: a dead "co-pilot" in the left seat with a seemingly endless supply of blood still draining onto the seat and floor. Ben had twenty minutes of flying time to his destination, and not even he could stand the sight and smell of all that blood for so long.

Ben's forehead pulled into a furrowed, narrow focus. *This is not in the brief.*

The final mission brief—the plans he'd received on the encrypted USB-stick two days earlier—had been meticulous and detailed. They'd planned every step and contingency.

Except for this.

*   *   *   *

Hobart

Constable Randall hated working traffic. But you got what you got each rotation, and that was that.

As he gunned the police car out of police headquarters and tore along Bathurst Street with lights and siren blaring, the shot of adrenaline was a welcome change, even if it meant skipping his McBreakfast. Something significant was happening and he'd be the one to take command. "What's up with the radio room?" he snarled at the constable in the passenger seat.

"They said to stand by. They're trying to allocate other units for us, but the radio is the only comms that's working."

"What the?"

"Yeah. The radio room guy said they'd all been logged out of the Bravo system. None of their passwords are working."

"That stupid new IT system up in the bloody cloud. Get back to the radio room and tell 'em to do things the old way. They need to tell all available units to get to the Tasman Bridge. *Now!*"

*   *   *   *

Thirty-two hundred feet above Storm Bay

Ben eased back the engine power and propeller-RPM controls, then pushed the Cessna's nose over into a shallow descent. He wound the elevator trim control wheel forward to keep the nose position steady.

He slid his seat all the way back on its tracks, released his harness, and clambered onto the passenger seat on the left side, immediately behind the dead pilot. With eyes closed, he put his arms around Sawyer's body and released the safety harness. The sticky, damp sensation meeting his hands was unmistakable.

Ben flipped the left-hand door control upwards to release the lock. The door opened a few centimetres and sat prone in the external slipstream. The effect was immediate: a sudden blast of freezing air and shrieking engine noise filled the plane, knocking the wind from Ben's lungs for an instant.

He reached around to the front of the pilot seat, yanked the seat-release lever upwards, then pulled back with his other hand to slide the seat all the way back. Sawyer's head flopped sideways and hit the side window, the headset skewed across his face.

I must do this, Ben told himself. *There is no other way.*

He stood as best he could into a stooped position beside and above the pilot seat, then pulled the headset away and dropped it to the floor. With a concerted push on the upper torso, he shoved the body to the left and as far off the edge of the seat as he could.

The propeller wash and slipstream blasted in as the door opened further, the dead weight of the body pushing it ajar. The body was half-out the door but clearly going no further.

Ben closed his eyes, put both hands under the right leg of the body, and heaved with everything he had. Sawyer's body dropped with an unceremonious thump out the wide-open door.

Almost.

*   *   *   *

PV Cape Portland—River Derwent

The constable sat low on the bridge of the police vessel, his feet perched atop the glare shield. Another long night on the river patrolling the exclusion zone around USS *John F. Kennedy* was ending. His shift had been uneventful—again—and they'd only needed to "encourage" two recreational vessels to stay clear of the zone that morning. The second police vessel would come out to meet them soon. They'd be relieved from patrol duty, get back to the dock, and enjoy the rest of their Sunday at home.

The radio traffic on the usual maritime channels chirped away in the background—communicating only benign and unremarkable events. Mostly quiet, as was usual for a Sunday.

The police radio channel, in contrast, was abuzz. The constable retrieved his feet off the glare shield, plonked them on the floor, and sat upright.

"All available units. Control. This is priority one," the radio message blared. "All available units east and west to the Tasman Bridge. Major traffic incidents. Multiple collisions—"

He dashed out the rear door and yelled to the sergeant on the deck below. "Hey, Sarge. What's up on the bridge?"

The sergeant didn't flinch. His binoculars were trained on the western approach to the Tasman Bridge, his handheld radio chattering loud in his other hand.

Even without binoculars, the constable could see the traffic building. The wail of sirens and the persistent bleat of car horns echoing across the river only confirmed what his eyes told him. Most vehicles were stopped, with only a few moving at a crawl. Lines of traffic were interspersed with red and blue flashes of police and ambulance vehicles.

"Get her underway!" the sergeant yelled. "*Now*. Head for the tugboat wharf on the western side."

"Yeah, Sarge, but what about the exclusion zone?"

"Bugger that. Something big's going down and we need to be there. The bloody aircraft carrier can look after itself."

The constable disappeared back inside, hit the starter buttons, and rammed the throttles forward.

*　　*　　*　　*

Thirty-four hundred feet above Storm Bay

The Cessna-206 climbed and turned, following the control inputs coming from the cockpit.

Ben could feel the nose-angle of the plane still rising. The steep roll to the left had mercifully stopped at close to forty degrees. He could sense the airspeed slowing at a rapid rate as the plane struggled upward in its ungainly spiral.

Ben grabbed the body's lower leg and boot. He pulled again, but it still wouldn't budge. The foot had gotten jammed in the angular corner of the control yoke when the body fell out of the plane. And thick leather boot laces had wrapped themselves around the narrow end. The yoke had flicked to the left in response, inducing the steep turn, and the control column slid much of the way backwards, pulling up the nose and launching the plane into the unwanted climb.

Ben let go of the leg. He grasped the control yoke on his side in a desperate attempt to get the plane back under control. He tried, with both hands, to roll the yoke right and push it forward, straining with all the force he could summon. It moved a fraction. He held it for five seconds before he had to let go, his muscles no match for the weight of the dead body, and the irrepressible force of gravity, both working against him.

And then the sound he'd been dreading. The stall-warning horn began its infernal squeak, bleating in rapid squawks. *Such a ridiculous sound*, Ben had often thought during his training, *so silly for something so serious.* If the condition was not recognised and managed—and fast—the plane would be headed back to earth, out of control and to certain oblivion.

Ben looked in horror at the airspeed indicator before him. The needle moved anti-clockwise, slow, and steady: *seventy-one knots ... sixty-nine knots ... sixty-eight ...*

At sixty-three knots a full stall was certain to come.

No ... think!

The intermittent squeak of the stall transcended into an unrelenting, shrill scream.

Think!

Ben struggled with the sharp spike in adrenalin coursing through his system, and a burning primeval instinct to either fight, freeze, or run.

Sixty-six knots ...

Ben closed his eyes and took in a long breath through his nose. *Only the breath, only the breath ... how it feels, how it sounds, the sensation of the basest human function as it rises and falls within.*

The sensations were similar. The emotions close to identical. That moment, years before, as he stood before the delicate green vase. The pivotal moment in the final test of his training. His hand outstretched to retrieve the object for Master Park, yet paused in mid-air—unsure of his next move.

Ben opened his eyes.

Sixty-four knots ...

A thought ignited in his brain. A flash of brilliance. And pure insanity.

Ben grabbed the yoke, but not to resume his fight against gravity. He rolled the yoke farther to the left—going *with* the weight. He eased the yoke back to let gravity have its way. And it responded smooth and easy, as if appreciating the change in strategy and the surrender to the laws of physics.

The boot laces and the jammed foot slid off the yoke and away.

Ben sensed a sudden freedom from weight and gravity just as the plane began to stall. He rolled the yoke to the right to level the wings and shoved it forward to extinguish the climb and the stall.

The airspeed indicator reversed its anti-clockwise turn towards hell.

The stall-warning horn fell silent.

The plane was steady once more. Straight and level, sixty-three hundred feet over Storm Bay and still heading for the Tasman Peninsula.

*　　*　　*　　*

A sudden violent splash.

A heavy spout of water rose like a mushroom cloud, then receded back to nothing. The waves and swell of Storm Bay recovered the scene within seconds. All back to normal, just as nature insists.

The arrival of a lifeless human body from six thousand feet? A mere drop in the ocean.

Nothing to see there. Except for a small rectangular object that floated to the surface. The black cotton object was partly torn and topped with gold. The morning sunlight sparkled off the three tiny gold bars as the epaulettes drifted away in the southbound current.

CHAPTER FORTY-ONE

*We are the ones we've been waiting for. We are the
change that we seek.*

—Barack Obama

Hobart Airport

Katherine sat in the open rear doorway of the helicopter. Her feet dangled outside, with one swinging in space. She reclined her shoulder and head against the frame, her eyes focused on her phone and oblivious to any movement on the airport freight apron.

The inbound commercial flight carrying the ship's mail bags had been delayed by forty minutes. Moretti and Perez had left on a mission to locate and capture coffees and were still nowhere in sight.

Her phone blipped again—another text in another exchange with Martin Brady:

How's dinner tonight at my place sound? he asked.

> *Hmm depends. Can you cook?*

> *Can you wash up?*

> *Back home we have things called dishwashers.. civilisation*

> *So you're a life-member of the American NDA?*

> *The what?*

> *The National Dishwasher Association.. they sponsor mass school wash-ups*

> *Piss off dish wipe boy*

> *So nasty whirly girl!*

"G'day."

Katherine sat up, transforming from slouched indifference to stiff-as-a-board attention. "Oh ... hi there."

"Sorry," he said. "Didn't mean to surprise you."

She took a second to take in the man standing before her, dressed in a navy-blue uniform, a yellow hi-vis jacket, and wrap-around sunglasses.

"Just thought I'd come and say hello, and visit an old friend?"

"Okay," Katherine replied, one eyebrow raised. "Um … which friend?"

"This bird," he said as he looked along the length of the Seahawk's fuselage. "It's been a while."

"You fly helos?"

"Yep." He turned and gestured to the far side of the apron, revealing the large blue letters emblazoned across the back of his jacket: POLICE. "I fly search and rescue now. The BK117 over there."

"Oh, right. Cool."

"I flew in the Australian Navy. I did five years in a Romeo just like this one." His eyes were wandering across Katherine's helicopter's curves as if gawking at a long-lost ex-girlfriend.

"Wow, for real," Katherine said as she plopped out onto the ground and shot a hand towards him. "Hey, good to meet you. I'm Katherine."

He took her hand and shook it. "You too. I'm Pete."

*　　*　　*　　*

The turquoise edge of Lagoon Bay emerged beyond the line of hills as the Cessna approached. Ben could see the stark white curve of the beach, the dark tree-covered headland to the north, and the flat area of open pasture stretching inland. He checked the map again, then the GPS position. His grip on the control yoke tensed as he peered again at the landscape ahead.

Ben turned the plane further north-west, reduced engine power, and eased the nose down a few degrees. He would manoeuvre inland in a low, wide arc to get a good look at the strip and windsock before setting up for the approach.

There would be no inbound radio call to alert any other aviation traffic in the area. He had switched off the transponder after taking control of the plane, rendering it invisible to electronic communications and surveillance. The former pilot's iPad and phone had met a watery grave in the middle of Storm Bay, and Ben had removed the SIM card from his temporary phone well before they left Bruny Island.

*   *   *   *

Tak jumped to his feet and looked southwards. He stood rigid, straining with all his senses toward the sky above the tree-lined hills. And there, in the direction of the rising sound, a small white object coming in low and fast.

Ryeon emerged from the coastal shrub, having left his surveillance position overlooking the beach.

Tak studied the plane with his binoculars. "This is him," he said. "Confirm the registration ... Hotel November Lima."

"Confirmed," Ryeon said.

"Get the flashlight," Tak ordered.

*   *   *   *

Even with partial flaps extended and the airspeed back at eighty knots, the valley and the airstrip were filling his view far quicker than Ben had expected. He edged the engine power back and rolled the wings into a hard right-hand turn, hoping not to hear the dreaded squeak of the stall-warning horn.

Ben had flown into a few smaller airfields in Victoria during his flight training, including a landing and take-off at an airfield with a grass strip. But nothing as remote or small as this one. And even then, those trips were in the Cessna-172—a plane he could fly with confidence. He had only six hours' experience in the larger Cessna-206, and only at airfields with long paved runways.

He'd studied the valley, the bay, and the airstrip with the knowledge that his life, and the mission, would ultimately depend on it. High-resolution images and detailed maps of the area were not in the mission brief—only a single medium-resolution image from a Chinese spy satellite. He'd practised the approach on his laptop flight simulator as best he could, though the simulator had no inkling of this tiny remote airstrip in the middle of nowhere. Such was the price of secrecy.

The windsock whipped past Ben's view on the right-hand side, a hundred feet below. The sock hung limp and still in the windless conditions. He levelled the wings and flew along the edge of the airstrip. The surface seemed free of any visible water, much to Ben's relief.

The bushes and trees ahead were racing toward him. At their boundary, a small but high-intensity light pulsed with a slow, steady flash.

All clear, Ben knew. *It's time to land this thing.*

*　　*　　*　　*

Hobart Airport

Their conversation had settled into an easy rhythm. They were comrades of a sort, who shared the bond of those who flew for their navy.

"So how's life, now that you're flying SAR?" Katherine asked.

The other pilot considered her question. "It's great, but different," Pete replied. "I'm still flying turbine choppers, but the missions are different. Some can be demanding, but most are fairly routine."

"Do you miss the navy?"

"There's a question," Pete said, smiling. "Sometimes. Yeah. I miss some of my old mates. Hunting things at sea. Getting away on deployment. All that."

Katherine tilted her head and squinted.

"But yeah, I knew when it was time. I wasn't sure where my career and my life would go, but things have worked out okay. And civilian life has some advantages."

"Hey Pete!" a man boomed as he ran towards them. "We gotta go, mate. Some accidents in the city. They've got injured people on the Tasman Bridge and need us to winch 'em out."

"Duty calls," Pete said. "It's been good to meet you, Katherine. Take care now." He gave the Seahawk an affectionate pat on the nose as he left.

Katherine watched the two pilots race across the apron to their red-and-yellow helicopter. They were gone a minute later, the Kawasaki BK117 flying out of sight.

Behind her, Perez cleared his throat. "Here ya go," he said. "Sorry if it ain't much good. The power's gone out at the terminal and they had to improvise."

"Thanks." Katherine continued to stare at the spot where the other helicopter had been.

"What you smiling at, Lieutenant Commander?" Moretti asked.

"Oh nothing," she said. "Just thinking ... that's all."

*   *   *   *

Ben had landed the plane from the east—over the beach-end of the airstrip—which meant he had to turn at the far end, then taxi back along the full length of the strip. The extra seconds would give him a chance to get his breathing back under control and for the tremors to leave his hands. Those waiting for him could not see such things.

The landing had been an alarming handful. There was no choice but to use an extreme short-field landing technique, right on the edge of the plane's performance envelope. He'd brought it in slow and steep, nose-high with the power up, then cut the engine power over the tree line. The plane just missed the top of a tree, hit the end of the airstrip, then bounced before settling to the ground. The wheels shimmied and skidded on the damp grass as he applied the brakes. He pulled up at the other end with only thirty metres to spare.

Ben turned the plane as close as he could to the trees, applied the brake, and pulled the mixture lever to the cut-off position. The engine sputtered and died and the propeller de-blurred to a reluctant stop. He waited a moment before opening the door. The hushed hum of the instrument gyros spinning down were the only sounds accompanying the silence. He looked at his hands, willing the remaining tremors to stop.

But there was no further time to waste. Ben grabbed the door lever and pulled. Two dark-clad figures had emerged from the scrub and were headed his way.

CHAPTER FORTY-TWO

I'm not overweight. I'm just nine inches too short.
—Shelley Winters

Princes Wharf, Hobart

"It's nearly ten o'clock," he said, "so where's the damned news crew?"

Lieutenant Emiko Nomura could read the agitation in Captain Thomas Vanbeck's voice alright, but she couldn't read the expression on his face. His form was in silhouette against the bright sunlight reflecting off the river behind him, and his features were hidden by the shadow of his officer's hat.

"I checked with the Deputy Premier's staff," Nomura replied. "There's traffic jams all over the city. The TV crew are caught in it, but they should be here soon."

"On a Sunday? In a backwater like this? This better be it for PR today, Lieutenant. I've got a ship to ready for sea."

"Yes, sir. This is the last engagement I have for you today."

Vanbeck blew out a sharp breath as he turned away and faced the river's glare.

Nomura contemplated the hours ahead, knowing this was their last full day in Hobart. Every eligible member of the crew was ashore, leaving only enough crew to keep the essential systems and departments operating. She expected Captain Collins to return to the ship in the early afternoon.

* * * *

Lagoon Bay
0958 hours

The three men had said few words since their rendezvous. A snapped salute, a sentence or two, and then straight to work with each man knowing precisely what to do.

The Cessna looked like it had vomited most of its internals onto the grass. The front-right seat, the four passenger seats from the back, all the internal linings, the safety equipment, and even the barrier between the passenger and freight cabins had been removed and dumped on the ground nearby.

Ben balanced himself on the left wing strut. He'd drained most of the fuel from the wing tanks, straight onto the grass.

Tak had been shuttling the payload containers from the scrub to the side of the plane. "This is the last one," he panted.

Ryeon grunted an acknowledgement from inside the plane. He was busy positioning the containers. Each had been designed to interlock with its neighbours and fill every square centimetre of space within the cabin. He moved with purpose and speed, but he handled each container with the trepidation of a Bohemia Crystal trainee on his first day on the job.

Before this mission, Ryeon had thought he'd seen it all. Specialised munitions were his thing, but he had never worked with such a cocktail of specialised weaponry. Some containers held conventional military-grade high-explosive materials. Others held incendiary compounds—some unconventional, a few experimental, and one volatile if exposed to extremes of heat or pressure. Others contained specialised chemical gels and emulsions of which he had little knowledge. He had complete trust, however, in those who had designed them.

The third and final layer of containers held thousands of miniature fragmentation objects and a set of cannisters filled with ultra-compressed gas that were specifically designed for the mission. Ryeon and Tak had also used electromagnetic fasteners to attach a sizeable electronic device pod to the underbelly of the Cessna.

Ryeon worked to weave ribbon cables through the layers of containers. Each cable had been designed with header-plugs at specific points along its length. He snapped each plug into its pre-determined socket throughout the containers. The daisy chain of cables wove between the growing rows and layers, then fed onto the floor where the front right-hand seat had once been.

Ben jumped off the strut and waited under the wing as Tak handed the final container to Ryeon. He shifted from one foot to the other, sniffing incessantly. "I'm concerned about the take-off distance," he finally blurted out. "I think we are too heavy."

Tak straightened up from under the wing and turned to Ben. "All of this has been pre-planned. You know this. The payload weight is calculated exactly."

"Yes. But the take-off distance was calculated assuming the grass strip would be dry, and with a headwind of at least five knots. I might not get airborne in time to clear those trees."

"Do you know more than the mission planners, Yong-sun?" Tak snapped. "You must trust their expertise. They worked all this out already."

Ben glared back at him. "I know what conditions they planned for, and they are *not* the conditions we have today."

"You must overcome this foolishness. Suppress your fear."

"Fear? The only way to overcome this is to reduce the weight. We must remove some payload."

"Impossible!" Ryeon had emerged from inside the plane after hearing their exchange. "The contents of each container are part of a carefully designed whole. If you take out even one of them, it will greatly reduce the combined reaction and effectiveness. This *cannot* happen. The mission objective depends on this."

"The mission will not happen if this plane does not clear those trees," Ben said. "Your fucking payload will be spread all over that beach if that happens. *Then* where is your mission?" Ben winced as he realised he should have said "our mission."

Ryeon and Tak exchanged glances. They were of superior rank to Ben, far more experienced in field operations, and unused to such spirited resistance from an underling. But Ben could see it in their faces—though they were highly skilled, resilient, determined, and fearless men of war, neither of them knew the first thing about planes, or how they flew. Few people in North Korea did.

The three stood awkwardly. The silence sudden and audible. Each looked at the plane, then at the airstrip. If they had known of a North Korean god, they could have petitioned their deity to stir the feeble winter sun to dry out the saturated grass, or maybe whip up a sea breeze to lift the windsock from its flaccid impotence. But Juche—the closest thing they had to a religion—was a mere state philosophy and not known for receiving the prayers of its citizens, much less acting upon them.

Ben took the initiative. "I will have to drain more fuel to reduce the weight. But this means I cannot take the planned route over unpopulated areas. I must fly a more direct route to the target."

Tak massaged his forehead. "There is more chance of you being spotted that way. More chance of an alarm being raised."

Ben did not gild his response. "Yes."

Tak rotated his head to the sky and closed his eyes. "Do as you must," he said. "But do not delay."

*   *   *   *

1018 hours

Ben sat in the only seat remaining in the plane—the left-hand pilot seat that was still tacky with the former pilot's blood. He was dwarfed by the stacks of interlocked containers surrounding him. Their black metallic presence darkened the cabin, robbing the incoming light from all but the front windshield and the pilot-side window.

Ryeon had positioned a rectangular box next to Ben and duct-taped it into place. Ribbon cables snaked into the unit from all sides and terminated into neat sockets. Two switches hung at the end of a short cable atop the unit, both guarded with protective covers.

Ryeon leaned in through the pilot door. "When you are on the final run, you pull out this isolator plate. Pull it straight out and discard it. All the circuits are then armed and ready. Keep the switches in your right hand. At three hundred metres, flip the black cover up and press the switch."

"Yes."

"At the final moment flip the *red* switch cover up, press the switch, and hold it in." Ryeon's next words were as soulless as those before. "The unit will do the rest."

"Understood," Ben responded, having repeatedly rehearsed the same actions in his mind since he'd first read the final mission brief.

Ryeon moved a step back to stand as straight as he could under the wing. Ben turned towards him, knowing this would be their last exchange. Ryeon's part in the mission was almost over, but from the glazed distance behind Ryeon's eyes, Ben could sense the man had more to say. *Something profound, maybe? Or even heartfelt?*

Ryeon's final words came only from his head. He took another step back, straightened further, and saluted. "For Korea. For the Supreme Leader," he managed, then marched away towards the tree line.

Ben braced in his seat with one hand resting on the glare shield. He closed his eyes in the silence and used the moment to clear his head, control his breathing, and slow his pulse. Whether it was mere seconds that then passed, or minutes, he had no clue.

"Yong-sun."

Ben opened his eyes.

Tak stood at the open door. "Two things before you leave," he said, hauling a case up into view. "Take this. Place it on the other side."

Ben took the case and heaved it over his lap to the far side of the cabin. Its surface felt like the black cold sheen of slate, and it was far heavier than he'd expected. "It's as heavy as lead," he protested.

"It is lead," Tak said with no hint of irony. "It contains something more for those bastard Yankee pigs. A special gift from the Supreme Leader. A gift even our Chinese comrades are not aware of."

Ben blinked. Part of him wanted to question the contents of the case; the other part knew he mustn't.

Tak picked up a rectangular foam packing box and placed it onto Ben's lap. "And this is for you."

Ben stared at the object. He felt across the smooth exterior of the box for a seam, found it halfway down the sides and pulled upwards. The top half of the box lifted to reveal a slender object.

Ben lifted it out with care. He cradled the object like a newborn child, laying its length along his right forearm. He took in its colour and quality for a moment. An exquisite blend of earthy green shades, each imperceptibly merging into the other in gracious, flowing long swirls, the delicate ceramic cool to the touch.

A handwritten note remained in the box: "The mission, Yong-sun. The mission only."

"From Master Park," Tak added.

Ben did not hear Tak's words. For he was there again—transported away in his memory. He stood in the dim, musty hall at the North Korean military camp. That same vase held outstretched before him in his hands, waiting for the master's acceptance.

"Yong-sun?"

Ben blinked. A shiver pulsed head to toe as the sound of his name thrust him back into the present. He reached into his pocket, withdrew a small envelope, and held it out to Tak. "See to it that Ryeon delivers this to my father when he gets to Hong Kong."

"It will be done."

Ben looked away. He pretended to examine something on the instrument panel while suppressing the tears he could feel building behind his eyes.

"Go now with the knowledge that you bring a new era to our magnificent state," Tak said. "This is the day our great nation will rise. You may be as an ant, Yong-sun, but *you will take down this elephant.*"

Tak stepped back and thumped the door shut. Ben caught a last glimpse of him as he retrieved the safety harness from beyond his left shoulder and locked his door. He started the Cessna's engine, turned the plane at the far end of the airstrip, and lined up for take-off. He looked down the length of the runway before him. Tak and Ryeon had cleared the plane debris and disappeared into the coastal scrub.

Ben checked the windsock. Were his eyes deceiving him? For a millisecond, he thought he detected movement.

Ben pushed hard with his toes. The tops of both rudder pedals rotated forwards to fully engage the plane's wheel brakes. After a final scan of the controls, he took hold of the engine-power control and advanced it all the way forward. The turbocharged engine responded with all of its three-hundred-and-ten horsepower growling to a fever pitch. The three-blade propeller blurred to invisibility and screamed a song of near-supersonic speed.

The plane bucked and shook but remained unmoved, shuddering as the thrust was held in check by the wheel brakes. And then, with the engine at maximum power, and the propeller at peak RPM ... *release.* With the toe brakes off, the Cessna-206 leapt like a thoroughbred from the gate.

Ben fixed his eyes on the far end of the strip to keep the plane aligned, then glanced at the instrument panel to check the airspeed gauge: ... *twenty-five knots ... twenty-eight knots ...*

He glanced back up: still aligned.

Thirty-nine knots ... forty-four knots ...

He looked up again just as the windsock flashed past to his left. His peripheral vision—and not his imagination—told him the sock was no longer hanging still. It had lifted and turned, reacting to a sea breeze from across the beach and coming straight down the strip.

A headwind. *An act of a god? Had Juche grown ears?*

The end of the strip raced towards Ben, the tree line growing ever taller in his view. The airspeed gauge needle remained sluggish as it struggled to fifty-eight knots.

Ben was under no illusion—it was still too early to get airborne. The wings didn't have enough speed for the magic of lift to happen. He eased the control yoke back towards him. He sensed the nose lighten, but the main wheels remained stubbornly on the grass.

Against all aviation instincts, Ben pulled the control yoke back further. He felt the first sensation of flight as the wheels left the ground and the nose pitched above the horizon. The plane was flying, but only just, and barely climbing. And the stall-warning horn was back to spoil proceedings, bleating its protest at the lack of airspeed over the wings.

Ben had seen bush pilots perform the manoeuvre. Alaskan pilots were among a revered elite—able to coax aeroplanes in and out of impossibly small airstrips and waterways in the steep sub-Arctic wilderness. Ben had watched their internet videos and he did as he'd seen them do. Against all logic, he pushed the control column *forward* to lower the nose. He held the Cessna level at ten feet above the ground and made straight for the line of trees a hundred metres away.

CHAPTER FORTY-THREE

What we see depends mainly on what we look for.
     —John Lubbock, *The Beauties of Nature*

Southwest National Park, 10:25 AM

The silence of calm weather in this place held a reverence all its own. Listening to the nothingness, and yet *hearing* a silence this pure, was a phenomenon few modern humans could experience.

Geoff Denman had left Collins at the airstrip and headed off to check on Parks and Wildlife monitoring installations around the uninhabited outpost. Collins stood in the centre of the empty runway, turning to take in a complete view of the valley and terrain surrounding him. The plane that would take them back to Hobart was due soon, and Collins would hear its approach from a good distance away. In the meantime, there'd be only the silence, compromised faintly by the sound of his own breath.

Mount Rugby stood tall above all else, beyond the Melaleuca Inlet from whence they'd come. He could see a line of hills bounding the west of the valley, their scarred slopes carved deep by wind and water over countless millennia. The valley itself was covered in an undulating carpet of grasses, shrubs, and tea trees. Bathurst Range guarded the south-east end of the valley and was matched by its partner—the imposing New Harbour Range—standing opposite. A narrow gap lay between the two, leading to Cox Bight and the Southern Ocean in the distance.

Low fog hung motionless in the gap, but not for long. It transformed from an opaque white to thinly transparent, and then to nothing as the late-winter sun provided just enough energy to warm the environs from near-freezing to a crisp cold.

As Collins listened, the mountains and the hills seemed to speak, their hushed words coming from somewhere in and beneath the silence.

We were here, they said. *We were here long before you.*

We were here when your species first arrived, they whispered.

Collins closed his eyes to drink in their counsel.

And we will be here long after you have gone.

Their whispers faded to nothing as the faint sound of a plane engine strengthened from the distant east.

*   *   *   *

Lagoon Bay

Ben chanced one last look at the instrument panel: ... *sixty-eight knots ... seventy-two ... seventy-five* ... the airspeed had jumped to life as the plane levelled out.

The yoke jammed into Ben's lower abdomen as he yanked the control backwards. The nose pitched toward the sky. The plane careened upwards, converting its newly-found airspeed into urgently needed altitude. But as the top of the impending tree line disappeared below the plane's raised nose, Ben could sense Isaac Newton's Third Law of Motion seeking its revenge. For every action, there is an equal and opposite reaction, one that registered all too clearly on the airspeed gauge: *seventy-one knots ... sixty-seven ... sixty-four* ... and was reinforced by the returning bleat of the stall-warning horn.

Ben shut his eyes in a tight grip as the line of trees whipped past. He cursed his reaction, hearing again Tak's earlier chastisement: *You must overcome this foolishness. Suppress your fear.*

The plane hit something with a thump. The nose pitched down and yawed to the right. But to Ben's amazement, the plane kept flying. He scanned the instruments and listened to the steady heartbeat of the engine. He could feel familiar vibrations through the control yoke and the base of his seat.

Must have clipped a tree top, he reasoned to himself, *but no damage done.*

Ben lowered the nose to a comfortable pitch angle. His heart rate eased back as the airspeed edged faster. The vertical speed gauge showed an upward trend of two hundred feet per minute as the Cessna-206 settled into a shallow climb. He held a steady course over the beach, then Lagoon Bay, and then out past the northern headland. He made a wide left-hand turn as the plane climbed, then rolled the wings level to take up a course of two hundred and fifty degrees. His destination: Hobart, thirty miles west.

*   *   *   *

Hobart Airport

"You wanna take this leg, Mets?" Katherine asked on the intercom.

"Why thank you, ma'am, I thought you'd never ask," Moretti replied as he got to work.

It wasn't unusual for a helicopter commander to hand control to their airborne tactical officer. Moretti was also a helicopter pilot and endorsed to fly the MH-60R Seahawk. His primary ATO role involved a host of complex tactical tasks, but he'd take any opportunity to keep his flying skills current.

Katherine was also at work—but on her phone. She used the spare seconds to sign off from her text conversation with Martin Brady—her fingers and thumbs working furiously:

Gotta go .. about to take off and head back to the ship

No worries C U this arvo

Yup, if u r lucky!

Im not into the whole luck thingy

Yeah well .... Im like a bird, I might just fly away xx

Im like a bad smell, I might just follow :) xox

"All clear your side?"

Katherine jumped a fraction and hoped Moretti hadn't noticed. "Oh, yeah. Sorry ... all clear on the right," she said without looking to her right.

"Do we run the pre-start checklist, Lieutenant Commander, or are you still sending lover boy your nudes?"

"Get on with it, Mets!"

"Yes, ma'am!" he said, punching the air in fake enthusiasm.

*   *   *   *

Dunalley, Tasmania

James Devereaux craned his head skywards. He used a spare hand to protect his eyes from the morning sun, seeing the silhouetted shape of a small plane coming toward their position alongside the Dunalley Canal.

Looking to the sky at the sound of a plane was an automatic response. James had been afflicted with the disease since the age of five. He'd never flown a plane in his twenty-four years on earth, and had no desire to, yet his love for anything that flew held strong. And he'd found others with the same disease. Enthusiasts who'd happily sit at an airport for hours, just to watch, or tune in to aviation radio channels to eavesdrop on the alien lingo between pilots and air traffic controllers.

He recognised the plane's type as it drew closer. No doubt in his mind: this was a high-wing Cessna. "Must be a 206," he muttered.

His partner had stopped a few metres ahead. "C'mon, James," he pleaded.

But James was spellbound by the sky. He often was, but this seemed something more. "Hold on ... look at that," he said as he pointed.

As the Cessna flew past it appeared to be trailing an odd-looking wiry object from one of the main wheels. James slipped his phone from his pocket, activated the camera, zoomed in on the plane, and began snapping away.

"Bit weird, yeah," his partner agreed.

"More than a bit," James said as he examined the shots. "Look

… that's a piece of a bush, or a tree, something caught up in the undercarriage."

"Yep," his partner said, hardly looking.

"And look at that! There's, like … dark red stuff all splattered along the left side."

James switched to the Facebook app on his phone and typed a quick group post for Plane Spotters Tasmania:

How weird is this? Cessna-206 flying past Dunalley real fast with half a tree caught underneath … and splattered in dark red!!

He tried to attach two of the best images, but they wouldn't load.

"Dammit," he said, "the bloody network is down."

"You can chat with your fellow nerds later, James. Now can we get on with our walk?"

James trudged off to follow his partner. His eyes remained on the sky as he tracked the plane disappearing to the west.

*   *   *   *

Hobart Airport

The Seahawk sang. Her engines purred. The rotor blades beat a slick rhythm. She was ready to escape terra firma and return to the sky.

"Checklist complete," Moretti reported. "Let's get our clearance."

"Okay, I'll go ahead and do that," Katherine said. She keyed the Hobart Ground Control frequency into their VHF1-radio, then slid her thumb over the transmit button ready to start her clearance request. Then she froze. Her heart thumped in her chest. She stared wide-eyed through the windshield at the man standing beyond the edge of the apron thirty metres away. For a moment—whether it was his frame, or his posture, or his tightly cropped steel-grey hair and beard—she'd mistaken him for her father. She could see him staring at her in her mind, with that look that could make her question her every belief, decision, and action. And even her career.

"Katherine … Katherine … You okay?" Moretti asked. "You look like you seen a ghost."

"Sorry. Not a ghost. Just thought I saw someone I knew."

"That guy?"

"Don't worry about it," Katherine said. She waved a hand as if to swat away the experience. "I'll get our clearance now."

But before she could press the transmit button, another pilot called in on the tower frequency. They listened as the radio call stretched into an elongated exchange between the air traffic controller and the captain of an inbound airliner. The captain seemed concerned about something he'd spotted, and his tone sounded none too happy.

*   *   *   *

Forty-two hundred feet above Frederick Henry Bay

Virgin Australia Flight 706 from Brisbane to Hobart was right on schedule. The Boeing 737-800 had slid down Tasmania's east coast in a hush, engines at idle, losing thirty-five thousand feet of altitude at a comfortable rate. The engines returned to a half-powered whine as the jet eased back on its descent as it passed the township of Dunalley.

Captain Ian Saunders glanced at the navigation display on his side of the cockpit. A magenta-coloured symbol with an accompanying label PIDOS sat one mile ahead on their projected flight path. Four miles beyond, another symbol—this one coloured white—sat further on their path and denoted the point where they'd turn the aircraft onto final approach for Runway 30 at Hobart Airport.

"Approaching PIDOS, coming up on four thousand," he said.

"Checked," she replied. Melanie Robinson—the first officer—was flying the approach from the right-hand seat, with Captain Saunders monitoring from the left-hand seat and working the radios.

"I'll call us established," he said.

"Roger that."

He keyed the transmit button. "Hobart Tower. Velocity Seven-Zero-Six. Overhead PIDOS, passing four thousand."

"Velocity Seven-Zero-Six," the controller replied. "Continue approach."

Saunders read back the instruction. "Continue approach, Velocity Seven-Zero-Six."

Robinson was a portrait of concentration. She monitored the aircraft path and descent on her navigation display, cross-checked the approach chart on the screen next to her, and monitored the 737's speed, altitude, and descent rate on the primary flight display. She made an occasional glance outside toward the airport still twelve miles distant.

But something to her left caught her attention. Something out of place. The captain was leaning forward with his face pressed against the cockpit window to his left. "What's up?" she asked.

"We got traffic," he said.

Robinson shot a glance at her navigation display. "Nothing on TCAS," she said, confirming there were no aircraft transmitting a nearby position to alert their onboard Terminal Collision and Avoidance System. If there had been another airplane nearby, the system would have flashed up a symbol on the navigation display and an auditory alert would have blared in the cockpit.

"I know," Saunders said. "But I got him visual. One mile ahead, eleven o'clock, and not far below us."

"What the—"

"Stand by," Saunders said. "I'll ask the tower."

"Right-o."

"Hobart Tower. Velocity Seven-Zero-Six. Ah … we got nearby traffic just below us. Looks like a Cessna. Is he with you?"

"Velocity Seven-Zero-Six," the controller replied. "Ah … negative. No reported traffic near your position."

"Well, I can *see* him. Less than a mile ahead now and also heading west. But we've got no TCAS indication. Is he below controlled airspace or something?"

The controller's tone shifted from cool to concerned. "Negative."

"So, you got unidentified traffic flying through your airspace, with no surveillance transmission, and not under your control?"

"Velocity Seven-Zero-Six, this is procedural airspace," the controller protested. "We don't use radar surveillance."

This wasn't the first time this fact had irritated Saunders. He'd been flying in and out of Hobart for twenty years and it hadn't ceased to amaze him how a busy pair of co-located airports—Hobart Airport and Cambridge Aerodrome—could operate safely without air traffic control radar. The tower controllers used position reporting by radio, binoculars, and their vision through the tower windows to monitor and manage the traffic—procedures from a century ago.

Saunders snapped an order to his first officer: "Go missed. Get us clear and out to the east side. *Now.*"

"Wilco," Robinson confirmed as she began flicking switches and spinning knobs on the autopilot mode control panel.

Saunders was not finished with the controller. "Tower. Velocity Seven-Zero-Six. We're conducting a missed approach. Request holding to the east while you get your damned airspace in order."

The controller's tone shifted from concerned to surprised. "Velocity Seven-Zero-Six. Copy that, and, ah ... stand by."

CHAPTER FORTY-FOUR

*If you want something said, ask a man; if you want
something done, ask a woman.*

                                        —Margaret Thatcher

Hobart Airport

"Aircraft in the vicinity of Sloping Island, this is Hobart Tower."
Silence.

"Aircraft ten miles south-east of Hobart Airport. Hobart Tower. *Do
you read?*"

Silence.

Katherine could sense the air traffic controller's frustration growing
with each transmission over the frequency. She was loath to interject,
but they had a flight to do and bags of mail to deliver for an eager
ship's crew. She waited for his next call to finish, then hit the transmit
button. "Hobart Tower. Black-Wolf Seven-Zero-Three on the freight
apron. Ready for departure. We have information Tango."

"Black-Wolf Seven-Zero-Three. Hobart Tower. Cleared for take-off
parallel Runway Three-Zero."

"Clear for take-off, parallel three-zero, Black-Wolf Seven-Zero-Three."

Katherine twirled an extended index finger upwards. Moretti
rotated the power grip on the helicopter's collective control in response,
sending the engines and rotor blades into a galloping roar. The Seahawk
vibrated, eager to be unleashed.

"*I say again.* Aircraft in Frederick Henry Bay, Hobart Tower, you
are inside controlled airspace without a clearance, advise intentions."

Silence.

*   *   *   *

Moretti guided the helicopter toward the nearby hills. The ridgeline formed a natural barrier between the Derwent Valley where the city of Hobart lay, and the southern end of the Coal River Valley and the airport. It was the shortest of flights—following the Tasman Highway, past the township of Cambridge, through the gap in the hills, over Hobart's eastern shore suburbs, and out to the ship. A ten-minute hop at most.

Katherine was studying an aviation map. "Mets. Slow her up while I call the tower."

"Will do."

Katherine waited for another break in the controller's repeated calls, then pressed the transmit button. "Tower. Black-Wolf Seven-Zero-Three. Departed parallel three-zero. Request change of track to remain in your airspace. We wanna track south over Frederick Henry Bay."

"Black-Wolf Seven-Zero-Three," the controller responded. "Track as required for Frederick Henry Bay. Remain west of the runway centreline, not above one-thousand five-hundred."

Moretti waited for Katherine to read back their new clearance. "Change of plan?" he asked.

"Yup. Let's go … left turn. Take us south."

"You got it," Moretti said as his hands and feet started the manoeuvre.

"Hey, Mets," Perez sang on the intercom. "The ship's thataway. Where we goin', man?"

"Standby, Perry," Katherine responded. "Change of plan."

Moretti rolled the helicopter level on its southerly heading. "What's up?" he asked.

"Something's—"

The tower controller's voice interrupted. "Black-Wolf Seven-Zero-Three, an unidentified aircraft was reported tracking west through Frederick Henry Bay. We believe it may be a Cessna; we've had no contact with him. Report if you get them in sight."

"Tower," Katherine responded. "Roger that. We're gonna go take a little look-see. Will report sighting the traffic."

Moretti shot a glance to his left as Katherine snapped the visor down on her helmet. "You got that look, Lieutenant Commander," he said.

"What look? Just a lil sight-seeing, that's all."

Katherine sat forward, straining to the extent of her safety harness. She peered hard through the windshield, scanning the blue expanse of Frederick Henry Bay. *Something light … maybe something white … something different in all this beautiful blue …*

*　*　*　*

Nine miles south-east of Hobart Airport

Endless, wide, magnificent blue.

A sea of sequins twinkling below and an infinite dome of pure azure above.

No radio to interrupt him. No procedures to follow. No airborne traffic to be concerned with. Just Ben, and a plane, and an open sky. And a mission.

Ben eased the propeller control back to steady the RPM. He adjusted the mixture control to maximise fuel efficiency, then scanned the instruments again. Airspeed one hundred and thirty-five knots and rising, altitude eight hundred feet, all else steady.

He ignored the fuel gauges. The two needles had been hovering dangerously close to the red "E" markers before take-off. Staring at them would not slow their brief journey to empty.

Ben eyed the western edge of Frederick Henry Bay, seven miles away. He could see the dreamy blueish shape of kunanyi/Mount Wellington in the distance. The city and the river, he knew, lay in between.

He re-checked his map and double-checked his compass heading. The southern tip of the South Arm Peninsula lay dead ahead.

*　*　*　*

Princes Wharf, Hobart

"Where's your little blonde torpedo today?" Captain Thomas Vanbeck asked.

Bruce Wardlaw paused as he adjusted Vanbeck's microphone pack. "Oh … you mean Steph? Steph Sadler?"

"Yeah, maybe. I forgot her name."

"She's, um … she's on leave."

"Vacation?"

"Something like that."

The over-pronounced nod from Bradfurd Rouse standing opposite all but confirmed the Network-8 journalist was on an extended leave of a different kind. Vanbeck saw the nod and ignored it.

A tall man in an impeccable royal blue suit stepped forward. "I'm Peter De Vries," he said. His deep-timbred fifty-something voice permeated the atmosphere like an earth tremor in slow motion. "I'll be conducting the interview with you and the Deputy Premier this morning." His broad smile revealed two rows of polished teeth.

Vanbeck adjusted his hat. "Very well. Let's get this over with."

*　　*　　*　　*

Two miles south of Hobart Airport

"Something doesn't feel right," Katherine said.

"It's weird, I guess," Moretti admitted. "No radio contact and no transponder in controlled airspace. But it's probably just a dumb student pilot or a weekend warrior out for a fly."

"Maybe. But it won't hurt to go take a look."

"Should we flick-on our search radar?"

"Nope. We don't wanna to fry all the local folk's electronics."

A local taxi driver had informed Katherine—in no uncertain terms the day before—of a "frying" episode involving a visiting U.S. Navy carrier. A search radar on USS *Carl Vinson* had been switched on by mistake while the ship was moored near Hobart. Many garage-door openers and TV remote controls across Hobart's eastern shore were rendered useless in an instant and never to work again.

"Perry, you got your ears on back there?" she asked.

"You betcha."

"We're looking for a light aircraft flying low. It's tracking from our left and near the southern edge of this bay. They think it's a Cessna. Eyes out now."

"Yeah. I'm lookin'—"

*   *   *   *

Ten miles south of Hobart Airport

With eleven miles left to run before the next turn, Ben had time to settle and re-focus. He ran through the final phase of the mission—playing through the steps in his mind.

His confidence grew as he reflected on the previous hours. Their small team had accomplished the unthinkable in a foreign place many thousands of miles from their homeland. They had overcome every obstacle they'd faced that morning. The plane was rigged, ready, and he'd taken off only a few minutes behind schedule. They hadn't been detected at Lagoon Bay. The mission had survived through all the significant risk points. Everything had come together.

Everything ... except for one. Ben stole a glance toward the case jammed into the only remaining space in the cabin. Its lifeless black surface exuded an unnatural cold. He recalled the knowing smirk on Tak's face as he'd said the words: *It contains something more for those bastard Yankee pigs. A special gift from the Supreme Leader.*

It irked Ben, although he didn't understand why. *Something more? Something even the Chinese were not aware of?*

Ben stretched out his right hand to feel the black surface.

Lead.

And then he understood.

* * * *

Princes Wharf, Hobart

"This visit has been a success, no doubt about it," Vanbeck enthused. Wardlaw had him framed to perfection, with USS *John F. Kennedy* in the distance to the right. "The United States Navy and the officers and crew of the *John F. Kennedy* have been welcomed here with open arms. We feel a strong connection with our friends here in Tasmania, and we won't forget that anytime soon."

"And what has been the highlight for you personally, Captain Vanbeck?" De Vries asked, his teeth beaming.

"Oh, too many things. But, for me, the kind hospitality of the people here. Many of our crew were billeted to stay in homes around Hobart. Others were dinner guests with your families. I think lifelong friendships have been formed. It shows how close our two nations are."

De Vries turned to Matthew Cash. The video camera panned left to bring him into the shot. "Deputy Premier. Has the visit been a success, from a Tasmanian perspective?"

Cash smiled. "It's been a fantastic week, yes, it really has. Everything has gone smoothly. I'm proud of what we've all been able to achieve. We hope this is the first of many visits by our American allies—our closest friends."

* * * *

Lagoon Bay

The two commandos had finished burying the aircraft seats and internals under the shrubs and made a last check of the beach and airstrip. There could be no visible trace of their activities.

Ryeon had changed into civilian clothes. He lifted a backpack, slung it over his shoulders, and tightened the waist strap.

"Until we meet again," Tak said.

Ryeon saluted. "Sir." He turned and headed along the airstrip.

Tak melted back into the shrubs. Night would fall before he could re-emerge. Then he'd recover the SDV from the hiding spot at the end of the beach, head out to sea, and submerge the craft. *Shaanxi-2* would wait for him at the top of the sea trench where she'd been hiding. Together with the submarine's divers, he would reverse the launch process to berth the SDV via *Shaanxi-2*'s dry dock shelter.

Their slow journey home would then begin.

*   *   *   *

Ryeon found the selected fire trail beyond the airstrip and headed north. His rendezvous point was four kilometres away at the remote end of the nearest public road. He broke into a run and regulated his pace for a balance of speed and endurance.

He felt out of sorts being in civilian clothes, and more so given the clothes were of Western origin. The athletic shoes were a size too small, the jeans stiff and restrictive. The jacket was a gregarious green colour with a ridiculous Western brand-name emblazoned across the front. They fitted Ryeon okay—which made sense. Their previous owner, Yong-sun, was the same height and build.

CHAPTER FORTY-FIVE

Our energy is in proportion to the resistance it meets.
—William Hazlitt

Sixteen miles west of Hobart

Ben wrenched the pilot-side door closed and re-engaged the lock. His heart thumped and nausea swilled in his abdomen as he stared at the now empty space near his right leg.

Have I done what is right? That gift was from the Supreme Leader! Was it my choice? It was not in the mission plan. Was it right to do this? It was a step too far, surely? But can there be such a thing as too far? But I swore allegiance to my nation, and our Supreme Leader, and—

Stop.

Ben shut his eyes, clenched his teeth, and hissed in frustration. *There's nothing to achieve in this! The decision cannot be reversed now.* He resisted the urge to keep fighting with himself and went to a place deep within. To a place of regulated behaviour and self-discipline.

Steady now.

A deep breath taken in through the nose ...

All other thoughts losing their grip ... only the breath, only the breath ...

And a long, slow exhale through the mouth ... how it feels ... how it sounds ... the basest human function as it rises and falls within.

Ben's heart rate eased as he re-took conscious control. The fog of frustration cleared. The next step of his mission re-materialised in his mind's eye.

* * * *

A sudden violent splash.

A heavy spout of water rose like a mushroom cloud, then receded back to nothing. The waves and swell of Frederick Henry Bay recovered the scene within seconds. All back to normal, just as nature insists.

The arrival of a heavy lead case from eight hundred feet? A mere drop in the ocean.

The case descended to the sea floor. The metal vials inside had remained intact in their shockproof casings, but the iridium-192 isotopes would not be performing the task their creators had intended. They would not transform a conventional military attack into a nuclear-dispersal assault on a civilian city. The spectre of a dirty bomb—a radioactive-laced weapon of heinous slow death—would not be coming to fruition.

The lead case would soon be covered by layers of shifting sand at the bottom of Frederick Henry Bay, and the iridium-192 isotopes in each vial would continue their natural radioactive decline and become harmless within three years.

*   *   *   *

"Hold on. I just saw something. In the water at two o'clock."

"What was it?" Katherine asked.

"It was like this sudden splash on the surface," Perez said. "It's gone now, but something went in."

Katherine scanned the water and air ahead and to the right of the helicopter, searching for something, anything, out of place. A sudden glint of sun on metal did the trick.

"*There!* Below us and going west. It's really moving too."

Perez had also spotted it. "Affirmative. Light aircraft. Looks like a high-wing Cessna. About a half-mile."

"Yup. Bring us around, Mets. We need to track this guy."

"Roger that," Moretti said as he rolled the helicopter and increased speed.

"Can you see it?" Katherine asked.

It took Moretti a few seconds. "Um … yep. Yeah, I got it now."

"Bring us up behind, but stay a hundred feet above."

"Will do."

The minutes it took for the helicopter to catch the plane seemed like the beginning of forever.

"It sure is moving," Moretti grumbled. "We're doing one-sixty knots just to match speed."

"Stick with it," Katherine said. "I'll call this in to the tower."

Katherine pressed the transmit button. "Hobart Tower. Black-Wolf Seven-Zero-Three. We're tracking a white-and-green Cessna heading west. Registration is Hotel November Lima. I noticed there's no lights active on the plane, not even an anti-collision light."

"Black-Wolf Seven-Zero-Three, understood," the controller replied "Stand by. We'll try to make contact."

* * * *

Fourteen miles south-west of Hobart

Ben brought the control yoke back towards him. The nose of the Cessna responded, lifting a few degrees above level. He adjusted the elevator trim wheel to hold the nose attitude and watched the altimeter gauge begin its upward count: *eight hundred and fifty … nine hundred …*

He checked the airspace chart again. The boundary of the Hobart Airport control zone was at least a mile behind and he could climb to forty-five hundred feet without being detected by Melbourne air traffic control radar. But it would be twenty-five hundred feet—the planned altitude for the start of the final run—that Ben would use.

* * * *

"He's climbing," Moretti said.

"Okay. Just stick with—"

"Black-Wolf Seven-Zero-Three," the radio interjected. "Hobart Tower again. We've tried all local frequencies. Melbourne Centre has also been trying. There's no response on any frequency. And we checked the registration. It's a Cessna 206 from a scenic operator at Bruny Island. Given its track, we think it's returning there."

"Copy that," Katherine responded, deep in thought.

"You're leaving my airspace now, so you're clear to close this frequency. But what's your intentions?"

Five seconds of silence ticked by before Moretti interjected: "Um, Katherine ... ATC wants to know our intentions."

"Sorry, yeah," Katherine said. "We'll keep an eye on things for a while before we return to the ship," she transmitted.

"Roger," the controller said.

"Mets. Bring us up level with the plane, and closer in."

"How close?"

"Close enough to communicate the old way," Katherine said.

*   *   *   *

Ben felt the urge to turn and look, like a driver slowing down to gawk at a pile-up beside the highway. But a base instinct kept his eyes locked forward. His conscious self seemed to slip out of his body, as if the temporary absence of his soul could secure his status quo.

He blinked, holding his eyes hard shut for a second. *Am I seeing things? Must be. Yes. It's nothing ...*

He looked to his right and shook his head, confident he'd cleared the illusion. The out-of-body sensation left him and another instinct took control. He kept his head forward while his eyes shifted left.

Still there. Shit!

An airborne object was a hundred metres to his left. Light grey and painted black at the rear. Two black wheels hung below at the front, and a smaller one at the back. It was flying in the same direction and at a similar speed. It was no illusion.

*   *   *   *

"Mets, take us down so we're below its wing," Katherine ordered. "Perry, see if you can get their attention."

Moretti eased the nose forward to reduce their climb—long enough for the helicopter to come level with the Cessna and then slip a few feet below.

"He ain't even looking at us!" Perry reported. "What the hell's up with this guy?"

Katherine strained to her right but couldn't see clearly. "Okay. Tell me what you can see, Perry."

"Looks like one person on board. A male, I think. I've been waving my arms out the door like a frickin' lunatic and he ain't even lookin'. And I might be seeing things, but looks like he's been pruning trees with the undercarriage!"

"How about I edge us forward? Get further into his view?" Moretti suggested.

"Do it," Katherine said.

*   *   *   *

It wasn't so much the physical sight of the helicopter. Nor its formidable size. Not even its unmistakable military origin. It was the small symbol in the centre of the fuselage that gripped him. A white star on a blue roundel overlayed on three horizontal stripes: the United States military aircraft insignia.

Jumbled pieces of the mission slid in and then out of Ben's mind. Maps. Images. Dates. Faces. Steps. Places. Instructions. They each danced in fleeting visions before him, like the work of a film director gone mad. He felt fear, a sense of having gripped something, yet feeling it sliding across the lengths of his fingers toward their tips. A sickening emptiness.

Then anger. Boiling. Rising in a seething fume. Intensifying for months, for years, and even decades. White-hot livid anger at those pigs who invaded the sovereign soil of his homeland and killed millions of his people.

And then resolve, harder than steel. Resolve as defiance, born from unrelenting oppression. And an unstoppable drive to be significant. To do something of great importance. To change the world.

And then a memory. A voice from his homeland. A flicker from his early training. The words coming to him as he remembered lying coiled in the snow in abject agony: *Do not deny your fear, or your anger, Yong-sun. Use them as a fuel to your next actions. Master this and you will master your world.*

Ben lowered the aeroplane's nose to level off at twenty-five hundred feet. The landscape beyond South Arm Peninsula had come into view. The full extent of the mountain, the city at its feet, and the length of the River Derwent were all visible in the morning light.

And USS *John F. Kennedy* sitting at anchor, twelve miles distant.

CHAPTER FORTY-SIX

*With most people, disbelief in a thing is founded on a
blind belief in some other thing.*

— Georg C. Lichtenberg

Twelve miles south-west of USS John F. Kennedy

"Like the controller said, chances are he's heading back home to Bruny Island," Moretti reasoned.

Katherine paused before she responded. "Which also means there's a chance he's not."

"Okay, so what's your point?"

"Well, you tell me, Mets. If by chance he's *not* heading for Bruny Island, then where is he going?"

"Due west right now and outside controlled airspace. I don't see what the problem is."

"You may be right. But I just got this feeling—"

"Yeah. And I've got liberty this afternoon. A tall glass of Tasmanian beer is waiting for me in a Hobart bar."

Perez had sensed the need for moral support. "And I got somethin' local and tall waiting for me too."

"Oh God," Moretti mumbled.

"No, a Goddess," Perez said. "Her name's Monique."

"Sorry guys, your local tall whatevers will have to wait," Katherine said. "We need to get a better look at what we're dealing with. I'm gonna take control from here, Mets."

Moretti lifted his hands clear of the controls. "Handing over. You want me to report our status to the ship?"

"Yeah, but wait a minute. Let's get some more info first," Katherine said. "Okay, hold tight ..." She increased the engine torque, lifted the collective arm, and eased the cyclic control forward and to the right. The Seahawk climbed, banked steeply, and sped away above the Cessna.

*　　*　　*　　*

Ben was still eyes forward as the plane approached the southern tip of South Arm Peninsula. A tiny island poked out of the river, just off the peninsula's rocky tip, with a stubby red-and-white lighthouse—the Iron Pot—sitting dead-centre. The lighthouse indicated to nautical types their journey to Hobart was almost complete. For Ben, it indicated his final turn.

He sensed the sudden change outside. A flash of shadow crossed above the plane, causing the sunlight to flicker in the cockpit. A look to his left … *it's gone.* He had hoped for as much. The stupid Americans would assume he would keep heading west. They'd return to their ship and leave him be.

*　　*　　*　　*

Forestier Peninsula, four kilometres from Lagoon Bay

Alix Zhao relaxed into the bright rhythm of her favourite K-Pop boy band in her earbuds. Her family in China would be horrified if they saw her playlist, but they were back in China.

It had been an hour since she'd found the cul-de-sac at the end of the gravel road. She'd parked her car and sat motionless for a time, attuned to the slightest sound or movement in the bushland surrounding her. But tension had given way to boredom, and boredom had been kept at bay by the Bangtan Boys.

A thump from outside made her sit up as erect as a meerkat. There was a face just outside her driver's side window. He gestured with one hand, his movements minimal and abrupt. She caught on after a few seconds and lowered the window.

"Could you give me directions to kunanyi?" he asked, his English clear and his accent thick.

The recognition phrase ...

"Um, yes, yes." Her mind raced while her mouth fumbled. "I am going to kunanyi. I can take you there."

He disappeared from her view. She searched for him in the rear-vision mirror, only to hear the passenger-side door opening.

"Two words out of place in your response phrase," he said as he clicked in his seat-belt. "Barely acceptable."

Alix glared at him, but with no words to say and no breath to speak. She recognised him—the man she'd delivered the USB thumb-drive to at Rosny Lookout days earlier. *Same clothes, same height, same build, same hair. But something is different?* His face seemed longer and narrower, his cheekbones more pronounced, and his eyes even deader than she recalled.

"Drive!" he growled. "No time to wait."

Alix fumbled for her car keys. *He's the same ignorant pig of a man,* she thought. *That's for sure.*

*   *   *   *

Katherine steadied the Seahawk in rapid forward flight. "Okay, Mets. Tell me what you got."

Moretti flipped up his helmet visor and focused his binoculars on the plane two hundred yards forward and left of the helicopter. "I can't see anyone else in there. I can't even see the pilot from this side."

"How come?"

"The windows on the right-hand side of the plane are blacked out. I think it's boxes or something. Like it's packed to the ceiling with freight."

"Okay. And so much freight, he took out a tree on take-off. Weird."

"Yeah. The seats must have been removed."

"A plane with a scenic tour company, with no seats, and carrying freight ... hmm."

"Yeah, well, who knows? Not my concern."

"It *is* our concern, Mets. Our ship is close."

"What? We know where he's from, and he's headed back there. No law against carrying freight."

"But his transponder is off. His lights are off. And he's not responding on the radio."

Perez re-joined the conversation on the intercom. "If it was just an electrical fault, you'd think he'd signal back, give us a thumbs-up to let us know he was okay. But nothing. Seems pretty darn strange to me."

"Right," Katherine said. "Let's take one more look." She allowed the helicopter to slip behind and below the Cessna, then eased up along its left side.

"Yeah, you're right, Mets," Perry confirmed. "I can see those boxes this side too. That thing is sure packed tight."

Katherine nudged the helicopter forward, but remained behind the pilot's eyeline and far enough from the plane's wingtip.

Perez held his binoculars steady and focused on the pilot. "Okay. This guy is young. He looks kinda Asian. Might be Chinese, I can't tell. What are we going to do?"

"We're gonna slip back some," Katherine said. "But if he shows any sign of turning north, we're gonna be playing a very different ballgame."

They each stayed silent for a time, all eyes on the plane, now two hundred yards ahead.

"We'll need to go defensive?" Moretti asked.

"We'll have no choice. If he even flinches, go ahead and report what's happening to the CDC."

Moretti tried to rehearse the radio call in his head. How does an airborne tactical officer, in a fifty-million-dollar U.S. Navy MH-60R Seahawk, report to the ship's Combat Direction Center that a Cessna carrying freight might be headed their way? He could almost hear them laughing. "What do you want me to say?"

Katherine's right hand tensed on the cyclic control. "You'll say we got a potential rogue civilian aircraft, with a suspect payload, ten miles south of the ship and headed inbound."

"Okay—"

"And tell them it may be a hostile. Defensive action may be needed."

Moretti's thumb rested on the button as he watched the Cessna ahead. The innocent green button seemed much more than a radio transmission switch. More like a switch to the ejection seat of his reputation, or the kill-switch on the electric chair of his navy career.

Don't you turn, Moretti said to himself. *Don't you dare fucking turn.*

CHAPTER FORTY-SEVEN

In any moment of decision the best thing you can do is
the right thing, the next best thing is the wrong thing,
and the worst thing you can do is nothing.

—Theodore Roosevelt

Eleven miles south of USS John F. Kennedy

Ben craned his head left. He looked to the sky, then towards the water as far as the Cessna's windows would allow. Nothing else in sight.

The Iron Pot slipped from view under the Cessna's nose. Ben would hold his present heading until the eastern shoreline of the River Derwent passed under the plane's right wing. Then it would be time.

*　　*　　*　　*

Just a gentle flicker of movement at first. A shallow wallow to the right. Maybe a reaction and a correction to light turbulence?

But then a turn. Unmistakable. Deliberate. The Cessna banked hard right.

Moretti winced. "Damn it. The bastard is turning."

"Shit. Here we go then," Perez said in a thin whisper.

Katherine rolled the helicopter hard-right to follow and cut the corner to make up ground.

The time for Moretti to hit the little green button had come. "Strike," he transmitted, referring to the ship's CDC by its tactical callsign. "Black-Wolf Seven-Zero-Three. Eleven miles south, inbound, two thousand five hundred, priority one report."

As seconds of empty radio silence ticked past, Moretti imagined the operations specialist in the ship's Combat Direction Center scrambling back to his station. Or perhaps choking on the remaining half of a hot dog as he tried to swallow it before responding to the radio call. Moretti realised the CDC would be almost empty with only a skeleton crew. At sea, the CDC is a coordinated melee of frenetic activity. The safety of the strike group and the carrier depends on the information and decisions flowing in, through, and out of the electronic nerve centre. But in port, Moretti knew, the only tactical issue for the few specialists and controllers left on watch would be looking busy while doing almost nothing at all.

"Black-Wolf Seven-Zero-Three," a female voice replied. "Strike. Copy. Go ahead your priority one."

"Yeah. We, uh … we've been monitoring a civilian aircraft. A Cessna. It flew through the Hobart control zone with no transponder ident and no radio calls. We tried to get the pilot's attention, but he doesn't acknowledge."

Moretti could almost hear the officer's mind scrambling at the other end.

"Roger," she said. "And what's the nature of your report?"

"He's headed your way, and we think he may be hostile."

"Um … a Cessna, you said?"

"Yeah, a Cessna two-zero-six."

The disbelief in her voice was clear. "You're reporting a civilian *Cessna two-zero-six* as hostile?"

"Yes," Moretti said. "My commander believes so."

Further radio silence.

"Black-Wolf Seven-Zero-Three. Continue monitoring your, uh … *bogie* … and report any significant developments."

Katherine had had enough. She thrust her hand in a stop signal towards Moretti, then pressed her transmit button. "This is Lieutenant Commander Marlowe, commanding officer, Black-Wolf Seven-Zero-Three."

"Yes, ma'am. This is Strike."

"What's your name?"

"McCarthy," she said, her voice constricting to a squeak. "CDC ops specialist, petty officer third class."

"Well cut the *bogie* bullshit, McCarthy. We got a serious situation unfolding here and you'd better goddam pull your finger out your ass and give us the support we need. *You got me?*"

If there had been a half-eaten hot dog in the mix, Moretti was sure it had just been coughed up over the officer's tactical display.

Her voice came back, the squeak getting tighter by the second. "Uh ... look ... sorry. I'll um, I'll have to refer this to my CDC watch officer."

"Do it now," Katherine ordered.

"I will, but he's, um ... the lieutenant on watch is ... he's outta the room right now."

"*Well, go find him.* There's no time for this!"

"Aye, ma'am. Stand by."

"Christ, Katherine. You bit her frickin' head off," Moretti said.

"We're eleven miles to the ship and closing, Mets. *Do the math.* That's about five minutes at this speed. There's no time to make tactical decisions, not on our own."

"Tactical decisions ... what the hell?"

"Damn right. The ship's tactical systems are mostly shut down. They can't use tracking radar in port. And they can't use their automated defences, not in the middle of a city."

"So what are you thinking? We're rigged to be a flying taxicab. We got no weapons. Nothing."

"I know that," she snapped. "We need a plan of action here."

The helicopter's intercom circuit fell silent.

"Katherine?" Moretti prompted.

But Katherine didn't hear him. She continued to guide the helicopter, tracking close behind the Cessna. More like an autopilot than a human one. A plan of action—a command decision—was nowhere to be found.

*   *   *   *

Arthur Highway, north of Dunalley

"We must not drive through the city. Keep this side of river to New Norfolk, then back road to Huon Valley. Then to ferry."

"It will take hours!" she protested.

"This not your concern. Only do as I say."

"My only instructions are to get you onto Bruny Island and—"

Ryeon withdrew his CZ-75 pistol and chambered a round.

Alix Zhao gulped, stared afresh at the highway ahead, then pressed down on the accelerator pedal.

*   *   *   *

Ten miles south of USS John F. Kennedy

You can fly alright, Marlowe, her simulator instructor said. *I can see that. But we don't just train you to fly. This is not a frickin' airline.*

… you can either do this or you can't. Some folks don't have it in 'em. If you're one of them, then transfer out of here and go fly medivac or something.

Make a decision! Katherine ordered herself. But what if she got this wrong?

And a submarine below. Or was that two?

My gut tells me we sink this prick, Moretti had insisted.

The navy instructor again: *In combat the bad guy is gonna kill you if you don't kill him first. It's black and white out there. It's kill or be killed. Simple as that.*

And the plane was still there. A hundred yards in front and two hundred below.

She could still see him as he spoke, even now, the officer on the *Princeton* all those years ago—the one with something emotional stuck way up his ass: *If you helo guys have a bad day, then we're all totally screwed. Or so I'm told.*

She stared afresh at the plane ahead.

*　　*　　*　　*

The prominent mound of the Droughty Point headland dominated his view. The ship was still visible in the river beyond and the headland was providing useful cover.

Ben adjusted his course ten degrees east. He would decide on a final course once he'd passed the headland. He'd re-check the angle and the ship with two miles to run, then make his final decision.

He shifted his eyes right. *Still there.* The switch hung innocently at the end of the short cable.

*　　*　　*　　*

Old Mitch Parker's croaky voice crackled in the headset of her long-term memory:

> *Whattya gonna do, my girl? Just sittin' there won't solve nothing. When in doubt, do something!*

The Seahawk banked left, descended, and accelerated in a singular velvet movement. They drew level with the Cessna before Katherine comprehended the actions she'd just taken.

> *That's better. Do nothin', you're dead. If ya do something, ya might just live to fly another day.*

"Perry?"

"Yeah. Talk to me," Perez replied.

"Last chance," Katherine said. "Do everything you can to get his attention. Do whatever you have to, I don't care. Just get his attention, then wave him off. Let him know he *has to* turn away."

"You got it."

"I'm gonna get ahead a few yards and get in *real* close now. So hang on tight—"

419

CHAPTER FORTY-EIGHT

History repeats itself, the first as tragedy, then as farce.
—Karl Marx

Nine miles from USS John F. Kennedy

His nightmare had returned—the unmistakable grey form of the helicopter out to his left. A sickening daydream that should not, and could not, be recurring.

The physical effect on the Cessna was equally unmistakable. The plane intermittently bucked and vibrated as turbulence from the helicopter's rotor blades struck the plane's wings and fuselage.

He kept his eyes stubbornly forward through the Cessna's front windshield. *Those stupid Americans will go away again. But only if I keep ignoring them.*

Yet a seven-ton, twenty-metre-long Seahawk helicopter is difficult to ignore for long. Ben noticed the distinct artwork—a trio of wolves painted in stark black on the helicopter's fuselage. Two of the wolves stood in a fierce attacking pose and a third was baying to the moon.

A momentary unwelcome shiver. Was the hunter being hunted?

Stop looking—

And then he saw the open side door. The man was there again and motioning to Ben like a Hong Kong traffic cop in peak-hour traffic. He kept signalling a sharp turn, pointed behind, and crossed his arms to form an X.

Ben added engine power to increase speed. But the pilot-side window of the helicopter drew level with the front of his Cessna.

Was it simple fascination? Just curiosity? An inner drive to see his counterpart—the pilot in the other aircraft? Ben gave in to his urge and turned to look. The other pilot raised her helmet visor, and his seething eyes locked in on hers. She shook her head from side to side and made a slashing motion across her throat. They were close enough that Ben could read her name printed immediately below her on the helicopter's fuselage: LT. CMDR. KATHERINE "FLARE" MARLOWE. He glanced back up at her as she made another slashing motion across her throat.

Ben had no conscious reason for his next move. His left hand came off the control column and into view in the side window. He gave her the middle finger and yelled "Fuck you, Katherine Marlowe," with hatred seething like venom through his lips.

*　　*　　*　　*

Katherine slumped back in her seat as the Cessna pulled away from the Seahawk.

"I'm guessing that didn't go well," Moretti said.

"Nope. But there's no doubt in my mind now that his intentions are hostile."

Moretti exhaled hard. "Dammit."

"Perry," Katherine asked, "did you get his attention at all?"

"Yeah, actually, for a few seconds," Perez said. "I gave him every signal I could to get him to turn around, but he just stared at me."

"Right. Well, no more trying to reason with this guy."

"What's next?" Perez asked. "I got nothing back here, other than these bags of mail. I could throw one at him, I guess."

"Black-Wolf Seven-Zero-Three, Strike," the radio crackled.

Katherine replied, "Strike. Black-Wolf Seven-Zero-Three. Roger, Lieutenant Commander Marlowe, go ahead."

"This is Lieutenant Lee Dealey, CDC watch officer. Your report's been referred to me. Are there any changes?"

"Negative. Still inbound from the south. Range now eight miles. We're confident he has hostile intent."

"How, exactly?"

"There's cargo on board that appears suspicious. And he refuses to respond to hand signals. He flipped us the bird when we tried."

"Is that it?"

"Look, I gotta terrible feeling about this. You gotta believe me. Something awful is unfolding here."

"No, I don't, actually. The CDC works on facts and data—not feelings."

"Your tactical computer systems are all switched off, are they? Or can't they handle a situation they're not pre-programmed for? I got something better than your damned AI … a pair of eyes and human intuition."

"Your intuition doesn't come into it—"

"*Come on,* Lieutenant! We got nothing on board to engage this plane with. You must take up a defensive posture to protect the ship."

"Look, Lieutenant Commander. We're in a quiet, friendly harbour a long way from anywhere. You, for whatever reason, decided to go follow a civilian plane. You have a pilot who doesn't want to wave back to you. We've had no intelligence to suggest a military or terrorist threat of any kind. This is just not happening."

Katherine slammed a fist against her side window. "Shit!" she shouted to herself. "What is wrong with these people? Where are we, *Pearl frickin' Harbor*?"

"Katherine, I—" Moretti tried to intervene.

But Katherine pressed the transmit button and cut across him. "Lieutenant Dealey, do you or anyone else in command aboard the ship have *any* orders for us?"

"Negative."

"Copy that. Black-Wolf Seven-Zero-Three, *out.*"

*　*　*　*

Droughty Point headland

Lauren Jack lifted the first of the white-painted car tyres off the ground and hoisted it into the back of the utility vehicle. Her only assistant— another protester—had lifted his first tyre and was on his way toward the ute.

The collection of tyres had spent a week at the top of the hill overlooking Droughty Point, spelling out a message facing Anchorage B, where the protestors had assumed the carrier would be stationed: USS JFK — KEEP YOUR FREEDOM. The carrier had anchored elsewhere, but the message had not gone unnoticed by the powers that be.

"Gives me the shits," Lauren grumbled as she lifted her second tyre. The protestors had planned to leave the message there for the departure of the carrier the next day, but Police Tasmania and their government overlords had other ideas. Two officers had knocked on her door early one morning with instructions to remove the tyres in a prompt and orderly fashion. The officers' barely concealed grins vanished when she told them to get off her property and take their instructions with them.

Their second visit the next day ended differently. A quiet conversation about Lauren's boyfriend and his recent history with cannabis distribution was all it took for her to come around.

She threw the third tyre in. "*Really* gives me the shits!"

A distinctive noise above caught her attention as she turned from the vehicle. She looked south to see two small shapes in the distance. Two aircraft, which she couldn't quite make out, seemed to be headed her way.

CHAPTER FORTY-NINE

A letter is an unannounced visit, the postman the agent
of rude surprises. One ought to reserve an hour a week
for receiving letters and afterwards take a bath.
—Friedrich Nietzsche

Six miles from USS John F. Kennedy

My student, you must focus upon your mission, and on the mission only, and do not fail me on this …

The helicopter had slid from Ben's view. He wouldn't waste time wondering where it might have gone. The American aircraft carrier getting larger by the second was his only focus.

Ben nudged the control yoke forward to steepen the Cessna's descent. He gave the elevator trim a quarter-turn to keep the rate of descent where it needed to be.

*   *   *   *

"Damn it, he's descending, isn't he?" Moretti's words were flat. Disbelieving.

"Yup," Katherine responded in the same tone.

"This prick is up to no good. Looks like it's game on."

"Agreed, but let's think it through. We got no weapons. Nothing. Not even a handgun. And even if we did, our rules of engagement here mean we couldn't take him out. Not until he actually attacked the ship."

"And by then it'll be too late, anyway."

Katherine eased the helicopter into a descent, holding position two hundred feet behind and one hundred feet above the Cessna. "Perry?" she asked.

"Yeah," he replied on the intercom.

"Those bags of mail. Choose the heaviest mailbag you can find. Tie it up tight, then hook it up to the hoist line. Drop the bag over the side and pay it out with a coupl'a-hundred feet of line."

"Roger that."

"What are we gonna do?" Moretti asked.

"We can't shoot this asshole, but we're gonna give him one hell of a very bad day. His airplane is about to get a visit from a long length of high-tensile steel wire."

Moretti nodded. "Got it. And the mailbag will keep the line steady."

"That's the plan," Katherine said.

"You got that look again. That look when you're hunting something."

Katherine snapped down her helmet visor, rotated the power grip, then dipped the helicopter's nose, allowing it to sprint ahead.

They had a plane to catch.

*   *   *   *

USS John F. Kennedy

The ship's bridge was a ghost town. Only Commander Jack Leavelle and a single ensign were on watch as the carrier sat at anchor, tranquil and silent.

Leavelle had drawn the short straw on the last full day of the port visit. The CO, Captain Collins, was still on liberty and not expected back till mid-afternoon. The XO, Captain Vanbeck, was ashore attending to public relations duties. That left him in charge.

Despite the inconvenience, it presented a rare opportunity to sit in the captain's chair, sip on a fresh cappuccino, and imagine his future. He'd be CO of his own ship within five years if all went to plan. And it was the perfect position to monitor the ship with a three-hundred-and-sixty-degree view of the flight deck and the fore, aft, port, and starboard sides. Together with the few watch-standers down in the CDC, and the lookouts posted around the ship, he would maintain security while the carrier lay at anchor.

A pair of bleeps heralded the arrival of a small orange diamond symbol on the TacOps plot—the tactical operations display in the centre of the bridge. Leavelle eased himself from the captain's chair and ambled over to check the source. The waterways and geographical features surrounding Hobart were overlayed with the tactical data available to the ship. With the ship's radar systems switched off while in port, the plot was mostly bare. Three civilian aircraft were depicted many miles away. Symbols for civilian maritime traffic were scattered around nearby. And five miles south, an orange diamond symbol with an accompanying text label: WOLF703-MH60.

He lifted a communications handset and hit the CDC button.

"CDC. Lieutenant Dealey."

"Acting CO Leavelle, bridge, what's up with our helo down south? I saw the caution on TacOps."

"They're keeping eyes on a civilian aircraft with no ident. Not a concern, though. We've classified it low risk."

"Very well."

Leavelle plopped back into the captain's chair, picked up his coffee cup, and took another sip.

*   *   *   *

Five miles from USS John F. Kennedy

"Okay. The hoist line is out. We're ready to rock and roll," Perez reported.

"Copy that," Katherine said. "You got clear eyes on the plane?"

"Yup. We're about three hundred feet above and gaining."

"Right. I'm gonna position us just ahead and directly above, but that means I'll lose sight of the plane. You'll have to guide me."

"Understood."

"Guys, I need to know … are you with me?"

"I'm not going anywhere," Perez chirped back. "Let's do this."

Moretti blinked and peered at the instrument panel. The tiny photo jammed in at the bottom edge was always there. The image of his wife, Lisa, smiling back at him, her presence with him on every flight. He'd change the photo on his next deployment to one of Lisa holding their new baby daughter. "Katherine," he said, "I'd follow you to hell."

The crew intercom fell silent. Katherine felt a welling from deep inside her that was begging to be free. A primeval drive to push her emotions up and out through her throat and eyes. To let fly her expression—her feelings of responsibility, of comradeship, and affection for her crew.

Katherine sucked in a quick breath and held it tight. Coping mechanisms she'd learned in childhood would sometimes prove useful, no matter how many adult years she'd accumulated.

"The bag's a hundred feet above and fifty in front," Perry reported. "Just come left a touch."

Katherine squeezed her left foot forward, advancing the left anti-torque pedal enough to make the course-correction.

"That's it. Dead ahead of him now."

"Roger that. Talk me down," Katherine said as she eased off on the collective control and reduced torque.

"Fifty now ... forty ... thirty ... twenty ... it's close now. Come five left—"

* * * *

A bird? Yes, must have been.

An elongated white blob had flashed past just ahead of the plane for the shortest of time, then disappeared.

Or am I seeing things? Ben asked himself.

Of course not. No.

* * * *

"It's really jerkin' around," Perry yelled. "It's about twenty in front and below now, and getting sucked back by the plane's prop."

"Okay, Perry," Katherine said as she reduced engine power and lifted the Seahawk's nose a few degrees to wash off speed. "Let's do this, keep talkin' to me ..."

Perry's voice had lifted to a screech. He was half out of the helicopter's side door to get a proper view below and holding on with everything he had. "*Shit!* Nearly there. Come right about three ... yep, yep, ... a touch more right ... yep ..."

"Okay, buddy," Katherine whispered to herself. "You're about to get a delivery of U.S. mail. Let's see how you like the news."

*　　*　　*　　*

It was over before it started.

Something had whipped into view. Thin and taut like a snake. Its appearance was announced by a fierce crunch, then a mechanical scream. The abrupt twang of metal fracturing as a propeller blade coiled something around it and then snapped free. And then violent thumping as an engine freed of its toil thrashed about in unbalanced chaos.

Ben released the flight controls by instinct, not understanding what was happening. He glared ahead in sheer disbelief as two blades of the three-bladed propeller spun to a halt before him.

The engine died and belched out a cloud of putrid black smoke. Fumes flashed through the Cessna's cockpit as a mix of aviation fuel and engine oil united in a toxic fog.

And then nothing. Just relative silence. Only the sound of air whistling past the Cessna's windshield and the distant pulse of a helicopter somewhere overhead.

CHAPTER FIFTY

The sky is the daily bread of the eyes.

—Ralph Waldo Emerson

Three and a half miles from USS John F. Kennedy

"**C**ontact on the Cessna!" Perez yelled over the intercom. "I think we nailed that sucker. I saw the line twist and snap, and black smoke come outta the plane's engine."

"Copy that," Katherine said as she rolled the Seahawk left, reduced speed, then steadied back on their previous course. She peered at the Cessna, three hundred feet below, as it slipped behind their position.

*   *   *   *

Ben gaped at the motionless propeller blades. Seconds evaporated as he struggled to make sense of his predicament.

Passing the second pair of men ... keep walking, eyes ahead. Another kick. This time into the pit of his stomach ...

And then the calm steady voice of Ben's military training asserted itself: *Assess the facts. Determine your options.*

He looked down at the instrument panel. Engine RPM: zero. Airspeed: ninety-five knots and reducing. Altitude: fifteen hundred feet and falling fast.

*   *   *   *

Droughty Point headland

Lauren Jack looked skyward again. The plane and the helicopter had just flown overhead, but it was the loud *bang* that got her full attention.

429

And then three objects arrived from the sky in succession. A large white sack came first, thumping to the ground midway between Lauren and her friend. A short length of steel wire snapped onto the ground beside it.

Spinning metal came next. A black steel object a metre long careened into a nearby shrub, slicing through the upper foliage of its unsuspecting victim before losing momentum and falling to the ground.

And then part of a tree—a bare branch and a few twigs—dropped from the sky five seconds later and pancaked onto the roof of the utility vehicle with a whoosh.

Lauren continued her stare at the sky, her mouth and eyes wide open. Her friend, after satisfying himself there were no further objects falling from the heavens, had squatted down to examine the white sack. "I dunno what the hell's going on," he said as he read the branding on the sack. "But we got mail."

*   *   *   *

Three miles from USS John F. Kennedy

> *Aeroplane engines rarely fail. But if one ever fails you, you can survive it if you follow the drill. Stick to the procedure, be decisive, take action, and you'll be okay.*

The flying instructor's words were imprinted on Ben's memory—as was the engine-failure procedure itself, which had been carved into his brain from relentless practice.

Ben skipped the usual steps to diagnose the cause of the engine failure and restart the engine. These things were clearly not relevant to his predicament. He worked the control yoke, adjusting the pitch angle of the plane to a few degrees below the horizon. The airspeed settled back to eighty knots as the Cessna's nose held a steady position. With the plane at this weight, Ben determined seventy-five knots would be the optimum glide speed and he'd keep a few knots up his sleeve. An unwanted meeting with the ground or water would be inevitable, but he could keep some control over where the meeting would be.

*   *   *   *

Katherine reduced power and brought the cyclic back to wash off the Seahawk's forward speed. The Cessna continued to slide back until it disappeared again from view. "Perry, keep eyes on him, I've lost him again."

"Roger that. He's two hundred down and about fifty behind us now. But how's the bastard still flying?"

"We got ourselves a cool customer," Katherine observed as she slowed the Seahawk further, allowing the Cessna to get ahead once more. "Must be well trained. He's set it up for a glide descent."

Moretti leaned forward against his harness and peered ahead. "What will he do ... try and set it down on that beach?"

"That would be the usual drill, yeah, and let's hope he does."

The plane landing on the beach, Katherine understood, would indicate either the pilot had given up on the attack—or that she'd completely misread the situation and seriously damaged a civilian aircraft in a foreign country.

But either outcome was preferable to the darker alternative—the plane continuing its glide towards the ship. The next sixty seconds would tell the other pilot's fate. And hers.

*   *   *   *

River Derwent foreshore, near Tranmere

The old man hobbled to a complete stop and gripped his walking frame. He twisted in tiny, shuffling steps to get a better view. "Did you tell command?" he asked.

The carer's first instinct was to ignore him. But he humoured the old man instead for entertainment's sake. "Tell them what, Henry?"

Henry pointed a crooked finger at the single-engine plane as it passed overhead—its engine silent, the propeller stationary. "Them little rice-paddy bastards. Did you inform the brigadier?"

The carer didn't bother to look. "Of course I did, Henry. He was thankful for your report."

"Good," Henry said with a wry smile. "The Yanks need to be ready."

"Which Yanks?"

A large helicopter burst into view from the hill behind them, its rotor blades beating a fury as it swept past and tore after the plane. Grass, leaves, loose garbage, and then the surface of the river jumped and spun as the rotors kicked up a localised storm.

"Those Yanks," Henry said.

CHAPTER FIFTY-ONE

Two and a half miles from USS John F. Kennedy

The wind had swung north-east as a sea breeze came in. The change shifted the carrier on its mooring, her bow pointing into the wind. The expansive starboard side of the carrier lay exposed to the morning sun and wide open to Ben's view as he approached.

He considered his options. The mission plan had been clear—the ship's flight deck and the island superstructure were the preferred targets. The deck bristled with aircraft, their wings folded and parked in neat rows. At the sharp right angle of his approach, however, he could easily mistime his final action. Milliseconds could make the difference between success and failure. And with no engine power, he'd lost the option of turning south to line up the length of the flight deck for the final run.

No. It will be Option Two—one of the hangar bays on the starboard side.

Ben could see them both clearly, even with the starboard edge of the flight deck looming over from above. Their spacious interiors were exposed with their sea-facing doors wide open. The crew working among the aircraft inside, he guessed, might be enjoying the sun and fresh air. *Perfect.*

His confidence grew as he noted the aircraft elevators in their stowed position on the flight deck. With both elevators clear of the hangar bays, he had an uninterrupted path into the hangars themselves.

Ben selected the hangar closest to the carrier's island. He adjusted course a few degrees to line up with the rectangular opening to the hangar bay, but it was moving ever so slowly up the Cessna's windshield—a sure sign the plane's current glidepath would not be enough.

Only one thing for it. A check of the airspeed gauge revealed he was still five knots faster than the best glide speed. Ben eased the yoke back to reduce the airspeed to seventy-five knots. The Cessna ballooned a fraction as the added lift from the wings took effect.

The hangar opening dropped lower in his windshield. Neither slipping down nor sliding up in his view. A sure sign the plane's current glidepath would be just enough.

*　　*　　*　　*

"Goddammit!" Moretti yelled, still straining against his harness. "He's passed the beach. He's headed straight for the ship!"

"Steady, Mets," Katherine said, doing her best to sound calm. "Get back on the radio, but get Pri-Fly, *not* CDC. Tell 'em they gotta scramble. Tell 'em they gotta *do something.*"

*　　*　　*　　*

USS John F. Kennedy

Primary Flight Control was almost as deserted as the bridge one level below. Pri-Fly would brim with activity while at sea as the air boss and mini-boss conducted their aviation ballet. They directed the primary task that carriers are designed for—to launch and recover aircraft. Every aircraft within five miles of the ship was their primary responsibility. Every catapult launch, approach, landing trap, and deck movement was a step in the complex dance they conducted.

Lieutenant Commander Houston—the mini-boss and second in command of the air department—was already at the starboard windows and peering through his binoculars when the radio call came. He'd seen the caution on the tactical display and was aware the Seahawk was within five miles of the ship without making their inbound call on the radio. With no other traffic to manage, he could give the approaching helo his full attention.

The voice on the incoming transmission was elevated and strained. "Tower ... Black-Wolf Seven-Zero-Three. We're inbound from the east with an emergency alert-one. We're tracking a civilian aircraft inbound two miles out. Hostile intent. Recommend defensive measures ... repeat, *recommend defensive measures.*"

Houston adjusted the focus ring. A high-wing, single-engine plane transformed from a blur to crystal-clear in his binoculars. The plane had appeared from behind a rounded hill, like an assassin emerging from a grassy knoll. "Tell the helo to stay with that plane and stand by for orders," he snapped to his junior officer managing the radio comms.

*   *   *   *

Commander Leavelle gulped his last swig of cappuccino, then answered the call. "Bridge. Acting CO."

"Sir, Pri-Fly. We got a helo reporting an airborne hostile inbound. Two miles east. Has CDC got 'em?"

"Damn it. Yeah, they flagged a small plane, but they said low risk."

"I got him in sight. Civilian plane. Looks disabled, but definitely inbound. Headed direct for our starboard."

"Can't be—"

"Our helo has recommended defensive measures."

Leavelle dropped his cup. "What the hell?"

"Sir, it's your call, sir. I got eyes on him and I say we got a real problem here. I concur we go defensive."

The word escaped Leavelle's lips before he realised: "*Shit!*" He raced to the rear of the bridge while yelling for the ensign to contact CDC and find out what the hell was happening. He flipped the 1MC communications panel open, reefed out the microphone unit, and went to key the transmit button. But he stopped. Leavelle shuddered for a second, not believing what he was about to do.

*   *   *   *

Two miles from USS John F. Kennedy

The "stand by for orders" directive on the radio was the last thing Katherine had wanted to hear. "Guys, I think we're on our own here."

"There's no way he can make it to the ship, right?" Moretti pleaded.

"He'll make it."

"We gotta get clear then. Give the ship's weapons a clear aim at this guy."

"No. They got no time to prepare."

Katherine added power, lowered the Seahawk's nose, and drove it forward to catch the Cessna. "This is up to us."

"Katherine!"

Moretti's shout slammed into her headset, but it transformed as it arrived. The spoken word was the same, but it came from someone else. Someone many years before …

> *"Katherine!" Sarah yelled from the starboard side, crouching to act as counterbalance as the boat keeled hard to port. "Watch his line!"*
>
> *Their adversary had done the unexpected and changed tack just ahead of them. Their boat was on the same line as Katherine's and just fifty yards away. Both crews could hear the flap of their opponents' sails, the barked commands of their skippers, the swish and thump of the hulls through the water as they drew closer.*

"What are we doing?" Perez asked.

"I don't know," Katherine said. "But we ain't gonna sit back here and watch. No way."

CHAPTER FIFTY-TWO

One and a half miles from USS John F. Kennedy

Katherine stole a last look as she guided the Seahawk past the Cessna. The pilot didn't acknowledge their presence. He sat like a stone, eyes forward, unflinching. He had a certain look, though. A confidence underpinned by arrogance. A subtle smirk Katherine thought she'd long forgotten, yet remembered all too well.

*   *   *   *

USS John F. Kennedy

Commander Leavelle keyed the 1MC microphone. His next words would be heard in every space, corridor, room, berth, and hangar: "General Quarters, General Quarters ..."

The ship's emergency claxon began pulsing its unrelenting shriek.

"All hands man your battle stations. The route of travel is forward and up to starboard, down and aft to port. Set material condition Zebra throughout the ship. Inbound hostile aircraft on the starboard side. *Repeat*, inbound hostile aircraft on the starboard side—"

*   *   *   *

One and a quarter miles from USS John F. Kennedy

The violence came from nowhere—the Cessna's steady glidepath assaulted by something unseen. The clear air turned to aerodynamic chaos, like river rapids playing with a leaf.

Ben jammed the control yoke left, then right, and left again, fighting on instinct and desperation to keep the plane flying and upright.

And as fast as it had come, the violence ceased.

* * * *

Perez leant half-out of the helicopter and looked behind as best he could. "What the hell?" he yelled.

"What's happening?" Katherine said.

"He nearly lost control just then. That plane was buckin' like a bronco."

Katherine swung her head right to get a look. But it wasn't the Cessna that caught her eye. A half-mile away, the white sails of a yacht flapped and stretched in the breeze as her skipper switched tack toward the river's eastern shore.

Katherine shifted her gaze from the white sails of the yacht and back to the white wings of the Cessna. And then her inspiration came.

* * * *

USS John F. Kennedy

The ship was a hive woken to action. Officers and sailors spilled out of spaces and berths. Hatches and ports were slammed shut and dogged tight. Sailors pulled on firefighting gear, masks, protective suits, and fire-resistant hoods as they ran to their stations. Security teams sprinted for weapons lockers. Corridors became funnels of fast-moving human streams. Each person had a place to be and an emergency role to play.

Some yelled for priority as they ran: "Make a hole" ... "Outta my way!" Others fired orders at their teams as they formed. Most of the crew moved quietly, though. Their brains in overdrive but their mouths not functioning. Limbs and torsos tense as their bodies teemed with adrenaline. They'd all get to their GQ stations like ever-reliable robots under common command. The endless repetition of emergency drills on the ship had that effect.

* * * *

One mile from USS John F. Kennedy

The Cessna adjusted its course for the hangar opening. The pilot had lost distance and altitude, but he was still on a path to the carrier.

Katherine shoved the cyclic hard right, held the bank angle for two seconds, then reversed hard left. "We're going to stay in front of him and get real close. Guys, you gotta be my eyes now ... I can't see him."

"Right behind us now, fifty left!" Perez shouted over the intercom.

"What the hell's he doing now? He can't do that!" Katherine was incredulous. Billy the Kid had changed the direction of his boat—just enough for his sails to be upwind of Katherine's.

Moretti jammed his head against his side window to watch the plane as the Seahawk banked right. "We're too close, Katherine. We're too close! What are we doing?"

Katherine slammed the cyclic left and added a sharp jab on the left anti-torque pedal. The Seahawk lurched sideways in response.

"We're gonna steal something," she said. "We're gonna steal his wind."

CHAPTER FIFTY-THREE

The shrill of the repeating emergency claxon clawed at Lieutenant Lee Dealey. The sound hit him like a murderous scream as he burst through the hatchway into the bridge. The acting CO—Commander Leavelle—stood at the starboard windows, his binoculars trained steady on the incoming plane.

"Sir, Lieutenant Dealey, CDC air defence," Dealey said, gasping for breath. He joined Leavelle at the window and spotted the Seahawk crossing right and left as it weaved toward the ship. And behind, he could see the Cessna flying low and slow and less than a mile away.

"What in God's name is going on down there?" Leavelle demanded as he faced Dealey. "How'd that goddamn Cessna get this close?"

Dealey ignored the question. He had just seconds to respond to the threat. His mind raced through his options. With the ship's radar systems off in port, most of her self-defence systems were blind to any close-in threat. He had no targeting data to feed to the RIM-116 Rolling Airframe Missiles—and in any case, the missiles were not designed to handle low-energy threats such as light aircraft. The automated Phalanx canons couldn't be activated and directed to engage the target in the seconds remaining. But the main issue confronting Dealey was what lay beyond the target itself. Hobart's eastern shore suburbs lay directly behind the low-flying plane. Any missile or cannon round that missed the plane could hit civilian houses. This was no place to fight a low-flying airborne intruder.

The Seahawk between the ship and the intruder was another limiting factor, but far more dispensable than civilian homes and lives.

Dealey lifted his handheld radio and pressed TRANSMIT: "Gunner on watch, starboard side. This is CDC watch officer air defense—"

* * * *

Gunner's Mate Steven Derilo had been enjoying the sun. The gunnery platform below the flight deck and off the main catwalk was the perfect spot to bask in the sun's warmth as it rose from the east. The warmth was nothing like the heat he enjoyed in West Texas, but it was the only sun on offer and would have to do.

The General Quarters call and the claxon had stirred him to his feet, although he'd somehow missed the usual "this is a drill" part of the call. He hadn't expected a GQ drill while in port, but such was life in the navy.

"Inbound light aircraft starboard side, range one mile," the CDC ordered. "You're cleared to engage the intruder. Set condition one."

Derilo shook his head and blinked. "Confirm condition one?"

The shouted reply left him in no doubt. "Affirm! Condition one. Condition One. Engage. *Engage with no delay.*"

Derilo grabbed the handles at the rear of the M2 .50-calibre machine gun. He swung it seaward around its pivot mount, cocked the bolt arm, flicked off the safety, and peered across the river.

* * * *

Fifteen hundred yards from USS John F. Kennedy

The aerodynamic violence was back. The Cessna thumped and groaned under the strain of rapid changes in airflow. Ben fought each shift in the air. He struggled with all his might to keep the wings level and the nose where it needed to be.

And then the whining screech from the stall warning horn. Ben flicked a look at the airspeed gauge. The needle danced like a lunatic as the plane rode the turbulence: *seventy knots ... sixty-six ... sixty-two ... seventy-one ...*

And then steady again. All turbulence gone.

How is this happening?

The helicopter crossed in front of him, its tail rotor close, then flicked out of view again as it rolled right. He saw the tips of the main rotor blades flash past and away. And the turbulence hit again with a vengeance.

*   *   *   *

"Holy crap!" Moretti shouted. "We missed him by yards. We're too damn close."

"Gotta be," Katherine managed as her hands and feet pummelled the controls. "Remember that safety directive last week?"

Moretti was wondering what the hell she was talking about when it came to him—the U.S. Navy safety directive about the hazards of rotor-induced turbulence had detailed incidents involving the severe downdraft and turbulence caused by the Seahawk's rotor. A plane had come close to a loss-of-control crash when it flew through a Seahawk's rotor-wash. The invisible vortices spewing from the tips of the rotor blades were like horizontal tornadoes. At the right distance, and at the right angle, they could wreak havoc on a plane. And the lower to the ground or water, the greater the effect.

"Climb above his level," Moretti shouted as Katherine's strategy gelled in his head. "The downwash and vortices will hit him harder."

Katherine raised the collective lever and gunned the power-grip. The Seahawk jerked into a rapid climb.

"He's fifty feet below and behind," Perez confirmed.

*   *   *   *

A sharp jab to his upper arm, another to his face, an intense thwack across the back of his head ... somehow, somehow, he kept moving forward ...

The bleat of the stall warning as the airspeed fluctuated: *sixty-eight knots ... sixty-two ... sixty-nine ...*

Eyes on the mission, focus on the vase. I must not fail—

As Ben fought the turbulence, he reached out for the electronic detonation unit beside him. His fingers felt the edge of the isolator plate. He pulled it out, dropped it to the floor, then grasped the black-guarded switch. He flicked the guard cover up, placed a thumb on the switch, and pressed it all the way in.

CHAPTER FIFTY-FOUR

One thousand yards from USS John F. Kennedy

Perez's observations had reached a fever pitch. "Something just fell to the water. Something fell off below the plane!"

"Ignore it," Katherine said. "Just tell me where he is."

"Still fifty down. A hundred back now."

*   *   *   *

USS John F. Kennedy

Gunner's Mate Derilo rested a finger on the trigger. One gentle pull would unleash a rapid stream of .50-calibre shells.

He was stooped over, his left eye aligned with the gunsight. His right eye looked along the matte-black barrel, between the two armour plates, and out to the river. The stark white form of the plane came clearer in his view, just a hundred feet off the water and coming straight down the path of his gun barrel.

*   *   *   *

The Cessna ballooned upwards as the weight of the pod dropped away. The extra altitude lifted the plane out of the helicopter's infernal rotor wash.

Ben seized the opportunity. He flicked the flap lever down two stages and re-trimmed the plane's attitude. The Cessna ballooned again, gaining another thirty feet of altitude. The hangar opening appeared stable ahead, though its doors were slowly closing.

I have time. There will be enough space.

And I will not fail.

*   *   *   *

"Twenty below and he's gaining again!" Perez shouted. "Forty back."

Katherine's left hand tensed on the collective control as she peered ahead. A hollow realisation began clawing at her. The edge of the flight deck was close to their level and disappearing from her view. The deck would soon be *above* the helicopter.

*   *   *   *

Derilo's finger remained on the trigger, but it was trembling. Somewhere away in the periphery of his awareness the radio continued to blare. His ears heard the shouted words—"Engage! Engage! Shoot that fucker!"—but his brain didn't process their meaning.

He squinted at the plane in his sights. It was closer. Close enough for him to see the stationary broken propeller on its nose and the silhouette of the pilot inside.

But it wasn't the plane that had induced his trembling. The many buildings on the riverside behind the plane were distant, yet still within the range of his gun. And not just any buildings. They were houses ... *civilian houses.*

*   *   *   *

The helicopter crossed in front again—and this time above him.

And then the fight. Ben's struggle on the controls against the invisible forces pounding the plane.

> *... a bamboo whip across his lower back ripping the skin*
> *deep and raw, and more kicks than he could comprehend ...*

Ben groped for the second switch. He found it, pulled it to onto his lap, and flicked up the guard cover.

*   *   *   *

Two hundred yards from USS John F. Kennedy

Katherine yelled an order over the intercom. It was an order to herself. *"Now!"*

She reefed the collective lever up at full torque and slammed the cyclic back, spearing the Seahawk into a near vertical climb to sprint for the sky.

* * * *

USS John F. Kennedy

Derilo let go of the gun handles and ducked.

The underbelly of the Seahawk screamed past him as it cleared the platform with inches to spare.

* * * *

One hundred yards from USS John F. Kennedy

Grey steel. All grey. Small waves cresting. Blue above shrinking.

People running. *Americans ... running.*

The gap ... level ahead ... still in reach.

Stall warning.

Pull back! Go for the gap!

* * * *

An arm's length of daylight flashed between the underside of the Seahawk and the edge of the flight deck as it thundered skywards. Rotor downwash boomed below the helicopter's vertical path. Rotor vortices—the invisible tornadoes flowing from its rotor-tips—thrust in crazed twisting coils at the river surface and the plane below.

Katherine didn't pray as the flight deck flashed past. She only whispered "Please" to someone, somewhere—she didn't know who. But all was done. Only chance and physics mattered now.

She knew but one thing for certain: the similarities of sails and wings. A yacht robbed of air would come to a stop. A plane robbed of air would fall from the sky.

> *The boat fell into the shadow of their adversary and the wind literally fell out of their sails. They looked up in unison at the mast and stared with disbelief as their sheets of cloth sagged and flapped impotently in the stale air.*

Katherine Marlowe closed her eyes. She could only remember those sagging sails, and hope.

*   *   *   *

Fifty yards from USS John F. Kennedy

A sudden surge of turbulence had belted the Cessna. The clean airflow was gone. Stolen. A vicious vertical torrent of aerodynamic chaos in its place.

Fifty-four knots ... forty-nine ...

And the gap? Above now, nearly out of sight.

> *His path took a drunken curve as he staggered to the table.*
> *He stopped and reached out to touch the vase—*

The river reaching up to take him ...

Ben shifted his thumb over the red detonation switch—

*   *   *   *

USS John F. Kennedy

Dealey screamed into his handheld radio like a man manifesting a demon.

Commander Leavelle's binoculars hit the deck with a shattering crunch. But any perception of sound had left Leavelle. As if the bridge, and the ship, no longer surrounded him. He was only aware of the plane dead below and too close to comprehend.

"My God—"

CHAPTER FIFTY-FIVE

White. Pure white.

An intense pulse of ethereal light.

Then weightless ... a freedom ... gravity's grip releasing.

Her eyes floated before him. Warm. Knowing. "Hush now, my silly child ..."

Then endless light.

And colour.

And peace.

CHAPTER FIFTY-SIX

Princes Wharf, Hobart

Bruce Wardlaw had the video shot framed to perfection. The sequence would combine with the journalist's warm voiceover and make the perfect ending to the good news story in Network-8's Sunday night bulletin.

Deputy Premier Matthew Cash stood left of frame with Captain Thomas Vanbeck on the right. They smiled and shook hands for the cameras. USS *John F. Kennedy* sat in the distance at the centre-top of frame.

Wardlaw relaxed as the scene played through the video-camera eyepiece. *Perfect.*

A pulse of light burst across the eyepiece.

Bloody camera ... what's wrong with it?

The surrounding air rushed past him, whooshing toward the river, then returned with a vengeance. A violent gust of thick wind slammed him onto his back. The camera and tripod joined him in the next instant.

Then a sonic boom like he'd never heard. Thundering for a second, then reverberating all around, then strangely muffled.

Vanbeck and Cash sprawled on the pier. Vanbeck struggling to get up—

A cloud on the river. First white, then orange and black. Mushrooming into the sky like a ferocious beast rising to scream.

Wardlaw shoved the camera equipment away. He rolled over and got to his knees. The carrier had heeled over to her port side and slammed back into the river as it recoiled from the blast. He could see objects sliding across the flight deck. White plumes and splashes erupted from the river surface as the objects met their watery end.

And from the near side of the rising mushroom cloud, something speared up and out, as if spat-out in disgust by the beast within.

Wardlaw squinted, and his vision began to clear.

Some sort of aircraft ... a helicopter. Large and painted grey. Navy—

He watched as the machine continued to scream upwards—its rate of climb impossible. He squinted again as he saw the helicopter's climb come to an abrupt end. The machine lurched tail over nose onto its back, then floated in a bizarre state of inverted suspension before falling back into the madness of the ever-growing mushroom cloud and disappearing from view.

CHAPTER FIFTY-SEVEN

White. Pure white.

An intense pulse of ethereal light.

Moving ... on a long journey, floating. A return to the whole, to the energy unseen.

> *"Steady on, my girl," Old Mitch Parker laughed. "It's just a*
> *bounce. Ain't none of us were born knowin' how to land."*

Then endless light.

And colour.

And peace.

CHAPTER FIFTY-EIGHT

*Dreams in the dusk, only dreams closing the day and
with the day's close going back to the grey things, the
dark things, the far, deep things of dreamland.*
          —Carl Sandburg, *Dreams in the Dusk*

Suffolk

Richard Marlowe was sound asleep on his recliner, as he often was. Rachel was used to him drifting off as they watched television in the evening. "Just resting my eyes," he'd say, although Rachel would sometimes hear him snore.

"*Katie!*" Richard shouted. His body flinched into a rigid state. Cold sweat beaded on his forehead and his eyes went to saucers, his attention fixated beyond the living room wall.

"Richard—" Rachel grasped his arm and shook it. "Richard, what's the matter?"

The alarm across his face faded. "It's nothing," he said. "Just a silly dream."

* * * *

Hong Kong

The sound of the shop doorbell and a rush of air took Jiang Cai by surprise. It was Sunday, which meant his tailoring business was closed. He worked alone to catch up on orders, as he often did.

Jiang came into the shop-front half-expecting to see a customer at the counter, but half-expecting not to. He was certain he'd locked the door earlier that morning. He pulled on the door and attempted to rotate the lock. *Yes ... still locked.*

He turned on his heel to return to the back of the shop, then stopped mid-step.

For an ephemeral moment he sensed a presence. Unseen. Unheard.

A sensation raced through his body. But not a chill. It was warm— like a breath.

And he knew.

*   *   *   *

Southwest National Park

The pilot had finished loading their bags into the baggage compartment of the Cessna-172. "Right, all set. We can get underway as soon as Geoff gets back."

The passenger standing near the tailplane paid him no attention at first. He looked in the opposite direction, toward the eastern sky. "How's the weather looking?"

"Yeah, all good. Some light scattered cloud on the way here this morning, but all pretty stable."

"Any storms?"

"Nah. Nothing forecast, and I sure didn't see any."

Captain William A. Collins looked back to the east. "That's strange," he said. "I coulda swore I just heard thunder."

*   *   *   *

North Sea Fleet Headquarters, Qingdao

The cloud of cigarette smoke in Rear Admiral Pengcheng Tao's office had almost cleared, although the rancid stench lingered. A mound of cigarette butts lay in the ashtray beside his lounge chair, their brief existences long since extinguished.

The calls he'd been waiting for had still not come. Instead, he was awoken by the morning light streaming in through a gap in the curtains. The narrow beam had made its slow journey across the room and crossed onto his face.

Pengcheng sat up with a start and threw his hands out sideways as if to keep from falling. His left hand hit something, and he turned to see the source of the clatter beside him. He'd shunted his chessboard sideways. Many of the pieces had fallen flat on the board and a few lay scattered on the floor.

His beloved game of chess was over without ever being finished.

CHAPTER FIFTY-NINE

To be a fine actor, when you're playing a role you've got to be honest. And if you can fake that, you've got it made.
—George Burns, The Third Time Around

USS John F. Kennedy
21 August 2023, 0600 hours

The hangar bay and nearby compartments had burned for twenty hours.

The starboard side had absorbed the primary explosion. The hangar bay opening—above the blast site—received a partial but substantial direct blow. The shock wave, shrapnel, and fragmentation objects at the top of the mission payload blasted into the open space, despite the outer doors being one-third closed. Intense smoke and heat raged out of control within minutes.

Fire-control partitions in the hangar had only partly closed and the explosive blast hit much of the internal structure. Internal surfaces were struck with incendiary compounds causing localised explosions and fireballs.

Automated damage control and fire-retardant systems activated within seconds of the first blast. Some systems did not activate as expected, their electronics unresponsive to computer-controlled or manual commands.

Firefighting and damage control teams swung into action, but they were significantly under-manned with many of the ship's crew ashore. It took ten hours from the time of the blast for all available officers and crew to return to the ship and join the firefight. The traffic chaos in Hobart, the hazards of ongoing fire and explosions on the ship, and a lack of watercraft and helicopters to transport personnel had meant the firefighting and damage control teams were not reinforced for hours. Exhaustion, smoke inhalation, burns, and casualties from fires and secondary explosions had taken their toll.

It became clear the ship had suffered a significant hit to many electronic and computer-controlled systems. Damage control, communication, and coordination were severely hampered across the ship, and ship-to-shore communication proved difficult.

But the secondary explosions in the hangar bay took the greatest physical toll. Aircraft were being prepared for flight operations when the attack occurred. They were to be ready for the recommencement of flying early the next day once the carrier had departed and cleared the coast. The fire suppression systems and teams largely prevented secondary explosions of fuelled aircraft, fuel lines, and ordnance— but five explosions and fires erupted within the first hour as aircraft and fuel caught fire, exploded, and burned, and as ordnance either exploded or cooked off in the hours that followed.

The flight deck took a substantial hit. The initial blast destroyed eleven aircraft parked on the starboard side. Some caught fire, others exploded into fireballs. Others were blown from their tie-down chains and shunted across the deck like toys. Many collided with other aircraft and deck equipment. Five aircraft were lost over the port side and into the river.

The upper levels of the island superstructure also took the blast. Almost all the windows were blown from their frames. Watch stations, equipment, and display consoles lay decimated. Structures buckled from the shock wave and heat. Radar and communications infrastructure atop the island were twisted into unrecognisable wreckage.

The XO, Captain Vanbeck, had taken command within fifteen minutes of the attack. He'd commandeered a local vessel and made it to the ship's fantail amongst the chaos.

Captain Collins came aboard two hours later and assumed command.

Collins and Vanbeck were assured of two significant facts as damage control reports and assessments flooded in. First, the attack had not fully infiltrated the ship because the rogue plane hadn't made it through the hangar bay opening. And second, the ship's critical infrastructure, including the nuclear reactors, fuel storage, and the weapons storage magazines, was not compromised. The protective armour and bulkheads of the critical spaces were holding firm.

It took close to a day, however, before any real semblance of order had been achieved. And crew members had been injured and killed with casualty numbers yet to be compiled.

USS *John F. Kennedy* itself was significantly damaged—that was also clear. The long trails of black and grey smoke pouring from its starboard side and flight deck were like streams of blood from a wounded beast.

A wounded vessel, yes. But stone dead in the water? Only time would reveal.

*   *   *   *

Melbourne Airport, 10:50 PM

The passport reader beeped and the screen displayed a large green tick. The gates to the departure lane opened and beckoned him forward.

Ryeon lifted his bag and strolled at an easy pace. He'd been anxious to see whether the system would accept his passport, although he'd never show it—not with Australian Border Force officers watching. The photograph on the document was not the issue—it was his image on display. But the printed name may have caused a problem—the passport belonged to a Ben Cai.

He picked up his pace once clear of the control point and made for the departure gate. His flight for Hong Kong would board in thirty minutes.

The previous day and a half had been crammed with tension and activity, but all had gone to plan. The local operative—a young woman with dubious skills—had dropped him at the specified location on Bruny Island. Ben's rental car was in the hiding spot nearby as expected. He caught an early afternoon ferry off the island, and he watched a tall plume of black smoke continue its churn into the atmosphere to the north as the ferry crossed the channel. He was careful to pay it little attention.

From there, it was a three-hour drive to Devonport. He returned the rental and boarded the *Spirit of Tasmania II* for the night crossing to Melbourne—all while using the pseudonym Ben had used to enter Tasmania.

He was met by a local operative after arriving in Melbourne and given replacement clothes, Ben's bag and mobile phone, the new passport in Ben's name, and documents for the flight to Hong Kong.

*   *   *   *

Ryeon took a seat in the departure lounge and pretended to study his phone. A television blared late-night news and held the attention of most of his fellow passengers: "Authorities have tonight released the names of two pilots," a reporter said. "The first—a Jacob Sawyer—the pilot of the Cessna involved in the attack. He was a resident of Kingston and aged 21 years. No indications have been given yet why this man would conduct a solo attack on a U.S. Navy aircraft carrier, or how he was able to organise such a thing. Investigations are continuing, but his name will no doubt go down in history with the likes of al-Zawahiri, Oswald, bin Laden, and Atta—"

Another passenger stared at the screen and shook his head. "Bloody world's gone mad," he said aloud to himself. "If an aircraft carrier isn't safe, then heaven help the rest of us."

"Yes, that's right, John," the reporter continued, responding to a question from the studio anchor. "The second pilot in this incredible story has been identified as a Lieutenant Commander Katherine Marlowe of the United States Navy. Details are sketchy at this stage, but sources are telling us she was involved in a remarkable act of bravery during the attack and may have saved many lives. In sad news, though, the navy has reported the helicopter she was flying was lost in the explosion. She and two other crew members are missing and presumed dead. Divers are currently searching for the wreckage in the river."

A public address announcement cut across the television audio: "China Southern Airlines welcomes passengers to board Flight 8076 to Hong Kong ..."

Ryeon stood and walked to the boarding lane. In fifty minutes' time his flight would lift off and he'd leave Australia, never to return.

*   *   *   *

22 August 2023

Ryeon disembarked China Southern Flight 8076 at Hong Kong Airport. Chinese agents met him at the gate, then accompanied him on a domestic flight to Beijing. He met with DPRK Colonel General Kim Hyun-woo and PLA Lieutenant Colonel Li Guoliang for a preliminary debrief on the mission. He would return to Pyongyang, North Korea, two days later.

Ryeon did not post Ben's letter to his parents. He was not aware of its existence. Tak had burned the envelope and buried the ashes at Lagoon Bay. A clandestine mission in a foreign land didn't allow for such sentimentalities.

*   *   *   *

23 August 2023

Horizons Commercial Pilot Academy received this email from Ben Cai:

> *Dear Sir,*
> *I regret to report my condition has not improved. I cannot return to study.*
> *I have returned to Hong Kong and made the difficult*

decision to withdraw from the course. Please dispose of my belongings. I do not require any refund.

Thank you for everything.

Yours sincerely,

Ben

The Academy administrator called Ben's phone four times, but all went unanswered.

Ben Cai's enrolment and student visa were cancelled the following week.

EPILOGUE

23 August 2023

USS *John F. Kennedy* was secure with all fires extinguished and all hazards under control. At the direction of the Australian government, the ship was towed to a remote anchorage in Storm Bay, twenty-five miles south of Hobart.

The guided missile destroyer USS *Stockdale* joined the carrier later that day. *Stockdale* and the submarine USS *Columbia* provided a protective screen for the disabled ship at the remote anchorage.

U.S. Navy engineers and technicians attempted to restore propulsion, guidance, and other systems to enable the carrier to return to the United States under her own power. This, however, quickly proved impossible. Damage to the ship's electronic systems and networks was so extensive the scope of repairs was not possible at anchor. Navy analysts suspected a non-nuclear electromagnetic pulse device had been used during the attack, but they could not find evidence of the device or how it was activated.

Launch and recovery of aircraft—other than the remaining helicopters—was not possible given the extensive damage to the MECALS system and the aircraft elevators. Seven of the electrically driven weapons elevators were also out of action. The remaining serviceable aeroplanes could not be removed from the ship until it returned to the United States.

Other damage—more insidious and not obvious to the eye—would be revealed much later in the repair process. Structures made from lighter alloys had buckled, shifted, and warped. Components that used to work in smooth harmony would shriek in painful protest or simply refuse to move.

*　　*　　*　　*

24 August 2023

Residents of Hobart's eastern shore suburbs were given the all-clear to return to their homes, businesses, and schools. Eight suburbs had been evacuated in the hours following the attack—as per the Hobart Port Safety Plan—with fears nuclear radiation might leak from the ship.

Investigations later determined nuclear radiation had not been emitted from the ship, and nuclear devices or materials had not been used in the attack.

The blast had killed fourteen residents: seven on nearby boats, three walking on the foreshore, and four killed by shards of flying glass in their homes. A further one hundred and eighteen residents on the foreshore and in nearby homes were injured after falling or being hit by secondary debris.

Henry was knocked onto his back, but survived.

*　　*　　*　　*

29 August 2023

USS *Oregon*—the other submarine in Carrier Strike Group 11—received orders from Third Fleet to proceed north into the Tasman Sea at high speed. They were to investigate a submerged contact detected near the surface by the Australian Navy. Sonar and satellite analysis indicated the contact was likely to be an unidentified diesel-electric submarine conducting a snorkelling procedure to replenish its batteries.

*　　*　　*　　*

3 September 2023

Most officers, chiefs, and sailors of USS *John F. Kennedy* and Carrier Air Wing 11 had been returned to the United States on U.S. Air Force and Royal Australian Air Force transport aircraft. A replacement crew—with only essential personnel for the ship's transit journey to the United States—flew to Australia on the incoming flights.

Captain William A. Collins was relieved of command and flown to San Diego. The navy re-assigned him to an administrative role in Third Fleet headquarters. He would later attend the funeral of every U.S. Navy officer and sailor who died during the attack.

* * * *

4 September 2023

A preliminary report published by the U.S. Navy listed the names of eleven officers, two chiefs, and twenty-seven enlisted sailors who were either killed in the attack or died soon after from their injuries. Their bodies were returned to the United States on a U.S. Air Force C-17 aircraft.

A further sixty-three personnel were injured in the attack and treated at civilian hospitals in Tasmania and Melbourne. Related outcomes, which were never documented or published, included instances of post-traumatic stress, substance abuse, and domestic violence. An untold number of people would suffer to varying degrees for the rest of their naval careers and civilian lives.

* * * *

5 September 2023

Lisa Moretti shivered where she stood. The night air at Dover Air Force Base in Delaware was uncharacteristically cool for the time of year. But it was the sight of the first party of seven navy personnel that had chilled her to a shiver and induced the trembling in her hands. The party moved past her in three pairs, followed by a commanding officer. They marched in perfect unison, their faces solemn, white-gloved hands held prone by their sides.

One hundred and sixty-one fellow civilians stood in three long rows

463

beside and behind her. She knew none of them—except for her mother—but they all had much in common.

As the party approached the loading ramp of the C-17 aircraft, she noticed a line of navy officers standing on the far side. They looked resplendent in their crisp uniforms and their many medals and ribbons glinted in the floodlights. A handful of civilians—all dressed in black—were interspersed along the line.

Is that the President? Lisa wondered. But she didn't bother to confirm his identity. It wasn't important, not now.

She had envisioned this day for weeks, for months, and almost every day since her husband had left on deployment aboard USS *John F. Kennedy*. She'd dreamt of the moment when the HSM-85 squadron would arrive at Naval Base Coronado and he'd sprint across the tarmac into her arms.

This day, however, was nothing as she'd imagined. No hot Californian sun radiating upon them. No coloured streamers. No band playing. No outstretched arms and hands. No smiles. Only tears of grief instead of pride and relief.

The chaplain and his entourage disembarked first, his prayer for the fallen completed.

And then they came. One by one—slow, reverent. Each silver casket lifted by the fallen's comrades, each draped in a red-and-white striped flag.

"Present arms!" an officer shouted. His order bellowed down the loading ramp and echoed across the apron. The six pallbearers lifted the casket encasing the remains and effects of the deceased officer and steadied themselves. The line of officers and civilians stood to attention as they brought his casket past. Officers saluted. Civilian dignitaries placed their right hands over their hearts.

"Order, arms," the officer shouted. The pallbearers lifted the casket into the waiting hearse.

The officers and the pallbearers performed a synchronised salute as the vehicle carrying the remains of Lieutenant Corey Moretti drove off into the cool Delaware night.

*   *   *   *

13 September 2023

Shaanxi-2 did not arrive on station for the planned rendezvous with the Chinese Navy tender vessel off the Solomon Islands. A clandestine search by Chinese surface vessels, a Chinese nuclear submarine, and Chinese and Russian satellites did not find any trace of the submarine in the months that followed. China made no requests to other nations in the South Pacific for information about the submarine or for assistance with the search.

Next of kin of each of the submarine crew were informed of the loss in person by pairs of Party officials. They were told the new submarine had been lost without trace in the Arctic Ocean during a deep-sea trial and instructed never to speak of the loss as a matter of national security.

Families of the crew did not hold public funerals. The Chinese state did not conduct public commemorations.

And North Korea did not acknowledge the continuing absence of Commander Tak.

*   *   *   *

29 September 2023

USS *John F. Kennedy* was towed out to sea by Australian Navy vessels in secret, and at night. Three U.S. Navy vessels, newly arrived from Pearl Harbor, met the carrier and, together with *Stockdale* and *Columbia,* formed a defensive escort for the long transit across the Pacific to the United States.

The U.S. Navy set a fifty-mile exclusion zone around the carrier and its defensive group during the journey. The U.S. government used all available means to suppress news media, video, and images of the ship while in transit. But it was a losing battle. Media organisations and freelancers competed for information and footage, which soon became an international phenomenon.

The story fuelled a public storm already raging across the United States. The backlash had started in the first days with shock and disbelief, then transformed to rage. Blame and rationalisation soon followed.

Calls for revenge, *but against whom?*

Calls to better protect, *but how?*

Calls for change, *but to what?*

* * * *

11 October 2023

How Martin Brady hated the sound of his doorbell. And even more so now. But he'd managed to answer the door and sign for the parcel delivery.

The non-descript parcel had sat on the kitchen bench for two days—along with a growing pile of unopened bills—before he found the motivation to open it.

It contained two items. The first: a letter on parchment, written in flowing script. Each word a small piece of art in itself:

Dear Martin,

Please accept my apologies for not sending this before now. I have not been able to bring myself to do this for some time — given the recent loss of our daughter, Katherine, whom you knew.

I want you to know Katherine called me the day before the accident and spoke warmly of you, Martin. I have not heard her as happy and at peace for many years. Your friendship, though short, obviously meant much to her.

So much so, she asked me to send this item to you. This was one of her most treasured possessions. Katherine wanted you to receive it while she was on her way back home. She said you would understand why.

Please accept this with our blessing.

With warm regards,

Rachel Marlowe

The second item in the parcel was square, flat, and separately wrapped. Brady peeled back the brown paper to reveal a record album in pristine condition and new as the day of purchase:

Bruce Springsteen: *Born in the U.S.A.*

* * * *

7 November 2023

USS *John F. Kennedy* was towed into Pearl Harbor, Hawaii, in the dead of night. The ship would remain in port to undergo repairs that would cost nearly four billion dollars. And this price tag didn't include the cost of thirteen aircraft either destroyed or damaged beyond repair, nor the cost of repairs to a further nineteen damaged aircraft. Losses and repairs to Carrier Air Wing 11 would total another two billion dollars.

USS *John F. Kennedy* would return to active service in late 2026. Engineering issues would plague the ship for much of its service life, and she would be given the unfortunate unofficial nickname of "PT-109" by some of those who served upon her.

* * * *

3 March 2024

A joint task force of the U.S. Navy, NCIS, the U.S. Federal Bureau of Investigation, Australian Federal Police, Police Tasmania, and the Australian Security Intelligence Organisation spent seven months investigating the attack before releasing their preliminary report.

The public report detailed the known facts including the lead up, the event itself, and the aftermath. They found the attack had been carried out by a single person—the Australian pilot, Jacob Sawyer—and though he must have been given significant assistance to organise the explosives and the attack, no clues of that assistance could be found. Investigators found no trace of anti-U.S. activity by Sawyer, or any interest in terrorism. The task force could not find plausible links between Sawyer and other persons of interest. They could only conclude he had been a sleeper operative with unknown motives and training.

There were no known foreign operatives in Tasmania at the time of the attack. CCTV footage from the Bruny Island ferry leading up to the attack did not reveal any person of interest. There was no booking recorded with the tour company for a scenic flight that Sunday morning, and so no plausible reason for Sawyer's solo flight. Limited testimony from witnesses on the ground, and a near complete lack of air traffic control data, left significant periods of time when the location of the aircraft was unknown. And the aircraft and pilot had been vaporised in the explosion, leaving no physical evidence for investigation.

Conclusions made in private, however, were going much further. High-level meetings between Australian and U.S. government and intelligence officials were exploring other troubling questions. Why did specific mobile phone towers, the Police Tasmania communications system, and parts of Hobart's road traffic system break down that morning? If computer hackers organised these events, why was there little traceable evidence of those hacks? Were the anti-nuclear protests in Hobart a factor? Were the disparate reports of submerged contacts in the Tasman Sea related?

The questions went unanswered and would remain that way, though when considered together, the evidence pointed to the strong possibility of involvement by a foreign state actor. But which country? Iran? China? Russia? Or was it a terrorist organisation? But which one?

Those in the know in the U.S. Navy and U.S. government would concede the attack had been carried out in a way they could not have foreseen, at a time they could not have predicted, and in a place they had never expected. These realisations and their effects on future carrier operations would never be made public, though some of their implications became clear in the years that followed. Several key ports in the Pacific Ocean and Indian Ocean refused further visits by aircraft carriers due to security concerns. Other ports became closed to all U.S. Navy ships. And with USS *John F. Kennedy* not in active service, and USS *Gerald R. Ford* not at full operational capability, the United States' ability to regularly deploy carrier strike groups around the globe faltered. Cutbacks and compromises became the new norm for their blue-water navy.

*   *   *   *

13 January 2025

The U.S. Navy released its Judge Advocate General Manual investigation into the conduct of senior officers of USS *John F. Kennedy* before, during, and after the attack. They concluded the CO, Captain William A. Collins, had acted in accordance with his orders and with U.S. Navy standing orders, had not been given specific intelligence to forewarn him of the attack, and could not have been reasonably expected to have the ship at a state of readiness beyond its state at the time. His time away from the ship, though unusual, was not in breach of navy regulations.

Collins resigned his commission and retired from the navy in the same week.

*   *   *   *

March 2025

A suite of U.S. Navy investigations and a board of enquiry concluded, and their reports were released. Recommendations from their findings included significant changes to the conduct of port visits by U.S. Navy vessels in foreign countries, including the responsibilities and duties of senior commanding officers, protocols, and procedures for all officers while in port, watch-keeping procedures, command and control, communication and coordination, and minimum requirements for the assurance of ship security in port.

U.S. Navy ships would never again anchor in harbours or rivers near foreign cities and their suburbs. They would be stationed at a distance where early warning and close-in weapons systems would be active and ready to engage threats.

Specific foreign ports were disallowed for future use under strict new security criteria. This included the port of Hobart. U.S. Navy ships would not visit any Australian ports—except for Darwin—for a further six years.

Training and drills on the handling of threats posed by light aircraft became a greater part of U.S. Navy doctrine—along with other close-in threats such as drone swarms and small high-speed surface vessels. The navy continued to develop A.I. and automation as a principal method to manage these threats.

Shore leave for crew, on-board crew comforts, and in-port public relations activities were all curtailed on U.S. Navy aircraft carriers from 2023 onwards. Security and readiness for battle were to be the priorities above all else.

Three U.S. government hearings had also concluded. A Congressional hearing on the incident insisted the U.S. Navy conduct earlier shock-testing on all new classes after they found the Ford-class carrier had been shock-tested at sea too late in the design phase. Another Congressional hearing concluded, given the costs of building and maintaining aircraft carriers and their increasing vulnerability to attack, that the United States should move away from the carrier strike group doctrine and look to new technologies. Carriers, they opined, should be primarily used to protect America closer to home. The Senate Committee on Armed Forces concluded the exact opposite. The attack on USS *John F. Kennedy*, they said, reinforced more than ever why the United States should bolster its carrier fleet and ramp up force projection across the world's oceans.

Policy decisions on the future of American aircraft carriers were a significant factor in the presidential election in 2024 and would resurface in 2028.

*   *   *   *

1 April 2025

Rear Admiral Pengcheng Tao (retired) leaned forward, his weight resting comfortably onto his hands atop the deck railing. The view overlooking the beach at Beidaihe, Qinhuangdao, in north-east China was always pleasing, no matter what the weather. He missed the comings and goings of navy ships in the port of Qingdao where he used to serve, but the occasional appearance of fishing vessels off his beachside residence would do.

Pengcheng grinned as he watched a worn and tired fishing vessel chug its way past his beach house and into the distance. *How things have changed on our seas*, he mused. *And what might the future bring? Prosperity, internal harmony, and a strong future for China on the world stage.*

China's coastal regions were enjoying a greater sense of ease. The past two years had seen a steady decrease in visits by foreign navy ships. The heat of contested territory had cooled. Instances of provocation and retaliation were reducing. Commercial ships, not navy ships, were again the most common on the South China Sea.

Perhaps, he told himself, *even in my lifetime I will see China rise to its place as a world power ... a respected equal among the greatest, with its borders and territory secure. Not a global hegemon, for such things are the folly of fools, but a true equal, nonetheless.*

"Here you are, old man," his wife said as she handed him a small glass.

Pengcheng grinned. "Thank you, my dear old woman."

He held the glass to the setting sun to marvel at its deep oakish blush, then took a first reverent sip. Satisfaction in simple liquid form. Port, of course.

* * * *

6 April 2025

Liling Cai hesitated at the thick steel gates. She hadn't visited the place since that dark day the previous year. But her sister had insisted she go and half-pushed her out of the house. "You must tend to the gravesite; you've put it off for too long!" she told her. Her sister was even more unstoppable than Liling, impossible as that might have seemed. And China's Ching Ming festival, or Ancestor's Day, came but once a year.

Liling reached the site and knelt down. The small gravestone was much as she remembered. A black plate covered the centre. Ornate gold lettering in vertical columns described the man interred there, and a small image of his face sat at the top.

She shook her head as she brushed away dust and cobwebs. So much had changed since that terrible night in late August 2023 when Chinese military police took Jiang and Liling from their apartment. They'd given the couple ten minutes to pack their things, then transported them under guard to the Chinese mainland. They were held in detention for three months with no outside contact. They were informed Ben had taken on a new identity in a foreign country and would not return. Any attempt to contact or find him, the officials said, would put their son's life in jeopardy and bring harsh retribution against them.

Jiang and Liling were forcibly resettled in a rural town in northern China, not far from Liling's older sister. They were forbidden to travel outside the province, use mobile devices, or access the Internet.

Jiang's request for their resettlement in North Korea had been denied—twice. He and Liling would never see Hong Kong again.

Forever denied the place of his birth and his second homeland, Jiang had weakened and withered before Liling's eyes. He died later that year. His last words, "Yong-sun," were spoken in a strained whisper before his final breath.

Liling stood and straightened her clothing. She'd performed her duty and it was time to go. Difficult emotions were stirring, and her son, Ben, might return any day. Her memories were to be hushed for now.

"No more of this, silly woman," she said as she shuffled off along the path.

*   *   *   *

14 May 2025

The United States Department of the Navy had received a formal recommendation from Third Fleet for the posthumous award of the Navy and Marine Corps Medal to Lieutenant Commander Katherine Marlowe, Lieutenant Corey Moretti, and Naval Air Crewman Second Class Emilio Perez. The medal was the highest non-combat decoration awarded for heroism.

The Department of the Navy declined the recommendation on the grounds of insufficient evidence of heroism at the time of the attack. The recommendation had not established the actions of the crew of MH-60R Black Wolf 703 involved a specific life-threatening risk, despite their deaths.

All three were later posthumously awarded the lesser Navy and Marine Corps Commendation Medal.

*   *   *   *

27 July 2025

Matthew Cash took his foot off the accelerator. His 4WD utility slowed as he headed south on the Midland Highway in Tasmania's central region. The reduced speed gave him time to eye the metallic monument in the paddock to his left—the marker that denoted a line on a map. This was the first time he'd crossed that divisive forty-second parallel in two years.

So much water had gone under his bridge since he'd left Hobart for good in September 2023. He'd resigned his position as Deputy Premier

473

and his ministerial portfolios. He resigned as an MP the next week, left Hobart, and never looked back.

His family farm up north had been waiting. Cows, not constituents. Paddocks, not parliament. Milking times, not media requests. And not a ship in sight. Or a Bradfurd Rouse.

Cash chuckled aloud as the monument slipped past and away from his view. He pressed down the vehicle's accelerator pedal and looked to the highway ahead. Three businessmen from China would be waiting for him at Hobart Airport, and he dared not be late.

*　　*　　*　　*

20 August 2025

"Dad."

Jacob Greenberg shifted in his recliner chair and looked up. There was so much he didn't recognise these days. Many things would bustle around him in the aged-care home and he would not care to notice. But a visit from Rachel was different. He'd have no words, but he would break into a beaming smile as he recognised his daughter.

Rachel Marlowe took the tray from Jacob's lap and placed it on a nearby table. "Richard is here too," she said.

Jacob turned further and stretched out his hand.

"Grandpa, it's good to see you," Richard said, taking the old man's trembling hand between his. He'd called his father-in-law "Grandpa" since Katherine first learned the word, and there'd been no need to alter the tradition.

"Dad. I have something for you," Rachel said. "It's something for your room." She turned the large rectangular object around and dropped the cloth cover away.

Jacob's smile drained away. His eyes lost their sharpness and took on a glaze, as if his soul were then somewhere else.

"Katherine gave me a set of acrylics, brushes, and a blank canvas before she left on her final deployment," Rachel said. "She told me I *had* to paint something for her for when she returned, and it *had* to be good."

One side of Jacob's mouth shifted upwards and a certain clarity was returning to his eyes.

"I didn't do what she asked. And after what ... happened ... I couldn't bear the thought of painting again. But today marks two years since our girl was taken from us, and, well, it just felt like the right time."

Jacob sat motionless, absorbing the painting. In the foreground the wide, dark, matte surface of a ship's flight deck dominated the view and stretched back to the empty horizon. A tall grey superstructure sat on the left edge. In the distance the form of a large helicopter lay at rest, its grey fuselage decorated with figures of wolves, one of them baying to the moon.

And standing in the centre of all this grey, a young woman in a flight suit had been beautifully painted in vibrant colour. She had an athletic frame, a squarish jawline, and a calm expression with a hint of dimples. Her tied-back hair was a mild brown that shone a radiant gold in the sunlight, and her hazel eyes were clear with a certain pure quality. And her smile was unmistakable. The colour returned to Jacob's face as he recognised the image of his granddaughter.

"Our girl," Richard said with a pained smile, his eyes soft and damp.

Jacob blinked and nodded.

*   *   *   *

28 August 2025

Captain William A. Collins (retired) swung the farm gate shut and felt the reassuring thump of timber on timber. The steel latch dropped into its cradle with a clunk.

Collins was not yet used to living alone on the remote property he'd purchased in the Wyoming steppes. He'd begun to find some sense of routine, but this was clearly going to take time. Twenty acres of open farmland thousands of miles from the sea was his home now. And he knew, somehow, he'd never see a coastline or an ocean again.

It was a desolate place and a beautiful place, this small valley. The mountains and hills surrounding him were different than the remote hills of south-west Tasmania, yet they served as a reminder all the same.

And as Collins sauntered home towards his cabin with his boots crunching the dry Wyoming grass, he heard their call yet again ...

We were here, the mountains whispered. *We were here long before you. And we will be here long after you have gone.*

Thank you for reading *Convergence on the 42nd Parallel*. I hope you enjoyed the experience.

I'd be grateful if you could post a review of the book at www.goodreads.com or any website where good books are sold or reviewed. If you post a review on social media, please use the tag *#convergenceonthe42ndparallel*

I welcome feedback and reviews by email, and your comments and questions are welcome on my social media pages – see my website for the links at **nicdalessandro.com/connect**

Bonus content for readers

You're invited to access reader-only content for this book, including background to the story, how it was produced, the characters, and behind-the-scenes elements – **nicdalessandro.com/fiction/convergence-on-the-42nd-parallel/bonus-content**

More for you to read and enjoy

Please visit nicdalessandro.com to check out my other books.

Subscribe to my newsletters at **nicdalessandro.com/updates** to be informed of new books and content.

AUTHOR'S NOTES

uthenticity was one of my primary goals as I wrote *Convergence on the 42ⁿᵈ Parallel*. It was important to me that readers enter a world as realistic and believable as I could make it—within the natural bounds of a fictional story. While there are some aspects of history and public knowledge that feed into the plot, the story itself is fiction. I used my own research and extensive input from subject-matter and technical experts, however, given the gamut of technical subjects in the book, this had to be tempered with a primary focus on the plot, the characters, and maintaining broad reader interest.

Compromises were made on some of the technical detail and especially around the military topics. I had access to quite an array of technical knowledge on these topics, but as a civilian there is further knowledge I could never access, and rightly so. In these cases, the technical and procedural information has been created as part of the fiction. I also chose not to use some technical information and to alter or fictionalise some information in the public interest.

I used the names of some actual ships and submarines as the names of fictional vessels in the story. The vessels in the book and their involvement in the story are entirely fictional. No meaning or conclusions about the real-life vessels should be made or inferred from this fictional story.

The real USS *John F. Kennedy* (CVN-79) will likely not enter full service until at least 2024, and I wish her, and all those who serve upon her, godspeed and the very best of service.

There is intentional variation in spelling and use of conventions such as time, distance, and altitude throughout the book. This was necessary given the many international locations; and various military and non-military contexts covered in the story.

Sources for quotations at the opening of chapters are variable in the public domain and not all can be singularly or directly attributed to an owner with absolute confidence. Corrections and further attributions are invited and will be further published on my website.

479

ACKNOWLEDGEMENTS

As I ponder these words and the many people I wish to thank, it astounds me how helpful and enthusiastic so many individuals have been in the two-year journey to produce this book.

Thanks to my incredible team of beta-readers: Ben Ippolito, Julie Poole, Lynden Leppard, Jenny Gallagher, Steve Bottomley, Donita Shadwick, Rosalie Bouwmeester, and Kent Whitmore. Your tireless reading of my drafts and your feedback were so important in the evolution of this book. Your enthusiasm, encouragement, and emotional responses to the story spurred me on. Donita and Jules—I'm sorry about what happened to your favourite character and I hope you've forgiven me by now!

Thanks Commander Ron 'Chadwick' Martin (USN) for putting up with my endless stream of questions about the navy and about your bird—the MH-60R 'Romeo'. Your comprehensive and kind assistance has been crucial to key parts of the book.

Thank you Vincent 'Jell-o' Aiello (USN, retired) for your assistance in finding information for the book, and for the awesome www.fighterpilotpodcast.com. It was your episodes on the MH-60R and the C2A which inspired me to include those noble steeds in the story.

To Ben Ippolito and Dain Cairns, thanks for your excellent technical advice on learning to fly and the flying sequences. You certainly brushed up my rusty hands-on flying knowledge. And special thanks to Ben for your air traffic control and airline expertise, our 'research' flying in Victoria, and an enjoyable Friday night at a certain bar near Moorabbin Airport which just so happens to feature in Chapter 15.

Thanks to Josh Hargreaves for the background materials and conversations on the world of submarines, to Greg Ross for helping me locate sources on helicopter flying, and Dave Flower for sharing your experience with port logistics.

To others who provided technical advice but cannot be named – thank you. As a civilian, it is reassuring to experience your unwavering professionalism and discretion. You are a credit to your service.

Thanks to the State Library of Tasmania for access to and help with so many of the historical materials and records I used in my research.

Thank you to the Tasmania History Facebook group for many great sources on early Tasmanian history, and to the Plane Spotters Tasmania Facebook group for allowing me to borrow their name.

Executive Chef Ainstie Wagner—thanks for your kind assistance with my fictional state dinner at Tasmania's Government House, and the sumptuous menu.

Thank you to Liz Dombrovskis for permission to include my favourite wilderness quote from the late Peter Dombrovskis—a legend of our wild places.

To Jack English, your review of the book and your encouragement and guidance on publishing came at a great time. And let's not forget, it was our conversation—while staring at USS *John C. Stennis* in the River Derwent in 2002—which accidently birthed this crazy idea.

To Peter at Bespoke Book Covers—thanks for your great work on the cover, you're a master of your craft. And thanks to Luke Harris at Working Type for your excellent work on the internal layouts and design.

Thank you Donita Shadwick (and Kent) for your painstaking work in proof-reading all 135,000 words. How many times have you read this book now?

To the many people and organisations out there in the publishing world who freely provide resources, advice, training, and inspiration – thank you. You may not realise just how useful and important your work is to new and aspiring authors, and especially for those on the self-publishing track. There are too many of these to name, but I want to pay particular thanks to reedsy.com for their amazing resources and services.

Thank you Geoff Smith—my trusty editor. Geoff, mate, your

professional and in-depth work on the book was more than I could have hoped for. I learned so much more about writing through this experience, and I thank you for staying true to your craft and for taking my book so passionately into your care. Thanks, too, for your awesome insights and additions on American and Chinese cultures, and for the 'shop talk' and answers to all my random questions 24/7.

And to my wife, Frances. It was your reaction to my first tentative draft of Chapter One that gave me the confidence to jump over the edge and into the world of writing a novel. You were my alpha reader, my sounding-board, and a never-ending source of encouragement throughout the process. Thanks for being so patient while I was lost in the endless hours of writing and editing. And thanks for your honest insights into many aspects of the story and the characters. Oh, and the endless supply of tasty treats from 'Frannie's Bakery'.

*   *   *   *

To all of you, including anyone I've missed, and to those who are not named, and to all the friends and family members who took an interest and encouraged me along the way, I thank you.

Nic D'Alessandro, June 2021.

ABOUT THE AUTHOR

Born and bred on an island state, Nic D'Alessandro is passionate about the wilderness, sea, and sky. He's a writer, landscape and aerial photographer, education consultant, keen on anything which sails or flies, fascinated by the human condition, and enjoys musing about the future of the world.

Prior to writing fiction, Nic forged a career as an education leader, manager in the public sector, and specialist in the aviation industry. He's now channelling his life and career experiences into written works to entertain, surprise, and stimulate thought.

Nic lives in Tasmania, Australia with his wife, and extended family.